War and Money
Book One

Sofia Diana Gabel

War and Money

Copyright © 2023 by Sofia Diana Gabel

ISBN 979-8-9893356-1-9

Dedication

To the three most influential women in my life; Alexandra, Olivia, and Andrianna. Life is so much more interesting with you in it.

Chapter One

Year 2187, Earth

How did this happen? I can't believe I'm strapped into this seat like a prisoner. I'm being sent away to die and if I don't find a way to escape, that's exactly what's going to happen. All I want is to be back home, wrapped up in my blanket like this never happened. But it did, and the stale air in this shuttle is making me sick. The transportation shuttles back home never felt this suffocating. This is the worst day of my life.

Everyone needs to stop staring at me like I'm a pariah. Especially Commander Viteri. Those close-set eyes of his are boring into mine, and I know I should look away, but I won't. I won't give him the satisfaction of seeing how scared I am. He told Ma and Da that I'm a non-conformist, well then, how's this for non-conforming. Go ahead and glare at me, I refuse to flinch.

His hatred is burning into me. He looks at me like I'm nothing, a stupid Single, the only child in my family. But why should that make me less than the Multiples, and who decided that being a Single was a stigma anyway. Ha! He looked away first. Sure it's because he brought up a projection in front of him, but it still feels like a little victory.

Lenora Averlowes is on my left. I remember her from school, but we were never friends. She's popular, taller, and prettier than me. Even her shiny auburn hair is better than my dull brown. And she's not a Single. She has a lot of siblings. She hasn't said a word to me and I know why. I'm nothing to her. I completely forgot that we have the same birthday, but I do remember that she volunteered to be advanced. Hard to forget, because she let everyone at school know, bragging like it made her special and better than those of us who didn't volunteer.

"Hi, Lenora, I'm not sure if you remember me, but I'm Dax." I'll shake her hand and be friends, if she wants to.

Look at her pulling away, repulsed by my offer of friendship. I should have known.

"I know who you are. You're a Single and your parents are poor. And you talk too much about things you shouldn't talk about. I don't want you talking to *me*." She turns away.

There are a few chuckles from the other kids, some I know and some I don't, and a few of them strain against their seat restraints like they want to get further away from me. So much for making friends.

"Orwan!" booms Viteri, staring right at me. He's out of his seat, holding onto a strap attached to the ceiling. "There's no talking on the shuttle! You've just brought on the first behavior modification." He touches a small metallic box attached to his belt.

Immediately, there's a stinging jolt that goes through my feet all the way to my head. Apparently, everyone got the same shock because they all jump and cry out as well. My fingers and toes are tingling. Viteri sits again and goes back to scanning through the projection.

Lenora glares at me, her bottom lip trembling. Her voice is barely above a whisper, "I knew you were trouble. Behavior modification before we even get to camp. Who's ever heard of that? I'm going to be made a Lead at training camp and I'll make you pay for this."

The other recruits nod and scowl at me.

How does she know she'll be a Lead? I thought ranks were given out at the camp, not ahead of time. It doesn't matter to me though, because I'll be slated to spend the rest of my life, however long that might be, fighting the Katarga aliens on the moon, unless I can find a way out of this. All Singles go straight to the moon and are never heard from again. Everyone knows that. I wish I never had to turn fifteen and go through my Date of Fate. I wanted to stay home and get a job, not get advanced into the Global Forces.

Soldiering is a world I know nothing about. All I have left are my memories of home. It seems like forever ago, but it was just this morning that I woke up and smelled the wonderful buttery aroma of birthday cake baking. Ma must have saved for weeks to buy eggs. Before it came out of the oven though, Viteri showed up at our door.

That was the moment my life changed. He ordered me out of my bedroom and made me stand against the wall in our tiny living room. He's so big, he took up most of the room and made Ma and Da look incredibly small with their heads drooped down. That's something I'll never forget because they looked defeated. I've never seen them like that. Even with us being poor and low status, they always had hope and made the best of things. That hope vanished this morning though and that's what scared me most.

When Viteri went on about how the only option Ma and Da had was to advance me instead of keeping me home where I could work in our outlier, I got all sweaty and almost fainted. That's when Ma yanked the cake out of the oven and tried to hand me a piece, but Viteri was fast and smacked it away, grinding it under his boot. The expression on Ma's face crushed me inside.

Looking back, I don't think I've ever heard of him showing up at anyone's house to pick up a recruit. So why me? I'm not exceptional in any way, so it's not that. He did stress how my child-rearing subsidies had ended since I turned fifteen today and that by advancing me, Ma and Da would get advancement subsidies now, almost double what they'd been getting. But that couldn't be the reason. Viteri doesn't care about low-status families.

I can't take it anymore.

I unfasten my restraints and get up. "Commander, I think there's been a mistake. I don't belong here. I'm not a soldier."

He shoots up out of his seat. "Orwan! There are no mistakes. I own you now." He rushes at me and gives me a hard slap across my cheek. "Sit down!"

What just happened? My legs are buckling and my cheek stings. I've never been hit before. He's hauling back for another slap, but before he can hurt me again, I sit and slip the restraints over my shoulders, even though my shaking hands make it almost impossible.

With his left eye twitching, he lowers his hand and strides back to his seat but doesn't sit.

"Recruits!" he bellows. "Any further outbursts will warrant a secondary intensified behavior modification." He glares at me. "I hope I'm understood. One last pick-up and then straight to training camp, where insolence will be met with a lethal penalty."

Lethal? My stomach's tight and it feels like the air's been knocked out of my lungs. We'll be at camp soon where things will be even worse. Only one stop left to pick up another recruit and then that's it. Maybe it'll be a girl who'll like me and be my friend. My only friend on a shuttle full of kids who hate me.

The shuttle banks to the left, descends, and settles at the mystery place to collect our last recruit. Viteri is out of his seat, standing by the entryway door as it opens. He has a hint of a smug smile. What does that mean? He steps aside and fires a scowl my way. I hold his look for a moment and then glance around. All of the kids have perked up and are craning their necks to see who's coming in. A second later, in strides a broad-shouldered boy with a long, jagged scar running from the bottom of his right eye all the way down to the right side of his upper lip. He has wavy, coppery hair, one of those barely-there mustaches, and a stern expression like he's better than everyone. I don't know him and I doubt he'll ever want to know me.

Unfortunately, Viteri tells him to take the empty seat next to me. If I could get up and move, I would. Now I'm sandwiched between him and Lenora.

I take one deep breath, let it out slowly, and then another. I'm still trembling. It's not working.

Before the boy sits, Viteri motions to him. "Recruits, for those of you too ignorant to know, this is Tablon Neemiss, Senior Lead recruit and heir to the Neemiss financial enterprise. He scored a perfect 100% on his exit exams and has won every Early Training Simulation game he's played. Take a good look at him because he's in charge of you. Your duty will be to protect him and die for him."

My *duty* is to die? Tablon marches down the aisle to his seat, with a sneer set on his face. I sneak a closer look at him while he's busy fastening his restraints and wonder how he got that scar. And what is an Early Training Simulation game? I've never heard of it. Nobody ever said I could practice training.

When he's strapped in, the ship zooms up into the sky again and Tablon lets out a whoop. Nobody receives an electric shock this time for the outburst.

He turns and looks at me with a cocky smirk. "Like what you see, smudge? Too bad because I don't associate with smudges." He laughs, leans back, and closes his eyes.

My jaw hurts from clenching my teeth. I've only heard the term "smudge" once before when one of the boys at school called his little sister a smudge. It meant she was worthless and if she was advanced, would end up as a smudge as the result of being on the frontlines. I may not know much, but one thing I do know is that I'm no smudge.

Chapter Two

The shuttle's gaining altitude and almost everyone is quiet, except for Tablon and Lenora. They've struck up a friendship, talking to each other like I'm not even in between them. Obviously they're allowed to chat, being higher status than me. All I can do is stare at the seat back in front of me and hope they don't start anything. Couldn't there be windows for us to look out? At least that'd give me something to do. I'd love to see where we're going and what the landscape looks like.

Tablon reaches across me, like he's handing something to Lenora, and smacks me right in the chest. "Out of my way, smudge."

"Where am I supposed to go?"

He continues, "Hold your breath until you die."

"I'd only pass out." I look directly at him.

He narrows his eyes. "Shut up. You smell like rotting garbage. Don't you ever shower?" He smacks me again.

"Orwan! No talking!" Viteri gets up but then sits down again. "I hear one more word from you, I'll shove you outside the shuttle."

Wonderful. I look forward again, at the seat back, and hope Tablon leaves me alone.

He does, but in my peripheral vision, I see him smirking.

I'm curious to see what Mid-World, where the camp is, looks like. I remember the lesson at school where we learned it used to be called Africa and had been filled with all sorts of wild animals like elephants and lions, but now those animals are extinct and their DNA is stored away at the Cryo-Center in the Polar Regions where there's still some remaining tundra. It was fascinating to learn that scientists maintain a gene bank of every animal that went extinct in the last hundred years, somewhere around 2085 or 2086. Those pictures of elephants and other animals I saw made me sad but when I asked if humans had forced them into extinction, I was shut down, as usual. I wonder if humans will end up like them and some other species will study us by looking at projections of us.

The shuttle banks left and levels off. If I could see outside, I bet we'd be cutting through fluffy white clouds, and every now and then when they got thin, I'd see a wild landscape or maybe the ocean below. Instead, all I can do is watch the other recruits once Lenora and Tablon finally stop talking and close their eyes. From my seat, I have a clear view of Viteri, who's scrolling through documents on a screen projected in front of him.

He looks up and points straight at me. "Orwan, step forward and salute."

Me? Why me? Did he notice me looking at him? I unfasten my restraints, ignoring the soft chuckles around me, and try to think if I've ever seen anyone salute before. If I don't do it right, I'm sure to get punished. I'm glad the ship's flying smoothly or I'd stumble and fall with my legs trembling so much.

I glance sideways to see if anyone is willing to help me out with the salute. They're not, or maybe they don't know what to do either. With the restraints off and draped across the seat back, I stand and take a deep breath, doing my best to prove that the slap across my cheek didn't faze me. I trip when Tablon sticks his foot out. Everyone laughs.

As expected, he laughs louder than anyone else and doesn't get yelled at for it. "You want help, little smudge? Beg me. Go ahead, get on your knees and beg me. I'll show you how to salute correctly."

Viteri shouts, "Orwan! Front and center with a salute!"

With my shoulders back and my head held high, I mumble, "I'd rather take my punishment than deal with you."

Tablon whispers that he'll snap my spine the first chance he gets.

"You'll never have the chance," I whisper back. With that, I walk to Viteri and wait.

Viteri stands, his fists balled up. "I said salute, Orwan!"

I stare straight ahead as a trickle of sweat rolls down my back. "Sir, I don't know how to salute."

"I guess that means Senior Lead Neemiss is right. You are a worthless smudge." Viteri grabs my shoulder and shoves me backwards.

I tumble to the ground but get right up. "No, sir, I'm not a smudge. I will salute if you show me how."

Again, he shoves me to the ground. This time though, he motions for me to stay down. "Senior Lead Neemiss! Come and show this ridiculous excuse for a recruit how to salute."

From the ground, I watch Tablon stomp down the aisle. He stops and hovers over me. "You salute your superior by placing your right hand on your left shoulder and raise your left arm, bent at the elbow, open palm facing outward." He bends down and whispers, "This is how you'll be saluting me, smudge." He faces Viteri and makes the salute.

Viteri gives Tablon a nod. "Well done, well done, Senior Lead. Please return to your seat while I conduct business with Orwan." He motions for me to stand.

I get up quickly and execute the salute perfectly.

"Sloppy," is all the Commander says.

How was it sloppy? I did exactly what Tablon did. "Yes, sir."

Viteri sits down again and points to the screen projection. "Now, I have your test scores for the exit exams and while you scored higher than most of your classmates, your lack of obedience and discipline is unacceptable. I have reduced all of your final scores to account for your non-conforming, destructive attitude. A notice of your lowered grades will be displayed at your school as incentive for other students to strive harder and mind their mouths."

I hear Lenora mumble that I'm stupid and lied about volunteering and should never have been advanced. I hate her so much. "Yes, sir."

He continues, "You'll be a foot soldier after training. You've already alienated yourself from your fellow recruits and that's a quality that won't allow you to be promoted into any position of responsibility. I'm placing you in the Lunar Seven encampment. You'll fight the Katarga. They're a nasty bunch of creatures. You might not survive your first day on the moon. Dismissed." He waves me away.

"Yes, sir." I spin around. *Don't cry, don't cry.* He already had his mind made up. I'm not anything but an expendable soldier. Maybe if I'd been given the opportunity to train on that early simulation thing like Tablon did, I could have been made a Lead, too.

When I get back to my seat, Lenora can't wait to rub my nose in my predicament. "You're a foot soldier? How humiliating for you. At least you'll get killed fast so you won't have to live long with the humiliation."

"Shut up," I mumble.

"Don't ever say that to me, smudge. I'm your superior. I thank the stars that we won't bunk together because you're disgusting. Leads have their own dormitory, you know." She stares at me with her nose wrinkled. "Didn't you have any nicer clothes to wear? Can't your parents afford any decent clothes? Look at you, you're repulsive." She makes a face and leans away from me as much as she can. "Singles are worthless."

As if things weren't bad enough, now she's starting in on my clothes. "What's your problem, Lenora? I have no idea how you were chosen as a Lead. You're horrible at math and barely passed the genetic recombination experiments in science. Just because you have new clothes doesn't mean you're better than me."

She shakes her head. "Don't even look at me, smudge."

"I'll look wherever I want." I shouldn't have said that, it'll only make the situation worse.

Tablon is in his restraints again and growls, "You don't ever speak to a Lead like that, smudge. I've decided to set a goal for myself; to make your life pure misery. I really wish you'd been assigned a job so I wouldn't have to look at you. Although you'd probably fail at factory work and put defects in our fighter ships. Why the Commander ever recruited you, I'll never know. You're not even good enough to be a smudge, you're vapor." He glances at Lenora and they both chuckle.

No matter how much I try to stop them, tears tumble down my cheeks. If they don't want me, why not send me back home? Working in a factory all day, coming home to Ma and Da and sleeping in my cot would be fine with me. Right now, any job would be better than being here. I wipe my eyes, slip the restraints on and fasten them in place, and do my best to block out the mocking laughter. Viteri calls up another recruit, who salutes and receives praise for it, even though it wasn't as good as the one I'd done.

Was Manti treated like this, too? She was my best friend and it hurts to think she might have been teased or called a smudge. When the weekly announcement came that she'd been killed, I cried at night for days.

Although since she'd volunteered, maybe her fellow recruits were nice to her. I really hope they were. I squeeze my eyes closed and imagine I'm snuggled in bed, with Ma singing the little song she always did when I was sad.

Sleep well, sleep well, my sweet baby,
Dream well, dream well of dead aliens,
They die, they die, and we live,
It's them or us, them or us,
So get ready to advance proudly,
Save the human race and sleep well my baby.

I dozed off at some point, for how long, I have no idea. But the shuttle is descending and everyone seems anxious. After a few minutes, we touch down. The other kids are smiling and Lenora and Tablon look giddy with joy, but joy is the last thing on *my* mind. We all get up when ordered and step into the aisle; I'm one of the last, behind Tablon and in front of Lenora, not a good place to be because they decide to crush me in between them.

Tablon is enormous, I know I have no chance of moving him, so I haul back with my elbow and catch Lenora right in the ribs. She grunts and I finally find something to smile about.

She whispers in my ear, "Better watch yourself, smudge. You've got no friends here."

"Yes, I know. I got your message loud and clear."

I'll have to be my own friend. Nobody else is standing in line for the job.

Chapter Three

We disembark and walk single-file down the ramp to where Viteri is standing on a small platform with his arms folded across his chest. It's incredibly hot and humid, with green trees and tall grass all around the perimeter of a large open area with rectangular buildings surrounding it. I've never seen anything like this. My outlier only has half-dead trees, with shriveled grass growing in small pitiful clumps from the six-year drought we've had. I'd love to walk through the grass here, but I'm sure it's off-limits.

I follow along as everyone lines up in front of Viteri's platform and salutes. I take my place in the second row when it's my turn. Nobody drops the salute.

Viteri hops off the platform and walks back and forth in each row, checking us out one-by-one. "End salute and stand at attention."

I don't know what 'at attention' means, but I carefully watch Tablon. In one quick movement, he slaps both arms against his legs and presses his palms to his thighs, shoulders back and head held high. Everyone makes the movement, but we're not together. Of course, this makes Viteri angry.

He gets up on the platform again. "Salute and repeat! As one! Senior Lead Neemiss, instruct the recruits."

Tablon steps out of line and takes a position in front of the platform. He's arrogant and orders us to follow his lead like he's a commander. For several minutes we work hard, sweating, until we're all in rhythm and Viteri is finally satisfied. My thighs sting and my shirt is soaking wet, but I now know how to do the perfect salute and stand at attention.

Viteri says something to Tablon and dismisses us. Nobody talks as we once again go in single-file, this time with Tablon in front. He's already the leader. I will not be happy until I see him fail. We go to a long, rectangular building with 'Holding Dormitory' written above the doorway, head to a ramp, and stop when Tablon turns and holds up his hand.

With an irritating smirk, he throws his shoulders back and clears his throat. "Listen up! This is your temporary quarters until you receive your permanent dorm assignment. Take the first bunk you see and change into the training camp uniform. Be prepared for inspection. I'll be right outside. Go!" He stands aside, with Lenora next to him. We go up the ramp and enter the dormitory. When I make it inside, I'm met with a blast of cold air that feels like winter. I wasn't expecting air conditioning.

There are two rows of bunks with an aisle between them. The greenish paint on the walls is faded and peeling and sort of reminds me of my bedroom back home, except mine is pale yellow. I'm glad I won't be staying here because it smells musty. It's half-full with recruits, most already dressed in the uniform; a bright red short-sleeved shirt, black pants, grey socks, and black lace-up boots. Everyone ahead of me grabs a bunk, making my choice limited to a couple of bunks at the far end of the dormitory; a bunk next to the wall, or one in between two frowning boys. I take the one next to the wall so I only have one pimple-faced boy on my left. He stares at me like I'm intruding on his space.

I give him a casual smile. "Hi. I'm Dax."

He doesn't smile. "Nikko." His uniform is still neatly folded beside him. He motions to my uniform at the end of my bunk. "That's yours. You pick out your boots over there." He points to some shelves with stacks of different-sized boots.

"Thanks. Nice to meet you, Nikko." I sit on my bunk and look around for somewhere to change. It looks like the uniform shirts are one size because some of the shirts on the kids who are dressed are stretched tight like they'll rip any second, and the skinny kids have baggy shirts as if two kids could fit in them.

How come nobody is doing or saying anything?

There's a whistle from outside and a second later, the kids without their uniforms on all strip off their clothes and get dressed without a second thought. How can they do that? Boys and girls together, undressing. I don't want to take my clothes off in front of anyone. They probably all have brothers or sisters and are used to changing in front of other people. I suppose it's not that bad, we all have underclothes on and we're all recruits, sort of brothers and sisters when you think of it. So why do I feel awkward?

Nikko's already dressed and kicks my bunk. "Put your uniform on. If you get us disciplined because you refuse to obey orders, I'll be the first one to break your spine."

Nikko isn't interested in being my friend either. Is there no one who wants to see me for who I am? I'm just an ordinary girl and I don't want to be here. Can't one person say something kind? Of course they can't, kind words seem very scarce around here. I nod to Nikko, turn away, and take my shirt off. I look over my shoulder and see that he appears satisfied because he fiddles with his boot laces, keeping an eye on me the whole time. I want to get dressed quickly since my underwear is old and worn, but Lenora rushes over before I have the chance. She's wearing a dark blue shirt. Where'd she come from?

She grabs me by the arm, pulls me to the middle of the dormitory, laughs, and tugs at my old undershirt. "Ew! Smudge has dirty underclothes!"

I pull away. "They're not dirty," I mumble as I wrench my arm until she lets go. "Leave me alone."

Stomping down the aisle, Tablon claps his hands together for attention. He's fully dressed in his uniform, which also is a blue shirt instead of our red, but his has a white stripe around the middle. "What's all the noise? You'd better shut up because the Commander is coming for inspection." He glares at me. "Why aren't you dressed, smudge?"

He puts his meaty hand on my shoulder and pushes me backward so I fall onto a bunk. I get up fast and ignore the jeers. "I was trying to get dressed, but..."

"No excuses, smudge!" he bellows. He thumps his way to the doorway and looks out. "The Commander is here. Recruits, get to your bunks and stand at attention."

I hurry to my bunk with no time to dress. Viteri has already entered the dormitory and is walking down the aisle slowly as the recruits stand up straight at the foot of their bunks. I do the same, wearing my regular pants and my undershirt. I can hear Nikko muttering under his breath that my spine will be snapped in half as soon as Viteri leaves. Breaking spines certainly seems to be a popular threat.

Viteri announces, "These are open-gender dormitories. There will be no sexual activity tolerated. You are here to train, not engage in sex. Control your urges. Anyone disregarding this rule will lose their subsidy forever, your family will be disgraced and you will be sent directly to the front lines without further training. It is your duty to report any sexual activity you might witness. All those accused will be examined by the verity-probe. For you uneducated vaporous nebulas, the verity-probe taps into your mind and detects deceit. If you report a verifiable incident, you will receive an extra ration of food and your family will receive a one-time bonus. If you falsely accuse someone, you will lose your subsidy for a month and receive half-rations for the entirety of your training. This is your only warning."

He continues on his way, screaming at a couple of recruits who evidently hadn't tied their boots correctly, but praises Tablon, of course, for his excellent military behavior. Now it's my turn.

"Orwan. I should have guessed you'd be the one to cause problems." Viteri's so close to me that I see the hard, deep lines etched into his face. He shakes his head. "How difficult is it to change clothes? I would have thought even you could manage that. Is this another of your rebellious traits?" He feels the fabric of my undershirt between his fingers. "This is the most pathetic thing I've ever seen. You might be a lowly Status 2, but in this camp, you're a recruit and will look like all the other recruits. Senior Lead Neemiss! Dress this pathetic waste of oxygen." He steps back and waits for Tablon.

I automatically back away. I don't want Tablon to touch me. Ever. I turn around and reach for my uniform shirt but Tablon grabs me, throws me to the ground on my back, straddles me, and pins my arms down. He's so strong, I can't move. He looks up at Viteri.

"Stop!" I shout.

Tablon slaps his hand over my mouth.

Viteri frowns and leans down. "Do I have to reiterate that a recruit does not argue or speak unless spoken to? When you are dressed in your regulation uniform, you will come to my office." He straightens and motions to Tablon. "Dress that recruit. And burn those underclothes. This is my camp and I have an image to uphold." He spins around and struts from the dormitory.

Nobody is talking or laughing, just staring at me, helpless on the ground. Tablon sneers and rips at my undershirt while I struggle. After a few seconds, he tears it off. "Well, at least you look like a girl under that filthy shirt. But you're nothing. A smudge. A trouble-making piece of galactic dust. You'll die so I can survive. Understand?"

I want to cover myself and scream out and push him off me, but I'm powerless. He works at my pants and underwear and with help from Lenora, gets them off me as well. I'm lying here, completely naked with everyone in the dormitory watching. Tablon finally gets off me, gives me a half-hearted kick, and throws my uniform on top of me. Lenora is laughing and pointing and tosses a pair of boots right at me.

Tablon chuckles. "Worthless smudge. Get dressed and go see the Commander." He peacocks around like he's just accomplished the greatest feat, and when he laughs, the other recruits follow suit, although a few hesitate, but ultimately join in.

I sit up with my shirt covering my chest, turn my back to everyone and dress faster than I ever have before, even with my hands shaking. Once I have my boots on, I rush from the dormitory as everyone laughs harder. I hate them all. Not one of them came to my rescue. Well, if they have no time for me, then I have no time for them.

Once outside, I take a few deep breaths and wipe my sweaty face with my new shirt. It's a bit loose and scratchy, but at least it's clean. The boots are a good fit, but I'm sure Lenora was hoping they wouldn't be. With my head clear again, I can see how the camp is set up in a semi-circular wheel-spoke pattern with the dormitories radiating out from the commander's offices, with the clearing at the center. It's similar to how our outliers are positioned around the city. It must be a popular planning design.

Viteri's is the nicest building in the camp, with a fresh coat of greenish-gray jungle camouflage paint and a precisely printed sign above the doorway that says *Viteri, Senior Commander*. The other commander's offices are located on either side of his and are much smaller.

I need to calm down before going in, or my mouth might blurt out something I'll regret. Just a few minutes to check out the camp and make Viteri wait. My personal rebellion. What's he going to do to me at this point if I don't rush to bow down to him? Deny me food, electro-shock me again? Sweat is dripping off my face, no matter how many times I wipe it on my shirt. Since there's no one in the area, I'll sneak around the back of the offices. That's amazing, ten fighter ships lined up in two rows of five each. They're beautiful ships; shiny silver and sleek with a main cockpit window located at the nose and smaller portholes on either side. Their wings are graceful, delta-shaped, and seem to be made of a solid piece of metal, no seams or rivets anywhere that I can see, and the ships are hovering off the ground without anything supporting them.

Across from the fighters are several small camo-colored buildings close together with an *armory* sign on them. I've never held a weapon; not a knife, not a laser gun, nothing. And I'm expected to fight against the enemy and kill as many as I can while protecting the likes of Tablon?

I wait a few more seconds, but I know I can't delay any longer. Back to Viteri's office I go and give one knock.

"Enter!" he shouts.

I walk in and salute. He paces back and forth behind his large, ornate desk, clicks his tongue, and comes to me, looking me up and down.

"At attention, recruit. You're late."

"Yes, sir." I press my lips together to stop from smiling, drop the salute and slap my hands to my thighs. At least I can salute perfectly.

He shakes his head and mumbles, "Can't even salute or stand at attention right. This only proves I was right to bring you here and get you away from prospective recruits. You'd have them questioning everything, wouldn't you? You're only good for one purpose." He lets the words hang in the air. "Senior Lead Neemiss and Lead Averlowes have already formed an opinion about you. And I agree with them. I can't justify wasting time and money on someone like you. You'll receive minimal training in weapons only." He goes behind his desk again, places his palms flat on his desk, and leans forward. "Your sole purpose is to serve my will and protect the lead soldiers when necessary. Got it?"

The last thing I want to do is protect Tablon, but I nod. "Yes, sir."

I don't plan on dying, no matter what he thinks. Ma and Da need my advancement subsidy, so the longer I stay alive, the more money they'll get. This isn't fair though. Nobody lasts long on the moon fighting the Katarga, but I have to find a way so Ma can save enough subsidies to get fertility treatments and have more children. It's kind of ironic though. She refused the government-sponsored fertility treatments because she wouldn't sign the waiver that the resulting child would automatically be advanced on their Date of Fate. And now, here *I* am, a soldier.

Viteri continues, "I called you out privately for a reason." He straightens, walks around me, and runs his thick, stubby fingers through my tangled hair. "I've come up with a practical way for you to serve the Global Forces regardless of your continued non-conformity. You're going to be an example and you'll be famous for it."

"Famous, sir?" Famous for what? Dying faster than any recruit in history?

He smirks like he read my mind. "Hopefully you won't die right away because I have plans for you. Being a Single, your sacrifice for the greater good will stand out and show other families that are as selfish as yours that they need to produce more children to keep their subsidies coming in, and to provide more soldiers for the wars. Nobody wants to lose a war. And for a Single to be a casualty of the enemy, well, it'll stir up the outliers. Parents will scramble to produce more kids and advance the ones they already have to keep the subsidies rolling in. We'll get a bump in advancements." He pauses for a moment and as an afterthought, mumbles, "And as a bonus, with you out of the way, there will be no more anti-Global Forces rants."

What does he mean? I've never ranted about the Global Forces. "I don't understand, sir."

"I didn't expect you to. You tested well, but you're really quite a simpleton, aren't you? Well, let me put it in words you can understand. You ask questions you have no right to ask. I have a way to shut you up. And you'll like this, your death will help the Global Forces grow. Your mother refuses to accept the fertility treatments we can provide free of charge, so when you die, your parents will have no subsidies at all and will be driven from their home, financially destitute. Living on the streets is a tough life and most people don't survive long. They'll starve or become victims of the roving scavenger gangs. Their demise will be broadcast to everyone on Earth, especially in the outliers." He nods to himself. "Oh, I didn't forget about you. *Your* death will be broadcast first, all over the planet. So, Orwan, you'll be famous for providing the world with proof that reproducing frequently and advancing children is a matter of survival. Families need money and we need recruits."

He has a full-on smile now. He stares off into the distance. "Advanced kids equals money."

I'm not going to be his propaganda. If I had the chance, I'd run from his office and wouldn't stop until I'm back home. My life means nothing to him, but my death is going to be used for his purposes. Am I supposed to react, to beg him not to let me die? If he expects me to crumble, he's in for a surprise. I throw my shoulders back a bit more and look straight ahead, willing myself not to break down.

He sits behind his desk and brings up a projection in front of him. "Tell Senior Lead Neemiss to report to me right away. Dismissed."

I salute, even though he's no longer looking at me, turn and leave the office. Once outside, I can't hold it in and run around the back of the building, crouch down and scream into my hands. Sweat drips down my face and mixes with my tears. I don't want to cry, but I can't stop myself. My life is over before it ever really started.

Chapter Four

I can't catch my breath and have to lean against the building so I don't fall. The hot damp air is thick and sticks to my lungs, and my face is dripping wet. I'm to die in one of the absurd, endless wars against beings I'll never get to know or understand.

The blaring sun is miserable and I'm too uncomfortable to stay outside any longer. My feet won't cooperate and I end up shuffling across the camp to my dormitory. My shirt is soaked through with sweat and tears. I'm sure this'll get me yelled at or disciplined. Does it matter? Do I really care?

I step into the air-conditioned dormitory and see Tablon's still there. I can't stand the thought of talking to him, so instead of telling him Viteri wants to see him, I walk down the aisle to my bunk. For whatever reason, nobody speaks to me, not even Tablon who's marching around glaring at everyone. Why doesn't he go to his own dorm and leave us alone? I lie down and stare up at the ceiling, listening to Nikko mumbling something to his other bunkmate, but I don't care enough about either of them to try to listen.

I'm not sure how much time passes before Viteri storms in and thunders for Tablon to stand at attention. "I will not tolerate a senior lead disobeying my orders! Are you learning bad habits from Orwan?"

Tablon snaps a salute. "What orders, sir?"

Viteri is red-faced. "To report to my office! Orwan was to tell you."

Now they both stare in my direction. In one smooth movement, I spring from my bed and salute. "I told him when I returned to the dormitory, sir."

"You liar! You didn't say a thing to me, smudge!" Tablon roars.

"Yes, Commander, I did. I passed him and told him, then went directly to my bunk, sir." I continue to hold the salute, but it's really hard not to smile.

Viteri glares at me. "At attention, recruit." He turns to Tablon. "Did you think it was unimportant because it came from Orwan? If I give an order, no matter who delivers it, it's to be obeyed!"

Tablon is pale. He looks at a girl next to him. "Did you hear her?"

The girl stands up, salutes, shakes her head, and motions to her bunkmate. "I was discussing strategy with Mayon. I wasn't paying attention to anyone else."

Viteri gets face-to-face with Tablon. "My office. You're a senior lead, act like one." He spins on his heels and strides away.

Tablon is obviously shaken. He straightens his uniform, points directly at me, and threatens, "You're dead, smudge. I'll make you pay for this."

I give him a salute and stare straight ahead, not at him. "Yes, sir." My lips curl up ever-so-slighty, even though I'm fighting it.

After Tablon stomps out of the dormitory, I sit, well aware that everyone is staring at me. This is the only good thing that's happened to me since I left home and I plan to cling to it and replay it in my mind many, many times.

With Tablon gone, there's mumbling and chatting among the recruits and I hear my name and smudge a couple of times. Thankfully nobody bothers me. After a while, the talking dies down and I'm left wondering what we're supposed to do. There's nothing in the dormitory, no books or computers. The only distraction from the boredom is to count the mismatched tiles that make up the ceiling and imagine ways that Tablon could get disciplined. I get to five hundred and thirty tiles by the time he returns and orders us to gather outside. He's angry judging by the scowl set on his face and I hope that means he was disciplined.

Everyone moves into the aisle, single-file, making me last, and trudges out. Tablon is waiting by the door and shoves me out, hard, and I fall face-first onto the dirt in front of the dormitory. As fast as I can, I scramble to my feet and hurry to join up with the other recruits. When Viteri comes out of his office, we all salute and Tablon stands in front of us, like we belong to him. My hatred for him is getting stronger.

Viteri, holding an open metal box, strolls down the row of recruits, passes me and slows, but doesn't stop. He continues down the line and finally stops at Tablon and Lenora, takes two swatches of fabric from the box, and presses one patch on the left shoulder of Tablon's shirt and the other onto Lenora's shoulder. They stick like they're sewn on. Tablon's patch is blue with SLS in white. Viteri announces that SLS stands for Senior Lead Soldier. Lenora's patch is light blue with LS in dark blue; LS means Lead Soldier. The rest of the recruits get patches with various initials; PS for Pilot Squadron, SC for Strategic Command, and IC for Intelligence Control. Nikko has a PS. Why was he chosen to be a pilot? I could be a pilot if someone would teach me. Everyone has a patch except for me. What's left? Viteri whispers to Tablon and hands him a patch. Without a word, Tablon slaps the patch onto my shoulder harder than he had to. It's a pale green rectangle with the letters AFGF in bold red print. Tablon steps back and Viteri comes to me.

He's smirking. "AFGF. Anti-foe Ground Forces. Bottom of the barrel. The loser squadron."

He goes and stands beside Tablon again, directly in front of us, and clears his throat. "Recruits, find your new dormitories and introduce yourselves to the RIC of your squadron."

I glance at the other recruits and a few are nodding like they know what RIC stands for. Tablon steps forward to seize the opportunity to assert his official status on those of us who know nothing.

He clears his throat just like Viteri did and receives a nod of approval. "Your RIC is the Recruit in Charge of your squad." He steps back with his chin jutting out.

Viteri gives one sharp nod to Tablon. "Thank you, Senior Lead Neemiss. Recruits, dismissed!"

Tablon follows Viteri into his office and the recruits separate and scatter in all directions looking for their new housing, but I stay where I am. The dormitories don't have any signs on them, so rather than wander into the various dormitories and get screamed at, I'll just stand in the middle of camp and wait until everyone vanishes into one of the units.

Most get it wrong on the first try and rush back out. The only one nobody goes in is the most run-down and shabby dorm in the whole camp. Process of elimination. That has to be mine.

Alone, I'll take the opportunity to enjoy the solitude and peace, although after a short time, the heat's too much. Hopefully my dormitory has air conditioning. I push the door and it creaks. From what I see, it's not too different from the first dormitory I was in, except it's a bit worse, with the floor boards worn with jagged splinters poking out. The bunks look really old, too. For a moment, I stand in the doorway and observe. The recruits are all sitting in a circle on the floor, but stop and stare at me. They have the same

23

patch as me. I point to my shoulder and they go back to what they're doing, playing some sort of game. One girl stands and smiles at me. She's small and skinny.

"Hi. You're an AFGF?"

"Yes. I'm Dax. I was just sent here."

She continues, "Hi, Dax. I'm Viga. You're tall and, ah, strong-looking. We never get many recruits in this squad, especially not anyone who looks like you." She comes to me and motions to the other recruits. "That's Kova, Mick, Brinna, Parna, and Big Pig."

I give them all a nod. "Hi. So there are only the seven of us?"

Viga shrugs. "Now there are. Four just graduated and were sent to the front lines. Parna's been here almost two weeks, so she goes next, then Mick. I'm the newest, here for another twelve days. We get the worst recruits every once in a while. Oh, no offense, but we're the rejects." She shrugs again and sits.

I'm not sure what to say. "I don't think any of you are rejects."

The boy named Big Pig laughs. His round belly jiggles. "Yeah, we are. I'm fat and stupid, that's why I couldn't be assigned a career and ended up here. I have three brothers and four sisters. They're all smart. I'm the oldest and the only worthless kid in my family. My Da couldn't wait to send me away. Laser fodder is what he said I am."

I'm so shocked at what I hear. How can any kid say things like that about himself? And how could his Da tell him that he's "laser fodder"? Big Pig looks like any other kid and I bet if he had training, he'd be just as good as any soldier. "What's your real name? It can't be Big Pig."

He looks down at the ground and wrings his hands. "It's Briett. But I've been Big Pig for as long as I can remember. It's okay, I'm used to it."

"Well, I'll call you Briett if that's all right." I come all the way into the dormitory. "I'm supposed to introduce myself to the RIC."

Viga raises her hand. "That's me. We appoint a different RIC each day so we all get a chance. You can be it tomorrow if you want."

"I don't think so." I sit on the floor when they make a space for me between Briett and Kova. Kova is a cute girl with long brown hair and a few freckles over her nose. She's also very small and scrawny. In fact, the only big kid is Briett. "So, what are we supposed to do?"

Briett looks up and flashes a smile. "They leave us alone, so we get to play games until it's time for weapons training. We only train for a couple hours a day. I stink at shooting. My Da's right, I'm laser fodder. I won't last a day on the front lines." He's still smiling.

"And you're okay with that?" I look around at the faces staring at me like I said something wrong.

With a heavy shrug, Briett sighs. "Don't have a choice, Dax. I knew from when I was a little boy that I'd never see sixteen, so I made the best of it and ate everything that tasted good! No reason not to. Had to steal some because my parents ration out the food. But I'm good at stealing. I didn't even pass my exit exams at school. My Da said he'll use my advancement bonus money for the early-pay marriage fee for my fourteen-year-old sister so she doesn't have to be advanced or assigned. When she's eighteen, she'll marry one of our outlier's teachers and have a heap of kids. So, that's good I guess, huh?"

I'm speechless. I can't think of a single response to what he said. How could any parent treat a child like that? Ma and Da love me. Then again, if they had other kids, would things be different?

Not a single AFGF recruit appears upset about Briett's acceptance of his fate, or maybe they all feel the same way about themselves as well. Maybe it's me who's weird for thinking this is all so wrong, after all, I am a "non-conformist". Viga hands me a small clay cube with a series of lines on each side.

She pats Briett on the back and gets up. "Big Pig, can you teach Dax how to play? I have to go to the toilet."

He nods and perks up. "Sure!"

I watch Viga to see where the toilet is. She goes to the end of the dormitory and vanishes behind a curtain. I nudge Briett. "We don't have an actual bathroom with doors?"

"Us? Of course not." He laughs. "There's a toilet behind the curtain and we get to use the communal shower outside."

"Communal shower?" I don't like the sound of that. It was horrifying when Tablon stripped me in front of everyone and the thought of repeating the experience makes me sick to my stomach.

Briett looks at me strangely. "It's not really a communal shower, that's just what we call it. It's a water hose. I use it at night so nobody sees me. Nobody wants to see my naked fat ass." He chuckles.

I look at the little clay cube in my hand as my mind spins in a thousand different directions. Here I am, in a broken-down dormitory with a toilet at one end, a hose outside, and a bunch of kids who are ready for death. What would Ma and Da say if they knew where I'd ended up? Will they ever know?

Briett nudges me. "It's called War and Money."

I'm brought back to reality. "What is?"

"The game." Briett points to the clay cube. "You have to roll the cube. If one line is face-up, you get assigned a bad job and die poor. You're out. But if you get a two, four, or six, you get advanced and you roll again."

"What happens if you get a three or five?" I ask, not fully understanding why they want to play a game that's too much like real life.

Briett takes the cube and turns it around several times. "Ah, I forget. I'm dumb."

Kova groans. "A three or five are lucky numbers. You get to be a pilot for a three and a Lead for a five. You don't roll a second time for a three or five, but when it's your turn again, the numbers are all different. A one means you get an advancement bonus, a two means you get two bonuses, and a four means your family gets subsidies for the rest of their lives. A six, now that's what you want to get. A six gets you fame as a Foe Buster."

And I thought my head was spinning before. "What's a Foe Buster?"

With a grin, Kova nudges Briett. "You know this, Big Pig."

"Oh, yeah." Briett smiles. "A Foe Buster means you win the game because you killed all of the aliens and you're a hero."

I drop the cube on the ground. "I don't want to play a game like that."

"Come on, Dax," Briett pleads. "Maybe you'll win."

None of us will win. Doesn't he understand that? A stupid game isn't going to change that. I get up and find a bunk that evidently hasn't been claimed. There's a thin blanket folded on top of the old mattress with an almost-flat pillow lying on top. I spread out the blanket, do my best to fluff the pillow, lie down and close my eyes, hoping to shut out everything around me.

A moment later, I hear Viga beside me. "Dax, what's wrong?" She squeezes onto my bunk, forcing us both to teeter on the edges. "You don't like War and Money?"

I open my eyes and shake my head. "No, I don't." I sit up. "Viga, it seems like everyone, including all of you, are ready to march into war and die. That's sick."

She looks at me as if she can't make sense of what I said. "It's just the way it is, Dax. Some people are born leaders or fighter ship pilots and some of us are born to protect them. We protect them for as long as we can. That's honorable, not sick. And look at us. We're the dregs of society and couldn't get a decent job in our outliers anyway. This is best because we get to protect the important soldiers. I feel like my life's worth something if I can save someone else."

"Come on, do you honestly believe we can protect anyone with only two hours of weapons training a day? I've never held a gun, ever. I have two weeks, two hours a day to learn how to shoot. I can't do it."

"You don't know that until you try. Kova and I have trouble holding the guns because they're so big and heavy, but the boys are doing all right." She lowers her voice to a whisper, "Well, except for Big Pig. He's awful. The instructor said he can put down cover fire since he doesn't have to be good for that. He just has to shoot in the general direction."

I flop back down and close my eyes again. "Don't you want to grow up to be somebody, have a career where you can do something you enjoy? Live each day without the fear of dying from an alien's weapon?"

"I guess I never thought of it. My parents advance us all. I have three younger brothers and my Ma's pregnant right now with another boy. I had four older brothers, but only one of them has survived so far. He's sixteen and on the lunar surface fighting the Katarga, I think. He was always kind of sickly growing up, but now he's beaten the odds. I'm hoping I'll see him on the moon and maybe we can team up and..."

I turn my head and look at Viga. "Hold on. Your parents are told where he is and what he's doing?" Maybe there's some hope that if Ma and Da know what's going on, they'll bring me back home.

Viga puts her hand on my arm. "Well, no. But the subsidy keeps coming, so that means he's still alive. And his name wasn't on the last death roster

I saw in our outlier. I like to think he's on the moon so I can look up at it and imagine he's there looking down at me. You know, they always send the skinny or sickly kids to the moon. As soon as someone dies, the subsidy's cut off and we're notified. The government doesn't waste any time either. If you die before the month is out, your parents will lose the whole month's subsidy. That's why it's best to try to stay alive until the very beginning of the month. Does that make sense?"

I give a half-hearted nod. "How can they do that? If we serve for every day except the last day of the month, the government takes the entire month's subsidy away from our parents? That's ridiculous. My parents need it all."

She shrugs. "Everyone needs it all. Without the child subsidies, nobody can make it on only a salary. Except for the rich people. That's why my parents keep having kids. Unless she pays the marriage fee for one of my brothers or sisters, our family will die out. But Ma's almost forty-four. It took her nine rounds of fertility treatments to get pregnant this last time. And those treatments don't come cheap. She gets a state-sponsored discount from Global Command, but even with the discount, the treatments cost a lot. With the discount, she had to advance the child or pay the marriage fee, but we never seem to have the money for the marriage fee."

"My ma refused to use the free treatments because she didn't want to be forced to advance her children. But, here I am."

"It's a hard decision, Dax. My ma's going to start accepting the free treatments so she'll save a bit of money and maybe one day have enough for a marriage fee. She'll have to advance the child, but if she can save enough, one day maybe she can have one child get married." She sighs. "Have you ever thought how it seems like Global Command handles just about everything? They make life so hard. Ma doesn't want to send us away to fight, but we don't qualify for decent jobs or careers. We're Status 3. My family is stuck in this cycle. See?"

"I do see. And like I said before, it's sick. If Global Command forces families to advance their children, soon the population will...maybe that's the plan. To reduce the population and only keep the wealthy reproducing."

"Don't talk like that, Dax. It's dangerous."

I roll over and watch the rest of my fellow AFGFs play War and Money. "Viga, what happens when your ma can't have kids anymore?"

She doesn't speak for a few seconds. "I don't like to think of that. Da puts tiny bits of his salary aside when he can by skimping on food, but I once heard him and Ma talking when they thought we were all asleep."

I roll back over and see tears in her eyes. "Talking about what, Viga?"

"Da said he'll divorce Ma once she's infertile and marry a young woman."

"What!" I spring up too fast and almost knock Viga off the bunk.

Viga wipes her tears and sits up as well. "No, listen, it's not so bad. He's going to give Ma money from the advancement bonuses once his new wife starts having kids. Ma can live in one of the underprivileged housing units so she won't be on the streets."

I know what the underprivileged housing units are. I saw them every day on my way to school. They're tall structures, walled in so no one in them can come out among regular society. The people in there are little more than animals kept in cages until they die. They're either too weak, too old, or too sick to work, or, according to Viga, they can't have kids. I didn't realize infertile women were shoved in there, too. Those poor people have scraps of food delivered to them. It's subsistence food, the stuff that's not fit for other people. It's the minimum to keep them alive. They can buy additional food, if they have the money. To think of Viga's ma, or my ma, in there makes me cry as well.

"Don't cry, Dax." Viga uses the end of the blanket to dab at my tears. "This is the world. We live, we die. There's not much in between."

"There are wars. That's what's in between, Viga. Never-ending wars!" I stand because I can't sit still any longer and my heart's pumping so hard it feels like I'll explode.

"Quiet, Dax," warns Kova as she tosses the cube. "If anyone hears you, you'll get us all disciplined."

I take in a deep breath. "Does it matter? We're all dead anyway."

A hush falls over the dormitory as they all jump to their feet and salute. What now? I straighten and salute as well when Tablon walks in with Lenora a few steps behind him.

Chapter Five

Like a factory auto-bot, Tablon stops, bends, and picks up the clay cube. He examines it and hands the cube to Lenora. "You Anti-foe's sit around all day playing child games? Is that why you're in training camp? Is it?"

Briett shakes his head. I'm willing him not to speak, but he does anyway, "No, we're here to get good with laser guns so we can kill the aliens before they vaporize us." He grins like he's proud of his answer.

For whatever reason, this infuriates Tablon and he pokes Briett in the stomach. "You must be that waste of oxygen, Big Pig. Did I say you could speak, piggy? No, I didn't. You don't open that fat mouth of yours until I give you permission. You've just earned your squadron a first-violation discipline."

Viga groans softly, "Oh, no."

I want to ask what a first-violation discipline is, but decide to wait and hear it from Tablon's mouth, just in case he gives me a second-violation discipline for asking what the first one is.

Tablon motions to Lenora. "Lead Lenora will be in charge of your discipline." He spins around and strides from the dormitory with his hands clasped behind his back.

Lenora's mouth is set in a slight smirk that makes me want to slap it off her. She walks slowly down the aisle, nose in the air. "This squadron is pathetic. I've never seen such pitiful alien bait." She stops at Briett. "Big Pig, you'll lead your squadron."

Poor Briett smiles and throws his shoulders back. "I'll be the leader?"

Lenora smirks more. "Yes, you will. You'll be 100% responsible for carrying out the discipline. If your squad fails, you'll incur a second-violation discipline. Okay, recruits, follow Big Pig into the gathering area in front of the dorms and get on your knees." She goes and waits by the door.

Briett nods and waves to us all to follow him. When I get near Lenora, she glares at me and gives me a shove in the back as I pass. I stumble like I always do when they shove me, but this time I was expecting it and I don't fall. I calmly continue outside and even though it's late afternoon, the sun seems even hotter now. I'm not outside for more than ten seconds before I'm drenched in sweat.

Briett is the first to drop to the ground on his knees, but he goes down too fast and hard and tumbles over. I rush and help him get back on his knees.

"Orwan!" Lenora screams. "Front and center!"

Apparently, I'm not allowed to help anyone. I come to her and salute. "Yes, ma'am," I spit the words like they're venom.

Lenora slaps my raised hand. "You don't call me ma'am and you don't salute me, stupid smudge."

"Fine." I drop the salute.

She walks around me. "You've got a tender heart, don't you, smudge? You think that fat lump is worth helping?" Now she's in my face. "He's not. And you're no better than him." She takes a step back and looks at the others. "The discipline for you AFGFs is to miss today's training session and to clean the other dormitories...in your underwear!" She laughs.

I'm panicked. "But I don't have any underwear on. Tablon ripped it off me and threw it away."

Lenora raises an eyebrow. "That's Senior Lead Neemiss. Then you'll clean naked. Doesn't matter to me, but you won't dirty your uniform. Now strip and clean my dormitory first, the Lead Squadron, third dormitory from the left. It better sparkle when we get back from training." She also clasps her hands behind her back.

A loud buzzing sounds throughout the camp and an announcement calls for all recruits to head to their assigned training areas. They all emerge from their various dormitories, some looking cocky, and others, terrified. I can't be naked, I just can't. I don't know what to do. I'm shaking so hard I might collapse. Briett is the first to strip off his uniform and fold it neatly on the ground. The others do the same until it's only me left fully dressed. Lenora grabs my arm, twists it, and throws me to the ground.

"I said take off your clothes, recruit!" She kicks me in the ribs.

It hurts, but I can't let her know that.

A crowd is starting to gather, pointing and giggling at us.

Briett pulls his undershirt over his head and carries it to me. "I don't need a shirt. It's too hot out for a shirt. And if they want to look at my tubby tummy, let them!"

I get up, keeping my eyes on Lenora, and accept Briett's gift. I'm about to take off my clothes when my fellow AFGFs make a circle around me, turn around facing out and close in so nobody can see me. I strip off my uniform and put on the shirt. It's so stretched out, it comes down almost to my knees.

I tap Briett on the shoulder. "I'm done. You're a life saver. Thanks."

My group breaks the circle and together we head to the Lead dormitory, doing our best to ignore the jeers. I glance over my shoulder at Lenora and know that I've just defied her in front of everyone, and it feels amazing. *Thank you, Briett!* At the dormitory, Viga takes my hand, turns to Lenora and grins.

Lenora takes off toward us, but Viga pulls me into the dorm and locks the door behind us. A barrage of hard thumps on the door makes Viga laugh out loud, but I'm mortified that we'll get in trouble.

Lenora shouts, "I can hear you laughing!"

Briett sits on the nearest bunk, shaking his head. "I'm such an idiot. I thought I was going to be a leader, but I'll never be anything. She said I was the leader, but she didn't mean it. I can't lead anyone. We'll get another discipline now and it's because of me."

When she stops laughing, Viga pats Briett on the back. "You're brave, Big Pig. That's better than being a leader."

I sit next to him. "You're a hero, *my* hero. You risked getting in trouble to give me your shirt. That makes you a hero, Briett."

He perks up a bit. "I guess." He looks around, his eyes getting bigger and bigger. "Wow, this dormitory is nice."

He's right, the bunks have sheets, fluffy blankets, and two pillows each, and the floor is polished tile with small area carpets near each bunk. It already looks spotless.

I get off the bunk. "What are we supposed to clean?"

The door unlocks and Lenora barges in. She has two other girl Leads with her, each holding two buckets. They walk around and empty the buckets, filled with mud and dirt, all over the floors and bunks, throw the buckets across the room, turn and leave without a word. Lenora grins and follows them out.

Viga and Kova are standing together, shaking their heads, looking absolutely disheartened. I feel the same way, but we don't have the luxury of feeling sorry for ourselves.

Over in the far corner, I see a few mops and brooms. "Briett, you're our leader, why don't you give us all assignments. We're going to clean this dormitory so it's cleaner than it was before."

He nods. "I don't know how to lead anyone."

"Yes, you do. It's up to you to tell us what to do."

He thinks for a few seconds, then grabs the buckets. "I'll fill these with water. Um, Mick and Parna, can you start sweeping up the dirt and mud? And Kova, Brinna, and Viga can mop up what's left. Dax, do you know how to do laundry? You can wash the bedding."

I smile at him. "Sure. I used to do all of our laundry at home and was pretty good at it."

Kova stomps her foot. "This isn't fair. I really need training. I was hoping to ask our instructor if I can use a lighter gun. What am I going to do if I can't shoot? I'll be killed as soon as I hit the ground." Tears fall.

I don't want to paint a rosy picture of our future, but it isn't doing any good to have our squadron crying and giving up. "Don't cry. Every tear you shed takes a bit of you with it. We have to be strong for our families back home." I grab one of the brooms and hand it to Kova. "How much heavier is the laser gun and how big?"

She holds the broom and points it like a gun. "I lot heavier than this. Maybe fifty times as heavy, I don't know. And the gun is about a meter long."

"Okay." I take the broom. When Manti and I were little, we'd play soldiers and aliens and I'd always prop my heavy toy wooden laser gun on my shoulder because I wasn't very strong. "Get on the ground, on your stomach, and lean on your elbows."

She lies down and props herself up on her elbows. "Now what?"

I hand her the broom again but put the handle on her shoulder. "Use your shoulder to take some of the weight. And what if you and Briett put down cover fire low to the ground. You'll be a smaller target that way and the gun won't be so heavy because you won't be carrying it."

With another sniff, Kova nods. "I get it. That might work. How did you think of that?"

I shrug. "Something I remembered."

Manti always said I was good at figuring things out, like the time I helped her fix the cracked leg on her school desk by making a splint with a stick and loose thread off her sweater. It saved her from getting detention, even though she hadn't broken the desk leg. Both of us suspected it was a boy who hated her because she scored higher than him on our advanced mathematics midterm exam. As terrible as school was sometimes, I'd rather go back there than be here.

Briett, with the two buckets in his hands, nods. "I can do that, too, Dax. I like the idea of being a smaller target for a change!" He bursts out laughing. "Think of that, me, small!"

We all laugh for a minute until Viga steps in as leader and puts us to work. I get the muddy sheets and blankets off the bunks and look around for a washtub or machine, but there isn't anything in the dormitory. I remember that Briett said we have a water hose outside of our dormitory, so off I go with my arms full of laundry to find a hose.

There's a strange humming sound echoing around the deserted camp, coming from the area behind Viteri's office where the fighter ships are. If it's a ship taking off, I want to see. I rush over to the office, peek around the corner and watch for a moment. The engines of the fighters are on and there are two recruits standing beside each fighter ship and a female instructor explaining the drill. I don't hear much of what she's saying, except for 'climb to altitude' and 'don't bank too steeply'. I'd rather learn to fly a fighter than be a foot soldier, but that's only a flicker of a dream that I really shouldn't allow into my head. But wouldn't it be wonderful to fly up through the clouds where nobody could tell me what to do? I'd be free.

The woman raises her arm and closes her fist. Right away, the pilots climb up a short ladder into their ships through a small entry door in the belly. A few seconds later, the engines roar. It's a magnificent sound; pure rumbling power and freedom, the only way to escape from the camp. I want to be in one of those ships.

"Orwan!" it's Viteri.

I spin around, drop the dirty laundry, and salute. He squints his eyes and shakes his head.

"What am I going to do with you, recruit? You refuse to obey even the simplest orders. Exactly how dumb are you? Did you cheat on your exit exams? You must have because I see no possible way you could have passed." He kicks at the laundry, steps on some of the sheets, and grinds them into the dirt with his boot. "There's a cleaning station behind the mess hall."

"Yes, sir."

"Drop the salute, Orwan."

"Yes, sir." I stand at attention.

He looks past me at the fighter ships. "Don't get any ideas. Your fate is determined, Orwan, and it doesn't involve a fighter ship. Your face will be on every pro-fertility, pro-Global Forces advertisement on Earth." He kicks at the laundry again. "You'll be famous. Posthumously. Your death has to come quickly because there have been grumblings that excessive childbearing is hard on the mother. That sort of thing needs to be nipped in the bud and your death is going to stress how vicious the Katarga are and how desperately we need more recruits to fight them. We lose hundreds of supplies every single day. Soldiers and their personal equipment and weapons. Big losses all around. We need more recruits to keep our supply up, Orwan, and you're going to be the one to help us keep them coming and get those whiny women to realize how Global Forces needs their children. It's a system of balance, you see. We need lots of children to be born and die before the world becomes overcrowded. Balance."

Sweat drips down my face and into my eyes, but I dare not wipe it away. I feel sick, whether from the heat or from what Viteri said, I don't know. He's staring at me. What does he expect me to say? "I'll do whatever I'm supposed to do, sir."

"Yes, you will. I told you, you're mine now to do with as I see fit. You will die for the Global Forces. And the bloodier, the better." He touches my cheek with the back of his hand. "A young girl's face covered in blood. Perhaps half your head blown off. That'll make an impact. Parents never see what happens to their kids. I'll spin it so they'll advance their kids to kill the Katarga before the same thing can happen to everyone on Earth. Ha, ha, it's perfect." He nods thoughtfully like he's talking to himself without me standing right in front of him. He snaps out of his wretched self-indulgent half-trance. "I'll make sure your family gets an extra bonus if your death is especially gruesome. A reward for your service. When you were inciting students to question the wars at your school, did you ever think you'd end up here?" He lifts the filthy sheets with his boot. "Finish that laundry. Meal time is at 1800. That gives you two hours."

He marches back to his office, leaving me alone with his horrible words floating and spinning in my head. A reward for my *service*? Not sacrifice, but service. And I wasn't inciting anyone to do anything. Is this his way of shutting me up for good? I stoop, pick up the bedding and go behind the mess hall with my knees wobbly.

The cleaning station is composed of two large, open vats with paddles inside that are turned by a solar-powered crank. I saw something similar once, only on a small scale, at the home of a friend who had a huge family. I can't even remember his name anymore. It was a long time ago.

Next to the vats are three rows of cord tied to posts and stretched out tight; the clothesline. After I dump the bedding into one of the vats and add water from a spigot, I turn on the crank and wait. Some sort of detergent is added automatically and soon suds bubble up and cover the laundry. I scoop out a handful of suds, rub them between my hands and over my face, and instantly feel cleaner than I have since I arrived. I stick my hands under the spigot and dump handfuls of water over my head.

While waiting, I climb onto the edge of the empty vat so I can get a view of the fighter ships as they hover along to a grassy field, in a single precise row. I saw a lot of transport ships flying overhead at home, but never a fighter. One after another, they gracefully lift higher off the ground by a few meters, tilt so their noses point straight to the sky, and shoot upward, disappearing into the clouds above. They're so fast! I want so badly to be in one of them, getting lost in the upper atmosphere where nobody can see me.

The water drains from the vats, leaving the sheets and blankets in a tangled pile. That's kind of how I feel, all tangled up inside. And I can't shake what Viteri said. What sort of person dreams of how a girl will die? That takes a special sort of demented mind.

It hurts too much to think of him and his plans for me, so I'll concentrate on hanging up the wash. The laundry is heavy, but I manage to drape it over the cords and relax in a lovely shady spot they've created. The coolness and the fresh smell of clean linen is wonderful and it takes me away for a few minutes. I feel like myself again, like when I'd hang our laundry at home.

Home. I remember the first day I went to school when I was five, ten years ago, and Ma made me a new shirt and walked with me all the way. My teachers were nice and I made a few friends, but not once did anyone tell me I was destined to die at fifteen. I couldn't wait to grow up, but now all I want is to be young again.

Enough dreaming, back to the real world. With the ships deployed and the rest of the recruits who-knows-where training, the camp is quiet and all I hear is the melodious chirping of exotic birds in the jungle surrounding the camp. They sound so happy and carefree. I can't help smiling in spite of the miserable situation I'm in.

"Hey, Dax!" calls Viga. "How's the laundry?"

I point to the bedding gently blowing in the light breeze. "Almost dry already."

She comes closer. "Looks good. We've got the dormitory clean." She shakes her head. "Big Pig stepped in a bucket and spilled dirty water all over the place, so we had to clean that up, too. But it's good now." She sits next to me.

"Listen," I whisper.

"To what?"

I motion around us. "The world."

A sweet scent drifts by. The perfume of flowers. Why didn't I smell that before?

Viga sniffs the air. "Oh, I love this time of day. That's when the jungle flowers come out. Did you have a flower garden at home, Dax?"

I shake my head. "No. The ground's too hard where we live. Nothing much grows there, except for a few wild flowers. I live in Village 77."

"Really?" She smiles. "I'm from Village 82. We're neighbors! Sort of."

I smile at her. "Yeah. Have you ever been to Jewel?"

"No. You?"

"No. I'd like to visit it, or any other city, but I don't think I'd like to *live* in a city. Too many people." I sigh.

"And no flowers!"

We giggle and enjoy the flowery perfume until it's time to take down the laundry. Viga helps me and we make up the bunks just in time, a minute before the Lead Squadron arrives from training. They collect in a group near the doorway. Thankfully Tablon isn't with them. My squad stands straight, not at attention, but proudly with their heads high and shoulders back.

Lenora steps forward. She looks around and checks the bunks, even underneath them. "Big Pig, did you really lead your squad?"

He nods. "I sure did."

"Well, Big Pig," Lenora says, "your squad did an acceptable job. Your discipline is hereby lifted, you don't have to clean any other dormitories. I can't be bothered with you AFGFs anymore. Go to your dorm and wash up. Meal time is in less than ten minutes. Your uniforms are already back in your dorm."

Briett licks his lips. "Meal time."

After taking a couple of steps toward the door, Lenora turns around. "And don't forget to tell the Commander and instructors that Lead Lenora Averlowes is fair and one of the best Leads in camp."

Briett glances at me for a second and then back at Lenora. "Oh, okay, I can do that."

"Good. Well done, recruits." She spins and strides from the dorm.

A compliment from Lenora? Did I hear that right? Although it's a self-serving move, still, we don't have to do any more cleaning. We hurry to our dorm and find our uniforms, which are in one big pile. Briett runs outside and comes right back with a wet towel for us to use to wash the dirt from our hands and faces, although I'm still quite clean from my brief wash with the suds. Kova passes around the only comb for our dormitory and helps me untangle the knots from my hair. For the first time since arriving, I feel good and hungry. I'm tired, but not tired enough to miss a meal.

When the dinner buzzer rings, we check each other to make sure our uniforms are neat and clean, then head out to the mess hall where Tablon is standing outside the entrance. Of course, he orders us to wait until everyone else goes in and is seated.

We start to move forward and the closer I get, the strong smell of food wafts by. There are so many aromas, I can't separate them. Potatoes, maybe? Roasted meat, probably. And bread, definitely. I haven't had anything to eat all day and my stomach's grumbling in anticipation.

Briett's in front of me and rubs his hands together. "I think that's roast chicken I smell. My mouth's watering."

"No talking in line!" screams Tablon. He stomps right to Briett. "Big Pig, of course it's you." He prods Briett in the stomach. "You could skip a few meals, you know. Shed a couple of pounds before the aliens splatter your fat carcass all over the lunar surface!" He laughs and pokes Briett again. "Go back to your dormitory, recruit."

"But I'm really hungry." Briett shuffles his feet in the dirt.

"You're a fat oaf and a disgrace to the Global Forces. Go to your dormitory!" Tablon balls up his fists.

I can't take it. "Leave him alone, Tablon. We all worked hard to complete Lenora's discipline and we deserve food." I push Briett forward as the line moves.

Tablon turns his fury on me now. "You address your superiors as Lead or Senior Lead!" He pokes me in the chest. "So, the smudge speaks in defense of an AFGF moron? I guess you don't want any food either. Both of you, go to your dormitory. Now." His eyes are burning into mine.

I know I shouldn't say anything, but I can't stop myself. "*Lead* Averlowes forced us to miss training and we did every single thing she told us to do. We deserve food."

Tablon threatens me with his fist. "You don't deserve anything, smudge. The Commander's right, you do poison people. Because of you, Big Pig misses that delicious, juicy chicken and seasoned potatoes in there. Now, both of you go to your dorm or I'll multiply your punishment by ten. You want that, smudge?"

There's no one around to help, not that they would. Nobody in camp seems to care what happens to me or my squad. I keep my eyes on Tablon. "I'm sorry, Briett. I'll make a formal complaint with the Commander."

"You'll do nothing, smudge!" Tablon unhooks what looks like an old-fashioned riding crop from his belt and whips me on the thigh. "You don't speak to the Commander!"

It stings and I yelp. My squad all turn around and without a word, run to get in front of me. Tablon swings the riding crop and manages to strike Mick and Parna before Briett snatches the crop out of Tablon's hands and starts whipping *him*! Tablon shouts and backs away, but trips and falls. Briett keeps whipping, over and over, ignoring me screaming for him to stop. Finally, Viteri arrives and pulls him off.

Viteri tosses Briett aside and helps Tablon to his feet. "How did this happen, Senior *Lead* Neemiss?"

Tablon's teeth are clenched and he has welts and cuts on his arms and neck. "He jumped me, Commander. No provocation. Just threw his lard ass at me and attacked me. Orwan told him to do it." He points at me.

Viteri turns and motions me forward. "Orwan? Why am I not surprised? Why did you make this porky recruit attack a superior? You'd better have a good answer."

I step forward and salute crisply. "I did not make Briett do anything, sir. He was defending me against an assault by Senior Lead Neemiss. Senior Lead Neemiss struck me on the leg, sir, because I objected to his command that Briett and I go without food simply for talking in line."

Viteri turns back to Tablon. "Is this true? You were going to deny them food for talking?"

"They attacked me, sir, and now they're lying." Tablon rubs a nasty welt on his neck.

"They?" Viteri shakes his head. "You said the fat recruit attacked. Now you say they? Which is it?"

Tablon is fuming. "I mean he attacked me. They both collaborated, that's what I meant."

Viteri nods. "Well, they deserve punishment and you are well within your right as Lead to deal punishment as you see fit, but we cannot starve recruits. A dead recruit isn't able to fight against the Katarga. Issue them a ration of bread and soup, but restrict them to their dormitory. I'd better not hear about any further incidents, *Senior Lead* Neemiss. Control these recruits and use whatever force you need. I'd suggest you administer an extra discipline for the recruit's assault on you." He glares at Briett and me and walks away.

I see that Briett is about to speak and probably get us in more trouble, so I open my mouth instead, "Senior Lead Neemiss, we apologize for any infraction and accept our punishment." The words are hard to get out, but they're only words. If it means protecting Briett from further punishment, then it's worth saying a few worthless words.

Tablon eyes me carefully. "Good. Seems like you're learning your place, smudge. Wait here and I'll fetch you a ration." He shoves his way inside.

Viga puts her arm around my shoulder. "You have to be careful, Dax. Lead Neemiss is out to get you and it's like you're not even trying to fit in and be a good soldier."

I'm not. I don't want to be a soldier and I certainly don't want to give in to Tablon. "Oh, don't forget, it's *Senior* Lead Neemiss, Viga. I'll be more careful, I promise. I'd never do anything on purpose to hurt any of you."

She steps back. "I know."

"Dax," Briett whispers. "I'm scared. I shouldn't have hit Lead Senior Neemo. Now he's going to kill me."

"No, he won't." I give him a pat on the shoulder. "And it's Neemis. Senior Lead Neemis. You heard the Commander. They need us alive." I wish I had something more positive to say, but I don't.

Lenora walks toward the mess hall but stops when Tablon comes out with one plate in his hand.

He glances at Lenora. "Where were you? You weren't in your dorm."

She shrugs. "I was waiting for the Commander. He just told me that you were disciplining the AFGFs with a reduced food ration. One plate? You can't starve them."

Tablon looks confused. "It's none of your business." He hands me the plate with a smirk. "Here." It contains one thin slice of bread and a small puddle of watery soup in a little cup with one spoon poking out. "Take it and get out of my sight. Big Pig gets nothing."

Briett groans. "But..."

I watch Lenora straighten and jut her chin out a bit, like she's trying to look authoritative. "Senior Lead Neemiss, the Commander said they both get a ration. Are you going against the Commander's orders? I would never do that. I give fair discipline. Don't I, Big Pig?"

Briett is completely confused. "I don't know. I mean, yes, I mean, I think so."

"Big Pig gets nothing!" Tablon shouts and stomps into the mess hall without looking back.

Instead of doing anything, Lenora shrugs and follows him with a smug look on her face.

I motion to Briett to follow me to our dorm. With his lower lip quivering, he shuffles along behind me, and once inside, I put the plate on his bunk. "Go ahead and eat, Briett. I had a big birthday breakfast this morning at home. I don't need it." I hope my lie sounds reasonable, although my growling stomach tells the truth. I didn't even get a piece of birthday cake because of Viteri.

Briett shakes his head. "No, we'll share. I can afford to lose a bit of weight, but you can't."

"Well, I'll have half of the bread. You take the rest." I tear the bread down the middle and go to my bunk before he can object.

The day is winding down, which means I only have thirteen more training days in the camp before I'm sent to the moon to fight the enemy. How do they expect any of us to kill without understanding the Katarga's motives for attacking us in the first place? I can't just kill on command. If the Katarga planned to invade Earth, shouldn't we find out why instead of trying to obliterate them? And what about the other aliens?

I gobble down my bread, which isn't that bad. Ma could only afford bread every couple of weeks, so it's a treat. I wonder what she's doing right now and if she misses me. I *really* miss her and would give anything for just one more hug.

Chapter Six

I'm about to drift off to sleep when the rest of my squad comes in from their meal, chatting. Viga runs right to me and hands me a small package wrapped in a paper napkin. Without unwrapping, I know what it is.

She sits on the edge of my bunk. "I hope you don't mind, but we all ate some of our food and saved the rest for you and Big Pig. It wasn't easy sneaking it out in front of Lead Tablon and Lead Lenora!" She giggled. "They were watching us the whole time."

I look over at Briett and see that Mick has handed him a package as well. Briett doesn't wait and downs the food as fast as he can. I carefully open the napkin and see two chunks of chicken, three tiny potatoes, two carrot sticks, and several small pieces of bread. It's the most wonderful sight.

I sit up and wave a carrot in the air for everyone to see. "Thank you. You have no idea how much this means." These kids are true friends, my friends. "Victory to the AFGFs!"

Viga smiles at me and hops off my bunk. "The Commander announced in the mess hall about the training times for tomorrow. We've got 0900. That's nine in the morning."

I nod. "I know." We learned about military time in school.

She continues, "Breakfast is at 0700. Oh, I almost forgot. Who wants to be the RIC tomorrow?"

Almost in unison, my squad says *Dax*. I suppose that since I'm the newest, it makes sense because everyone has already had a chance. But being in charge of other people isn't something I've ever done before. I learned about it in Leadership class, but this is real life. What if I let them all down and open my big mouth like I've already done a hundred times? I might get everyone disciplined, again.

Briett wipes his mouth on the back of his hand and crumples the napkin. "What do you say, Dax?"

I shrug. "I suppose I can do it. What's involved?"

Viga takes a deep breath. "You have to report to Commander Viteri first thing in the morning with an update on your recruits. You know, if anyone is sick or hurt. Then you have to go to the mess hall a few minutes before 0700 to set your squad's table. After breakfast, you take your squad back to the dorm to clean up for training. We don't do this part because we don't have bathroom facilities. Like Big Pig said before, most of us try to use the hose at night. Um, I think that's about it."

That doesn't sound so bad. At least it'll be better than sitting around staring at the walls. "Okay, I'll do it, but if I mess up, you have to tell me."

"You won't mess up, it's easy. Hey, if you want to wash, you should go out now while it's somewhat dark." Viga jumps on her bunk. "Who wants to play War and Money?"

I don't want to play or bathe so I curl up under the ratty blanket and close my eyes, imagining that I'm back home in my bed listening to Ma and Da in the living room softly talking about their jobs and how the only way our outlier stays solvent is because of the weapons factories up north.

The factories run 24 hours, seven days a week, and produce crates full of supplies each day. The Global Forces own the factories and the families who lease them are super-rich. So rich that their children never have to be assigned or advanced, and they have dishes without any cracks and new furniture, or so I'm told.

With constant wars and soldiers dying each day, the factories will never close down because they have to constantly crank out uniforms, armor, weapons, and fighter ships to keep up with the demand. That means the families will stay rich and maybe even get richer if more aliens attack us. They never have to worry about anything.

I hear Briett whoop when he wins at War and Money. I want to ask when he'll graduate and be sent to the front lines, but I'm not sure I really want to know. And I don't want to upset him. I can't imagine what it'll be like in a war, and I don't want him to start thinking about it. How am I going to feel pressing a trigger and blasting a hole into another living thing? One second a Katarga is alive, the next, dead. Do they have feelings like we do? Do they send their children into battle to die? Do they have nasty people like Tablon and Lenora? Maybe the Katarga are vicious and unthinking and deserve to die. Maybe.

I'd love to sleep, but I'm not tired and my mind's churning.

"Dax, are you asleep?" It's Kova.

I open my eyes. "No, I'm too wound up to sleep."

"Can I ask you something?" She kneels by my bunk.

"Sure."

She bites her lip and keeps her voice quiet, "I'm scared. I'm graduating in four days. I don't want to die. I know I'm supposed to accept it, but I'm so scared. And I won't have you with me."

My heart is breaking. "Kova, you'll be all right. Remember what I said about holding the gun and you'll do all right. We can practice that tomorrow in training. Can we ask for more training time?"

She shakes her head and wipes her eyes. "They don't waste much instructor time on us." She leans close to me. "I'm ashamed of feeling like this. I'm supposed to be a brave soldier, but I'm not. I'm thinking of running away."

"What? You can't do that. Where would you go? There's a jungle all around the camp and then there's the security fence as well, not to mention dangerous animals. I've heard horrible creatures still live in jungles." I put my hand on her thin shoulder. "Running away isn't the answer." If it was, I'd be the first one to escape. "Don't be embarrassed, I'm scared, too."

"You are?" She looks directly into my eyes. "But you're so brave and not afraid to speak up."

"That's not bravery, Kova, that's stupidity. If I thought before I spoke, I wouldn't get into so much trouble."

Kova wipes her eyes again. "Well, I still say you're brave. I'm always scared. I don't even like sleeping by myself."

"Do you want to sleep in my bed with me tonight?" I shift over so she can have some room. I hope she will because I don't want to be alone either.

She nods and climbs under my blanket. Her body is so small, there's enough room for her and me without either of us hanging over the sides. Even though we're the same age, I feel like an older sister. One day I'll probably have a sister, although I'll never get to meet her.

I listen to Kova's breathing as she settles down and falls asleep. After a while, Viga comes over and I place my finger on my lips. She smiles and pulls the blanket up to Kova's chin.

Viga bends down and whispers, "Big Pig ships out the day after tomorrow. He doesn't remember and I don't want to tell him tonight. Let him have one last night of peace. Get some sleep." She tries to force a smile, but her lips can't quite turn up and sort of quiver.

Now I'm really glad I didn't ask Briett when he was leaving. It's absurd to send him into battle. What's the point? Even if he can lay down cover fire, he's sure to get killed right away. There's no sense in denying that. He's too bulky to move quickly and he has absolutely no sense of stealth. I watch as Viga pats Briett on the back and tells everyone that game time is over and it's time to clean up and go to sleep.

Briett is still chattering on about how he won the game and didn't die. I wonder if they let him win. I feel so bad for him that it hurts and I can't stand the sight of him being happy like he has nothing to worry about. All I want is to block out everything and not think. I shut my eyes tightly and press my head into the pillow.

When morning comes, Viga shakes me awake. "Come on, RIC, time for you to take the helm."

I didn't sleep well and wake up with a headache. "Okay."

Kova is still sleeping, so I slip out of my bunk and run my hands through my hair. Somehow I've lost the bit of yarn Ma tied in my hair. I'll have to look for it later because it's all I have of her. Ever since I was little, she'd always have a piece of yarn in her pocket. Outside, I'm shocked that even this early, it's hot and humid. Of all the places on Earth, why choose the equatorial zone of Mid-World for a training camp? I remember reading about how Africa used to be divided into multiple countries a long time ago, but when Global Command was elected to govern the world, Africa was united into one big country under the World Military Leadership's control and called Mid-World. That's when the Council of Commanders was set up. Maybe that's why they united it, so they could use it for their own purposes. If that was the case, how many other training camps are in Mid-World?

I have to stop thinking. It's a waste of time and energy to wonder about what's left of my life. Before heading to Viteri's office, I stop by the water hose to freshen up and let the cool water cascade over my head and face. How can something this simple feel so luxurious?

Even with the water splashing on the ground, I hear something else, like grunting, not too far away. What if a wild animal sneaked into camp? I shut the water off, wring out my hair and listen. The sound's coming from near Tablon's dorm. My heart's racing and I'm shaking all over, but if I save his squad from an animal attack, I'll be a hero and then he'll have to leave me alone. Maybe I can leverage a brave act like that and request pilot training instead of certain death on the moon.

It's hard to be quiet in boots, but I manage to tiptoe close to the dorm and see movement to the side where there's a stack of storage boxes up against the building. But I don't have any weapons or anything at all to fight off an animal attack. The biggest animal I've ever encountered was a stray cat in my neighborhood at home. *Oh, come on Dax.* Improvise. That's what Da always says when I can't figure something out. Okay, I'll improvise. There are rocks all around the camp and rocks can make effective weapons. There! By my feet. A fist-sized rock that'd do damage even to a big animal.

With a good grip on the rock, I creep closer. The grunting is coming in fast bursts now. I'm sure that means the animal is about to pounce. Sweat is pouring down my face and into my eyes. I'm not more than three meters from the storage boxes. With a couple of deep breaths, I run to the other side of the boxes.

"Argh!" I shout to scare whatever is there and prepare to throw my rock.

In an instant, I let the rock drop from my hand. It's not an animal at all, but Tablon and Lenora. Both have their pants off and she's on top of him. They're having sex! I've never seen anyone having sex before, but there's no mistaking what's going on. We learned about it in Reproductive Science.

Lenora waves her arms around and shouts at me to leave. Tablon pushes her off and pulls on his pants. I have no words at all. I should look away and run, but I can't, my feet won't move. He jumps up and gets in my face.

"You tell anyone, smudge, and I'll kill you. I'll snap your spine and leave you to die in the jungle." His face is bright red and sweat's streaming off his face.

I glance at Lenora, who now has her pants on, too. She's furious and glaring at me. I let out my breath, realizing I'd been holding it the whole time. She makes a motion across her neck like she wants to cut my throat.

I back away and hear Tablon whisper to Lenora. "I told you we'd get caught. Why did I listen to you?" He sees me and narrows his eyes.

Without waiting for him to do anything to me, I rush back to my dorm where I lean against the outer wall to catch my breath. I'm still stunned and my head's spinning. I knew Tablon and Lenora had teamed up, but to go this far? The thought of anyone having sex never crossed my mind, especially since Viteria made a point of stressing how it was forbidden.

If they hadn't seen me, I could have sneaked away without them knowing I saw them. Then again, perhaps this isn't so bad. Why ignore an opportunity? This is a huge secret that I can use to my advantage. Viteri said if anyone was caught engaging in sexual activity, they'd lose their subsidy forever and would go to the front lines. I don't want anyone, not even Tablon or Lenora sent to the front lines, but they don't have to know that. If I threaten to tell, I can hold it over Tablon's head. Best to keep quiet for the time being and pull out my blackmail when I need it. *See, Da, I'm improvising!*

I splash more cold water over my face to cool off and go right to Viteri's office. There's a line out front, the other RICs I presume, and as usual, I'm the last one. A couple of kids turn and glare at me like I shouldn't be here. I ignore them, still thinking of Tablon and Lenora. I don't want my mind to go where it's going, but I can't help it. All I can think of is sex and what it would feel like to have someone touch me all over and kiss me and...I have to stop. I'll never know what it's like.

The closest I've ever come to having a boyfriend was Marckon. We had lunch together every day and played games during recess and we got along really well. I still remember his gorgeous brown eyes and skin. And when he'd smile, his eyes seemed to shine. If I could, I'd have sex with Marckon. He's about four months younger than me and is planning to advance on his Date of Fate, but I won't be around to see him when he gets here. I'm sure he'll be made a Lead or maybe a fighter ship pilot because he's a higher status and smart and he catches on to new things fast. He'll do okay in the Global Forces. And I'm glad.

It's almost my turn to go into the office when Tablon runs up to me and drags me out of line by the arm. He's breathing hard and looks a mess. "Orwan, what are you going to tell the Commander?"

He's scared. I give him a casual shrug. "Nothing. Yet. But I will if you keep treating me and my squad like dirt." I pull away. "Do you think they randomly use the verity-probe on us to see if we're hiding anything."

We had one at school and they used it on me once to ask if I was against Global Command. I said no, but got detention anyway. I'm not sure how it detects a lie because it's just a small bowl-like thing that sat on my head without any attachments.

"Keep your mouth shut, smudge. Don't you mention the verity-probe to the Commander. Ever."

"It's all up to you, *Tablon*. You heard the Commander, it's my duty to report any...activity."

"I know, but...just don't say anything." He wipes his sweaty forehead and glances around. "Don't say anything."

I give him another small shrug. "I have to go." I get back in line.

Tablon stands for a few seconds, staring at me, then shuffles off toward his dorm.

"Next!" shouts Viteri.

It's my turn and I walk into the office and do my perfect salute. "Good morning, sir."

"Orwan, you're the RIC?"

"Yes, sir." I hold my salute and look straight ahead.

"Interesting. End salute."

I drop the salute and stand at attention.

He comes out from behind his desk. "You've got your first training this morning, recruit. Use the time well. You're being shipped out tomorrow. I won't spend any more time with you here in training camp, wasting resources on you. You're an instigator and have to be removed. We're on the brink of an uprising." He rubs his chin. "Over a hundred women have been arrested as of yesterday for refusing to breed. There's talk of organized protests and factory walk-outs. People are saying they don't want their children to die in war. Idiots. Why do they think they have children? Not to mention how it would hurt sales and the factories would lose money. The instigators must

51

be stopped like I stopped you. Why can't women see the importance of reproducing and sending their offspring to war? Production has to continue no matter what." He's basically talking to himself at this point.

Production? Of what, baby-making or weapon-making? Maybe both. He's got it all worked out. Get rid of anyone who doesn't go along with the system. Does this happen to other kids who ask questions? My squad doesn't cause trouble, but they're weak. Is that why they're AFGFs? To get rid of them too? Culling the weak from the population?

When he looks up, I straighten my shoulders a bit more. "Yes, sir." My hair's almost dry and sweat's trickling down my face and back even though it's cool in the office. He's sending me to the front lines without hardly any training. How is that fair? I was supposed to have two weeks. "Sir?"

"What."

"I need training, sir. I've never fired a weapon. I've never even seen a battle. This isn't right. You can't..."

"Shut your mouth. You'll have training today. Not that it'll do you any good. Orwan, we've gone over this. I realize your brain's the size of a sub-atomic particle and you can't comprehend the simplest of things, so let me impart a bit of strategy on you. We have wars with aliens to keep our global populations united to prevent uprisings. A common enemy creates unity. Wars with aliens mean no wars on Earth. Then there's the economical factor. The more wars going on, the more equipment and materials we need. And soldiers. If women refuse to breed, we lose our recruits. If we lose our recruits, we lose the wars, and Earth is obliterated. We die. Wars are excellent for the economy, Orwan. A lot of people rely on that economy. People rely on wars to generate an income." He chuckles to himself.

I stand still, but my brain is whirring fast. War and money. It isn't just a game, it's real life. I feel bile rising up my throat. Where's the line between right and wrong? *Is* there a line or has it been redrawn to suit the commanders?

"I'm going to be sick, sir," I mumble.

He scrunches his face. "Then get out of my office." He waves me away. "You weak kids can't handle the heat."

I stumble out, collapse in the dirt, and vomit. The sun is burning my head and my stomach is roiling. What's happening? How can any of this be true?

I breathe in the hot, damp air and retch. After a few minutes, my stomach settles and I take a moment to collect myself before shuffling back to my dorm. The cool air inside revives me somewhat and I see that everyone except Briett is awake and playing War and Money.

My stomach tightens and I scream out, "It's not a game!" I grab the cube from Kova's hand. "They make money off us."

Kova looks at me. "Who does?" She reaches for the cube.

I drop it on the floor. "The commanders. The rich people. We're a commodity to them."

"What's a commodity?" Briett mumbles from his bunk.

Viga picks up the cube. "Big Pig, don't you know anything? It's something that's used to make money, make a profit. Get it?"

Briett comes over, stretches, and sits down. "Oh. So I'm a commodity because my Da advanced me so he could get money?"

Viga nods. "Exactly. Wait, Dax, what are you talking about? Are you saying our parents use us as commodities or the government does?"

I'm feeling sick again, so sit on my bunk and take a few breaths. "Both. And I don't get two weeks, I'm being shipped out tomorrow."

"What?" Kova jumps up and runs to me. "You can't. You only just got here. We all get two weeks of training."

I shake my head and lie down. "I don't. Commander Viteri wants me on the front lines tomorrow." I'm so drained I can't even cry. "I'm an instigator."

Kova hovers over me with tears in her eyes. "He can't do that. You'll get killed for sure. How are you an instigator?"

I sit up. "It doesn't matter. Kova, we're all going to get killed. Don't you realize that? They take us from our homes and put us in a war, knowing we can't win it. In fact, they don't want us to win. We're expendable commodities. And if you dare question this *logic*, you're named an instigator or non-conformist."

Everyone gathers around my bunk as if they're waiting for some words of wisdom. I don't have any. There's nothing I can say to make sense of anything that's going on. I hug Kova, but she keeps crying.

"Attention!" shouts Tablon from our doorway.

Not one of us has the energy to jump up as we should. Instead, we rise and dangle our arms at our sides.

Tablon stomps down the aisle to my bunk. "All of you, go away. Smudge, stay." He waves his hand to dismiss them.

Is he going to discipline me for catching him and Lenora? If he tries, I'll go straight to Viteri. If I tell him, maybe then he won't send me away tomorrow.

When everyone's gone, I prepare for the worst. "What do you want, Tablon?" I refuse to address him as Senior Lead.

He looks around and lowers his voice, "I want to make sure you keep your mouth shut."

"I didn't tell the Commander. I said I wouldn't, but I will if…"

"Good. Because you didn't see what you thought you saw. Lenora fell down and I was helping her up. That's all."

"With her on top of you? And with your pants off? I know what I saw, Tablon."

He groans. "What'll it take for you to forget this?"

Might as well try something. "Get me training in a fighter ship and don't let me ship out tomorrow."

With a snort, he shakes his head. "You're scheduled for the front lines, smudge. And believe me, no AFGF will ever fly a fighter. Maybe I can try to delay your deployment or get you extra rations of food, but that's about it."

"That's not good enough." I have to stand my ground, after all, I'm a non-conformist. This is my only opportunity for leverage. "I want to fly. And I want my squad to get extra rations and all of us stay together, nobody gets deployed until we're all fully trained. And I mean fully trained, not just worthless training for two hours a day."

He's sweating. "Forget it, smudge." He turns to leave.

"Okay, no problem. I didn't think you had the power to do anything. If you'll excuse me, I have to go to the Commander now and tell him I heard kids were having sex and suggest he use the verity-probe on, oh, I don't know, maybe the Leads. See you around, Tablon." I push past him, but he grabs me by the arm.

"Wait! Ah, don't do anything just yet. Let me talk to the Commander. Maybe there's something I can do. He listens to me and asks me about the recruits. Go to the mess hall and set up your squad's table. Don't talk to anyone." He lets go of me and rushes from the dorm.

I've actually got him on the run and it feels good. After a minute, my squad comes back in.

Briett rubs his stomach. "Is it time for breakfast? I'm starving."

Viga rolls her eyes. "You're always starving, Big Pig. Dax, what did Lead Neemis want?"

What should I say? I can't very well tell the truth or my blackmail might backfire. I have to keep this secret to myself. But I hate to lie to my friends. "I think he feels sorry for us. He's going to see if he can get us extra rations."

"Really?" Kova shakes her head. "He's a decayed personality. Why would he ever help?"

I know that term, it fits Tablon perfectly.

"I don't know why, Kova, but I'm glad he's willing to try. I have to go the mess hall. I'll be back in a few." I give Briett a pat on the back as I pass.

The other RICs are also on their way to the mess hall, but nobody acknowledges me. I haven't been in the mess hall before so have no idea where to go and decide to stand near the doorway and watch. The floor isn't really a floor at all, but sand and there are skylights in the thatched roof. The RICs wipe off smooth, wooden tables and set out plates and cups. Some have two tables and a few have four or five. My squad is so small, we'll all fit around one. There's an empty table in the far corner which must belong to the AFGF dorm. As I set the wobbly table, a few RICs make nasty remarks and while it's hard to ignore them, I do and continue working. They're not worth the effort of responding.

"Orwan!" calls Tablon.

Not smudge? I turn. "I'm done here, Senior Lead Neemiss. Do you have news for me?"

"Not here." He motions for me to follow him out the back door. Once outside, he checks the vicinity and paces. "Here's the deal, smudge. The Commander is giving your entire squad seven days of training, together, no deployments until the seven days are up."

How did he manage that? I never thought he'd actually do it. "And? That's not the whole deal, Tablon."

His hands are trembling. "Your squad gets as much to eat as they want."

"And?"

He looks around again. "And I have a friend who's a fighter ship pilot. He's agreed to give you a few lessons, for a price."

"What price? I don't have any money." I glare at him.

"Not money, stupid."

Oh, no. I know the only other 'price' a boy is interested in. I shake my head. "No, no, no."

Tablon rolls his eyes. "Not sex either, smudge. He'd never jeopardize his training. Jarmer has a twin sister, Jarmella, who's getting shipped out today. He'll train you, in secret, if you agree to take Jarmella into your squad so she won't be shipped out. She gets deployed before him because she's not a fighter pilot and flyboys get longer training. The flyboys get three hours of free flight time every day, so he can sneak you into his ship during that time. That's when they don't have any instructors around. That's the deal, smudge. Take it or leave it. I can't do anymore." Sweat is dripping off his face and his shirt is damp all over.

I'm relieved the price I have to pay isn't what I thought, but I don't want Jarmella in our squad. I'm happy the way we are, although if it means keeping us all together for another seven days with extra food and training, plus getting me in a ship, then I'll have to make sacrifices. "Okay, deal."

He nods and wipes his face. "I'll get the Commander to make the transfer to your squad."

"Out of curiosity, Tablon, how are you going to do that? The Commander hates me and my squad."

"I know. That's why he'll do it. I already told him that it'll look so much better if your whole squad is deployed together and gets killed together. Adding one more female recruit to your pathetic squad will be even better. One more recruit means one more death." He shrugs and almost looks sympathetic.

"Nice, Tablon, real nice. What about the extra training? Why is he agreeing to that?" I can't figure that part out. Viteri didn't want me trained at all, so why give us all seven days of training?

Tablon looks down and seems a bit apologetic, or what I assume is apologetic for him. "I said your deaths will be more dramatic if you can actually fight a little. He's going to record your battle scene and broadcast it when you die. He wants gore and blood." He glances at me and says softly, "Did you know he wants to show the world your death?"

"Yes, I did. He made a point of telling me that already. If this all comes together, we've got a deal and I won't say a word about you-know-what."

"Good. I'll tell Jarmer. Get back to your dorm and act like everything's normal."

"Sure." I wait until Tablon jogs away before I leave.

I take my time because I have a lot to think about. Deep down I know it's a foolish thing to hope seven days of training will give my squad a chance against the Katarga fighters, but it's all I have. Hope is a strong motivator.

Chapter Seven

I walk extra slowly to my dorm to give myself time to absorb everything that Tablon's done. I pass by several squads on their way to the mess hall and thankfully they don't sneer or make fun of me. By the time I get to my dorm, the projected clock on Viteri's office says it's a few minutes after 0700. Briett is sitting on his bunk, tapping his foot, but when he sees me, he jumps up.

He smiles. "Breakfast?"

I give him a nod. "Yes. Single file, like we're real soldiers, and no talking in line." I smile. "If *I* start to open my mouth, somebody shove a dirty sock in there."

They all laugh and exit the dorm. I'm glad everyone's in a good mood, even though Kova still thinks she's shipping out. I can't wait to tell them the news. Briett's the first in the mess hall line and I bring up the rear. We file in, but our table's gone. I go to the kitchen counter and ask the chubby kid who's serving food where we're supposed to sit.

He puts his finger to his lips. "Shhh. Your table's outside. Senior Lead Neemiss said it's so nobody will know you get extra food. They'll think you're outside because you're the AFGFs and nobody wants to sit near you. But you get whatever you want. Tell me and I'll bring it to you."

I'm stunned. It'll look like we're being punished, but in reality, the loser squadron is getting preferential treatment. When I turn around, I see quite a few kids pointing and laughing. Everyone else is already stuffing food into their mouths. I turn back and keep my voice low, "Thanks. Can we get an extra helping of everything? And give Briett an extra-extra helping."

"Briett? A new recruit? There's no one here named Briett. I get a roster and I've never seen that name." The kid looks around.

I motion to Briett. "Big Pig." Can't they even put his real name on the damn roster?

"Oh, sure, Big Pig. His name's Briett?" The kid begins scooping food onto plates. "He's Big Pig on the roster." He winks. "I like you AFGFs. If I hadn't broken my ankle first day of training, I'd be an AFGF like you."

"Well, we'd be happy to have you." I smile.

I go and tell my squad what's happening and we leave through the back door where our table is. It's half in the shade of the mess hall, so it won't be too bad. After everyone sits, I stay standing and smile.

Viga frowns at me. "Why are you smiling? Kova's getting shipped out. That's not funny."

I sit down. "I have good news, that's why I'm smiling. Really good news."

Before I can tell them, the chubby kitchen boy limps out of the kitchen with a tray piled high with food and pitchers of light purple fruit juice. "Here you go. I got another tray coming." He slides the tray onto the table as another boy comes out with the second tray.

There's so much food. I glance at Briett and see he's crying, really crying. When the kitchen boys leave, we all dive in and scoop mounds of scrambled eggs and potatoes onto our plates.

I say softly, "Okay, here's the news. None of us are getting shipped out for seven days. And we get training for those seven days, more than two hours each day."

"What?" Kova drops her fork. "I'm not..."

I continue, "You're not shipping out, Kova. We also get as much food as we want."

That last one gets to Briett. "As much food as we want? You're not teasing, are you?" He wipes his eyes with the back of his hand. "Please say you're not teasing."

I shake my head. "No, no joke. I had a talk with Tablon and he got the Commander to approve it all. But, we only have seven days, so we'd better make good use of that time."

Viga nods. "Definitely. Maybe Tablon's not so decayed after all."

"No, he is," I say in a whisper. "This is all for his benefit. Trust me."

"How does he benefit from us getting treated better?" Kova asks.

I said too much as usual. "Well, he looks like a better Lead if he's fair to all the recruits. Like why Lenora didn't force us to clean the other dorms. They're all trying to impress the Commander." That sounded good.

Viga nods again. "That makes sense. Now we might actually learn how to shoot."

"Not me." Briett stuffs a huge forkful of eggs into his mouth. "I'm pathetic." Egg pieces spit out over the table. "But at least I'll die with a full belly!" He chuckles.

I don't think it's funny, but when everyone around the table giggles, I force a smile so Briett won't feel bad. My stomach is so empty that I gobble down two plates of food and three glasses of juice. I thought it was grape juice, but it's not. It has a sweet, exotic flavor that I've never had before. It's probably from a local fruit, a delicious local fruit. I know nothing about the world and won't have the chance to learn anything other than how to shoot at aliens.

We nibble on the scraps for a while before we notice the other squads are walking through the camp, heading off to their training. That reminds me, I don't have any idea where we go for training. "Viga, who's our instructor?"

Viga wipes her mouth with a cloth napkin. "I'm so full. We have a woman instructor. She's not so bad. All she does is hand out the laser guns, but she's not mean. We're on our own after that."

That doesn't sound much like training to me. "How can we learn how to aim or shoot if she doesn't show us?"

Briett finally stops eating. "We don't really need to know. Remember? Laser fodder."

"I can't accept that. None of us are laser fodder. And I don't plan on dying after seven days." I get up. "And I won't let you either. We're going to learn to shoot and stay alive." Regardless of what Viteri wants.

Viga leads the way through a path in the jungle where there's a large clearing with a rope strung across the whole width at the far end, and a curtain hanging over it. Viga points to the curtain. "That's where the aliens are hiding."

"Aliens?" My heart's thumping.

She laughs. "Not real aliens. Holograms, projections. The instructor pulls the curtain and we shoot."

"Do they shoot back?"

"Dax, they're holograms. They just kind of float there and we try to shoot at them. If we get a direct hit, it registers on the instructor's computer." Viga looks around. "Instructor Milo, we're ready."

From behind the curtain, a tall woman with the blackest hair I've ever seen strolls out. She looks bored or tired or maybe a combination of both. "I was told you have the entire day to practice. Except for whoever Dax is. She has specialized training or something at midday." She goes to a shed behind a shrub and drags out a couple of crates. "Come and get your guns."

Kova nudges me. "What specialized training?"

"Oh." What should I say? "It's because I'm the RIC. Tablon said he's changing things so the RICs get special training."

"That's not fair." Viga stomps her foot. "I didn't get any special training when I was RIC. None of us did."

"It's a new rule I guess." I shrug and head to the crate of guns. I stand at attention in front of Instructor Milo. "Could we please get more directed training? Can you show us how to aim?"

Instructor Milo stares at me. "Directed training? Aim? You're AFGF. You don't need to know how to do anything but fire and die. What's the point?"

I maintain my stance. "At least you'll be doing something instead of standing around sweating and watching us make fools of ourselves."

She sighs. "I suppose that's right. Okay, why not. But I've got to tell you, there's no hope for Big Pig. His fingers are too pudgy to hit the trigger button accurately, so he misfires all the time. He won't last more than a second after he exits the lunar transport. The Katarga are merciless. *They* know how to hit a target."

"Then teach us accuracy. I'll work with Briett myself. Please give us a fighting chance." I relax my stance a bit. "Please."

She looks at me for a moment. "I'll do what I can for you. You have seven days, I was told. Not much I can do with you in a week." She reaches into a crate and takes out a laser gun, hands it to me, and gets another one for herself. "Recruits! Pay attention."

My squad gathers around her and everyone looks eager to learn, even Briett. Instructor Milo gives us an in-depth lesson about the weapon, how it recharges, how it fires, and how it's best to shoot for the head or heart. After that, she tells us a little about the Katarga.

They're big, about two meters tall, with an armored skin of overlapping scales. That makes it hard to kill them unless you hit them directly in the heart or head. The scales are thinner on their chest and head. Other than that, they're pretty much like us, except they have a different language that nobody on Earth seems to understand.

After the lesson, we get down to shooting. Instructor Milo gives us tips on how to hold the guns, which like Kova said, are big and heavy. She agrees with me that Kova and Briett should lie on their stomachs to fire, while the rest of us manage to hold the gun from a standing position. Instructor Milo raises the curtain and a line of Katarga holograms, which look just like how she described them, weave back and forth. After I shoot at them for a while, my shoulder and arm start to ache terribly. We continue for a while longer until everyone is struggling.

"Can we take a break?" I ask.

Instructor Milo shrugs. "Sure. Not one of you is any good, so I wouldn't rest for long. You need the practice."

I motion for my squad to put their guns down and follow me under a tree. "We'll rest for a few minutes and then get back to it."

Viga stretches out on her back. "I'm getting the hang of firing at the target. Did you see how close I got to one of the Katargas? Almost got him in the brain."

With a sigh, Briett lies down next to Viga. "I missed every one of them by a million kilometers."

"We've only been at it for a couple of hours." I rub my shoulder and move it around. "We'll all get better."

After a little while, Instructor Milo comes over. "Back to practice. I've set the Katarga holograms to attack mode."

"What does that mean?" I look over at the curtained area and see that the curtain is once again closed. How can a hologram attack?

With a smirk, Instructor Milo winks. "You'll see. Be alert and do your best to aim straight." She wanders away toward the curtain. "Recruits! Arm yourselves!"

I jump up. "You heard her. We're in battle!" I run to my gun and wait until the rest of my squad is armed before I shout 'ready'.

The curtain opens and right away the holograms rush at us, firing bursts of lasers that explode into the trees behind us. How can they do that? I thought the lasers weren't real. I duck and roll on the ground to avoid being hit. The holograms disappear before they reach us and start over again from the curtain area.

Everyone has avoided getting hit, but Briett is shaking so hard, he can't hold his gun steady. I hurry to him, drop down, lie beside him, and reach over to help him keep his gun from jiggling all over the place. He wipes his brow and presses the trigger button. One shot actually hits a Katarga!

"Whoo!" he shouts. The next second, he gets a shot to the head. "Ow!"

"Are you all right?" I check him out and he already has a bruise forming on his forehead. What exactly are the Katarga holograms firing? Obviously not lethal lasers. "Keep low, Briett. Take a deep breath and hold it before you press the trigger!"

I roll away and get to my feet in time to fire a couple of shots before getting a hit to my left arm and right thigh. It stings, like a bolt of electricity. I press the trigger button but my laser gun doesn't fire.

Instructor Milo shouts, "When you get hit, you're out! Your weapon won't shoot! Lie prone on the ground and put your weapon down and the Katarga won't shoot at you!"

I do what she says and lie face down with my gun at my side. Briett is quick to do the same. All I can do is watch as my entire squad gets out in less than a minute. The Katarga go back to the starting position and float.

I'm already exhausted and my clothes are drenched in sweat, but I know we have to keep going. "AFGFs! Are we ready?"

Everyone shouts 'yes', except Briett, who mumbles, 'I guess'. Kova and Briett stay on the ground while the rest of us stand and aim our guns. The Katarga rush as us, firing continuously. We don't stand a chance and I'm hit first, in the stomach. It knocks the wind out of me. Viga falls next, then Mick, Brinna and Parna. Only Kova and Briett are left. They seem to have worked out a strategy. One of them fires until all of the Katarga aim at them, then the other takes over and draws the Katargas' attention. It works, for a while, until the Katarga realize and split their shooting, and aim at Kova *and* Briett. That gets them both out.

We practice and practice, but don't seem to get much better. We need to develop a strategy like what Kova and Briett figured out. Before I can collect my squad together for a strategy meeting, Tablon walks right onto the playing field and points at me. The game halts.

"Smudge, come with me." He turns and strides off the field.

I stand up and address my squad. "Keep going without me. I'll be back as soon as I can."

Viga runs over to me. "Are you getting disciplined for something? I'll come with you if you want."

"No, it's all right. I think it's that RIC training." My heart's beating fast. This is my first flight training session. "I'll be back soon, Viga." I have to run to catch up to Tablon because he doesn't slow down at all.

I hurry behind him as he goes to the fighter ship area. There's only one ship still on the ground with a boy, dressed in a snug-fitting black one-piece uniform, standing beside it. He's wearing a helmet with a clear faceplate and carrying another.

Tablon stops and motions to the boy. "That's Jarmer. Don't breathe a word of this to anyone, smudge. Go." He glances around and hurries away.

Jarmer waves me over. "Hurry up, dwarf star!"

Great, another stupid nickname. When I get to the ship, Jarmer shoves the helmet at me. "What am I supposed to do, sir?"

"You don't call me *sir* for one thing. You'll sit in the co-pilot seat. This is free flying time so I don't have an instructor co-pilot. I'm doing you this favor and risking discipline because Tablon says my sister will be safe for at least the next seven days by going to your squad. She's better than any of you AFGFs, so don't think you can treat her like she's decayed or stupid." He points to the ship. "You enter through the cockpit hatch under the belly. Co-pilot's seat is on the right."

I nod and squeeze the helmet over my head and instantly feel like I'm suffocating. "I can't breathe in here." My head tingles like something is tickling my scalp.

With the ship hovering off the ground, Jarmer ducks, goes underneath, and slides open the hatch where the ladder descends. "When you're inside, there's an oxygen delivery system that attaches to the helmet. Don't panic, there's plenty of oxygen in your helmet until you're seated. Leave the helmet on because it has to acclimate to you before we fly." He climbs up the ladder and vanishes into the ship.

I can't believe I'm about to go inside a real fighter ship. Unfortunately, I've fogged up my helmet with my rapid breathing and have to feel my way to the ladder. I manage to climb up the four rungs completely blind but have to pull off my helmet so I can see where to go next. What I see makes me gasp. The cockpit is beautiful, even though it's small with only two seats. There's an array of colorful buttons on a panel in front of the pilot's seat and several switches on the right side of the panel. The front window is black, I can't see out of it at all. How can I ever learn what all the buttons are for? I planned to learn to fly so I could escape from camp and go home. Now I'm thinking it was a dumb plan.

I put the helmet back on before Jarmer yells at me. Maybe I am being a dwarf star, a small-minded person with no sense. Did I honestly think I could go home? Even if I did, they'd come and take me back and send me straight to the front lines.

"Sit down and buckle in, recruit," Jarmer orders, sounding a little less bossy.

I slip into the seat and get into the restraints, which are exactly the same as in the shuttle. They tighten automatically and Jarmer reaches over and snaps a tiny hose into the left side of my helmet. My helmet defogs completely and I can breathe easily. He then attaches his oxygen hose.

"Watch what I do, recruit."

"My name's Dax." I shake my head, but the tingling continues. "I think my helmet's too tight. It feels funny."

"Just relax. Okay, Dax, first thing you do is push the engine warm-up button and then go through the pre-flight checklist. There's a copy attached to the side of your seat, so you can follow along."

I find it and keep track as he goes down his list clicking switches and pressing buttons. It's complicated, but I can see how, once I realize the order, it'll be easy, especially with the checklist. The engine hums to life and warms up while the other systems are started one by one. There's the weapons prep button, the propulsion exhaust system, the avionics, and the heads-up display, which is a transparent depiction of instruments that appears in front of the window, like the projection I saw Viteri using. I'm not as nervous now and feel comfortable with Jarmer at the controls. He doesn't need the checklist, but I think he's scanning through it for my benefit. He's calm. I want to be like him one day.

"Jarmer, where do you fly?"

"I'll go into the stratosphere because the other pilots are in the mesosphere and troposphere doing maneuvers. Once we're at altitude, I'll show you how to actually fly."

"Fly?" I didn't expect to take the controls this soon, but I'm excited at the thought. "I've never flown anything before."

He looks at me like I said something stupid. I hadn't realized before how handsome he is. His skin is light brown, like Marckon's back home, and he has amazing green eyes. I've never seen eyes like that.

"Dax, we're all novices. But if you want to learn to fly a fighter in seven days, you'll have to trust me completely. I've been in camp for five weeks and can handle this ship better than any other flyboy. I know what I'm doing."

"Five weeks? Senior Lead Neemiss said you got longer training, but I had no idea it was that long." I shake my head again, but the tingling is still there.

He smiles. "Pilots have to fly a lot to get proficient. We get six weeks of training. And only boys become pilots, so you're the first girl recruit I've ever flown with." His smile drops. "If the Commander finds out, we'll both be deployed to the Katarga base camp without any weapons or armor."

"I'm not going to tell anyone. Why only boys?" I can't get over how green his eyes are.

Jarmer raises an eyebrow. "Because flying a fighter means shooting at the enemy without hesitation. They used to train girls I was told, but every one of them washed out. The Commander said girls tend to be too compassionate, even toward the enemy. It's hard to train that out of someone. I don't know why boys do better, but we do. I always thought I was compassionate." He shrugs. "Oh, you'll probably vomit in your helmet, so be prepared. There's a suction system that'll clean it up if you do."

That's not a very appealing thought. "I'll be okay." I never thought of myself as compassionate, well, not really. I do care about people, but that doesn't mean I'll care about the enemy if it comes down to them or me. I don't want to kill, but I suppose I *could*. "How come your sister is still in camp? Shouldn't she have been deployed after two weeks?"

He's quiet for a few seconds. "She went into pilot training for three weeks, but like I said, girls always wash out. The Commander said she wasn't good enough. She's been in regular recruit training for two weeks now and was getting deployed. That's why I agreed to this. I don't want her..."

"I understand. She's in my squad now. I'll look after her for you."

"Thanks." He stares at me for a moment. "I mean it. Now get ready for launch."

He winks and grabs the control stick that's attached to the floor in front of his legs. Right away, a shield across the front window slides open and the heads-up display flickers in front of the window. I don't have a control stick at my seat, so I don't know how he expects me to fly. He tells me not to touch anything and then yanks back on the stick. The fighter tilts up almost vertically and shoots up into the air. My insides feel like they're compressed into one solid lump. It's uncomfortable, but I don't feel sick, I feel thrilled. I'm already in love with flying.

Chapter Eight

O nce Jarmer climbs to altitude, 40 kilometers above the Earth, he levels off. I'm not feeling bad at all, no vomiting, and even the tingling around my head has eased off a bit. Another shield has slid open to reveal a small oval window to my right and when I look out, the view takes my breath away. I've never seen the world from this vantage point before. It's gorgeous, patches of lush green landscape interspersed with bare brown areas and incredibly blue rivers that snake through it all like veins. I have no idea exactly where the camp is below us and I don't care. This is freedom, true freedom.

Jarmer taps me on the shoulder. "You doing okay?"

I nod. "Fine. Really fine. You get to do this every day?"

He smiles and lets out a light laugh. "I do. Free flying time is my favorite time. Training is rough though, too regimented. Sit tight for a minute, Dax." He reaches out to the heads-up display in front of him with one hand and slides his finger around like he's drawing in mid-air.

There are no other ships near us and other than a few wispy clouds, we're alone in the sky. I see the moon in the distance and the dark areas that are the Katarga encampments; I've seen them before through a telescope at school. "Jarmer, why don't the Global Forces just launch a bunch of bombs at the moon and destroy the Katarga once and for all?" I turn away from the window.

He gives me a brief smile. "You don't know much about the wars, do you?"

"We didn't learn *anything* about the wars in school. All they teach us is that the aliens are intent on killing us."

He turns serious. "The Katarga have a protective shield around the moon. Otherwise, we'd have won years ago."

"How do we get our troops on the ground then?" I stare at the moon and wonder how many of our recruits are lying dead on the surface.

"Dax, it's not a solid shield or anything like that. It's an energy shield that interferes with our weapons. It deflects any incoming weapon attacks. Our troop delivery transport ships can make it through the shield because they don't have advanced techno-systems like the fighters so the shield doesn't interfere with them. But if they try to shoot lasers from an airborne transport ship, the lasers deflect off the shield and bounce back at the transport. That's why the transports drop off ground forces, like you and your squad, and exit right after drop off."

"Wait, Jarmer. I'm confused. If the shield deflects lasers, then how can our ground forces use the laser guns? And why don't the Katarga leave?"

Jarmer takes his hands off the control stick for a moment and motions with his hands. "This is about the size of a laser gun. It's a very small-scale weapon and can get through the shield at ground level where the shield is weakest. Anything mounted on the fighters or transports won't get through. Our fighters are equipped with large-scale laser guns and priz-spec, but the Katarga shield interferes with both weapons. Get it? Only from ground level. Even if we had small laser guns, we'd still be firing from the air." He takes hold of the control stick again. "And the Katarga can't leave. We shoot them down if they try."

"That doesn't make sense. Why not let them leave?" Well, I suppose I know the answer to that. Wars make money. "So, what's priz-spec?"

He lets out a breath like he's fed up of my questions. "Prismatic spectrum rounds are our weapons system. It works by collecting energy that comes when the spectrum of light is diffracted by a prism and then forced back. The photons emit energy that's used as a pulse weapon. Don't worry about it, it's powerful and can knock out any techno-system. But we still can't get through the shield. If the AFGFs ever knock out the tech, we can fly in."

There's so much I don't know. "All right, so the fighters can't use the priz-spec either, but what about using lasers on the transports at ground level? The transports drop off troops, so why not fire from the ground? At least a transport would give the AFGFs some protection."

He shakes his head. "No, it doesn't work. Commander Viteri mounted small lasers on the transports and had them fly low, only a meter above ground, but they were ineffectual because the transports make big targets and once the Katarga saw the transports were attacking, they took out every transport within minutes by using their own type of pulse weapon. I heard we lost a lot of good soldiers back then. Ground forces are our only way to get in close. They wear beige tactical gear that blends in with the lunar surface. They're hard to see. It's your job to try to get in close. It's not as hopeless as the Commander makes us believe. I heard that a year or so ago, the AFGFs blew up one techno-system and were able to come close to infiltrating the Katarga base."

"So what happened? Did they send in the fighter ships?"

He's quiet for a moment. "No, for some reason, the fighters weren't deployed. Or at least that's what I heard. Dax, fighter ships and fighter ship pilots are valuable. I guess the commanders didn't send them in because the Katarga base wasn't completely without tech. I imagine it was too risky. So, the AFGFs advanced alone, but the Katarga rebuilt their systems and vaporized them all. They didn't stand a chance."

"If the fighters were deployed, they could have helped the AFGFs."

"I'm sure the commanders had a good reason. When I learned about it, the first thing I thought was that they weren't deployed for some strategic reason, but that doesn't make sense because Global Command never sent in more troops or anything. That allowed the Katarga to have enough time to repair their systems." He shrugs. "Whatever the reason, those decayed Katarga are still contained on the lunar surface and we're still at war with them. If the AFGFs manage to knock out the shield again, they'll do their best to make it into the base and try to completely disable the techno-systems so the fighters can be deployed." He looks at me. "You AFGFs are given a laser gun with enough energy to disable their techno-systems."

"Disable? Not destroy?"

He continues, "Don't know what to tell you about that. From what I know, the laser guns can't fully destroy the Katarga tech. Anyway, the laser gun can be fired point-blank at the Katarga main control mechanism. Unfortunately, the Katarga repair their techno-systems real fast, which means the AFGFs have to be faster. The problem with that is that the AFGFs are always scrawny, pathetic kids. No offense. My opinion, I don't think the Katarga war is ever going to end unless Global Command changes their strategy. Anyway, I'm being trained to battle the approaching Piltraks, not the Katarga. The Commander says there's a fleet of more than ten thousand Piltrak ships on their way and a thousand ships already waiting at Saturn's rings. My squad is going to launch next week. You know what a Piltrak is?"

"Not really." I can't believe nobody is going to fight the Katarga except for me, my squad, and the other AFGFs. There must be a better way. And now we have more aliens ready to attack. "Are the Piltraks like the Katarga?"

"No. The Piltraks are these small, hunched creatures with four arms and six eyes."

I swallow a lump in my throat. "What do they want?"

"What do you think? To conquer us and kill everyone. That's what they all want." Jarmer pushes a button on the heads-up display, takes his hand off the control stick, and unhooks his oxygen hose. With a smile, he unfastens his restraints and gets out of his seat. "Switch with me." He pulls out my oxygen hose.

"Excuse me?" My hands are shaking, but I manage to take off my restraints and stand. "You want me...I can't..." There's gravity in the ship. Amazing.

He motions to his seat. "Sit down. We need a pilot at the controls." He pushes past me. "Wait until you see what this ship can do!"

I get into the pilot's seat and secure myself. "What do...how...?"

He motions to the oxygen hose and I connect it.

With his restraints secured, he cautions me, "Don't touch the control stick. It's for launch and landing only. I'm going to show you something really stellar. Use the synap-trodes to make small movements. See that instrument on the heads-up display, right in the middle? That's your horizon and the star-compass is next to it on the right. Keep the ship on a steady course so you don't deviate. The compass uses the stars to help you maintain your position. Just pick a direction and hold steady. Make a few slight turns, without touching anything, and come back to level flight again so you get used to the synaptic-controls."

I can hardly breathe. "The what?" I put both hands in my lap and stare at Jarmer. "What's a synap-trode?"

"Use your brain, Dax."

"I'm not stupid, I just don't know what you're talking about."

Jarmer groans. "I didn't mean it like that. When you put the helmet on, the synap-trodes attach to your head and receive signals from your brain. You control the ship with your mind. It makes for faster responses. See, use your brain."

"Okay, I understand." Synap-trodes? So that's what the tingling is. I concentrate on making the ship tilt to the left in a turn, but I'm all over the place, dipping and rolling the ship this way and that. It's hard to get it to fly where I want. Jarmer doesn't say a thing, he's letting me figure it out for myself. What will happen if I make a mistake? Will he take over? Can he do that if I'm in control of the ship?

When I finally learn how to keep the ship on the horizon by anticipating how it will react to my thoughts, Jarmer says, "Well done, Dax. Took me more than two hours to figure out how not to roll the ship. My instructor had to step in twice!" He laughed.

Now I know he could have taken over at any time. I'm out of breath from the thrill of flying. "How did the instructor step in?"

"Another pilot can override the synaptic-control and seize it away from a pilot, but it's hard to do. Takes a real lot of focus and concentration" He points to the heads-up display. "It's best to fly from the pilot's seat because that's where the display is. But if I need to take control, I can. I know how. Although I don't think I'll need to because you're a natural."

"Thanks." That's the first encouragement I've had. I like Jarmer already. "So, you said the Piltraks are these weird little creatures."

He nods. "Yes. Hey, make a turn to starboard, to the right. Watch the compass heading and your horizon and make it exactly 90 degrees."

I find the compass display and begin the turn, doing my best to keep the ship lined up with the horizon. It takes a lot of concentration, but I'm getting much better. "Well, how do we know what the Piltraks look like? Who's seen them? If they aren't even here yet, who's seen them? And how do we know what they want?"

I complete my turn. It wasn't perfect by a long shot, but good enough for a beginner, according to Jarmer. He gives me a few more instructions on how to turn, dive and climb, then turns to me.

"Dax, you ask too many questions about things we're not supposed to ask questions about. Our military commanders know everything there is to know about our enemies. They have intelligence gathering squads who get all the information. As soldiers, we obey our commanders and don't ask questions. Got it?"

"No, I don't. What's wrong with wanting to understand the world we live in? Like, where do the Piltraks come from? What planet? How far away? Why do they want to hurt us?"

He groans. "It doesn't matter. They're already in our solar system, that's all we need to know."

A red light flashes on the heads-up display. "What's that, Jarmer? Did I do something wrong? Are we going to crash?"

"No, Dax. That's the command center telling us free flight time is over. Listen to me carefully, recruit. You can't be seen. I got away with sneaking you in because I was the last one to leave the field, but everyone comes back at the same time. You'll have to exit the ship before I land."

"What? How?" Blood is pounding in my ears. What does he mean? How can I exit in mid-air? My stomach's tightening.

"Oh, calm down, Dax." He lets out a laugh. "These ships hover. I'll hover over a clearing and you'll drop down to the ground. But you have to be fast because if anyone notices me hovering, it'll raise questions. Come on, switch seats again."

He gets up and we switch seats. I watch everything he does as he brings the ship through the atmosphere. He's so smooth on the synaptic-controls, like it's instinct. I want to be that good. We descend quickly and for a moment, I swear we're going to crash, but Jarmer brings the ship to a clearing in the jungle, hovers, and descends to about four meters above the ground.

He motions for me to open the hatch and leave. "See you tomorrow, Dax. Same time?"

I nod, take off my helmet, slide the hatch open and wait until the ladder drops down. I climb down, but still have almost three meters remaining. The last thing I want is to break my leg falling. "Jarmer, can you get lower?"

"No! Exit now!" He rocks the ship back and forth violently.

I lose my grip and fall. Before I hit the ground, the ship is gone. I land hard on my feet and tumble over. Luckily I'm not hurt, although my feet sting from the impact. I look around and have no idea how to get to camp.

"Over here, smudge." It's Tablon, waving to me from the undergrowth. "How was it?"

I run to him. "Amazing. Better than anything I've ever experienced."

Tablon glances at the ground. "Smudge, there's a slight change of plans. No more training, you're getting shipped out. Well, we all are. The Piltrak war is starting early."

Chapter Nine

I follow Tablon through the jungle hoping he'll explain what he's talking about, but he doesn't say a thing. Within a few more seconds, I hear voices, which means we're close to camp. I have to know what happened.

I grab him by the back of his uniform. "Tablon, why is this new war starting? I need more training. I'll go to the Commander and tell him about you and Lenora if..."

He stops and shakes free from my grasp. "It's Senior Lead...oh, who cares. Nothing matters anymore, smudge. We're *all* getting shipped out. Every last one of us. Even the flyboys. Three days from today."

"Why?" I'm not sure I'm ready for the answer. If everyone is deployed without any further training, there's no chance my squad or I can survive. And I'll never get another flying lesson.

"Global Command had already identified more than a thousand Piltrak ships hiding among the rings of Saturn, but now they're getting into battle formation. They can attack any time, so we have to be ready. The Leads, flyboys, and Intelligence recruits are getting specialized training for the next two days, but I don't think you will."

My head spins. So now it's not only Jarmer's flyboys that are going to fight the Piltrak. "Does my squad know?"

"No. Only the Senior Leads have been briefed." He shrugs. "I'll try to get you another flying lesson with Jarmer, but no guarantees. We're all shipping out on the transports. You ground forces recruits won't go to the moon after all. So I guess that's good, right?"

"Then how do we fight?" I was getting prepared to fight against the Katarga on the lunar surface, but how does a ground force soldier fight against an airborne enemy?

"You really want to know?" He wipes his forehead. "Your squad is scheduled for spacial hand-to-hand combat."

I don't like the sound of that. "Is that what I think it is?"

"If you think it's you and your squad floating around space with propulsion packs and laser guns, then you're right. It's the same as fighting on the ground, except you're in space." He wipes his face again. "You still lay down cover fire, but this time it's so the fighter ships can move into position. I'll be in charge of Jarmer's squad."

"But there's nowhere to hide in space. We'll be slaughtered." My throat's too dry and I can't swallow.

"You were going to be slaughtered anyway. Commander Viteri is still going to broadcast your deaths. He says to tell you that if you can manage to get a hit to your head so your helmet shatters and your face explodes, he'll make sure to give your parents an extra bonus. I know that sounds gruesome, Orwan, but that's why you're here and your parents will get more money." He shuffles his foot in the dirt. "Your death will keep the Global Forces strong. Death comes to us all, but a brave death is a good death."

I never thought I'd hear that idiotic phrase again. I'm lightheaded and sick. "And the rest of my squad? Are they being sacrificed, too?"

"Of course, stupid. This battle is going to end with a lot of deaths, not just yours. I'm not going to be safe either. I'll be on a transport and those are big targets. You better cover us before you die. I've got plans to move up in the Global Forces and maybe be a commander one day. Don't mess this up for me, smudge. I did what you wanted, now it's your turn to keep me safe."

I don't respond. I'm supposed to die protecting Tablon, the most decayed personality I've ever met. Of course he did get me a flying lesson and more food, but that was really for his benefit. I rush away from him and go directly to my dorm where I find my squad restless. They're pacing, rocking back and forth on their bunks or hugging one another. Kova is sobbing and Briett is wringing his hands. They all run to me when I come in.

Viga speaks first, "What's going on, Dax? Training was canceled for today and we were all sent to our dorms. And you never came back. Nobody will tell us a thing."

"It's bad," I mumble. "Really bad." I can't bring myself to say anything more because I don't want to upset them. They're good kids who don't deserve the treatment they're getting.

Briett groans. "I don't want to die, Dax. I'm scared. They're shipping me out, aren't they?"

"You're my friends," I start, not sure how to give them the news. "We're in this together. And I can't imagine a better group of soldiers to be with."

"What does that mean?" Briett asks, obviously puzzled. "Am I getting shipped out or not?"

It's Kova who puts it together. "Big Pig, we're all being deployed, together. Right, Dax?"

I nod. "Yes. Tablon just told me. Three more days until we're deployed."

Viga shakes her head. "So much for our seven days. Okay, we train like crazy for those three days." She pats Briett on the back. "You'll get better in three days, Big Pig."

I hold up my hand. "Wait. There's something else." I take a few deep breaths. "There's a new enemy and that's who we'll be fighting. In space, not on the lunar surface."

There's complete silence, nobody so much as breathes out loud. I look at each of my friends and can't imagine them floating around without any cover. We haven't even practiced with an armored spacesuit on. That's going to impact how we move and how we fire the laser gun. I go to my bunk and lie down with my eyes closed. I don't want to see anything. But my darkness is intruded upon when the image of Ma tucking me in at night pops into my head. I see her clearly. She leans over me, kisses me on my forehead, and pulls my beautiful blanket up to my chin. It took her months to make that blanket, scavenging scraps of yarn from old discarded sweaters she'd find in the communal dump. Each piece of yarn was different in color and texture. That's what made my blanket so special. That, and how Ma stayed up each night after a long day at work, knitting the strands together.

The image vanishes. In three days, she'll get the news that I'm dead. And everyone on Earth will see pictures of my disfigured dead body.

"Dax?" It's Viga. "There's a girl here asking for you."

I open my eyes. The girl has to be Jarmella, Jarmer's twin sister. She looks remarkably like her brother; same skin color and the same green eyes. I drag my body off my bed and stand up. "I'm Dax. You're Jarmella?"

She nods and looks around. "This is a deplorable dormitory."

I'm in no mood to deal with her attitude. "You can sleep outside if you'd prefer."

Her eyes narrow. "Show me my bunk."

I motion to Jarmella. "This recruit is joining our squad. Make her feel welcome like you did to me."

Viga points to an empty bunk. "You can take that one. Not that it matters much anymore."

Jarmella grunts. "The mattress is filthy. Hey, does anyone know what's going on? I can't get any information out of anyone, not even my brother."

With a friendly smile, Briett approaches Jarmella. "I'm Big Pig, nice to meet you. I know what's going on. The whole camp is getting deployed and we're going to die in space instead of on the moon." His smile drops. "Maybe I shouldn't have said it like that. Sorry."

"I'm not getting deployed for a week. That's why I'm here." Jarmella glares at me. "I'm not getting deployed with your AFGFs."

Kova and Parna shake their heads but don't say anything. I can see by the sour expressions plastered on everyone that nobody cares to make Jarmella their friend. The morale of my squad has bottomed out. I have to do something.

I hate everything about the Global Forces, but I need to be strong now. "The fact is that we were all advanced. We're soldiers. We have our duty to do. But that doesn't mean we have to give up and accept that we're going to die." I put my hand on Viga's shoulder. "I flew a fighter ship today."

"You what?" Viga raises her eyebrow. "What are you talking about? You've been out in the sun too long."

"I took a lesson from Jarmella's brother. I didn't do too bad. So, if I can learn to fly a fighter, then we can all learn something new, like how to fight better. I have no intention of being a floating target with a propulsion pack. We need armor or shields or something for protection." I point to Jarmella. "What have you been trained in? You flew for three weeks, so what are you now? Jarmer said you've been in regular training."

Jarmella looks down. "I was, but they put me in training for transport pilot since I knew some basics. Girls can fly those, you know. I was a good fighter pilot, but they washed me out. I think they don't trust girls as fighter pilots. But I'm not a pilot anymore because I'm in this decayed squad now."

I go up to her. "These people are my friends. None of them are decayed. And you've got a good skill. I'm sure you are a good fighter pilot, and who knows, you might need to fly one at some point. But for now, we have to figure out how to fight in formation with propulsion packs and we need to get some armor. I'll try to find out when we can continue with training. Jarmella, while I'm gone, can you tell the squad everything you know about fighting with aliens. I'm sure Jarmer's told you things and you must have learned something useful in flight school. And if you have any tricks to fight them, please let us know. You're with us now so the more you help us, the more you'll help yourself. I'll be back soon."

I hurry from the dorm and go to Viteri's office. Tablon and several other Leads are coming out. Tablon gives me a sideways glance but doesn't say anything. I go in and salute.

"Commander Viteri, may I speak to you please?"

He's sitting behind his desk and doesn't look up. "Not now, the camp is on alert. Why aren't you in your dormitory as ordered?"

"I apologize, sir, but my squad needs to continue training. Can we resume?" I hold the salute.

He glances at me and stands. "End salute. Training your squad is a useless endeavor, Orwan."

I drop the salute and relax. "I understand that sir, but I'll make you a deal. If you let us train, I'll put myself at risk and give you the graphic death you want. My squad's so demoralized that they won't do any good at all and won't have the will to put down cover fire. They'll die without ever having got off a single shot and the fighter ships will get shot down."

He shakes his head. "Worthless AFGFs. I have better things to do than deal with your pathetic squad. Go ahead and train, but you'd better hold up your end of the bargain and give me a death I can use. Get out of my sight, Orwan."

If he's willing to deal, then I might as well ask for more. "Wait, sir. We need armor and shields."

His jaw twitches. "Watch it, recruit. You're testing the limits of my patience." He eyes me carefully. "There might be a few out-of-date body armor suits in the storage building behind the Lead's dormitory, but there aren't any shields. You get new shields when you're deployed." He sits down again.

Before he changes his mind, I hurry to the storage building behind Tablon's dorm and look inside. A light flickers on and I see that it looks like it's been recently picked through. There isn't much in here. Tipped over empty crates, a few torn up uniforms, an open crate filled with broken pieces of laser guns and finally, what I'm looking for; a pile of old, worn body armor suits. Apparently they weren't good enough for anyone else, but I'm happy to take them.

There aren't enough suits for everyone, but maybe we can figure a way to share them or piece them together so everyone has some sort of protection over the regular spacesuits. If only Ma was here, she'd know how to do that. I never got good with a needle and thread. With the suits in my arms, I rush from the building.

For the next two days, we train and I get to fly with Jarmer, learning and improving with each flight. My flying is much smoother now that I've practiced with the synap-trodes and I can execute a 90-degree turn with the horizon completely level. This is the most fun I've ever had.

Kova managed to scavenge two more half-ruined body armor suits and used them to patch up the others, leaving us with four decent suits. I've managed to keep a low profile and Tablon hasn't given me more than a passing glance, but on the morning of the third day, our last day before deployment, I take a few minutes before training to search for additional armor suits. Right when I head back to my dorm, Lenora and three other girls I don't know stop me. There's nobody else around because they're all off training.

Lenora grabs my arm and throws me off balance. "I've been waiting to get you alone, without your worthless bunch of idiots. I know this is your fault. You told on me and Tablon, didn't you? That's why we're getting deployed. The whole camp is getting disciplined because of you. I'm not ready."

I stumble. "I didn't tell anyone. Ask Tablon, he'll explain it." Lenora shoves me harder and I topple over onto the dirt.

"I knew you'd be trouble the second I saw you in the shuttle." She kicks me in the ribs. "You're making me look bad. The Commander will never respect me now."

Before I can do anything, the other girls join in, kicking and punching. I curl up to protect my gut. "Stop it! I didn't do anything," I scream.

When they stop for a moment, I get to my knees and try crawling away, blood dripping from my mouth onto the soil, only to have Lenora crouch in front of me and put her hand around my throat. I try to struggle, but another girl grabs my arm.

Lenora's panting and sweating. "Because we're getting shipped out early, I haven't been trained properly in Leadership yet, so I'm getting put on a transport with the other inexperienced Leads. I should be on the command transport, but I'm not. You know what that means, *smudge*? Do you?"

With each breath, my ribs hurt, but I manage to speak, "No, I don't."

"Well," she continues, "It means I'll have to fight alongside everyone else. I don't know how to fight. We were learning how to be Leads, not fight. And you're useless, so you'll be long dead before you can cover us with laser fire." She stands and brushes her damp hair off her forehead. "What if the Commander decides to use the verity-probe on us Leads? I've heard that happens sometimes to test for loyalty. You might as well die right now, smudge, before that happens and they find out that I..." her voice drifts off.

The girls close in and someone smacks me over the head with a heavy object. I fall over and feel blows striking me everywhere. Everything is black and muffled and my ears are pounding. I'm about to pass out and can't do anything about it. Is this really how I'm going to die? Bloodied and beaten, lying in the dirt, unable to help my squad. My head throbs and I think I hear laughter. I can't die. Not yet.

Chapter Ten

I'm cold, shivering, and hurting all over. But that's good. It means I'm alive. I force my eyes open, but can't see a thing. Just where am I and why am I cold? I'm in the equatorial zone, nothing here is cold. It's a struggle to get to my feet because every time I move, my body reminds me that Lenora and her friends beat me senseless. But, I'm not going to let them get the better of me.

On my feet, I shout into the darkness, "Hello?" My raspy voice is lost as it echoes a few times and fades away. My throat's so dry and sore.

If only I could see where I am, but it's completely black. With my arms stretched out in front of me, I take one step at a time, feeling for anything. I'm walking on a hard surface and after maybe a dozen steps or so, my fingers brush against a hard, frosty surface. It's a wall made of metal and it's curved. I'm in a circular duct of some sort, a duct big enough for me to stand upright with room to spare. Am I inside the cargo area of a transport ship? I continue walking with one hand touching the side of the duct and the other feeling the space in front.

Finally, after I don't know how long, I hear a sound—a droning or humming—and follow it as it gets louder and louder. My head hurts, my ribs hurt and I'm aching all over. Even my face hurts where they were hitting me. I never expected Lenora to do something like this. I know she hates me, but to do this?

I keep walking and find that every now and then there's a turn in the duct. I keep going so I can find the origin of the noise and hopefully find a way out of this prison. It's louder now and clanking. The sound is coming from something straight ahead where there's a faint light, enough for me to see a placard on the wall a meter or so ahead. When I'm close, I read it: AC Duct A-4, Mid-WorldETC. Okay, so I *am* in a duct, which must be the air conditioning system. And evidently I'm still on Earth in Mid-World, but what's ETC? Oh! Equatorial Training Camp. This is the air duct that runs under the camp and into the dorms. All I have to do is find an upward vent.

Ahead I see the source of the noise, a large generator that's rattling and clanking like it's half-broken, with a small light above it. A label says 'Cooling System by Mil-Tech Products Inc.'. To the right of the generator is a metal ladder leading up to a trapdoor. My escape. I put my foot on the first rung and pull myself off the ground. It's really hard to climb up the ladder because every muscle hurts with even the slightest movement. At the top, I can see the trapdoor has no lock and with a big shove, it opens, and a blast of hot air from outside slams into my face. The sun's going down. Was I in the duct all day? I can't wait to get my hands on Lenora and smack her right in the nose....but I have to get to her first.

Once above ground, I see that I've come out near Viteri's office. It takes a moment to catch my breath and when I see a nearby spigot, I gulp down a bunch of cool water. I check myself over in the last of the sunlight and can't believe how bruised my arms are, and how much caked blood is on my shirt. Thankfully nothing seems to be broken though. My throat is still raw, but the water helped to revive me a bit more, enough for me to make my way, limping, to Viteri's office and knock. No answer. What am I going to tell him? If I say Lenora beat me, then he'll want to know why and I'll lose any leverage I have with Tablon. I knock again. Nothing. This time I try the door; it's not locked.

"Commander Viteri?" I call out, but the office is deserted, papers strewn over the desk.

I step out and look around the camp. Where is everyone? I don't see a single recruit. It's deathly quiet, no voices, no movement. Only a few birds are singing. The camp must have all shipped out early. Does that mean the aliens are closer than anyone thought?

"Hello!" I shout as loud as I can. "Hello?" Am I alone in camp? Why didn't anyone go looking for me?

I make my way around the back of Viteri's office, stopping briefly for some more water, and see all of the fighter ships missing, except for one that's still hover-parked in Jarmer's spot. Could he be worried about me, waiting for me to show up? I knew I felt a connection between us and I guess he feels the same way. He's the only boy who's ever complimented me. I can't wait to see him again.

My aching legs won't let me run, so I stumble to the ship in a half-jog. "Jarmer? Are you there?"

The hatch is open underneath and the ladder is down. At least it isn't as long as the vent ladder and only takes me a few seconds to ascend. Unfortunately, the ship is empty, although there's a box filled with tools near the pilot's seat and the control stick is disassembled. What if Jarmer isn't here at all? Why did I think he'd be waiting for me? The ship's here because it's broken. He shipped out in another fighter or left on a transport ship.

What am I supposed to do now? Maybe I can go home, if I can find how to communicate with my outlier. I hurry back toward Viteri's office, but as I turn the corner, I bump right into an old man in coveralls and knock him off his feet.

"I'm so sorry." I extend my hand to help him up. I've never seen this man before.

With a shake of his head, he shows his greasy, stained hands. "Better not touch me, young lady." He stands and looks me up and down. "What happened to you? In fact, where'd you come from?" He touches the AFGF patch on my arm. "Ground forces? Your squad shipped out with the rest of the camp just yesterday right after breakfast. How come you weren't with them?"

What? That can't be right. "Yesterday? You mean today? They left early?" I lean against the side of the office.

"Early? No, the deployment was on time. Are you sure you're okay?"

We still had one day left. Unless I was down in the duct for almost two days. Viteri never bothered to search for me? He probably figured I ran away. But what about my squad? They must all think I'm a coward, running off and leaving them to fight the battle while I hide. "I was attacked and left for dead in the air cooling ventilation system."

"Oh. That explains it. Commander Viteri had several guards on patrol in the jungle for a full day. You must be that girl who deserted...I mean the girl everyone thought deserted. That's right, from the AFGF squad. Well, ah..."

"Dax."

"Well, Dax, nice to meet you. Glad to know you're not a deserter. I'm Trab, maintenance specialist." He wipes his hands on his coveralls. "Been trying to get one of the damn fighter ships operational."

"That's Jarmer's ship, right?" I feel a little better knowing that at least I was missed. Although I'm sure Viteri wanted to find me so he wouldn't lose his prized victim. But now my squad is on their own. They won't know what to do. Not that I'd know either, but I wanted to be there with them, to help.

"Jarmer? You know him?"

I nod. "Yes, I met him a few times. And his sister. Took three flight lessons with him."

Trab smiles. "Really? Lessons from Jarmer? He's a skilled pilot, so you were lucky. Well, they're both good kids, and good pilots. But Jarmella washed out. I think it has to do with Commander Viteri not liking girls very much. He thinks girls can never be as good as boys, and when they are, he washes them out. But, he's the Commander, so he knows best."

"If you say so."

Trab smiles a little. "You might as well hang out with me, Dax. Communications are down until the battle transports are in position, which means I can't contact the Commander. Hey, do you need medical attention? There's no doctor here, but I know first aid." He studies me.

I shake my head. Other than the stiffness and bruises, I don't need first aid. What I want is to go home. "I think I'll be fine. Is it possible to go home?"

"Home? The Global Forces is your home, Dax. Once you're advanced, you never leave."

Never leave? Those are the worst words I've ever heard. I knew it, I suppose, but somewhere down deep, I still clung to a shred of hope that one day I'd see Ma and Da again. It's finally sinking in; I don't belong to my family anymore, I'm a soldier and my squad is my new family. "Trab, how did my squad look? I mean, were they afraid?"

He looks up at the sky and nods. "Everyone is afraid when they get shipped out. Some don't show it, but they're all afraid. I've been in this camp since I was advanced and I've seen plenty of kids come and go, so I know. But I didn't actually see your squad get on the transport. Sorry." He points to Tablon's dorm. "Why don't you go and clean up a bit? There's a nice bathroom in the Lead dorm. Nobody here to see you use it." He gives me a nod and heads off to Jarmer's ship.

I watch him for a while and wonder how old he is. He looks quite a bit older than Da, with gray hair, a slight stoop and a limp. I shuffle toward Tablon's dorm and still can't believe how lavish it is with carpets and fresh linens. At the back of the dorm is the bathroom.

Like the dorm itself, the bathroom is incredible. It's luxurious, with two bathtubs and showers separated by tiled walls, and clean, white towels piled up near the bathtubs. That's my destination, the tub.

The faucet is like nothing I've ever seen before. It has a temperature gauge across the bottom, but nothing else. How do I turn it on? With my finger, I touch the gauge and it lights up. As I slide my finger to the right, the water automatically flows out. I stop at 30 degrees Celsius and feel the water; warm. When it reaches about ten centimeters from the rim of the tub, it shuts off. I strip and slip in, giving my shirt a quick scrub. I wring it out and lay it over the tub's rim.

I always wanted a bathtub at home instead of a shower, and the one time I got to use Manti's tub made me want one even more. Sinking until my entire body is submerged except for my face feels indulgent and my sore muscles relax to the point where I actually feel good as the pain eases. With my eyes closed, I let my mind wander and the first image to pop in is of Jarmer sitting at the controls of his ship. He's so handsome in his flight suit and he's smiling at me. As clear as if I'm sitting beside him again, I see him go through the checklist and start the engine. I can hear it; that rush of power just waiting to propel the ship into the atmosphere. He pulls back on the control stick and the engine roars in my ears. Wait a second, something's not right. I open my eyes. It's not a dream, I really hear a ship's engine.

As fast as I can, I rub myself with a ball of unscented soap, rinse and dry off, get dressed, and run my fingers through my wet hair. My shirt is still wet, but it'll dry fast in the outside heat. The warm water soothed my muscles until they hardly hurt, so I can hurry out to the airfield faster than before.

Jarmer's ship is working! The entry hatch is still open and I climb up into the cockpit where Trab is sitting in the pilot's seat.

"You got it fixed!" I shout.

He turns with a huge smile. "You look much better now. Ship just needed a little love from old Trab."

"So what now? Do we leave the camp?" I sit in the co-pilot's seat and squeeze my dripping hair.

Trab laughs. "I don't fly, young lady. Once the recruits are in position, they'll resume communications and I'll get notified to open the camp for the next advancees. When there's an urgent battle launch like this, all new recruits gather for temporary training at the Arctic Holding Camp, then they're shipped over here when the commanders return. We'll get a new supply of fighters then, too. This one will be given to the worst flyboy, just in case he crashes. Then they'll order a new one."

"Fighter or flyboy?"

"Both."

"That's so cold." Kids are commodities here. "Trab, what do you mean 'when the commanders return'? They don't stay and fight? And what about Jarmer? Will he come back?"

"They didn't tell you much, did they? Dax, the commanders accompany the battle squads and oversee the strategic positioning, but then they come back here before the actual battle starts. Wouldn't do any good to lose our commanders in battle, now would it? That's what the Senior Leads are for. They carry out the commanders' orders in battle."

I wonder if Tablon knows that the commanders escape harm while leaving the Leads to risk their lives. "This is all overwhelming, Trab."

He laughs. "I can imagine. They'll be back in a day or so to supervise the new recruits and supplies. Jarmer won't be back though. He'll stay and fight the enemy until..." he pauses and pats the armrest. "I swear, Dax, if I owned one of the manufacturing plants, I'd be richer than rich. New fighters for new recruits. Fighter ships are either lost in battle or kept on the transports. The ships never come back here. Just like the recruits." He stares through the window.

I slump in the seat. I'll never see Jarmer again. I hope he'll be all right.

"You okay, Dax?"

"Sure."

At least it seems like Trab also understands how the Global Forces are run. Money is at the center of everything and it makes me sick. There must be more people out there who can see through the propaganda and the corrupt Global Forces. I can't be the only non-conformer. Of course, they were probably rounded up and shipped off to fight the Piltraks or Katarga as well. That seems like the preferred method of silencing people.

I can't believe Viteri is coming back. He'll send me directly into battle with the Piltraks. It wouldn't be so bad if I could join my squad, but I know in my heart they won't last long enough for me to get to them. I'll be all alone again without any friends. I have to force myself not to cry. Why couldn't *my* parents own a manufacturing plant? Then I'd live a long life without having to die in space at the hands of aliens.

Trab shuts down the engine and looks at me. "Did I say something wrong, young lady?"

"No. It's just that...I don't want to die." I wipe the tears that finally fall.

He avoids looking at me. "We all die, Dax. The only reason I'm still alive is because I have an aptitude for fixing these ships. Every time we get a new shipment, they break down right away. There's always some issue. Every single time." He locks eyes with mine. "The engine components are faulty, the synaptic-controls won't trigger or the heads-up displays don't work. I have to order an entire set of new parts and then they work like a dream. One time I had to order new seats! Almost seems like they build them shoddy in the first place."

I nod. "They do. I'm sure of it. It's so the manufacturing plants can get more money."

He lets out a sigh. "I think you're right." He glances around. "Not that you heard that from me. Ah, but I'd rather be up there fighting alongside those flyboys instead of sitting out the battles down here."

If Trab suspects the truth, why doesn't he say something? I guess he's afraid. He's too old to fight, but he'd end up on the front lines anyway if they declared him a non-conformist.

Trab gets out of the seat, stretches, and wipes his hands on his coveralls. "It's almost mealtime, young lady. You hungry? Must be if you were in the AC duct for two days."

I *am* hungry, hungrier than I've ever been. "I could eat something. Is the cook in the kitchen?"

He shakes his head. "No, we have to get our own food until the commanders return. Even the cooks ship out with the recruits to prepare meals up there." He reaches into his toolbox and hands me something wrapped in foil. "Here, take this for now. It's a protein-mash bar."

"Thank you." I unwrap the bar and it smells awful, but I eat it anyway. The texture is coarse and gritty, with small, soft bits mashed together. "What is this, Trab?"

"Protein-mash is an old family recipe. Learned how to make it before I was advanced. Made up of whatever nuts I can get my hands on, fruit, insects, and honey, all mashed up together. Disgusting, I know, but it gives a body what it needs."

I give him a nod of agreement and finish the bar as fast as I can. It almost comes up a couple of times, but I manage to keep it down.

With a slight smile, he takes the foil from my hand and tosses it into the toolbox. "I sure hope they can get a handle on those Piltraks."

"Trab, what do you know about the Piltraks?"

He shrugs. "Only what I hear. They're supposedly a vicious, conquering species with no conscience. Worse even than the Katarga. If I could, I'd be up there shooting holes in those creatures. I want to be up in the clouds instead of stuck down here on Earth."

"I used to think the same thing, but now I'm not so sure. I want to be with my squad, but once I'm in space, I'll die." I want to change the subject. "Have you seen any pictures of the Katarga or the Piltraks?"

"Curious about the enemy, eh? That's good. Never seen any of them. Nobody has, except the soldiers who come face-to-face with them, and that never ends well for the soldiers. I suppose the commanders know what they look like, but what we hear about the aliens is basically just rumor, never really confirmed by the commanders. Okay, young lady, I'm going to clean up and then I'll get to cooking. Unless you'd rather have another protein-mash bar." He grins.

I shake my head. "No, thank you. I think I'll sit here for a while, if that's all right." I've got a lot to think about.

"Sure. Just don't mess around with anything." He climbs down the ladder.

I watch him cross the field and disappear around Viteris's office. I sit in the pilot's seat and slip the restraints over my head, snapping them in place, feeling like I belong here. If I was a fighter pilot, I'd be on my way to fight the Piltraks and I'd be with my squad again. Imagine what it would be like to speed through the atmosphere toward the moon or even the outer solar system, past meteors, and comets.

What if I could actually fly the fighter by myself? I did a good job, even impressed Jarmer. I remember exactly how he started the engine and there's a checklist to help. First thing, press the engine warm-up switch.

With the engine revving, I go through the checklist like before and prepare for lift-off. I'm sure Trab can hear the engine, but I don't care. I don't want to shut it down. The ladder automatically retracts and the entry hatch closes with a soft click. My heart's thumping so fast and my hands are shaking. I can fly this ship, I know I can. Whatever it takes, I'll find my squad. The control stick is in my hands and I pull back like Jarmer did. The ship launches into the air and as I shoot upward, I glance out the side window and see Trab running across the field waving his hands.

I bet he's furious with me. Sorry, Trab, I can't land even if I wanted to. I never saw how Jarmer set the ship down and don't know the first thing about landing, but I'll worry about that later. As I climb up through the atmospheric layers, I begin to feel faint and cold. Damn it! I forgot to put on a helmet. I'm running out of oxygen and I don't see a helmet anywhere in the cockpit! What was I thinking? I'm not fit to be a pilot.

Chapter Eleven

It's hard to breathe now, my chest hurts and I'm lightheaded. How could I be so stupid? I see nothing but clouds out the side window and pure blackness in front. Why did I think I could fly a fighter? Without a helmet, not only do I not have an oxygen supply, but I won't have the synap-trodes. I'm going to die in Jarmer's ship.

Everything's getting blurry and it's hard to keep my eyes open. Ma's face flashes in front of me, then Da, then Jarmer. I force my eyes fully open and Jarmer vanishes. But I see, half under the side of the co-pilot seat, a helmet! It must have rolled out during my ascent. I stretch my hand as far as it'll go and brush against the helmet, but I can't get a grip. I'm so weak and sleepy.

I hear Jarmer's voice, "Put on a helmet and attach the oxygen hose, Dax!"

"Okay," I mumble as I unfasten the restraints and lean over, grab the helmet and slip it on. The oxygen hose is situated on the ceiling, but with the ship pointing straight up, I have to sort of crouch on the seat to reach the hose. With the g-force, it's hard to move, but after a moment, I have the hose and push it into the slot on the helmet.

Right away there's a hissing and I can breathe! I suck in oxygen for a few seconds before getting back into the restraints.

"You did it, Dax!" comes the voice again, but it's not Jarmer, it's Trab.

"Where are you, Trab?" I glance around, but he's not in the ship.

"Young lady, you scared me to death. I'm on ground-to-ship communications, the only way we can talk until the commanders return. A warning sounded that your biological readings were dangerously low. The moment a pilot sits down, he, or she in this case, is continuously monitored. I figured you forgot to put on your helmet. I don't know what you've got in mind, and although I'm very impressed that you launched without killing yourself or destroying my fighter, you're in big trouble."

"Sorry, Trab."

"Too late for sorry. If you're not planning on coming back, then you'll have to listen to me carefully. You've violated quite a few regulations, so you have to be extremely alert to avoid getting your butt blown into oblivion. I'll put out an alert that I'm field-testing a repaired ship and pray that's good enough to save you. Okay, now, you'll pass through the exosphere in a few minutes, but the ship's temperature and gravitational controls should keep you warm and intact without a flight suit. For the time being. So, Dax, what exactly is your plan?"

What's my plan? I don't have one. All I want is to be away from camp when Viteri returns. I suppose I succeeded in that. But what now? "Trab, I want to find my squad. How do I do that?"

"That's what I figured you'd want. Soldiers, even AFGFs, don't like being left behind. I was so angry when I was told I wouldn't fight, that I had to stay in camp as the maintenance..."

"Trab! How do I find my squad?" I didn't mean to shout, but I'm about to pass through Earth's atmosphere and leave behind everything I've ever known.

"Oh, sorry. I do ramble on sometimes. Give me a little time...oh."

"What? What? Trab?"

I heard him whistle. "Dax, your squad's only about a day away from the battle zone at Saturn."

My ship suddenly slows and changes course. "Trab, where's my ship heading? I didn't do anything. What did you do?"

"I didn't do anything either, young lady, although the ship will automatically place you in orbit if you don't program in coordinates. You didn't program anything in, did you? Dax, do you know how to fly?"

"Jarmer was a good teacher, Trab, but I don't know anything about coordinates." I have an idea. "Can you program in the coordinates for the transport?"

"You want to go to a transport, where they'll know you broke regulations and stole a fighter ship? That's as bad, or worse, than flying into enemy territory." He whistles again. "You'd be safer finding a nice outlier somewhere on Earth where nobody's ever heard of you."

"Trab, please. I want to be with my friends. They need me." And I need them. I look out the side window and see Earth far below me. It's a beautiful sight. The most beautiful sight I've ever seen. Never in a million years did I expect to see my world from this perspective. Ma and Da are down there somewhere, living out their lives without me. I hope they never find out what I've done.

The Earth's getting smaller. I'm flying free, no longer held down. No rules, no teasing, no discipline; I'm a fighter pilot. I can do anything I want now. This is the greatest feeling I've ever had. It's terrifying, but incredible at the same time.

After a while, Trab announces, "Coordinates programmed. Dax, are you sure you know what you're doing? A couple of lessons doesn't make you a pilot."

"I'll be all right. If I'm going to die, I want to do it with my squad, on my terms."

He laughs. "Now that's spoken like someone who thinks for themselves. Do you know how to fire the laser guns or priz-spec, if you need to, and use the synaptic-control?"

I tell him no on the weapons, but yes on the synaptic-control. He goes through the procedure for firing the laser guns and compared to the heavy laser guns I practiced with, shooting lasers from a ship will be easy. Aiming requires activating the heads-up display and positioning the target with the synap-trodes. I can do that.

The ship accelerates and changes course again, flying away from the Earth at incredible speed, but something's not right. The moon, big, round and whitish-yellow, is on my left and getting closer. I squint and see little explosions on the surface. Why am I going to the moon? The Katarga war is happening right before my eyes. That's a real war with humans and aliens shooting and trying to kill one another. But that's not where I'm supposed to be heading. Trab was supposed to take me to the transport.

My ship lurches and I'm thrown forward against the restraints. What does that mean? "Trab? What's going on?"

Silence. Where's Trab when I need him? Probably went to make his lunch. *Great timing, Trab.* My ship lurches again. He must have put in the wrong coordinates! I have to do something or I'll crash onto the surface. I activate the heads-up display and search for the coordinate setting, but don't understand a single thing I see. Why didn't I ask Jarmer to explain things more?

My ship's spinning and the horizon on the heads-up display is out of control. I concentrate on making the ship rotate in the opposite direction to the spin, but nothing happens. I grab the stick and shove it forward, backward, and side to side. It's dead, like someone else is guiding my ship. Can it be Trab? Can he do that?

Watching the moon as I spiral toward it makes me dizzy, so I shut my eyes. If I don't do something, I'll die without ever fighting the enemy or finding my squad. But what can I do? At least the impact will end everything fast. But I don't want to die! What if Viteri came back and he's controlling my ship? He wants a spectacular death and crashing into the moon would certainly give him what he wants. I can't let that happen, I don't want him to have the satisfaction of watching me die as a worthless smudge. I'm going to go down fighting.

I open my eyes and focus on one point on the moon's surface, a ragged crater, so I don't get too dizzy. I'm closing in and I can see that the explosions I saw before are back-and-forth laser fire between a large horseshoe-shaped structure and ground forces that are doing their best to advance their position. There are no fighter ships to help them. This is the Katarga war and I'm watching it happen. Trab told me how to fire my lasers, so maybe I can get off a few shots and save the ground forces before I die.

I engage my synap-trodes and position the target-finder on the Katarga stronghold until it's dead center. I have them and they're evidently not expecting me because they're not shooting at my ship. I wait until I'm a little closer and then open fire, directly at the structure. I keep firing and hit the structure with every shot, but don't receive any counterfire from the Katarga. Why not? Why aren't they shooting at me? I don't know how my lasers are penetrating the shield, but they are! After about a hundred shots or so, my ship veers off to one side and starts spinning end-over-end, out of control. For whatever reason, I'm no longer heading to the moon, but back into space. I've broken free from whatever or whoever was controlling my ship.

After a few minutes of tumbling wildly, I manage to gain control and stop the spinning. The last thing I see is the ground forces rushing toward the stronghold. I did it! I managed to attack the Katarga and escape. I wish Tablon could see me. He'd be shocked and maybe even a little jealous. Jarmer would be proud, I'm sure of it. What a great day this is! I'm free and unharmed. I watch the AFGFs advance, but suddenly, my ship shakes and there's a loud crack. Sparks fly around the cockpit, showering down over me. I've been hit!

Chapter Twelve

There are sparks everywhere, but with limited oxygen in the cockpit, there aren't any fires. I have to find out where the ship was hit and assess any damage. The good thing is that I'm heading away from the moon and hopefully out of range of the Katarga. The damage doesn't seem too bad, a few charred places on the walls, and a couple of broken instruments, and thankfully the heads-up display is still working.

The ship's mine again, so where do I go? If Trab lied to me and programmed in the lunar coordinates, then he'll gain control again and turn my ship around. But I have no idea how to stop him or how to reprogram new coordinates. Why did I ever trust him?

"Young lady?" It's Trab. "Dax! You there?"

"Barely." So now he knows I'm alive. "Why did you do that? I thought we were friends. I almost died."

"Me? Oh, you have it wrong. That wasn't me. Your ship was caught in a tracker vortex from the Katarga base. They had your ship and I couldn't do anything about it. Lost communication with you, too. How'd you get away? Nobody gets away once they're in the vortex."

"So it wasn't you..." I'm glad he didn't betray me because I need a friend now more than ever before. "I don't know how I did it. My lasers worked, so I started shooting and hit their base with everything I had."

He laughs. "Dax the hero! Well, you must have disabled their vortex since you got away. If your lasers got through, it means the Katarga have a weak spot. The shield mustn't work within the vortex!" He lets out a whoop. "We have to notify the commanders. Our fighters can purposely enter the vortex and get in nice and close. No more keeping their distance. You did what the ground forces are supposed to do. You just might have saved them."

"I hope so. Trab, the Katarga didn't fire on me until I was out of the vortex. What does that mean?"

He pauses for a moment. "That's even better. I guess they can't fire through their own vortex. They don't need to. Any ship caught in it is broken into pieces and it crashes onto the surface."

If I hadn't destroyed their vortex, I'd be dead on the moon. That was too close. I turn in my seat so I can see the moon through the side window. As it grows smaller and smaller, I lose sight of the laser fire. "You were right. We do have to contact the commanders. Now. But how? You said the communications are down."

"Yeah, they are and I can't contact them until they start them up again. But you can give them the intel. You'll have to fly to them and tell them. You were planning on going there anyway. It's a stupid system to disable all contact, but it's set up like that so there are no false communications. Listen, Dax, the Katarga will figure out what happened real soon, so you have to push your ship to its limits. Do you still have the transport coordinates programmed?"

"I don't know. I was hit and some of my instruments got messed up. Can you check?"

"Well, I can't see your ship anymore. When you were sucked into the vortex, it messed up your transponder. I'm amazed I got ground-to-ship communications back. Is the heads-up display working?"

"Yes."

Trab pauses. "You'll need to activate a backup system. I think your avionics are blown. You'll have to use synap-trodes from here on. There's a button in front of you, marked with a green triangle. Activate it with the synap-trodes and tell me if the coordinates appear on the heads-up display."

The control panel has so many buttons that it takes me a while to locate the right one. I activate it successfully and wait. The heads-up display flickers and two sets of coordinates flash in red. I read the coordinates to Trab.

After a moment, he replies, "The first coordinates show your position relative to your launch point and the second ones are to the transport. You'll receive avoidance alerts on your heads-up if your ship approaches any obstacles in your flight path, including the other transports. All of the transports follow the same coordinates to the staging area, but your ship will avoid a collision and take you to your transport. You're a long way from them, Dax. You have to go sub-light and try to accelerate to 2% lightspeed."

"What? I don't know how to do that." I check the instrument readings on the heads-up display, but can't find anything about acceleration. Jarmer never showed me how to accelerate. And that's not even the worse thing running through my mind; can a fighter go sub-lightspeed without disintegrating?

"Listen to me, young lady. The only way to catch the transport is by forcing your ship to go 2%. To do that, activate the small black star-shaped button on the left side of the heads-up display, down a couple centimeters from the top. Press it twice for 2% acceleration. Remember to use the synap-trodes. Hurry up, you can't afford time to think."

The button is right where Trab said it is, but I'm not so sure I want to press it. What if the ship falls apart? Or what if it doesn't and I actually manage to find the commanders and tell them how they can get through the shield by using the vortex and then they order a full-scale attack. The Katarga will be wiped out and I'll be responsible. I don't think I can handle that sort of guilt.

"Dax!"

"I can't do it, Trab. They'll kill the Katarga." I look away from the button.

"If you don't tell the commanders, the ground forces will continue to die. The Katarga are going to realize their weakness and fix the vortex so they can shoot into it! Do you want that? You and your squad are ground forces. What if it was them down there getting slaughtered?"

I squeeze my eyes shut and see Briett, Viga, Kova...kids just like them are on the moon fighting. Those kids deserve to live every bit as much as my squad. I concentrate on the button and draw in a deep breath. What if Viteri is angry that I stole Jarmer's ship? What if he punishes my squad because of what I did? What if, what if, what if? Does it matter what happens? What could be *worse* than having us fight the Piltrak in outer space? Nothing. I just need to see my friends again.

I trigger the synap-trodes and press the button twice and I'm instantly thrown back into my seat as my ship is propelled forward in a blur of speed. The distant stars are lost in a haze as I'm hurtled through space. A small box appears on the heads-up and says Obstacles: 0.

"That's my girl, Dax!" shouts Trab. "You'll be out of communication range soon, so I'll say goodbye now. Good luck, young lady. Oh, once you're in range of the command squadron, they'll detect you and bring you into the main transport with a retrieval device, kind of like what the Katarga use. Tell them everything. I hope I see you again, young lady." His voice is faint.

"So do I. It's been a wonderful experience and pleasure knowing you, Trab." I feel this weird sense of loss because Trab is my lifeline to Earth and that lifeline is going to be cut. How odd that I don't like being alone anymore. "Goodbye, Trab."

"Kill a few aliens for me, will you, Dax?"

I don't want to kill any aliens. "Sure."

"Young lady, you're almost out of range," his voice crackles and is hard to hear now. "Take care of yourself."

"I will. Trab? Are you still there? Trab?"

That's it, no more communication. No more Trab. The only thing I have with me now is the blackness of space and my own thoughts torturing me. I'm going through this suffocating emptiness toward my destiny, and my end. Viteri will send me into space with my squad and I won't even get a thank you for destroying the Katarga vortex. Instead, Ma will see her little girl, the one she used to tuck in at night and sing to, bloodied, the grotesque result of a senseless battle.

Why was I born into a world like this? What's the point? We're born only to die at the whim of the commanders. It doesn't seem right, a waste of life. And what about the aliens? How many of them are dying? What if they're just like me and want to live in peace instead of fighting wars that mean nothing? I must have killed at least a few of the Katarga when I shot through the vortex, which makes me a murderer.

I don't want to kill anyone else. How am I supposed to be brave and shoot without thinking? My head hurts and I wish I could turn off my brain. Just as I manage to drift off to sleep, I startle myself awake with a nightmare about my ship exploding.

Time's passing slowly and I have no idea how long I've been flying. An hour, two, three? The heads-up display hasn't changed; it still says zero obstacles. That's odd. Trab said there'd be other transports. Shouldn't I have encountered at least one other ship?

The display now says I'm approaching the transport, but I don't see it. As soon as it comes into view, my ship lurches and shakes. They must have turned on the retrieval device Trab told me about. At least I'm not spinning like I was when I was caught in the vortex. I wonder what they're thinking? They sure won't be expecting me, a lowly AFGF recruit, to be at the controls. Under different circumstances, this would be a pivotal moment in my life where I'd get recognition for doing the unbelievable, but I won't get praise today. Not for knocking out the Katarga vortex and not for flying a fighter ship. But my goal isn't praise, although it would be nice. My only goal is to tell them about the vortex and help my squad as much as I can.

The transport is huge. All I can do is sit and wait while my ship is pulled into a tunnel-like opening at the back. It's completely dark, like my ship has been swallowed up in the blackness. I don't like this at all. I have no control.

Finally, there's a light ahead but I can't make out anything else until my ship pops out of the tunnel into a cavernous hangar with rounded walls that reminds me of being back in the ventilation duct, only this is far, far bigger. There are fighters everywhere, each one docked on a platform attached to the wall. They're stacked twenty per column with at least thirty in each row. I'm not sure what I was expecting, but I had no idea the transport would be this big with so many fighters. No wonder transports don't do any fighting, they're definitely a large target like Jarmer said.

My ship's drifting slowly toward a large landing platform above the hangar floor where there's one other fighter to the side and a group of people standing directly in line with my ship's heading. There aren't any recruits doing drills or pilots readying their ships, but I recognize Viteri right away from the way he has his thick arms folded across his chest, standing in front of everyone else.

After my ship glides over the platform and settles into a low hover, the engine shuts off and the hatch opens without me doing anything. Time to think about what I'm going to say. There's no logical excuse I can come up with other than to admit I stole the ship.

A voice echoes through the hangar: *Pilot, remain in your ship and prepare for boarding.*

I take off my helmet, wriggle free of the restraints and stand, holding a salute in preparation for what's coming. Sure enough, Viteri is the first one to climb up the ladder.

"Orwan?" His mouth gapes and he glances around the cockpit. "How is this possible? You're alone?" He comes closer and points at my face. "What happened to you?"

"Yes, sir, I'm alone. I was beaten and left in the ventilation duct under the camp." He'll have to be sympathetic.

He continues with a frown, "I don't want excuses. You couldn't have flown this ship. Where's the pilot?"

"I *am* the pilot, sir. I have to report some vital intel. I knocked out the Katarga vortex and if our fighters purposely enter the vortex, they can fire at the Katarga stronghold because the shield doesn't work in there." My arm is getting tired from the salute. "We can destroy their techno-systems."

"Drop the salute, Orwan. You didn't do anything to be proud of, recruit. You don't know what you're talking about. You've racked up a lot of charges. Dereliction of duty, theft of warcraft, and anything else I can think of. Report to Senior Lead Neemiss on the platform. He'll take you to your squad until I figure out what to do with you." His voice is tense-sounding like he's holding back a barrage of insults. "You are poison. You didn't attack the Katarga. Any more talk and I'll have you executed right here for insubordination and making up inflammatory lies!" His fists are balled up and his cheeks are scarlet. "Dismissed!"

I want to object, tell him how he can't ignore what I just told him, make him understand that he has to send a squadron of fighters to the moon before it's too late. But I don't say a thing. He doesn't want to hear what I have to say. He shut me down. I should have known he'd do that. I drop the salute and hurry down the ladder where Tablon is standing about five meters away, staring at me, stunned. After a moment, he motions for me to come close. He's confused like I'm the last person he was expecting, and I'm sure I am.

He looks very Global Forces in a new uniform; a crisp shirt and pants in black, a white patch on his arm with the black letters SL in the center, and a strange little hat that fits snugly and is pointed at the front. I go to him, not sure if I should salute or not. He doesn't order me to, so I guess I'm all right.

"Smudge?" His brow is pinched. "How are you...how did...you look like you were pummeled by a Piltrak death squad."

"Yes, sir." Should I tell him it was his precious Lenora who did this to me?

"You stole a fighter?" He whispers, "You'd better not tell anyone I arranged for Jarmer to teach you to fly. We'll be dragged down with you. Theft is punishable by death." He straightens his shoulders. "Death, smudge."

I lower my voice so the other people standing around can't hear, "Is that supposed to be a threat? I'm going to die no matter what. I don't particularly care how it happens. Which means I've got nothing to lose by telling everyone about you and Lenora, and the flight lessons. I don't think there's anything you can do to me now. The Commander wants a spectacular death, remember? Maybe you'll be joining me."

He's grinding his teeth. "If you tell on me, I'll make sure your parents have to repay the advancement subsidy and are declared traitors. Your whole family will be dishonored." He takes a step backward and points to a metal door behind him on the platform. "Go. Your pathetic, worthless squad is down on the yellow level."

Whatever he says to me now is meaningless. I'm on a transport filled with commanders and Leads who want to see me die. This is it for me, I'm done. "Fine. How do I get to the yellow level? You're supposed to take me." I can't wait to see my friends again. I also can't wait to find Lenora. Only this time, I'll make sure she's alone.

Tablon shakes his head. "I'm not going down to that festering yellow level. There's a magnetic lift, take it. Can you handle that, smudge?" He motions to the door again.

I nod and stride past him with my head held high. The door slides open and shuts once I pass through. Wait until my squad knows that I didn't abandon them. I hope they believe me. I don't have any real proof that I was left for dead, except for my bruises.

The area I'm in is an open space maybe three or four meters wide and equally as long. There are recessed lights up near the low ceiling and panels of monitor screens that show the view outside; pinpoints of distant stars and the black expanse of space.

I'm not sure where the magnetic lift is because all I see are the monitors covering the walls, and there doesn't appear to be another doorway. Is Tablon playing a joke on me, trying to embarrass me and make me look like the idiot he thinks I am? There has to be a way out. I look back, but Tablon hasn't come in after me. Great, what am I supposed to do, wait here or go back and ask him how to get to the lift?

"Dax?"

I spin around and see Viga standing against the far wall. How did she get there? "Viga, where did you come from?"

She runs over and flings her arms around me. "They didn't say it was you up here. I was sent up to bring a recruit to our level. We all thought you ran away! Or worse." She pulls back and gapes. "What happened to you? Are you all right? Your face is all bruised."

I give a quick nod. "I'm fine. Lenora decided I shouldn't live and did her best to get rid of me. It's so good to see you." I hug her again.

She squeezes me tightly, which hurts my ribs. "Dax, how did you get here?"

"Oh, well, I flew Jarmer's fighter." I smile.

"What? You didn't. Did you? I can't believe it. You *have* to tell me all about it. However you got here, I'm glad you did! Dax, they have us in training. We're learning how to use a spacesuit and propulsion pack. I'm okay, but Big Pig does nothing but spin in circles. Oh, and he put himself on a diet." She giggles. "We know he steals food when nobody's looking, but we don't say anything. Tell him he looks thinner when you see him, okay?"

"Sure." I let go and point to where she'd been standing before. "Where's the lift? I don't see anything."

She smiles. "Right there. You stand on the pressure pad to activate the lift. It's big enough for about ten recruits. Here, I'll show you."

She takes my hand and leads me to a circular area on the floor with a series of colored buttons around the perimeter. As soon as we get on, she steps on a yellow button and there's a sharp click. Right away, a clear outer tube rotates to enclose us and we start descending. The first level contains sleeping quarters, very comfortable with wealthy-people beds, according to Viga. It's where the commanders sleep. All I see are fancy screens though, that block everything. As we pass through the next level, I smell food although it's too dark to see much. My stomach grumbles and I realize just how hungry I am. Trab's protein-mash bar didn't exactly fill me up.

The next five levels, color-coded in blue, red, green, purple, and orange, are training levels Viga tells me. Below those are two levels, white and black, that are the other sleeping quarters for the rest of the recruits and Leads. Our level, the yellow level is in the bowels of the transport. Not surprising. The lift stops and the tube rotates so there's an opening for us to step through. A strong, nasty smell rushes in and overwhelms me. It's stale and damp with a horrid rotten stench mixed in. But when I see my squad lined up, the smell doesn't matter, I'm home.

Chapter Thirteen

Everyone surrounds me and bombards me with questions, one after the other in rapid-fire. It's hard to focus on any one person. "Slow down!"

"Okay, but, Dax, what happened?"

"Did the Commander beat you?"

"Who brought you here?"

It takes a while, but I do my best to answer each one and tell them all about how Lenora ambushed me. They're appalled, except for Briett who isn't sure what ambush means. When I tell him, he gets tears in his eyes.

He's such a sweet boy. I pat him on the back. "Don't worry about it, Briett. I'm here now, that's all that matters." I smile at my friends. "I have so many questions to ask you."

"I'm sure you do. Let's get you comfortable first." Viga leads me to a spare bunk that, incredibly, is worse than my old bunk at the training camp. There's no pillow and only a thin sheet instead of a blanket.

Once I'm on the grimy mattress, everyone sits on the floor around me, although Jarmella hangs back. I wish she'd accept that she's with us now, but at this point, it's up to her.

I take a breath. "You have no idea how happy I am to be here with you all." I feel like crying, but I have to be strong. "Did anyone tell you when we're arriving at Saturn's rings or how many transports were sent ahead? Viga, you said we get training, how long do we train?"

Kova groans and holds up her hand. "Hold on, Dax. One thing at a time. We do get training in the spacesuits, but only after everyone else has been training in them all day. It's not really fair because we were told we're the only ones who fight in the suits. Anyway, we won't get assigned a spacesuit until we're deployed. For now, we have to use the training suits and that doesn't give us much time since we're last in line. But it's better than nothing. Viga tried to get us more time, but Senior Lead Neemis threatened to snap her

111

spine for asking." She pauses. "What else did you want to know? Oh, yes. I don't know how many transports were sent after us, but we were the first to launch. At least that's what I heard. And we should be at the rings in three days."

Three days? We only have three days to live. "Aren't there any other AFGFs on our transport? I mean, from other training camps in other outliers? I didn't see any recruits training in the hangar. And there are a ton of fighters docked. All I've seen are kids from our camp."

This time Viga speaks up, "This is the AFGF level, but it's just us. Maybe they're on the other transports or maybe there aren't any more AFGFs. Each transport is made up of several training camps, but I've only seen our camp here, too. But I remember Instructor Milo saying that Mid-World is filled with training camps, so there have to be a lot of transports. Since we launched first, we're the first line of defense against the Piltraks." She glances at the floor. "I'm scared. We're all scared."

So am I, more than I want them to know. "Wait, if we were the first to launch, where are the other transports? I didn't see any and my fighter didn't detect any obstacles in its path. I came from the moon directly to the transport. I should have encountered..."

"What?" Viga paces. "They should be behind us. You must have missed them."

"Well, there was nothing between the moon and this transport. I was told that all of the transports follow the same flight path. Maybe after I blasted the Katarga stronghold I somehow went a different...no, that's impossible. Viga, what if there aren't any other transports coming to help us?" I get up.

"Of course there are. Wait. What do you mean you blasted the Katarga?" Viga stares at me.

There's no time to explain everything. "I'll tell you later."

Briett stands and holds his head. "What are you talking about? I'm really lost."

"You're always lost, Big Pig," Viga says, but then gives him a pat on the arm.

I go to him. "You're not the only one lost, Briett, I'm confused, too."

I don't understand what's going on. I need to think, so I wander away from the group to give myself a bit of space. Viga has to be wrong about us being the first transport to launch. It doesn't make sense that we'd be the only transport to fight against an entire Piltrak fleet. There is only a handful of us AFGFs, including me now that I'm here. How do they expect us, with hardly any training, to break through the Piltrak defenses? It's impossible. This isn't right. I saw the fighters in the hangar, which means they intend to fight, but if we're the only line of defense, we'll all be killed.

As cruel as Viteri is, and as much as he wants me dead, he wouldn't have agreed with the other commanders to only send our transport. Why jeopardize all of the fighter pilots? There's got to be more to it. I need to speak to Tablon and find out the truth. He'll know.

I turn to Viga. "Can you take me to Tablon?"

She shrugs. "I guess. He's still our Lead. Why do you want to see him? He hates us. You most of all."

"I know." I head toward the magnetic lift. "This is wrong and I have to find out where the other transports are. Tablon has to know what's going on. Do you know that Jarmer told me ten thousand Piltrak ships are coming and a thousand already waiting at the rings?" I stop at the lift and turn around. "How many soldiers do we have on this transport?"

Kova comes over and pauses. "I overheard the Leads talking when they were leaving a training session. They said each transport has fourteen hundred recruits, but I didn't hear what else they were talking about. Dax, it sounded like they thought there were more transports, too. What if the others got destroyed by the aliens and we're the only one left?"

I shake my head. "I don't think so, Kova. You said we're the first transport. That means the Piltrak are still in front of us. I came up from behind and trust me, there aren't any others and there's no debris floating around. We're it. There aren't any aliens around here. Nobody fired on me, well, the Katarga did, but that was at the moon. Please, Viga, take me to Tablon."

"Okay, but I don't think you'll get anywhere with him. When he's not yelling at us, he's ignoring us." Viga enters the lift. "If we run into Lenora, I'm going to bite her nose right off."

I follow her into the lift and try not to laugh, but I do anyway. That's quite an image. The tube rotates and seals, and starts to ascend.

We ride to the white level where the lift stops and the tube rotates again. But Viga hesitates and doesn't get off. Unlike our yellow level, which is empty except for the bunks, this one is sectioned off with dividing walls and has a large sitting area with couches, tables, and some sort of computers with heads-up displays. I've never seen anything like that in my life. Two boys are standing in front of their computers, playing what looks like a game. They have gloves on their hands and they're acting like they have imaginary laser guns, shooting at the display.

"Viga, what are they doing?" I ask, fascinated.

She whispers, "It's a training game for the Leads. At least that's what I heard. It's so they can learn to shoot a laser or something."

"But I thought the Leads didn't fight. Don't they stay on the transport?"

"I don't know." She shrugs. "We're not told anything, Dax."

Now I remember. Lenora was angry because she said the Leads were going to have to fight. "Maybe I can ask Tablon if we can play so we'll get better."

"Really?" She raises an eyebrow.

"No harm in asking."

I go to step out of the lift, but Viga grabs my arm and pulls me back. "Wait, Dax. We can't enter the Lead's level until we're recognized. We were told that much."

Recognized? All of these rules and regulations are absurd, just designed to make us feel inferior. It's strange, but I don't feel like a 'smudge' anymore. Maybe it's because I flew a fighter and did what nobody else was able to do with the Katarga vortex, and even though it was an accident, I actually succeeded in something. Whatever the reason, it makes me angry that I have to wait for permission to leave the lift.

After a moment, one of the boys playing the game looks up. "What do you vaporous nebulas want?"

Viga looks too scared to talk, so I figure I might as well say something. "I'm looking for Senior Lead Neemiss," my voice comes out bold and assured.

The boy strides to the lift. "What do you want with Tablon?" He points at the patch on my arm. "You're an AFGF. Tablon doesn't speak to worthless bilge scrapings like you." He laughs, glances at his friend and sneers at me. "Go back to your squad."

"No." I step out of the lift and right away notice a couple of other boys and girls coming out from behind the dividing walls. "I need to speak to Senior Lead Neemiss. And I'm not leaving until I do."

"Is that the smudge?" Tablon shouts as he comes around a wall. "On my level?"

I lean around the boy. "Senior Lead Neemis, I have to talk to you for a minute."

He glares at me. "I have nothing to say to you, smudge. Get off my level."

It's hard, but I stop myself from rolling my eyes. "Senior Lead Neemiss, I only need one minute and then you'll never see me again." I keep my eyes on him. "Or maybe I should go and talk to Commander Viteri."

"No. You don't bother the Commander. I'll give you one minute, smudge," Tablon says through clenched teeth, his cheeks turning red.

"That's all I need. Will Viga be all right here? Nobody will hurt her?"

Tablon grunts. "She'll be safe. But only for that one minute. You waste my time and I'll add to those bruises on your face." He chuckles and glances at his friends. While they nod and laugh at me, he points to a door to the right that I hadn't noticed. "Over here."

How big is this level? Ours is so much smaller. This one has to be more than twice the size of ours. I know I shouldn't worry about the unfairness of it all, but I do. My squad is every bit as important as these Leads. We're all recruits. I hold my tongue and follow after him as he presses a silver button in the center of the door and steps inside the room when the door silently slides open.

The room is small, with another computer game sitting on a desk. The door slides shut and Tablon sits with his feet up on the desk. "What do you want, Orwan? You can't keep threatening to tell the Commander. You know, at this point, I don't think it would matter anyway. So, what do you want?"

I feel confident being alone with him, like we're on equal footing. "Tablon, first of all, did you put Lenora up to beating me?"

His brow pinches. "Why would you ask me that? Lenora beat you?"

"Yes, she and her friends beat me unconscious and left me in the ventilation duct."

I notice a slight frown on his face. After a bit, he shrugs. "You probably deserved it. But no, I didn't have anything to do with that. You've got less than thirty seconds. What do you want?"

"Do you know that we're the only transport heading to the Piltrak fleet?"

He shakes his head like he thinks I'm an idiot. "What are you talking about? You really are brainless, Orwan. We're at the head of a fleet of a hundred transports with a total of nearly a hundred and fifty thousand troops. We're going to eradicate the Piltraks before they can start their attack." He chuckles. "You must have been in the ventilation system too long, your mind's gone." He takes his feet off the desk and slides the chair back. "Get out of my sight and stop wasting my time."

I stand firm. "Listen to me, Tablon, there aren't any more transports. I flew here in Jarmer's fighter ship, following the same coordinates as the supposed fleet. Trust me, there's nothing between Earth and here. We're alone. And it looks like only our camp is onboard."

He stares at me and his mouth gapes slightly. "I don't understand how you could fly a fighter after only a few lessons with Jarmer. He told me you were good, but—"

"But nothing. I flew the fighter. And I could have flown anywhere, but I chose to come here to be with my squad. Tablon, Jarmer told me a thousand Piltrak ships are getting ready to mount an attack and thousands more coming. If that's true, then our single transport doesn't have enough flyboys or recruits to defend ourselves. I saw maybe a couple of hundred fighter ships in the hangar when I came in, but our camp doesn't have that many pilots. Something's not right here. Think about it. There should be at least fourteen hundred recruits on this transport and I know our camp didn't have that many."

Tablon stands, breathing hard. "Orwan, you must have missed the other transports. A couple of flying lessons doesn't make you a pilot, you know. You probably flew under them or over them and didn't notice them."

"Didn't notice a hundred transport ships? Really? I know you don't like me, Tablon, but just check it out. Do it." If only he'd believe me. "And look into why no other camps are on this ship."

He pauses for a moment, staring at the ground, then looks up. "You don't know what you're talking about, smudge. The commanders don't lie.

The other recruits must all be on some other level. We were made soldiers so we can fight the aliens and save the world. Why would they lie to us and let us get killed? I'm a Senior Lead, they won't risk getting me killed. I'm important."

"Can you just look into it and let me know what you find out? I promise you, I won't say another word if you find that I'm wrong."

He gives me a nod. "Yeah, fine. But I can't wait to prove you wrong. Talking bad about the commanders is insubordination and traitorous. You'll pay, and this time, it won't only be Lenora pummeling your face."

"I'm not a traitor, Tablon. And it won't be me you want to punch when you find out I'm telling the truth." I turn and go to the door. "I'll be with my squad."

It slides open and I hurry to Viga, who's standing by the lift, eyes closed and head down, hands clasped together. I nudge her, we get in and I go to step on the yellow button, but change my mind and step on the clear button. Since the buttons are in a circle and it's next to the yellow button, I figure it means that since yellow is the last level, the clear button must be the first level, the commanders' level with the comfortable beds. If they're all still in the hangar, I can explore and see what they're hiding. It's time for a reconnaissance mission.

Chapter Fourteen

The lift keeps going up and my heart pounds harder. Even a couple of deep breaths can't calm me down and Viga's ragged breathing isn't helping. When we get to the clear level, I'll have to come up with something to say if the commanders are there. Maybe I can ask for a meeting with Viteri. That way I'll have a little time to look around until he comes and yells at me. I haven't thought this through very well. That seems to be my biggest fault lately, as if I need another fault.

"Dax, what are you doing?" Viga whispers frantically. "You're going to get us in trouble. I want to go back down."

"We're already in trouble. Don't you remember, we're going to die? They need us to die. What have we got to lose. They won't punish us at this point." I'm tired of everything, of how I'm treated and how my squad is treated, how the commanders are lying to us, how my parents were tricked into advancing me. That's the sick game the commanders are playing; forcing parents to advance their children to keep a steady supply of troops available to be slaughtered by this alien or that alien. "This isn't right."

"What isn't? You're scaring me, Dax. You have a...crazy look on your face."

"I'm not crazy. I'm determined."

The lift climbs up past the levels and I see some recruits that I recognize from our camp training with real lasers that burn holes into the padding on the wall of the orange level. On the purple level, more kids are doing some sort of flight training in simulators. Why bother to train the recruits at all if we're so outnumbered? Wouldn't it be better to wait for more transports or not fight at all? Did the commanders already try to reason with the Piltraks? Maybe that's it, they're in negotiations and there won't be a war after all. If that's the case, then it makes sense that they didn't send more transports. A whole detachment of transports would look aggressive.

Viga taps me on the shoulder. "What are you thinking? I wish I could see into that brain of yours."

"Unless we're negotiating with the Piltrak, it doesn't make sense that we're going to Saturn alone without support."

"Oh." She relaxes a bit. "So you think there won't be a war?"

We go past the blue level where recruits are studying maps and charts projected in front of them. "Maybe. But Tablon seems to think we're still getting ready to fight. He could be right because you were all rushed out of camp in an emergency. But that'll be suicide. The only chance we have is if there's an announcement telling us there won't be any fighting because the Piltrak agreed to go home."

"Okay, that makes sense. The commanders must know what they're doing."

I take a deep breath again. "I wish I had your confidence. I need to find out what they're up to, just in case Tablon doesn't."

Viga shakes her head. "Why? Dax, this isn't some sort of conspiracy. We're soldiers and we have to do what we're commanded to do. If we're told to fight the Piltraks, then that's what we'll do. It's that simple."

"No, it isn't."

Viga's expression shows that she's frustrated with me, but she doesn't argue anymore and stands facing the front of the lift. We stop on the clear level, and it looks empty. The tube rotates and I step through the opening without waiting and listen. There's not a single sound or voice.

To my right is a display case of sorts, a clear box hovering a meter off the ground with a shiny silver and blue object the size of my hand, floating inside. The object is elegant; smooth and oval-shaped with a thin groove going lengthwise across the top. There are strange symbols, ⅃⅃ ⅃⅂ ꝺə, imprinted on the object, but I have no idea what they mean. I do know, however, that I want the object because it must be special if it's kept on the commanders' level. If it's valuable, it might be the leverage I need now that my threat about Tablon and Lenora isn't likely to hold up.

I examine the box, but can't find a way to open it. *Think, Dax, think.* There has to be a way to get inside.

"Dax," Viga whispers.

I ignore her and run my hands over the box until my left index finger hits a hidden button on the side that slides the top open. I reach in and grab the object, which starts to glow slightly. It's got some weight to it and it's warm. I place it in my pants pocket and wander around. Each bunk, well bed is a more appropriate word, has a machine, maybe a computer, on a desk to the side. That's where I'll start. If I can access it, I might find data or instructions or the reason why there aren't any other transports. I was always good at computers in school.

"Dax," Viga says softly. "Come on, let's go."

I turn around and see that she's still standing in the lift. "Viga, come here. If someone else calls for the lift, you'll be trapped inside."

"Oh." She dashes out and hesitates for a moment before running to me. "What are you looking for?" She glances around. "Where is everyone?"

"I don't know, maybe training or still in the hangar." I sit on the first bed and check out the computer thing. It's nothing like the computers at school. Our computers had a flat finger-pad with a small screen and we had to place our thumb on the recognition space to start it. This has nothing like that. This thing looks look like a ball that was cut in half so the round part is face-up, smooth all over, and about the size of someone's head. And the screen, if it is a screen, isn't attached, but is standing to the side. It's possible these aren't computers after all.

"Do you know how to work that, Dax?"

I shake my head. "Do you?"

"Kind of. My Da has one. It's a cerebral impulse interpreter."

I stare at her. "A what? Is that a computer?" The synap-trodes in the fighter use brainwaves, so this might not be so different.

"Well, sort of, but it's not artificial, it works by tapping into your brain. It's an organic computer. You've never seen one? They're amazing, really galactic."

My friend Manti used to say galactic. She was popular and the popular kids always said things like that. She didn't care that I'm poor and hearing galactic again makes me feel better like I haven't completely lost touch with my old life. "Viga, back in your outlier, were you popular? Did you have a lot of friends? I don't mean to pry, but does your family have money because of the advancement subsidies from your brothers?"

She shrugs. "Um, I don't know. We have a nice house and like I said, my Da has a cerebral interpreter. I guess I have, had, a lot of friends. But our outlier is bigger than yours so there're more kids. Doesn't mean I was popular though. Besides, what does it matter now, I'm still an AFGF soldier."

She's right. Our past lives don't matter anymore. "We'll be friends for the rest of our lives, won't we, Viga?"

She nods and smiles. "Definitely. Except..."

"Except what?" My heart stops. Doesn't she want to be my friend?

She takes my hand. "Except, I feel more like your sister than just a friend. I've never had a sister."

That was easily the nicest thing anyone has ever said to me. I'm so lucky to be back with her, and the rest of my squad. "I've never had a sister either. We'll be sisters then." I squeeze her hand and turn my attention back to the cerebral interpreter. "How does it work?"

"I watched my Da a couple of times, but I never actually used it. He wouldn't let me, said it was too expensive for a kid to use." She picks up a small button-like thing that's next to the screen. "You put this electrode on your forehead. Then you have to place your hands around the interpreter, that's the round thing. It activates and uses your thoughts."

I take the electrode and study it. How does it read my thoughts? It's so small and not attached to anything. "What am I supposed to do?"

She sighs like she expects me to know. "Didn't you ever learn about thought-synthesis in school?"

"No." I feel dumb. I thought my school was up-to-date. Apparently it wasn't.

"That's okay. I told you my outlier is bigger than yours, maybe our schools have better teachers or whatever. Anyway, the organic computer takes your thoughts and synthesizes them into an operating system. You become the computer and can access anything that's stored in the interpreter or any system the interpreter has access to. Make sense?" She raises an eyebrow.

I nod even though I'm not completely clear about how it works. The electrode is about the size of my fingernail and I press it to my forehead as Viga said. It sticks without me holding it and I feel a slight tingle. I glance at Viga and put my hands around the interpreter. Right away, the screen lights up in a multi-colored display, changing from red to blue to green and back again.

"What do I do, Viga?"

"Think of something you want to know. Um, try something simple first, like the names of the recruits on board."

I close my eyes and think how I'd like to know who's on board. My whole head tingles and when I hear Viga gasp, I open my eyes. On the screen is a scrolling list of names. "Did I do that?"

She nods. "You sure did. You've got a knack for this. It took my Da a bit longer to get his to work correctly. Okay, think of something else."

"Like what?" What should I think about? I want to know why the commanders are sending only our transport to battle against thousands of Piltraks. But how do I phrase that so the interpreter will understand?

I look over at Viga and see her smiling. She points to the screen. "Dax, what does that mean?"

The screen shows a depiction of Saturn with red x's among the outer rings. "I don't know. It doesn't say what the x's represent."

As soon as I say that, a sentence appears above Saturn; *51 Piltrak vessels holding course.*

Viga gets closer to the screen and starts counting the red x's. "Fifty-one? That can't be right. There should be a thousand. Maybe the rest of them are on the back side of the rings."

I wonder the same thing and right away, another message pops up. *51 Piltrak vessels total. Holding course. No hostile actions detected.*

I stare at the screen. "No hostile actions? Then we must be in negotiations. But why do the commanders think there're a thousand Piltrak ships? Where are the other transports?"

Another message: *Commanders have planned a manageable war with anticipated human casualties. No additional transports are necessary. No negotiations planned. Attack on Piltrak scouting fleet projected to cause full-on war with Piltrak species. Transport soldiers, minus commanders, projected to be eliminated, minimal human loss. Significant equipment and supply loss. Full-scale war to commence once commanders are safe. Estimated revenue generated from future Piltrak war, 400 trillion global tokens. Commander share of revenue, one trillion global tokens per commander.*

How can that be right? Sweat drips down my back and I tear the electrode off, drop it on the desk and pull my hands off the interpreter. The screen goes blank. I can't believe it, a manageable war? There's no such thing. And how is the death of everyone on the transport minimal human loss?

Viga nudges me. "Did I read that right, the commanders are creating a war?"

I nod. "That's exactly what it said. They're going to murder the Piltrak scouts so there'll be a war."

Viga gasps. "The lift's moving."

My head's spinning and it takes me a second to realize what she said. "We'll wait until it stops and then call it back. Do you know how to call it back?"

"Yeah. There's a recall button near the shaft. We're going to get caught if we're not careful. Dax, why would they cause a war?" She points to the blank screen.

"Money. We're being sacrificed to make the commanders rich. They're going to create another war by provoking an attack from the Piltraks." Is this what they've been doing all along?

"Dax!" Viga motions to the lift.

It's going slowly and I see the platform coming down. It's about to stop at this level. We have to hide!

Chapter Fifteen

I grab Viga by the hand and pull her to one of the beds where we both slide underneath, hidden by a blanket that's draped down over the side. I hold my breath and hear two men talking as they leave the lift. One I recognize as Viteri, with his smarmy, sickening voice.

He says, "I can't wait to sleep in my own bed again. These lousy bunks make my back ache."

The other man replies, "Same here. The return speed-transport better get here soon. We'll be in range of the Piltraks before long and I don't intend to be anywhere in the vicinity."

Viteri again, "Don't worry. We'll be back home before the fighting ever starts. Don't forget, once this war's in full swing, we'll be rich beyond imagining. The sacrifice of my camp is well worth it. I'll get a whole new batch of recruits, which means more uniforms, weapons, and fighters. We'll lose all three hundred fighter ships that are on this transport as well. You know how much each ship costs? My stocks in the factories will surge like never before!"

Laughter. The other man says through fading chuckles, "And once your sacrificial recruit's death is broadcast, we'll have the populace demanding revenge. It worked out perfectly that she actually came to the transport. She could have gone home and nobody would have known. Dumb girl. And when your plan works, parents will send all of their children to us and we'll have to order even more supplies. And that means a freighter full of additional revenue!" More laughter.

I feel sick. How can they laugh? Viga wraps her fingers around my arm.

Heavy footsteps approach the bed and Viteri clears his throat. "Yeah, Orwan's death is going to make us an incredible sum of money. Shame though. She did quite well on her educational exit exams, but her attitude made her a danger. We have enough problems with women thinking twice about cranking out future recruits. If Orwan wasn't a nebulous smudge, she could have made something of herself."

"Stupid girl. Why's she scheduled to die? I mean, why'd you slate *her* for death?"

"Well," Viteri starts, "She's a potential instigator. You know what happens to those!" He snorts. "The educational schools have been doing a good job at keeping the children under control, but every now and then, one slips through. This one, Orwan, asks questions about the war and our motives. Causes others to question us. Can't have that, now can we? Two of the new Leads, Tablon Neemiss and Lenora Averlowes both agreed that Orwan's a trouble maker. Averlowes doesn't like her and Neemiss is my star, so if he agrees with Averlowes, then Orwan's my sacrificial recruit. His recommendation swayed me."

"Why? What's so great about this Tablon Neemiss?"

There's a pause before Viteri speaks again. "His family paid me fifteen million global tokens to keep him off the front lines, with another fifteen million in a year if I keep him alive. He's my thirty million token prize and he showed an incredible sense of patriotism toward Earth on his exit exams, so I made him a Senior Lead. He wants to destroy anyone or anything that jeopardizes the planet. That kind of bloodlust-loyalty has to be rewarded. He's coming back with us on the speed-transport. It's all basic strategic maneuvering."

A brief throaty chuckle. "Wise decision, Viteri, very wise. What about the AFGF squad? Are they scheduled to die together with Orwan? That'd be quite the show for the people on Earth."

"Not quite. I want them to last a bit longer. I've given them some training to keep them alive for a while. It'll look like they're avenging Orwan's death, fighting the evil aliens. Once we have outrage over Orwan's death, we'll broadcast the total annihilation of the entire AFGF squad. Those weaklings fighting to the death will get everyone glued to their projections." He laughs. "See, I've got it all planned out to the last detail. Orwan's a Single, which means her parents will be destitute without any subsidies and when the people see her pretty face all bloodied, and the dim future of her parents all because of the alien menace, they'll be outraged. Women will do everything to avoid producing Singles as well. So, more recruits to generate income for us. And on top of that, Orwan's entire squad will follow her in death. That'll clinch it. The people have never seen what the aliens do to their children and when they do, they'll be appalled and demand war with the Piltraks as revenge. And they'll think it was their idea!"

Viga's nails are cutting into my skin. I try to shake her off, but she won't budge. I grit my teeth against the pain because I can't let out even a slight sound.

The other commander continues, "She's pretty, eh?"

Viteri lets out a long sigh. "Yeah, a dead pretty face is excellent propaganda. It's her fault. That rebellious mouth of hers brought her here." He laughs. "Ah, well, it's beneficial for all of us to have her die. That girl is mine to do with as I please."

I feel disgusted and sick to my stomach, and with Viga squeezing my arm so tightly, I almost scream out.

Viteri continues, "Once we have full support from Global Command, we'll attack the Piltraks. We had intel that there were over a thousand Piltrak ships, but then we found out those alien morons only sent fifty-one scout vessels. Our intelligence squad has been punished for that bit of misinformation. Total incompetent idiots."

"Good thing you verified it and only identified fifty-one or we would have sent all of our transports."

"Definitely. Although we could have destroyed all of the transports and generated even more revenue. And blamed it on the Piltraks."

"Oh, that's true."

Viteri continues, "Too late now though. Oh, Averlowes actually discovered that the other ships we thought we saw were ghost projections, false images. She detected an anomaly at the training camp and determined that they weren't ships after all. She's the only one in the intelligence squad with any brains at all. Good with computers and coding. She and Neemis are close and if he trusts her, then I'll trust her, too. I had my doubts about her, but if they've become friends, I'll keep her around. Don't want to upset my meal ticket." He laughs.

"You're absolutely right to keep the Neemis kid happy. Happy kid, happy parents."

"And a happy income!" Viteri laughs so hard he starts to cough. "Anyway, I'll have Averlowes sent back with us and Neemis. I'll make sure that once we've taken out most of those scout alien black holes and left a few to report back to their commanders, not a single member of the intelligence squad remains alive, except for Averlowes. I'll have them fighting alongside the AFGFs."

A slight chuckle. "I'm in agreement with that, Viteri. I'm honored to serve under you."

I can't wait to get off this level and go back to my squad.

Viteri continues, "As you should be. I've estimated that we'll have nearly eleven months to prepare once the Piltrak make it back to their planet and begin gathering a large enough battle squadron. The factories will run day and night to make enough equipment for the impending war. And kids will be standing in line to be advanced. Maybe even before their Date of Fate. The more kids..."

"The more money for us!"

Viteri laughs. "Indeed. The people of Earth won't ever know we orchestrated the whole thing."

"They're certainly easy to dupe. And then in eleven months, we'll be sitting on a pile of money from our investments. Maybe I should buy up a few more shares in the factories. How did I ever doubt you, Viteri?"

They act like wars and death are business transactions. Their casual attitude about killing makes my blood boil. And Viga, she's shaking and digging her nails into my arm even harder.

After another chuckle, Viteri sighs. "I told you not to worry. Between the Katarga, the sporadic attacks by the Jurale and a new war with the Piltraks, we'll be able to retire early. I'm already thinking of a way to get the Jurale to step up their attacks. Oh, I forgot to tell you that Orwan accidentally knocked out the Katarga vortex. She said we can fly into the vortex and fire at the Katarga. Imagine that, she expected me to congratulate her and send in our fighters. As if I actually want to end that war."

"Viteri, you're a genius. Totally agree with you that this Orwan is nothing but trouble for us. You always know which kids to get rid of. If not for you, my investments in the Katarga war would have bottomed out and I'd lose a sizeable income. I have a lot of money tied up in stocks for ground forces' lunar laser weaponry. I think maybe now I'll buy my own moon somewhere to live on in my golden years." He laughs again.

Viga is taking quick gulps of air. I want to say something to her to calm her down, but I can't. What I really want is for Viteri and his cohort to leave so I can take Viga back to the yellow level.

Viteri stops laughing. "Quiet. You hear something? Like..."

"Like what?"

I move ever so slightly so I can reach Viga and put my hand over her mouth.

"I don't know. I thought I heard something."

Footsteps are moving around the room, coming near the bed, then moving away again. I hold my breath and hope Viga doesn't panic.

"Viteri, you've got space sickness! I'm going to get some sleep."

"I guess I'm hearing things. You know, I'm not really that tired after all. Thinking about the Jurale and another war has got me excited. I'm going to check on the Leads, make sure Tablon is comfortable, then join the others for supper."

I hear one set of footsteps go past the bed toward the rear of the room and one set go back to the lift. How are we going to escape if the other commander is still on this level? When Viga struggles, I take my hand off her mouth.

Even from under the bed, I can detect the soft whisper of the lift as it moves. It's just me, Viga, and the other commander. I'm not sure where he went, so I lift an edge of the blanket and peek out. There's nothing in front of the bed, but behind, toward the far end of the room, I see a pair of boots at the foot of another bed. If we wait a little while longer, he'll be asleep and we can sneak into the lift.

I drop the blanket and shift around so I'm face-to-face with Viga. I smile at her. As quietly as I can, I whisper, "We'll give it another few minutes."

She nods. "They want our whole camp to die for nothing, don't they?"

"Yes. But I won't let that happen." I put my finger to my lips when I hear movement. I peek under the blanket again and slide out enough to see the commander settling into his bed.

He yawns, chuckles to himself, and rolls over. I still can't believe how casually they were talking about me and my squad dying and using our deaths to cause another war. Nobody in my squad should die and I'm going to do whatever I can to see they don't. I won't let them down.

The sound of steady, rhythmic breathing gives me the opportunity I've been waiting for. I slide out from under the bed and accidentally roll onto the object in my pocket. I'd forgotten all about that, but now I'm not so sure it'll do any good to have it. After a moment, I stand, and sure enough, the commander is softly snoring. I help Viga out and we tiptoe to the lift, but before she presses the small recall button, I tap her on the shoulder.

"Viga, hold on. I need to do something first." I touch the object in my pocket and jog over to the cerebral interpreter, press the electrode onto my forehead and place my hands in position. I think to myself, *what is the object in my pocket*? The screen blinks on and says, *Object is a Jurale weapon, illegal to own and with reported lethal capabilities*. Really? A weapon? Well, maybe it can be useful after all.

How do I use it? One word pops up on the screen: *unknown*.

I hear the lift coming down and see that nobody is inside. I don't know what I would have done if Viteri or Tablon were inside. This whole thing was a huge risk, not just for me, but for Viga. I can't be so reckless. I peel off the electrode and run back to the lift.

Viga points to the cerebral interpreter. "I couldn't read that, what did it say? What did you ask?"

I take out the Jurale weapon and keep my voice low, "I wanted to know what this is."

She touches it. "And what is it?"

"It doesn't matter, I don't think it'll do me any good anyway. Come on, let's go." She doesn't need the added stress of knowing I have an illegal alien weapon.

We get in and I step on the yellow button, but instead of heading down, the lift goes up. I stomp on the yellow button over and over, yet the lift continues upward.

Viga whimpers. "We're going up to the main level. What are we going to do, Dax?"

What should I say to her? I don't know what to do. Panic is rising up in me, but I don't want Viga to see so I draw in a few breaths and I force a smile. "We'll be fine. They're not expecting us. As soon as the lift stops, we'll just make it go back down again." Of course, I know if the lift is going up, it means someone called for it before I pressed the yellow button.

"Oh, that's a good idea. Why didn't I think of that? You're so smart, Dax." She's trembling.

No, I'm not. I'm an idiot for thinking I can get away with snooping around off our level. "I'm a fool."

Viga continues, "You are not. I heard Commander Viteri say you scored well on your exits. I passed, but not by much. You're smart, Dax."

"If I'm so smart, why am I on this transport about to be sacrificed to the Piltraks? A smart girl would be a thousand light-years from here."

"Don't put yourself down. What the Commander said about you, well, it's super-massively repugnant. He doesn't own you, or any of us. If anyone can get out of this, you can."

Maybe, but Viteri does own me, and that hurts. I'd put my palm print on the projected recruitment form, nobody forced me. I can still remember what he said to Da on my Date of Fate; *your daughter belongs to me*. Those words sting my heart, but if I'm going to die, I want it on my terms. As the lift begins to decelerate, I hold my breath. I don't know why I'm so terrified. What's the worst that'll happen? What can they possibly do to me? I let out my breath and watch Viga.

"Dax, I'm so frightened."

"Get down low, on your stomach." I push her down and curl up next to her. "If anyone is waiting to get on, they'll notice someone standing right in front of them, but they won't be looking at the floor. If we can press the yellow level button before they get on, maybe we can make it."

"Dax, the lift won't go down until the shaft rotates open and then closes again. It has to lock in place or it won't descend."

I nod. "That's okay. We'll make it." I have very little confidence that we'll be safe, but so long as Viga thinks we will, she won't panic.

The interior of the lift is dim, which should give us a little cover. As scared as I am, I'm also weirdly excited, like when I was flying the fighter ship. I remember how our teachers at school used to tell us that being a soldier was one of the most thrilling occupations a person can have. I always figured it was their way of trying to get us to volunteer for advancement, but maybe they were right. It's exhilarating doing something terrifying. Is it wrong to feel that way?

When the lift stops at the top level, I instinctively press my body as close to the ground as possible and hold my breath as the shaft rotates. Thankfully, there isn't anyone waiting close by. They must have called for it and wandered off. I reach over and press the yellow button and the shaft begins to rotate closed again. Just as I think we've made it, I hear an all too familiar voice.

It's Tablon and he's calling out to another recruit, "The lift's here. I'm going down to the purple training level for a while."

The shaft continues to rotate slower than I thought was possible. Tablon is maybe three meters away, but it's obvious he hasn't seen us yet. I hear a small click and feel the lift drop slightly. My hand rests on my pocket and I feel the weapon under my fingers. If only I knew how to use it.

"Hey, why didn't the lift...Orwan?" Tablon runs toward the lift and bangs on the closed shaft. "Come back here, smudge!"

Chapter Sixteen

The lift descends below the top level, taking us away from Tablon. Viga is whining and I'm sweating. Now Tablon has the right to say anything about me, like how I should be shoved out into space or sent out by myself to fight the Piltrak, or worse, he can do anything to my squad. Whatever he says, Viteri will listen. But he won't listen to a thing I say.

I get up and offer Viga my hand. "You have to calm down. If Tablon doesn't know the truth about what's going on with the Piltrak, I'll tell him, and if he does, he'll know there's no point in punishing us. We'll be fine."

She takes my hand and stands. "I doubt it. He's mean and decayed. He can still make our lives miserable. What if he stops our training or our food? What then?"

She has a point. "Well, if we lose our food, Briett will lose weight for real." I smile. "If we all stick together, we'll be all right. We'll show them all what a great squad the AFGFs are. I won't let you get hurt."

"Promise?"

"I promise." I don't like making a promise I know I can't keep. It's like I'm betraying my friends. I have to find a way to keep them alive or stay alive myself so I can help them. What will the commanders do if I *don't* die and somehow manage to escape? Sacrifice someone else? I can't let *that* happen, I just can't.

We stop at the yellow level and as soon as the shaft rotates around, Viga runs out and throws herself on her bunk. I follow, not wanting to tell my friends what we heard, but I know I have to.

Briett comes forward. "Dax, we've been ordered to the, um, the..."

"Oh, Big Pig!" Kova gives him a shove and pushes past him. "We got orders to go to the purple level. Do you know anything about this, Dax? The purple level is for Leads. Why would they tell us to go there?"

I glance over at Viga, who has her head buried under her arms. It's completely up to me to explain. I sit on the edge of my bunk. "Tablon saw me in the lift so he's probably going to discipline us. But that's not all."

"Isn't that enough?" Kova groans. "Are we all getting punished because you and Viga went roaming around? That's not fair. Why can't you obey the rules?"

What's not fair is that our squad is doomed and there's nothing I can do about it. I want to tell everyone that everything will be fine, we'll all be safe, but that'd be a lie. I'm done with lying and I'm done with getting blamed for everything. "Listen to me for a minute. The Piltraks are being used, just like we're being used. The commanders are designing a war so they'll get even richer. That's all they care about. They don't care about us or our parents. They want money and they need a constant supply of soldiers to put in these ridiculous wars."

My stomach aches and I want to get as far away from here as I can. I wish I could hop in a fighter ship and fly and fly and fly until I'm in another solar system. I look at the faces around me. Even if I could do that, I wouldn't.

I grip my mattress. "Kids like us die so the commanders can order more uniforms, more flight suits, more fighters, more everything. They invest in manufacturing plants. And Trab, the mechanic at the training camp, told me he always has to order new parts for the fighters. They purposely build them shoddy so the Global Forces has to order new parts. That's more money going to the manufacturing plants, and the shareholders. Do you understand? Viteri told me there are rumblings among the people and so that's why we're being sacrificed. To be used for propaganda. I was advanced so he could kill me off to shut me up."

Briett gasps. "I didn't know the commanders were making money off the wars. That's not something we ever learned in school. Or maybe we did and I didn't understand it. That happened to me a lot. But why does the Commander want you dead?"

"You're such a smudge, Big Pig." Kova sits on Viga's bunk. "Because Dax says what's on her mind. They don't like that. Get it?"

"Hey, don't call him a smudge," I say. "Do you understand, Briett?"

Briett shrugs. "I guess. So why am I in the AFGFs? I never say what's on my mind."

"It doesn't matter. Your family advanced you for the money." I lie down and stare up at the ceiling. Was that a harsh thing to say?

Kova clears her throat. "Um, we have to go to the purple level. Did you all forget?"

"Let's go." Viga jumps off her bunk and stomps to the lift. "We're all dead anyway."

"I'm not dead yet. Training!" Briett shouts as he stumbles after Viga. "Purple level training!"

As much as I like Briett, and feel sorry for him, he's making me angry with his oblivious behavior. I want to shake some sense into him. It's not training we'll get on the purple level.

Jarmella, who's been very quiet and sitting by herself, finally speaks up, "You people are brainless. You deserve to die." She rushes to the lift and pushes Viga out of the way. "I don't belong in this squad."

I'm not in the mood to deal with her attitude. "You do. You're an AFGF, just like the rest of us. I made a deal with Jarmer to have you in our squad. You *will* stand with us and you *will* fight. If any of us are going to have a chance at surviving, we have to fight as a team." I motion for everyone else to go to the lift.

Jarmella gets in first and scowls at me. I don't care about being popular or liked, not anymore. All of us enter the lift and since nobody steps on the purple button, I do. I don't realize I'm stomping on it over and over until Viga tugs on my arm and tells me to stop. The lift rotates, closes, and heads upward. Nobody talks on the way to the dreaded purple level.

When the lift stops, Tablon is standing in front of five other Leads, his arms folded like Viteri's. His thin lips form a tight, flat line and he's glaring straight at me. His eyes have a sparkle to them and I bet that means he's looking forward to whatever he's going to do. As soon as the lift opens, he lunges forward and grabs me by the front of my shirt, pulls me out, and pushes me to the floor. My body still hurts from the beating at training camp and when I slam down, every bruise screams out in pain, but I'm not about to cry out.

Tablon stands over me. "Smudge, you don't seem to understand orders, do you? You were to stay on the yellow level with your squad, not ride around in the lift. So now because of your insubordination, you're here. Why is it so hard for you to do what you're told? I know you have the brain of a decaying star, but just once I'd like to see you act like a soldier. Stand up and salute, smudge!"

"Yes, sir." I scramble to my feet and perform a perfect salute, regardless of the pain I'm in. "I thought you said I'm not supposed to salute you."

He comes near and lowers his voice to an angry growl, "If I say salute, you salute. I told you one day you'd salute me. I was starting to feel sorry for you getting beat up, but now I think you deserve every single one of those bruises." He gets so close that his lips are almost touching my ear. "Commander Viteri told me to isolate you from your squad. He thinks you're a bad influence. I agree. But if you continue to keep your mouth shut about you-know-what, I'll sneak you some food. That's about all I can do."

So he's still afraid I'll tell on him and Lenora. Good. He must know he's going back with the commanders and doesn't want to jeopardize his future. At least he's got a future. "Where am I supposed to go for isolation?" I don't want to leave my squad, especially since I only just got them back. "Can't I stay with my squad?"

Tablon steps back and shakes his head. "No. *I'm* not going to disobey the Commander. I have a career with the Global Forces and I don't intend to risk it. You'll be restricted to the storage level until we get to Saturn. I'll personally escort you later. But right now, take your squad to the Organic Synaptic Link-up port." He points to a strange circular platform about five meters or so behind him.

"What's an Organic Synaptic Link-up port?" I ask, hoping he'll tell me without berating me. It doesn't sound like anything I want to be near. Does everything link to our brains?

He exhales. "I should have known I'd have to explain every little detail. The OSL port links all of the players' minds together into a simulation program for a computer-based battlefield. Your pathetic squad is going to train with my Lead squad. You'll be the Piltraks." He smirks.

I hear Briett gasp and Kova whimper. This is Tablon's idea of punishment. Well, at least I'll have one more training session with my squad before being banished to the storage level, wherever that is. I pat Briett on the arm and motion for my squad to follow me to the platform at the far end of the room. The platform is floating off the ground about half a meter and is big enough to hold perhaps fifteen or twenty recruits. Around the perimeter, maybe three meters above the platform is a shimmering blue ring of light with a transparent blue curtain that drops down about a meter. Dead-center on the platform floating in a column, are rings of multi-colored buttons. It's a strange control panel, if that's what it is. There's nothing solid on the OSL port, except for the actual platform.

Briett taps me on the shoulder. "Dax, I don't want to step on that and I don't want to be a Piltrak."

I completely understand his hesitancy, but it's best to get it over with. "It'll be all right, Briett. We're not going to get hurt, it's only a practice session."

Tablon stomps over and shoves Briett in the back, making him fall forward onto the platform. "Yeah, Big Pig, everything's going to be just fine. But you will get hurt." He laughs and pushes Viga, Jarmella, and Kova onto the platform.

I glare at Tablon. "How can we get hurt if it's a simulation? What are we supposed to do? I've never trained like this before. I'm not doing anything until you explain how we play. We won't stand a chance otherwise."

The rest of my squad rushes up onto the platform, but I'm still waiting for an answer.

Tablon raises his hand to strike me, but stops. "Shut up, smudge. You'll do exactly what I say and you won't ask questions. This training is for the Leads, not for the AFGFs. You don't get training or weapons. You don't matter."

I do matter and my squad matters. Damn, how I want to scream that in his face. It hurts me to see how afraid my squad is and how they blindly go along out of terror. I don't accept that my fate is to die for the glory of the war and as stupid as this might be, I'm not afraid either.

My mind's made up at this point and I'm going to fight and try to stay alive as long as I can. I'm not about to stop trying and I certainly won't give Viteri the spectacular death he wants, if I can help it. If I survive for a while, my parents will collect a few more subsidy payments and I can show everyone I'm not worthless. And I'll find a way to report back to the people of Earth and tell them the truth about the wars.

I stare at Tablon. "What's the point in training with us if you're going to slaughter us? If you give us weapons, you and the rest of the Leads can get better practice."

He narrows his eyes and watches me without saying anything for a few seconds. "AFGFs with weapons might be a hilarious addition." He turns to another Lead, a girl who's very tall with her blue-black hair twisted around her head almost like a halo. "Pyla, you be the controller and add enemy weapons to the training program. We'll give the smudge and her pathetic squad of losers some weaponry, just for fun!" He glances at me again. "Just so you know, the weapons are simulations, but you can hold them, if you know how. Oh, and they fire real pulses of directed-energy, if you can figure that out, too! And the directed-energy pulse, well, it hurts. You'll find that out soon enough." He laughs, grabs me by my arm, and drags me onto the platform.

The rest of the Lead squad, except for Pyla, hops up and surrounds us. I wish Lenora was with them so I could blast her. I look over Tablon's shoulder and see Pyla sit at a projection panel and push a bunch of buttons, but out of nowhere, here comes Lenora. She sits down when Pyla gets up. My eyes connect with Lenora's and I'm positive there's the smallest hint of a smile on her lips.

Tablon takes hold of the front of my shirt and pulls me to him. "Ready, smudge?"

No, I'm not ready. Not ready at all, but I nod anyway. "Of course." If Lenora's involved, this isn't going to be any ordinary simulated training program.

"Good." He lets go of me. "Then go ahead and press the green, yellow and blue buttons, in that order, and get ready."

I try to swallow a lump that's formed in my throat, but it's stuck there and won't budge. All eyes are on me, waiting for me to initiate the training session. The Leads are all smiling, which makes me want to smack each and every one of them right in the face, but instead, I put my finger on the green button. It's a hologram and my finger goes right through. Next, I touch the yellow and blue buttons and before I can take a breath, I'm standing in a desert; sand, rocks, and cacti all around. It looks vaguely like my outlier, except we actually have a few plants and less desert. I don't see anyone else at all. Where's my squad?

I rush for cover behind a large boulder, press my body against it and peek over the top. It feels real, but how can it be? This is a simulation. A second later, I fall through the boulder, into the open. It's a hologram! Right away, I feel a sharp sting on the side of my neck followed by another and another pelting my body. Why was the boulder solid before? As fast as I can, I roll back through it. Shots continue to come through and a couple more hit me in the leg. Where are my weapons? I reach for a rock, but my hand goes right through it. I don't see a single thing to use and since everything appears to be projections, I can't even pick anything up. Tablon lied about giving me a weapon. No, it has to be Lenora who changed things.

I hear a shout, "I found a Piltrak behind the boulder!" It's Tablon. "Concentrate on the enemy combatant but maintain cover!"

Great, now they all know my position. I have to move. Even though I was only in the open for a few seconds, I saw several other boulders about five meters ahead of me. That has to be where the Leads are hiding. But where's my squad? I check the area behind me and to the sides, but other than a shallow strip of depressed land about ten meters away that looks like a small dry riverbed, there isn't much. The dry riverbed doesn't seem very deep, maybe a meter, if that. Not much cover if I can even make it that far. This is completely unfair. Especially since hiding behind a hologram boulder doesn't give me any protection from the lasers. But how can that be? I leaned against it before.

I hear a few screams and I'm sure it's Briett's voice above the rest. My heart hurts knowing they're under attack, but what can I do? I'm helpless. Just as I'm about to make a run for the riverbed and hope for the best, I hear a thud right next to me. A strange sort of gun appears on the ground. I grab it and as soon as my hand is on the butt, it flashes blue. The word 'armed' glows on the barrel and vanishes a second later. Wait, this doesn't seem right. Tablon said the weapons were simulations, yet here I am, holding the gun, and it's heavy. What if it's a projection, like the boulder?

A split-second later, it falls from my hand. What's going on? The only way something like this could happen is if when I first picked up the gun, I thought it was real. Is that what Tablon was talking about, believing something is real? But how can I convince myself that the weapon is real when it's not? It has to be possible. That's why Tablon shot through the boulder. He knows the boulder is a hologram, but he convinced himself that his weapon is real. Well, if he can do it, so can I.

Making sure I don't touch the boulder, I get to my feet and pop my head up and right back down again. That was long enough to see Tablon and three other Leads advancing on me. The weapon at my feet is different from the guns we used at the training camp, but a gun's a gun. All I have to do is pick it up and fire. Simple. I reach down, but my fingers go right through. That didn't work. Manti used to tell me that I questioned things too much and was never satisfied with reality. Well, Manti, you're absolutely right. Here I am in a simulation where everything I see is *not* real, but I have to *believe* it is. How's that for an altered reality?

With the Leads' positions in my mind, I pick up the weapon, aim right into the boulder and fire a multi-shot burst through it. There's a shrill scream and then nothing. Ha! I must have hit someone. I aim again, but before I can get off another shot, Tablon shouts for his Leads to "blast the smudge into oblivion". I'm not about to be blasted anywhere, so I keep low and sprint to the dry riverbed. A barrage of blasts whiz by my head and several shots get me in the back, but I keep going and dive into the riverbed. I get to my knees and peek over the bank, squeeze off another multi-shot burst and duck down in time to avoid getting struck by the Leads' rounds.

"Orwan! Halt your fire!" Tablon orders.

Why should I? If I surrender, he wins, and I'm tired of losing. More than anything, I want to win this battle and show everyone that I'm as good as any soldier and not a *smudge*. I pop my head above the riverbank again, but this time I don't fire. Tablon has Briett on his knees with a gun pressed against his head.

Tablon is breathing hard. "Put down that weapon, smudge. I don't know how you did it, but when the Commander finds out, you'll be in more trouble than you ever imagined. If you don't surrender, I'll shoot Big Pig. I told him a direct shot to the head will scramble his brains. He believes it will, so it will. Do you want that?"

What's he talking about? What am I supposed to have done? He's the one who forced me into the simulation. "Is this a new tactic, Tablon? Did you learn bluffing in your advanced training back home?" I aim my weapon right at him. "Let Briett go."

"Orwan, surrender the game! You wounded Maron really bad. This was supposed to be a training simulation with no *alien* weapons. I don't know how you got hold of an alien weapon, but you'll pay for violating the training code. Surrender!"

I keep it pointed directly at him and take a moment to look at my weapon and his. They're different. Very different. His has a short barrel with a narrow muzzle, while mine has a barrel about the length of my arm with glowing blue lights running along the top and a flared muzzle. Is mine actually an alien weapon? The Jurale weapon I have looks nothing like this one.

I lock my eyes on his. "Aren't I supposed to shoot my enemy, Tablon? Isn't that what training is all about?"

His voice is quieter now, "Not in a *simulation*, idiot. Alien weapons are live, even in the simulation. That's why they're against regs for normal training. They're only used for super-advanced training."

Did he say my weapon is live?

He continues, "Maron's a good Lead and you'll pay for hurting him, you galactic waste of space. Why did you do it? He's probably got internal injuries."

There's no way my weapon could really hurt someone other than a mild sting, even if I believed it was real. Like he said, the directed-energy hurts, but it sure doesn't cause internal injuries. This is a training simulation. Fake weapons can't do real harm. Unless...Lenora. She must hate that I'm alive and on the transport. But would she do something so horrible?

"Tablon, listen." I point my gun barrel up. "I didn't know this weapon could hurt anyone. Lenora did it. She was at the computer console when we got onto the port. How would I have been able to do anything?"

"You're such a liar, smudge. She's on the other training level." Tablon kicks Briett over and aims his weapon right at me. "I can't kill you, Orwan, but I can hurt you." He fires.

Before I can get out of the way, a shot gets me in the head and I instantly remember what he said about a direct shot scrambling Briett's brains. But nothing happens to me, except for the pain I feel where I was hit.

There's a bright flash of green light all around, so bright I have to close my eyes. When I open them again, I'm no longer in the desert, but in the middle of a blizzard where the freezing wind is biting into my skin and snow's swirling around me. What's Lenora up to now?

Chapter Seventeen

I'm shivering uncontrollably. It's only a matter of time before my fingers will be too numb to hold my weapon.

"Smudge! I'm coming for you," screams Tablon. "I made my weapon go hot just like yours!"

He's close, but there's no way I can see him in this white-out. This isn't a battle simulation game anymore, I'll have to fight for my life. A "hot" weapon means lethal, I know that from training. So that's what Lenora's plan is; to make Tablon so angry, he kills me. I still don't understand how a weapon can be hot in a simulation.

I hold my breath and listen for any sound other than the whistle of the wind, but there aren't any footsteps. The only thing I hear is my own chattering teeth. Then I detect something, the slight crunch of a lone foot settling down into the snow, and it's no more than a meter away to my right. I swing my weapon around, fire a single shot and throw myself to the ground. A miss, I think.

Immediately, there's return fire, but he also misses. This is ridiculous! Isn't there a way to end the simulation? The wind is easing, I'll soon be visible, if I don't freeze to death first. On my stomach, I crawl away, but someone grabs my hair and pulls me to my feet.

The wind dies completely and I see that it *is* Tablon. There's no way he could move that fast. Lenora must be moving him around in the game. His fingers twist in my hair and his face contorts into a furious scowl. I have to get away.

"Tablon, stop! I didn't do anything wrong. Lenora's doing this. Didn't you see her at the console before the simulation started?" I'm sure he won't listen, but I have to try.

He lets go of my hair and slaps me hard across my cheek. "I should let the Commander take care of you, but this is too personal. You made me look like a fool. I'm Senior Lead and this is my training program. You're only a worthless AFGF and you violated the rules in *my* sim." With a violent shove, he knocks me to the ground. "I want to see your face when I crush the life out of you. I'm going to end you once and for all."

I roll away from him a second before his boot would have stomped on my throat. As I scramble to my feet, I notice someone in the distance. I can't believe it, it's Lenora. So it wasn't Tablon I heard before, it was her! She's put herself in play. I take my chances and run through the snow away from both of them, only to find I'm standing in the middle of an empty expanse of ice. At least I still have my weapon.

I hear the whir of a gun and dive to the ground. Several bursts whiz by, but when I turn my head to look, the snow turns into a blizzard again and I can't see anything. If Lenora is in the simulation, then who's at the controls? From the direction of the bursts, they're right behind me.

Okay, so if they're expecting me to keep going, why not double back and come at *them*? I stay low, shielding my eyes with one hand and aiming my weapon with the other, and creep toward them.

After a short time, I hear the snow crunch. Lenora and Tablon can't be more than three or four meters away and since they're not shooting anymore, they mustn't know where I am. This is the opportunity I need. Quietly and smoothly, I concentrate on the footsteps and fire a continuous burst.

There's a loud shriek. It's Lenora. A direct hit!

"Tablon!" I shout, "Stop the simulation now or I'll keep firing!"

The blizzard stops and the remaining snow falls in heavy flakes until there're none left. I see Lenora on the ground, lying still. Her image pixelates a second later. Tablon is standing over her with his gun at his side. I lower my weapon and run to her. Her image begins to fade and then vanishes completely.

Tablon sees me and raises his gun at the same time I raise mine. It's a standoff. His hand is shaking so much that he can't aim straight. His brow is wrinkled and his cheeks are flushed. "Orwan, what did you do?"

I can't tell if he's angry or shocked, or both. I lower my weapon again, shove his arm away and drop to my knees where Lenora was. "Where did she go?"

He raises his gun again. "She's gone. You killed her. You killed her!"

"I didn't...Tablon, stop the simulation. She's still on the port like the rest of us. Even a hot weapon can't kill someone in a simulation."

His eyes are glassy. "Yes, it can. She's not on the platform. You shoot her in the simulation with a hot weapon and she dies for real and disintegrates off the port and becomes part of the sim forever. She's dead. She told me all about it. She knows code writing. If a hot weapon hits a person, their body on the platform gets an overload of epsilon-wave energy and disintegrates. The energy that's left goes through the port and into the sim-code. She told me that's why nobody ever programs a weapon to go hot in our sims. There are safeguards, but I guess you found a way around them, didn't you? She's...she was...so much better than you at everything. Now she's dead. You're going to follow her."

"No, listen. This isn't right. It doesn't make sense." I put my weapon on the ground and look up at him. "She can't be dead."

Tablon presses a button on a silver cuff around his wrist and within a couple of seconds, I'm warm again and we're no longer on the ice field, but back on the OSL platform. Three Leads rush up to us, but Tablon raises his hand to keep them away. He stares at me, his breathing heavy. I know I'm in serious trouble. I back away and jump off the platform.

"You killed Lenora," his voice is deep, pained. He points at me. "Take Orwan to Commander Viteri."

The girl Pyla stares at me. "I was monitoring the sim and as soon as Orwan blasted Lenora, she vanished from the platform."

"Orwan killed her." Tablon hops off the platform. "Belay my last order, I'll take the smudge to the Commander myself."

I back up some more, toward the lift. "Tablon, I told you I didn't mean to. She messed with the programming. I didn't even know my weapon was hot. Pyla, tell him. Lenora took over for you."

He shoots a glare at Pyla and focuses back on me with wide, crazed eyes. "You're blaming Lenora? Easy to blame the dead, isn't it, smudge!"

I look around, but all I see are the Leads, no member of my squad anywhere. Shouldn't they still be on the platform? "Tablon, we need to talk about this. Where's my squad?"

One of the Leads speaks up, "Your squad was out a few minutes into the game. They're back on your decayed level."

With a sneer, Tablon takes a heavy step toward me. "It's just you and us now. You should never have been advanced."

I agree. "Tablon, this isn't my fault. If it was, I'd admit to it, but it isn't. Lenora put my weapon in the simulation and she must have made it hot. Think about it, how could I possibly do anything to the program?"

He stops and seems to think for a moment. "Why would Lenora do that? She wouldn't. We were all in the simulation. There's no way she'd jeopardize me getting hurt. And she came into the sim as well." Now he frowns. "Stop trying to confuse me, Orwan. You hacked the system somehow."

If Lenora was trying to get me killed by having me hurt someone, she must have been desperate. But why? I didn't tell Viteri about her and Tablon, and in truth, I wasn't going to. It was a bluff, pure and simple. "Why *was* Lenora in the simulation? Something's not right, Tablon."

"Yeah, something's definitely not right, Orwan. And I know you're at the heart of it." He massages his forehead like he's frustrated or confused. "I specifically told Lenora not to enter into the sim and stay on the other training level so she couldn't be implicated in what I was going to do...I mean, if your squad got hurt. AFGFs aren't allowed in a Lead training sim, so I told her to stay away. Then when I saw her inside the game, I asked her what she was doing. Know what she said?"

"No." I take another step backward toward the lift.

One of the Leads approaches. "You need some help, Tab?"

"No. I've got this." Tablon continues and lowers his voice, "She told me that the only way to make sure you never said a word was to lose you in the simulation."

"Lose me? What does that mean?"

Tablon glances around. "I thought she meant to make you get separated from your squad, so you'd be all alone, and then unplug you from the game so you lose on a technicality. I've heard of it, but nobody's ever done it. If you get unplugged, you die in the game, but not for real."

"Tablon, I don't think that's quite what she meant, do you? She wanted me dead and didn't care if I killed someone along the way. I could have killed you or any of the other Leads. What was she thinking?"

"Just...shut up. She was scared." He waves the other Leads away and comes close to me. In a whisper, he says, "I tried to keep her calm by telling her you and I had an arrangement, but she wouldn't listen. That must be why she tried to kill you at camp." He shakes his head. "I never meant for anything like this to happen."

I'm speechless. Is that guilt I detect? "Can't we hack into the simulation and reverse it or something? It's just a computer after all. I'm sure someone else knows code."

"Lenora is the one who modified it for me. In the old version, the weapons couldn't hurt you. She said it would be more realistic if they could, so she coded the sim to cause a directed-energy jolt on the platform if anyone was hit in the sim." He shakes his head and looks at the ground. "You need to go. Her death will already have been reported to the commanders. Spend your last few minutes with your squad because the Commander will execute you immediately for this. And you deserve it."

"What? But I..." Even though Lenora set me up, I'm the one who gets punished. "He won't execute me, he wants me to die in battle. You know that, right?"

Tablon shrugs.

"Is my squad really back on yellow level?"

He gives a dismissive wave. "Of course. Go and wait with them and say goodbye or whatever." He turns, goes back to the platform, and just stares at it.

The other Leads run to him and point at me, but he just shakes his head and tells them to let me leave.

I head for the lift and hit the recall button. If Lenora is dead, that means I've killed someone. How am I supposed to live with that? Then again, I might have killed some Katarga when I blew up their stronghold, but it isn't the same. I didn't *see* them. If everyone had to stare into the eyes of their victims, it would be harder to pull the trigger.

A disembodied voice booms, "AFGF recruit Orwan report to the main level immediately!"

No chance to see my squad. Maybe I deserve to be punished for killing Lenora, even if I didn't mean to, but if Viteri decides to kill me now, I won't be around to help my squad. And while the people of Earth will get their show earlier than planned, it won't have the impact Viteri hoped for. We haven't engaged the Piltraks yet, so if my body is scattered in pieces, floating around the rings of Saturn, it'll be nothing more than a sad tragedy. He's spent too much time planning; he'll keep me alive.

The lift's coming. Now I won't get to explain to my squad exactly what happened. I can't even fully explain my side to Viteri without implicating Tablon, and I promised I wouldn't do that. He's a decayed personality like everyone says, but he did hold up his end of the arrangement. Although if I don't tell my side I'll be accused of cold-blooded murder. I don't want Ma or Da to think that of me. What do I do? I feel sick and I'm sweating through my shirt.

The lift slows and of all people, Jarmer is inside. He's wearing his flight suit and has a silver cuff around his wrist like Tablon does. When the shaft rotates into position, he hops out and looks around. By this time, the Leads have all gone to console Tablon and nobody is looking at us.

Jarmer puts his finger to his lips and whispers, "Dax, listen to me carefully. I know what happened. You have to trust me. You're in danger."

"Yes, I know. That's nothing new."

He glances down and then back up. "I received a ground-to-ship communication from Trab when I was running a training mission outside the transport. He told me everything. How Lenora beat you and left you for dead, how you flew my ship all by yourself. He says you're special, so I watched a display of the training sim to see just how special you are and saw what Lenora did. If there's one thing I detest, it's dishonorable conduct. She got what she deserved. But I can help you. Will you trust me?"

I'm still not sure what Jarmer wants. "I suppose. You can tell Commander Viteri what happened with Lenora. He'll understand." There's a glimmer of hope bubbling.

Jarmer puts his hand on my shoulder. "That can't happen. He won't listen. But you did me a favor by taking my sister into your squad so I could have time to get her a position as a transport pilot before she was shipped out. Not that it matters now, but still, you did that. I can repay the favor, but not by talking to the Commander. Obviously you can fly a fighter, right?"

We get into the lift, but Jarmer doesn't press any of the buttons.

I nod. "Sort of. I got caught in the Katarga vortex and only got out of it because I blasted my lasers at them. It was an accident. I didn't know it'd get

148

me free. Then Trab punched in the coordinates to the transport. Not sure if that qualifies me as a pilot though."

He smiles and moves his hand so it's resting on my cheek. He leans in close. "It does." He gets even closer and kisses me on the cheek. "I've never met a girl like you. You're like a meteor that can't be stopped. You're the bravest..." He pulls back. "Sorry, I don't know what I'm thinking. Okay, here's what you have to do if you want to live past the next few minutes."

He kissed me. I've never been kissed by a boy. "Wait. Does that mean the Commander *is* going to kill me right away?" That moment of joy over the kiss is gone and now my whole body feels heavy.

"Yes. You've ruined his plans of making your death heroic. Now I think he just wants you dead. Jarmella told me how you sneaked onto the commanders' level and heard what's going on. I suspected something like that, but I didn't want to believe it. Some kids in my school said the wars keep going because they keep the economy going and keep the planet united. I get the part about keeping us all united against the aliens, but money can be made in other ways. We need to take a stand and tell everyone on Earth what's going on, with you as the leader. It has to be you because you keep beating the odds and I think you have what it takes. You'll be the non-conformist who saves the world. You're going to escape this transport and I'm going to help you do it."

Chapter Eighteen

Jarmer wants to help me escape. That's not what I expected because I thought he was dedicated to the Global Forces, yet here he is, willing to help an AFGF smudge get away. Although I appreciate it, I don't think we can pull it off. Does he expect me to get into a fighter and fly to Earth? Even if the commanders don't shoot me into dust, they'll capture me when I land. Jarmer is capable of doing it, but not me. I'm not good enough. It's a horrible plan.

But I want to agree with him and try since he has such faith in me. And that smile of his makes me want to believe anything he says.

"Dax, I'm going to fly beside you in my fighter and throw up a deflective holo-energy mask that'll conceal us both...for a time." He holds up his wrist with the silver cuff. "This projects holograms and can create a mask for a little while. Not long though." He raises an eyebrow and gazes into my eyes.

"I don't see how we can get out of the transport alive, let alone all the way to Earth. I want this to work, but it won't."

He sighs. "It will. You have to do it, Dax. It has to be you. You're a low-status, non-conformist, you flew a stolen fighter out of camp, alone, and you knocked out the Katarga vortex. And when the people realize that nothing was done to defeat the Katarga with the information you provided, they'll rally around you. The dissidence on Earth is growing every day. Trab is going to make sure everyone on Earth knows what's happening. You're the one who found proof about the wars. We could have saved multitudes of kids on the moon, if only the commanders would have listened. That won't sit well with the majority of families on Earth."

"I heard Commander Viteri tell another commander that he had no intention of doing anything about my intel. They had a narrow window to concentrate all their attacks on the stronghold but did nothing. Trab said the Katarga would repair it quickly. It's too late now, isn't it?"

He raises an eyebrow and nods. "Of course they didn't do anything. If we defeat the Katarga, that'd end one of the wars. It's beneficial for them to sit on the intelligence and give the Katarga time to fix the vortex. I've lost more than half my family to the Katarga and I've reached my limit. No more. I won't let my sister die like the others." He presses the yellow and clear lift buttons together. "Come on, we don't have long. I was sent to bring you to Commander Viteri. He'll send a Lead to find me soon if I don't report to him with you."

Instead of going up or down, we move sideways! "Where are we going?"

"Relax. This is a shortcut to the fighter hangar. They won't be expecting us to come this way."

"Jarmer, I can't do this. I can't leave my squad behind. You know what the Commander is planning for them." I think of Viga, Kova, Briett, and the others. They're my friends and they've trusted me with their lives. I can't betray that trust and abandon them. "They have to come."

Jarmer groans. "That's too many people. I'm taking Jarmella with me and your fighter has an extra seat, so you can take one person. There's no room for more."

"Then we have to figure something out." After a few minutes, we pass through a dimly lighted tube and come to a stop at a small room filled with tables and projected maps showing Saturn, the moon, and Earth. "What's all this?"

When the lift rotates open, he takes my hand and leads me to one of the maps. "This is the pilot's ready room, where we plot our courses. Everyone is out on maneuvers. I came back early because I'm the PIC, Pilot in Command, and was going to plot a few extra maneuvers for my flyboys. Dax, we've been told our whole lives that there's glory and honor in battling these aliens, but you confirmed what I suspected. Provoking aliens into a war is dishonorable. Anybody would attack if threatened. Jarmella agrees with me and said you have her full support."

"Great, but we still need to save my *squad*." I check the map of Saturn and see little blips among the rings and a bunch more on the back side of the planet. "Are those the Piltrak ships?" There are so many.

He sighs and moves his fingers over the rings and the blips fade away. "Jarmella told me what you heard, so I ran a diagnostic program on our avionics and couldn't locate a thousand other ships, only the fifty-one closest to us. There's a weird energy signature, but that must be from some sort of ghost projection. The commanders fooled us and we flyboys don't like to be fooled."

"Jarmer, my squad."

He sighs heavier. "We don't have time to worry about them. Jarmella will be here soon and then we're launching. I've already programmed Earth's coordinates into my new ship and my old ship, well, your ship. If you want to bring one of your squad, you have to send for them right now. Jarmella can bring them."

I can't make that decision and leave any of my friends behind, but I don't know how to bring them along. I look into the hangar through a small window in a door marked *Hangar Bay*. The hangar still has most of the fighters in their docking stations.

"Jarmer, did you know the commanders are letting all of those ships get destroyed just so they'll have to have more built?" I turn and face him.

There's a frown on his face. "All of those beautiful fighters...all of them destroyed. It makes me sick."

"Just another way for the commanders and factory owners to get revenue."

He nods and stands at the window with me.

In addition to the fighters, there's a wall at the far end filled with shelves of equipment and supplies. At least we can stock up on body armor and spacesuits. But what good will that do? My squad can't float around in space and follow my ship.

Or can they? I remember something I saw back home one day. One of the local transport shuttles broke down and was towed by another shuttle. "Why can't we tow them?"

"What?" Jarmer pinches his brow and stares at me like I've gone crazy. "Fighters can't tow ships. We don't have the power. And there aren't any passenger ships we could tow anyway."

"Not ships, people. They've been training in the spacesuits and propulsion packs. We can tow them all the way. It won't be much weight if we distribute them between our ships." I raise an eyebrow. "I saw a shuttle once towed behind another. It can't be much different to tow people."

He looks back at the map, then at me, peeks through the window, and stares at me again. At the map, he drags his finger from the far left of the projection, brings up a small schematic of a fighter ship and studies it. Next, he scrolls down the schematic and types in some information. Up pops a list of mathematical formulas that I can't understand. He cocks his head to the side and types some more.

After a short time, he turns to me. "I can't believe it, but it'll work. I knew I was right to trust you. It's a crazy scheme, but we can do it. There's a somewhat protected zone about ten meters long behind the ships that should reduce stress on them and will also be shadowed by the mask. But *I* can't tow anyone because it'll interfere with my ship's mask. And you won't be able to fly too fast. And, we'll need three fighters. Jarmella can fly one. She's not bad. Okay, to balance things, you and Jarmella have to tow two recruits each. That leaves two. I can take one in my cockpit and either you or Jarmella can take another."

"Why don't I take one and Jarmella can take the other. That way you don't have to worry about any passengers."

He smiles. "Good idea. Of course, it'll only work if we don't get blown to bits."

"Then let's avoid that, okay?" It's unusual to have someone believe in me. Abandoning the transport in three fighters towing a bunch of AFGF recruits behind us doesn't seem like the best strategy, but if Jarmer says it could work, I'll trust him. There are so many variables though. What if the commanders see us steal the fighters? They'll come after us or send Jarmer's flyboys to get us. And then there's my squad to think about. They'll be trailing behind me and Jarmella like tails of a couple of comets. Easy targets. Sure they'll be safe so long as the energy mask works, but Jarmer said it won't last forever.

The only part of the plan I'm excited about is seeing Ma and Da again so they'll know I'm alive. They'll be humiliated though when everyone finds out I've run away from my duty.

"Jarmer, this is a crazy plan. Isn't it?"

His eyes widen. "What are you talking about? It's *your* plan. I've got the coordinates set and my flyboys are away. We have to do this. Look, Dax, I don't intend to wait around while the commanders push us into a war against the Piltrak. I want to get Jarmella home safe. She didn't want to be advanced, but I convinced her to. If she gets hurt, it's on me. I love my sister and I won't let anything happen to her. She was supposed to get married and stay in our outlier. *I* brought her here."

"Wait, are you doing this only for Jarmella?" My heart sinks. I thought he was trying to rescue *me* and my squad, and help me reveal the truth to the world. Can't anyone be trusted? "Is that why you don't care about my squad?"

With a sweep of his hand, Jarmer shuts off the map projections and then stares at me with his eyes slightly squinted. He's angry. "Of course I'm doing this for my sister, but I'm doing it for you, too. I'm doing it for everyone. If I didn't care about you, I would have been halfway to Earth already with Jarmella. I care about you, Dax, and I don't think it's right how Lenora, Tablon, *and* Commander Viteri are so set against you."

"Why do you care?"

He sighs and glances toward the lift. "Jarmella should be here soon. I've never told anyone this before, but there was a boy in school who was always picked on. Everyone made fun of him and did awful things to him. I felt so bad for him, but you know what? I never did a thing to help him. He had no friends and I heard from Trab that he died the first day he was deployed to the moon. He died without any friends. I could have talked to him, been his friend, done something to make his life better. That guilt gnaws at me every single day."

That wasn't what I expected him to say. He's got a heart, not like Tablon or Lenora. "Jarmer, I understand what you're saying, but why do you care about *me*? You don't even know me. You gave me a couple of flight lessons and tossed me out each time like I was nothing."

He frowns at me. "You don't really trust anyone, do you? I'm not using you, Dax. I had to get you out of my fighter fast before you were found out. I know I only flew with you a few times, but it's possible to learn about someone by the way they handle things. Like my fighter for instance. Remember when I told you how girls wash out because they're too compassionate? I believe you are, too, but not to the point where it interferes with whatever you've got your heart set on doing. You flew my fighter from Earth to the moon and to this transport without giving up or panicking, even after you knew you'd probably killed some of the Katarga. That takes someone special. I don't even know if I could have done that. I've never faced the enemy. You got my attention, and you have my respect. And the thought that someone like you is being discarded like you're nothing is...repulsive."

I'm stunned. Can it be that I have another friend, one who not only *wants* to help me, but *can* help me? He's willing to put his life on the line for me and my squad. "I didn't mean to doubt you, but I haven't had the best of luck with people so, yeah, I'm a little cautious. And I think Lenora would have been an excellent fighter pilot. She had no conscience or compassion."

He laughs a little. "You're probably right about that."

"Okay, how can we get my squad up to the hangar?"

He lets out a breath and flashes his wonderful smile. "Let me take care of that. You go and get into your fighter and don't let anyone see you."

"Oh, sure, I'll just walk into the hangar and say *excuse me, I need to escape now.*"

"Stop doubting yourself. You *can* do it, Dax. If I didn't think you could, I wouldn't have brought you here. There shouldn't be anyone around, but just in case, stay low." He leans over and gives me another kiss on my cheek. With a grin, he turns and rushes back to the lift, calling over his shoulder, "I'll bring your squad and meet you in the hangar!" He hops into the lift and disappears as it descends.

Over by the hangar doorway on the right is a green button. I peek through the window again and don't see anyone wandering about. This is my chance, maybe my only chance. As soon as I press the green button, the door slides open and a burst of cool air comes in. There aren't any of the commanders or leads in the hangar, which gives me more confidence. I stay low while hurrying to my ship as it hovers above the hangar floor near the platform. Seeing my ship again is like finding a long-lost friend. Soon I'll be flying with that freedom of not being tethered down, with nobody to control me or order me around. That's the best feeling in the world.

The hatch is still open and the ladder is down, making it easy to climb up into the cockpit where I belong. Once inside, I see my helmet on the pilot's seat, like it hasn't been touched. I poke my head out through the hatch to get a better view of the pilot's ready-room and hear a voice echo, but it's not Jarmer's. It's Viteri's! After retracting my head, I hold my breath.

"Senior Lead Neemiss, you will locate PIC Jarmer and find out why he hasn't obeyed a direct order to bring Orwan to me. He's never disobeyed an order before and I want to know what's going on. I'd hate to have to discipline my best pilot."

"Yes, sir. I'll locate him for you. His fighter's still here, so he didn't go back out on maneuvers," Tablon says in a loud, sycophantic voice.

"Tablon, don't point out the obvious. You're a Senior Lead, you're supposed to have a brain. If you're not careful, I'll leave you here with the rest of the troops and tell your parents the Piltraks killed you. You want that, *Senior Lead*?"

Is Tablon losing favor with Viteri? I hope so. As carefully as I can, I look out again to make sure Jarmer doesn't come into the hangar. I wish there was some way to warn him. If he doesn't check through the window first, he won't know Viteri and Tablon are here.

Tablon speaks again, "Sir, I do have a brain and I'll prove to you that I'm more than qualified to be a Senior Lead. Some day I hope to be as great a commander like you. My parents paid you to keep me safe and I promise you I won't give you any reason to regret it. I'll bring Orwan to you personally."

"After you locate Jarmer."

"Yes, sir, after I locate Jarmer."

Somehow I have to let Jarmer know that Tablon's looking for him. I spring to my feet, staying away from the windows, and check the cockpit for anything I can use to communicate with Jarmer. I can't activate the heads-up display because it'll be seen from the platform since all of the windows are uncovered, but I think I know a way to get a message to Jarmer. I crouch on the floor and slip the helmet on. Right away I feel the tingle of the synap-trodes and concentrate on using the ship-to-land communicator to reach Trab. Hopefully the commanders haven't blocked all communications.

"Trab? Can you hear me? Trab? Are you there?" I have a quick look out the window and see Tablon riding an open lift from the platform down to the hangar floor. "Trab?"

"Mid-World Equatorial Training Camp here, this is Trab. Who's that? Dax?"

Thank goodness. "Yes, it's me. It's so good to hear your voice, Trab. I need help and I don't know who else to ask."

"Well, young lady, I'm here to help. Tell me what you need."

"I'm on the transport and hiding in my fighter. I have to find a way to get a message to Jarmer, but he's in the lift. Do you have any ideas?" I take another peek through the window, but can't see Tablon anymore.

There's a brief pause. "You can explain to me later why you're hiding and why Jarmer is involved. I can't wait to hear it. All right, young lady, here's what you do. You'll need to connect your synap-trodes to the transport's tech system. It's not hard. Look for a white toggle switch on the control stick and move it to the position that says 'on'. Once you've done that, press a small button on the top of your helmet. It's flush with the helmet. You got it?"

"Ah, hold on." I find the white toggle switch and move it, but can't feel anything on the top of my helmet. "There's nothing on my helmet, Trab."

"Are you sure?"

I feel again. "Nothing." I hear footsteps near my ship. "Trab, what do I do?" I whisper.

Trab groans. "They must have revamped the helmets. Always doing that. The factories are constantly using new materials and developing new equipment. The upgrades always cost a lot more and the old supplies get scrapped. Generates a lot of revenue for the factories, you know."

Panic is rising. "I don't care about that right at the moment. Hurry!"

Silence.

"Trab?"

"Patience, young lady, I was checking a schematic of fighter ship equipment. I tell you, they're always changing something around here. If it's not a new type of flight suit then it's..."

"Trab!"

"All right, all right. Okay, this is no problem. Toggle the white switch back to its original position and activate the heads-up display."

"I can't do that. Think of something else."

Now Trab grunts. "There is nothing else. You have to use the heads-up display to link to the transport's system. Why can't you do it?"

"I just can't. I told you, I'm hiding." If my heart beats any harder, it'll beat right out of my chest.

"Well, then give me a minute to think of a way to circumvent the system."

"Thanks. Don't take too long."

I don't hear the footsteps any longer and raise my head enough to check through the main window. Nobody is on the platform or on the open lift. Where exactly is Tablon? If he finds me in the ship, there'll be no way to escape.

Tablon shouts, "Jarmer! What are you doing here? And where's the smudge?"

I take off my helmet, crawl on my stomach to the hatch and peer out. Jarmer is standing in the doorway of the pilot's ready room. It's obvious that he's blocking anyone from leaving and that must mean he has my squad with him.

He glances behind him and faces Tablon again. "Tab. I wasn't expecting to see you here. You're not allowed on the hangar bay floor, you know. This is only for secured flight personnel." Jarmer's eyes meet mine.

Tablon throws his shoulders back. "I have orders from Commander Viteri to find you and Orwan. Where is she?"

Jarmer shrugs. "I couldn't find her. Her squad said she has a bout of space sickness and went to the medical wing. I was heading there now. If you have no more accusations, I'll be on my way." His voice has a tinge of irritation to it.

"Accusations? You like using big words, flyboy? On the transport, we're not friends. I'm a Senior Lead and I outrank you." With a snort, Tablon goes to grab Jarmer by the arm, but Jarmer slaps his hand away.

"You have no authority on the hangar floor, Tab. I'm PIC and down here, I outrank the hell out of you. Get out of my way." Jarmer shoves Tablon.

Hauling back, Tablon swings at Jarmer, who ducks, causing Tablon to miss. Jarmer is fast and lunges, puts his arm around Tablon's throat, sweeps a leg around Tablon's legs, and throws him to the ground.

With a thud, Tablon lets out a huff. "You've done it now, flyboy. I guess we're really not friends anymore. You and the smudge are going to spend the last seconds of your lives floating in space without any weapons."

Jarmer is standing over Tablon. "You've always been a decayed pile of space garbage. Come to think of it, you're not just decayed, you're a festering black hole that sucks the good out of everything around you."

Tablon jumps to his feet. "You'll regret every one of those words. And don't think I don't know that you can't get to the medical wing through the hangar, flyboy. What are you doing down here?" He reaches under the jacket of his uniform and pulls out a small laser pistol. "Go to the platform lift and we'll see Commander Viteri together. I can't wait to hear how you're going to explain your way out of this."

Jarmer doesn't move and looks right at me. I have to do something. I roll away from the hatch and feel the oval weapon in my pocket. That's it! I grab it and descend the ladder to the hangar floor. With the weapon in my hand, I run across the floor and get right behind Tablon.

"Drop your gun, Tablon!" I shout.

It takes him a few seconds to react, but when he spins around, his eyes widen and he drops the gun. I point the weapon at him. He's shaking and starts walking backward, but bumps into Jarmer, who pushes him away.

Tablon stops and holds up his hands. "Don't fire that. What are you doing? Where'd you get that? Those are illegal."

Jarmer rushes over to me and I see Jarmella, Viga, Kova, and the others in the ready-room. Briett is behind them, jumping up and down, trying to see around them. I motion them to come out and when Briett walks past Tablon, he purposely bumps right into him and almost knocks him off his feet.

Jarmer's by my side. "Dax, do you know how to use that?"

"Of course I know how to use it," I say loudly, then whisper, "No, do you?"

He whispers back, "I've read about them. You run your thumb along the groove in the top to activate it, but I don't know how they fire." He moves my thumb to the groove.

Tablon is trembling all over. Obviously he knows what the weapon can do. I don't, but he does. He wipes his forehead. "Orwan...Dax...put the weapon down. We can talk about this. I'll speak to the Commander and tell him Lenora's death was an accident. He'll listen, he trusts me. Maybe he'll spare your squad. But like I said, that's an illegal weapon and the penalty for having one is death. I can't do anything about that, but you're going to die anyway."

I shake my head and trace my thumb the full length of the groove. It emits a few sparks at the end that's facing Tablon. "Everything I'm doing is illegal, you black hole, do you think I care at this point. I'm leaving this transport and you're not standing in my way."

"Stop pointing that at me!" Tablon stumbles backward.

I nudge Jarmer. "Get everyone suited up. Take Kova with you and put Mick and Brinna behind Jarmella's ship. I'll take Briett and Parna behind mine. Viga can be my copilot."

Viga runs to me. "Dax, this is insane. They'll shoot us down."

"No they won't, I'm taking care of that," Jarmer calls out.

My squad follows after him.

Viga objects, "But I don't understand."

"Just go with Jarmer." I wait until she finally shrugs and hurries to catch up to him and the rest of the squad. When they get down the spacesuits off the equipment rack, I concentrate on Tablon again. "I heard you with the Commander. You know this whole thing is a suicide mission. The commanders have set this up so every recruit onboard will die, except for you. You're in on it. You don't even care if Jarmer dies, and he's your friend. Did you know Lenora was going to be saved as well?"

"Of course I'll be safe." Lenora comes out of the ready room with a laser gun in her hand. "I've positioned myself to be the Commander's right hand."

Tablon spins around. "Lenora? How...when...you're dead. I saw you die. What's going on?"

How is she alive? I shot her and saw her disappear. "Lenora, what have you done? Why aren't you dead?"

She aims the gun at me and winks at Tablon. "Sorry, Tablon, but I couldn't let anyone know, not even you. I rigged the sim and put a hologram image of myself on the platform and made everyone think Orwan killed me."

Tablon glances at me and back at Lenora. "Why? You *wanted* me to go weapons hot and kill Orwan? For nothing?"

Lenora shakes her head. "Not for nothing, Tablon. She knows about us. She'll tell the Commander and we'll be shamed and put on the front lines and our parents won't get any more subsidies. I'm not risking my future because of Orwan. I'm among one of the Commander's trusted circle now, because of my affiliation with you. But I don't need you any longer. I was the one who discovered there weren't thousands of Piltraks and that makes me incredibly valuable. I'll be a commander one day." She comes closer to me. "You just won't die, will you, smudge?"

Tablon moves in front of me like he's protecting me. "Lenora, Orwan isn't going to tell. She's had the opportunity, but she's kept her mouth shut. You don't need to kill her because she's going to die in battle anyway. Besides, Commander Viteri told me what's going on."

"The smudge has to die now, Tablon." Lenora glares at me. "What if she doesn't get killed by the Piltrak? What then? It's us or her."

I am so sick of everyone telling me I'm going to die, but Lenora doesn't intimidate me anymore. I survived her attempt at murdering me and setting me up in the simulation and I'm not about to let her dictate my life anymore. My thumb glides along the groove of my weapon again making more sparks shoot out of the end. "Put your gun down, Lenora."

"What is that thing?" she asks, without lowering her gun.

Tablon answers, "It's an illegal alien weapon. It dissociates solids in a split second. If Orwan fires it, we'll all die."

How can such a small thing do that? "Lenora, you have no idea what it's like to take a life. Once you kill someone, you'll always have that lodged in your heart like a weight that never goes away. I should know. I destroyed a part of the Katarga stronghold and murdered some of them. Those deaths follow me around wherever I go. Do *you* want that?"

She's staring at me with a strange look on her face. "You think killing is bad?"

I nod. "It is."

She continues, "And you regret killing those Katarga?"

I nod again. "Of course I do. I just reacted without thinking about what I was doing."

With a smirk, she takes a step toward me with her thumb moving closer to the trigger button of her laser gun. "You're bluffing, smudge. You're a coward and you have no intention of killing me. I'm calling your bluff."

I take a glance at my squad and see they're suited up and tethered to tow lines, one line attached to Jarmella's ship and one to mine. Jarmer is waiting by his fighter, helmet in hand, nervously tapping his foot. He motions to my ship.

"Be right there!" I shout. What do I do now? Lenora knows I won't shoot the weapon.

In a split second, Lenora fires a short laser burst at Tablon and hits him in the thigh. He cries out in pain and collapses. "Lenora! What are you doing?"

She smiles. "Next shot will be in his head unless you put down that weapon, smudge. You want his death on your hands, too?"

Clutching his leg, Tablon looks from me to Lenora. "You're going to kill me? I thought you..."

She rolls her eyes and keeps her laser gun on me. "What? Love you? Please. You're a pampered mess, Tablon. I researched all of the recruits and found evidence that your family paid the Commander to keep you alive. From the second you got on the shuttle back home, I knew I had to get on your side so you'd make sure I'd have protection as well. I could never love a paid-for trash heap like you. I used you."

The hurt look on Tablon's face makes me hate Lenora even more. Before I can do anything, he jumps up on his good leg, grabs Lenora's arm, and wrestles the gun away from her. He pushes her back and points it at her. "You made me think Orwan killed you and made me go weapons hot. That's an illegal maneuver in training. How could you do that to me? You made me think we were a great team." He pauses and stares at her. "The Commander's been questioning my decisions lately. Is that your doing?"

"I told you I don't need you anymore." She rolls her eyes again. "You can't kill me. That'd be treason."

He gives her another shove and aims the laser gun at her head. "I'm not letting you get away with this."

I keep my thumb in the groove of the weapon. "Tablon."

He holds up his hand. "This is my problem, Orwan. Go and get into your ship. I'll hold them off as long as I can. Go!"

"But what about Lenora?" I keep my weapon aimed at her, just for effect.

He's looking at Lenora with such intensity. "If I don't kill her, she'll turn me in as soon as she can and make sure you and your squad are blown to pieces."

Lenora smiles. "I won't have to. Commander Viteri isn't far behind me. I told him you and Orwan teamed up and tried to murder me in the sim. I'll be a hero for turning you both in and I'll be in line for Senior Lead, taking it from you once you're gone. You'll all end up as Piltrak fodder and I'll be sitting pretty in my new role, safe and sound."

Jarmer runs to me. "Dax, we have to go right now. Maneuvers will end soon and my flyboys will come straight into the hangar. There's no time to stand around and chat."

"Just go," I say. "I can't let Tablon get punished for what I'm doing. Take my fighter and get my squad home, Jarmer."

With a firm shake of his head, he puts his hand on my shoulder. "No. We all go or nobody goes. That's what Viga just told me."

We all turn when the sound of the lift echoes through the quiet hangar. So many lives are at stake because of me. If I don't do something right now, we'll all be captured.

I take a few breaths, but it does no good, I'm still terrified. "Jarmer, get Tablon suited up and put him in your ship. He's wounded. Parna is smaller than Kova, so let's put her behind Jarmella's ship and I'll take Kova. Briett's, ah, bigger, so it's probably best I only have two kids behind my ship."

Jarmer nods and gets busy switching everyone around.

With my eyes back on Lenora, I rub the weapon again. "Get out of here before I change my mind and use this on you."

Lenora frowns and backs away, her fingers squeezed into tight fists. While Jarmer has Tablon at the wall where the spacesuits are hanging, I urge Lenora into the ready-room by continuing to stroke my thumb along the groove of the weapon so sparks pop out in a continuous stream. It works. She spins around and stomps to the room. I close the door and see her go right to one of the communication computers.

It doesn't matter what she does, because the lift's already here and Viteri is about to step out onto the platform above. I hurry to my squad and see Tablon in a spacesuit, waiting near Jarmer's fighter. He points to the platform. Viteri and the other commander who was with him when I stole the weapon are both standing there, glaring at us.

"Dax!" Jarmer shouts. "Get in your fighter! Use the synap-trodes to fire it up and head to Earth via Trab's coordinates. I rigged the fighters so that once we start the engines, the jet propulsion packs will fire and we can go. Jarmella knows the plan and she's ready."

Viteri bellows, "Recruits! Stand away from the fighters and drop to your knees!"

Instinctively, I hide the weapon behind my back and stand straight, but realize a second later that I'm breaking every regulation possible, and standing at attention isn't going to fix that. I bring my hand back around and point the weapon at him.

"Don't try to stop us. We're leaving. This is not our war, it's yours. How many more soldiers have to die so you and the other commanders can get richer? People are starving, but all you care about is money."

He comes to the edge of the platform and points at me. "I should have taken care of you a long time ago." He leans forward and stares. "Is that a Jurale Electro-Magnetic Resonator in your hand? Where did you get that?"

"From your level, *sir*. If they're so illegal, why did you have one?" I make the weapon spark. "Did you kill a Jurale to get it?"

Jarmer rushes to me. "Dax, time's up. My flyboys are coming back. We have to go now. Now, Dax." He tugs on my arm.

I keep my eyes on Viteri. "I'll use the weapon to destroy the entire transport unless you let us go." I keep the Jurale weapon aimed as I walk backward to my fighter and hope he doesn't realize that I have no idea how to actually use it.

Viteri shakes his head at me. "You're a traitor, Orwan. As of this moment, all of you are marked for execution as traitors."

I run to my fighter and scamper up the ladder where Viga is already seated with her helmet on. She's shaking and breathing hard. I grab my helmet and put it on, then attach the oxygen hose to Viga's helmet before I sit down and attach my own oxygen hose.

After fastening my restraints, I glance over at her. "Are you ready?"

She shakes her head. "No. This is madness, Dax. You can't fly a fighter. Even if you can, we'll be shot down as soon as we leave the transport. And this helmet's making my head tingle."

"We won't get shot down. Jarmer said he'll create a holo-energy mask around us to protect us. And don't worry about the helmet." I wave the Jurale weapon in front of the window so Viteri will see. "Besides, I have this."

Once I engage the synap-trodes and start the engine, I hear the other fighters start as well. My ship turns slowly until it's facing away from the platform and I see Jarmer come beside me on the left and Jarmella on the right. He gives me a nod and we all head out of the hangar bay side-by-side.

I wish I could see my squad to make sure they're all right. In a flash, the heads-up display comes on and a small square in the center shows a view from behind my ship; Parna and Briett are floating along in a line as I pick up speed. I can't see behind Jarmella's ship, but I know she'll take care of the others. We're going to make it.

Chapter Nineteen

The sense of relief I feel when our fighter ships slip effortlessly from the transport into the blackness of space is almost overwhelming. Somehow space no longer feels empty and dead, but alive and buzzing with hope, and that's exactly what I need right now. I steal a sideways look at Viga and see how she's gripping the straps of her restraints with her eyes tightly closed. There's nothing I can say that'll help. Best to leave her alone.

I can still see the rear of the ship where Briett and Parna are floating behind. I'm sure they're every bit as scared as Viga.

Finally, she reaches over and taps me on the shoulder. "Dax, was I dreaming, or did you have Jarmer take Tablon with him? And put Parna outside?"

"You're not dreaming. I couldn't leave him. He was shot and I couldn't have him floating around outside."

"Why not? He's decayed. Galactically decayed. He'll betray us as soon as he can, if he hasn't already. I wish you'd left him."

"It wouldn't be right. He helped me. We couldn't have escaped without him. Parna will be fine. They all will."

With a frown, Viga shakes her head. "I guess you know what you're doing. At least I hope you do." She points to the display. "What are those coordinates?"

"Earth. We're going home."

"Home?" She starts to smile, but her lips start to quiver. "With Tablon. He'll have us all killed once we get there."

"He won't. He's just as guilty as we are now." Outside the window on my left, I see that Jarmer has put some distance between us and has gained on me a bit. Jarmella is on my right and slightly ahead, enough so I can see my friends behind her ship. "Viga, look." I point and lean back so she can see.

"Our squad!" she shouts.

"They're fine." What a relief to know everyone is safe.

Jarmella falls back and I lose sight of my squad. She did that so I could see them.

Viga turns from the window. "Why are we going to Earth? The Council of Commanders won't let us return home. Don't you know that?"

She still doubts me. "No, Viga, evidently I don't know as much as you do because our schools only taught us the basics. I don't know much about politics or Global Command or the Council of Commanders or why everyone is so willing to keep fighting and dying in these stupid alien wars."

She's quiet and turns away. After a moment, she says softly, "Dax, the Council of Commanders have all of the real power. Whatever they say, goes. We've just disobeyed the main directive of the Council."

"What's the main directive?" How come I don't even know that? Are most kids like me or do they all have a better understanding of how the world is run?

I hear Viga sigh. "I'm not supposed to know this, but I heard my Da's boss say once that the main directive forbids any advancee to ever return to Earth on penalty of death. That's why when a recruit dies, the coffin is empty. The Council doesn't want anyone demoralized by seeing the bodies, and no living recruit can come home because the Council doesn't want them to talk about the Global Forces or give away any secrets. At least I think that's why. We can't go home, Dax. They won't let us. It doesn't matter if you have some sort of weapon or not. We'll be blown up long before we enter Earth's atmosphere. Not even Jarmer can prevent that."

"I won't let that happen." Our teachers always said recruits are so dedicated and loyal that they never leave the Global Forces. I had no idea there was a directive *preventing* us from coming home.

Viga isn't talking, only staring out the front window. Is she mad at me for bringing her and the rest of the squad along? Or maybe it's because we're all now deserters. I watch the stars through the window and wonder what it would be like if I managed to get Global Forces to listen. It could just be the commanders who are profiting.

"Dax," it's Jarmer.

"I'm here." I look out the window, but can't see his ship. "Where are you?"

"I'm several hundred kilometers ahead of you and a hundred to your starboard. Jarmella's a bit behind you. I've discontinued the mask, but if we need it again, I'll get closer and project it again. We can't be too close together in case...well, you know."

I do know. In case we're fired upon, having us separated would give at least one of us a chance of surviving. "Did you hear from Jarmella? How's my squad doing?"

He laughs. "You sound like a worried mother. They're fine. Jarmella's keeping an eye on them. Ah, Dax, there might be a problem."

I don't want to hear about any problems, although I should have expected something to go wrong. "What sort of problem?"

He pauses. "I made a miscalculation. When I figured the configuration for the ships and the mask, I didn't consider the limitations of the propulsion packs. They only supply enough oxygen for one battle, which means about an hour."

"But we won't be anywhere near Earth in an hour. Can we use the black star-shaped button to jump to 2% lightspeed as I did before?"

Jarmer whistles. "So that's how you got to the transport so fast. I've never done that. Trab didn't mention he told you how to do a speed-jump. But no, we can't, not with a trail of recruits dangling behind. Well, I could, but I'm not leaving you. Any other ideas?"

"What about 1%? I can just press the button once for 1%. Is it still too much?"

"Dax, even going this speed is dangerous for them."

Viga taps me on the shoulder. "I heard Jarmer. What are you going to do? Don't let our squad die."

I turn to her. "I'm doing my best." I scan the heads-up display and check on Briett and Parna again, but no solution is coming to me. We can't turn back and we can't go forward. I need an answer, fast. "Viga, did you learn about the planets in school? Specifically, Saturn?"

She nods. "Sure. It's mandatory."

"Good. Do you remember learning something about one of the outer rings? Isn't there an asteroid in the ring that has a probe on it?" I engage the synap-trodes and bring up a display of Saturn's rings. "Or maybe I'm wrong..."

SOFIA DIANA GABEL

"No, Dax, I think you're right, but what good will that do?" She points to the display. "Can you enlarge the outer rings?"

I do and see the multitudes of rocks and asteroids that make up the rings. "But which one is it?"

Jarmer comes back, "Dax, what are you thinking?"

"Give me a minute, Jarmer. Trab? Hello, Trab?" I ask. "Are you there, Trab?"

"Of course, young lady, I've been monitoring your communications. I've made sure to disable all other ground-to-ship channels so no one else can hear us. What do you need?"

I think for a second. "Trab, can you plug in the coordinates for the location where the Saturn ring probe is?"

"Ah, that probe hasn't transmitted any data in years, young lady. It was decommissioned a long way back. It's nothing more than scrap metal. No use to you whatsoever."

"I don't want to activate the probe, Trab, I want to use its energy source. Does it still have a latent energy source?" I'm trying hard to remember everything I ever learned in school about science, math, physics, and astronomy.

"Sure, but your fighters have a renewable energy source onboard, you don't need additional..."

I cut him off, "Listen, Trab, if we can somehow hook the propulsion packs to the energy source of the probe, won't it regenerate the oxygen?"

"Wait," Jarmer says, "how do you know that?"

"I don't know, it sort of popped into my head. I must have read it somewhere. A propulsion pack regenerates oxygen from the scant elemental oxygen in space if it's connected to an energy source. But a fighter doesn't have sufficient energy to recharge anything but its own oxygen. This is why if the airborne troops survive a battle, their packs are hooked up to an energy pod on one of the small transports, and then the recruits are sent right back into battle. Is this right, Trab?" I can't believe this just came to me. I don't remember learning it in school, so how do I know it?

"Ah, I, ah...I don't know. Hold on, young lady, let me check."

Viga is staring at me. "Dax, how did you know that? I've never heard that before. Even when they were training us with the propulsion packs, they never said we could recharge."

I'm not sure how I know about the regeneration process, but I do. "Maybe they didn't tell you because they didn't expect any of us to live long enough to need a recharge. Trab, did you find out anything?"

A moment later, he replies, "I did. You're absolutely correct, young lady. But nobody except the commanders are supposed to know about the regeneration capability. The information is buried deep in the files. How did you get this information?"

"I have no idea. I must have learned about it at school."

Viga blurts, "No, you couldn't have. I didn't know about it and we had a better education system than your outlier. I think you got that from the cerebral interpreter on the transport. But what good will it do? Even if we recharge all of the propulsion packs, we still won't have enough oxygen to go all the way to Earth if Jarmer's right and a full recharge is about an hour. And don't forget Piltrak ships are hiding within the rings. They'll find us."

"Fifty-one Piltrak ships to be exact." It'd only be a temporary fix anyway, and not a good one at that, even if we could get to the probe. Plus, we'd have to fly to the rings first, the opposite direction to Earth. We'd be farther away. "I didn't think it through."

"Young lady, you're smart," Trab says. "If there's an answer, you'll find it. I'm sure you're on the right track. And I just found an energy signature from the probe. I've programmed in the coordinates that'll take you right to it."

"Thanks, Trab, but sorry to disappoint. I'm not smart at all." I check the heads-up display and see my friends. They trusted me and depended on me to take them away from certain death, and yet now that's exactly what they're facing. And I'm responsible. I'm killing my own squad. I use the synap-trodes to lock onto the coordinates so I can see the exact position of the asteroid in relation to where the Piltrak ships are stationed.

The probe is on a ring that's facing Earth and the Piltrak are on the back side of the planet. We could get there without the Piltrak attacking us, unless they flew around the planet. But what about Viteri? I'm sure he's sent all of the fighters to find us. There are so many variables.

"Dax." Viga touches me on the arm. "Can't we turn back and take our chances with the commanders?"

"I thought about that." I shake my head. "If we stayed there, we'd die. If we go back now, we'll die."

"We're probably going to die anyway."

"Viga, I'd rather die out in space than at the hands of Commander Viteri." I know she's scared, but I wish she'd stop adding to my guilt. "We'll be all right. You'll see. I have an idea. Trab?"

"Right here, young lady."

I give Viga a smile that hopefully looks like I know what I'm talking about. "Trab, Jarmer had calculated that we have enough power to tow my squad, but do you think we could possibly tow another object? Perhaps the probe?"

Jarmer shouts, "Are you serious?"

Trab laughs. "I knew you'd figure something out. What do you have in mind? You're already pushing the limits of reason here, young lady."

I hope my idea will work because I have nothing else. "Well, if we can secure the probe to one of the fighters, then we can recharge the propulsion packs' oxygen as we go if we connect them all together. On the fly, so to speak. Will that work?"

Silence.

"Still calculating," says Trab after a while. "For stability, you'd have to attach all of the human cargo onto one ship and secure the probe to the other, with a connection tube from the probe to the last recruit and connect that recruit to all the others. If you can do that, it might just be possible. But I'm not so sure one fighter is capable of towing your whole squad." He's quiet for a moment. "We can't get a break. I've got some bad news." He pauses again. "I just intercepted a transmission from the transport and you're not going to like it."

Jarmer bursts in, "Stop messing around, Trab, what did it say?"

Trab continues, "Don't yell at me, Jarmer, I'm doing everything I can to help. Commander Viteri sent a message to Global Command. He's requested legions of fighters from the East-World, Mid-World, and Arctic Training Camps to stand ready. They'll be dispatched when you're within range of the atmosphere. You can't return to Earth, young lady."

No! Now what can I do? I thought I had it all figured out. Get the probe and take my squad somewhere on Earth where they'd never find us. Then tell everyone who'll listen about how the wars are orchestrated. "Where are we supposed to go, Trab? We have to go to Earth. There's nowhere else!"

Viga slaps me on the arm and points to the display showing the squad. "Dax, we have to do something. They'll run out of oxygen soon." She has tears in her eyes.

What have I done? We can't go home and we can't go back to the transport. "Trab, can you adjust the coordinates to the probe to take us as far away from the transport so the commanders can't see us?" I need the probe's energy if we're to have any chance of surviving. But then what? I need a permanent solution.

Jarmer speaks again, "Dax, I'm not sure if this will work. We'll still be visible until I'm close enough to cast the mask. But if the commanders realize I'm using a mask, they'll find us."

"We don't have a choice."

After a moment, Trab comes back. "Dax, I've programmed the probe's coordinates into all three of your ships. You'll have to accelerate to .5 lightspeed or your squad will die before you reach the probe. The acceleration will cause strain on the tether lines, so keep an eye on that. I have to break communications now because I've been found out. Young lady, listen to Jarmer. He knows more than I do about flying those fighters. Good luck to you all. Mid-World Camp out."

I stare out the window at the stars in the distance and feel so alone. We can't get help from Trab anymore. He's gone. *Please don't get caught, Trab.* "Jarmer, are you there?"

"Yes," his voice sounds hollow.

"Did I get Trab in trouble?"

"Yes."

I feel my ship begin a turn. "Will he be okay?"

A pause. "Dax, by helping us, he'll be tried for treason. So, no, he won't be okay." Another pause. "He decided to help us, Dax. He knew the consequences. Don't blame yourself."

"But still..."

173

"There is no 'but still', Dax." Jarmer sighs loudly. "We need to concentrate on getting to that probe. To accelerate to .5 lightspeed, depress the white button next to the black star button at the same time you press the black star button. Only press them once, exactly at the same time. Got it?"

"Yes."

"Jarmella, you read me?"

"Of course, brother."

"Okay then, on my count, 1...2...3...engage!"

I press the white and black buttons and right away I'm pressed into the seat. I glance at Viga and see she's already looking at me. "How are you doing, Viga?"

She shrugs. "I'll let you know. Can you bring up the view of the squad?"

I hadn't noticed that the rear display was gone, and as hard as I try, the synap-trodes won't bring it back. "Jarmer, I can't see my squad anymore."

"That's because we're in lightspeed mode. All systems focus on flight control, not viewing. They're fine." He sounds confident. "I'm sure they're fine." Now he doesn't sound so confident.

Viga squeezes my arm. "Dax, I'm sorry. I know this is the right thing to do. If you didn't get us all off the transport, we would have died trying to fight the Piltrak. That's a wasted death. Now that we know the commanders are creating the wars, dying as a soldier has no honor. It's a waste."

It's all a waste. Everything. Our minds are being wasted and teenagers are being wasted, thrown away like we don't matter.

Before I can say anything, I see a field of rocks ahead, nothing but jagged rocks of every size and shape imaginable. The heads-up display says the nearest asteroid is less than 500 meters from my ship.

"Jarmer, I'm going to impact an asteroid!" I shout.

He responds right away, "Calm down, Dax, you're not. The fighter will avoid all impacts. Just let it take you to the probe."

"Okay." I take a few breaths and watch out the window as my ship banks and dips beneath the asteroid. It does this several more times to avoid others until it turns suddenly and heads right for a large asteroid with a flattened area on the bottom. Or maybe it's the top. Who knows which end is up in space. I hope all of the erratic movement hasn't hurt my friends trailing behind me.

Viga points to the asteroid as we close in on it. "We're landing on that?"

"I think so." I lean forward when I see something small glinting on the flat surface. "Is that the probe?"

Jarmer answers, "My display says it's the Council of Commanders Saturn Exploration Probe."

My display doesn't say that. "Council of Commanders?"

"Yeah." Jarmer continues, "That's odd. I thought the probe was a scientific exploratory probe."

I glance at Viga. She stares back. She looks out the front window again and points without saying anything. Words aren't necessary, I know what she's thinking. We're heading right to the asteroid at a fast speed.

"Jarmer! How do I slow down?" I shout.

"Didn't you listen? I said let the ship take you to the probe. Don't do a thing." He sounds frustrated.

"Sorry, but it looks like we're going to crash. Where are you? I can't see you."

"I'm a little behind you, alongside Jarmella. Everyone's okay on the tethers. Once you land, wait for me and I'll come to you. You're not wearing a flight suit, so you can't leave the ship."

"Oh. Right." I forgot to get a suit for myself in the rush back at the transport. "Viga, we're almost there."

She nods. "Good. But what are you going to do without a spacesuit?"

"I'll have to help from inside the ship." What a stupid mistake to make.

My ship begins to slow as it approaches the asteroid. I want to grab the control stick or engage the synap-trodes, but resist the temptation and allow the ship to land on its own like Jarmer said. It hovers over the ground, about ten meters from the probe, and slowly descends. From the side window on my left, I see the other fighters descending, too, and can just make out the tether attached to the rear of Jarmella's ship.

I point to the window. "Look, Viga, our squad's out there."

Viga nods and makes a little sad-sounding groan. "I hope they're not too scared. I can't imagine floating around space like that. Thank you for helping us all escape. At least now we have some sort of chance to survive."

I smile at her. "That means a lot to me, Viga."

When the engine shuts down, I remove my restraints, run right to the window and peer out. I see my squad still tethered to Jarmella's ship. They're floating off the surface, moving slightly. Everyone behind my ship must be fine, too. After a bit, I see Jarmer climbing down the hatch ladder and walking slowly toward the probe. I want to be out there with him.

The probe is a fascinating piece of machinery. It's about two meters tall, cylindrical, flat on top, with a silver metallic mesh material wrapped around it, and a lone blinking light on the very top. Instead of legs or landing gear, it seems to be implanted into the ground with a slight impact crater around it. Jarmer shuffles and sends little plumes of dust floating up from the ground. I'd love to explore the asteroid with him and help figure out a way to secure the probe to one of the fighters. I hate waiting here and doing nothing.

I look around the cockpit for a spare spacesuit. "Viga, did you happen to see an extra..."

Before I can do anything, a blindingly bright reddish light fills the cockpit.

"Dax!" Viga screams.

"Where's that light coming from?"

"I don't know! Dax, are we going to blow up?"

"Launch!" shouts Jarmer. "Jarmella, Dax, get out of there! The Piltrak are on the asteroid!"

Chapter Twenty

I can't see a thing, the red light is too strong. Where are the Piltraks? I didn't see any near the probe. "Jarmer! Jarmer, talk to me!"

He's out there, all alone with my helpless squad and no weapons. I have to get to him and do something to protect them all. Why didn't I think to grab a spacesuit from the hangar bay?

"Dax!" yells Viga. "Help them!"

"What am I supposed to do?"

I drop to my knees and shield my eyes hoping the light won't be so bad down low. Thankfully, the pilot's seat blocks it a bit, but I don't see anything I can use for defense. Jarmer isn't far from my ship, although he might as well be a million light-years away. How did the Piltrak get on the asteroid and what's the light? I didn't see any other ships when we were approaching and my readings didn't indicate anything.

Just when I'm about to get up, I take a breath and tap Viga on the shoulder. "Give me your spacesuit." As fast as I can, I slip into the suit when she wriggles out of it and secure the Jurale weapon into a pocket on the front of the suit. A hood on the suit automatically tightens around my helmet for a snug fit. I'm all set now, but a sudden thought strikes me. I've never had any experience walking anywhere but on Earth.

"Viga, you trained in the spacesuits, is there anything I should know?"

The light dims enough so I can once again look out the front window. Jarmer's and Jarmella's ships are still there, but Jarmer isn't, and neither is the probe.

Viga stares through the window beside me. "Once you have the suit on and leave the ship, the bio-supports trigger and you have oxygen. Apparently only an hour. The suit will provide kind of a gravitational field around you, so you won't float away. I hope. Dax, did the Piltrak take the probe? If they did, our squad won't last long. That was our only hope. Don't let them die."

"I'm doing my best!" I snap. "Sorry, Viga. Can you see Jarmer? What did they do to him?"

"No idea. I don't see a Piltrak ship. Do you?"

I shake my head. "No, but the light is still there, so there has to be a ship somewhere. Maybe behind us. I'm going out." I engage the synap-trodes and bring up a schematic of my ship to see how I can exit without the ship's oxygen getting sucked out.

While I'm studying it, Viga crouches down beneath the window and kneads her hands together. "We're going to die. I don't want to die. Not here on some rock at the hands of the Piltrak. Dax, I don't want to die!"

"Neither do I. But listen, I think I found how to get out of the ship safely. There's a negative air pressure system that automatically turns on when there's no atmosphere outside the ship. Instead of the oxygen in the ship getting sucked out, it forms a barrier so I can go through the hatch without putting you in danger. Like how the transport hangar bay is open, yet we can breathe inside the bay. I'm going out there to make sure the squad's okay and to look for Jarmer. Since the Piltrak haven't destroyed us, it either means they don't know we're in here or they don't care enough about us to kill us. Hide and don't make any noise. Okay?"

She squeezes my hand so tight it hurts through the gloves. "Why don't you blast them with the ship's guns?"

"I don't want to kill anyone unless I have to. Jarmer said the fighters have priz-spec weapons as well, but I don't know how to use them. Ever hear of those?"

"No."

"Well, hopefully I won't have to use any weapons at all. But I want to find that Piltrak ship and see what they want."

"Wait. You *want* to or *need* to?" She drops my hand. "You want to go out there and see those vaporous aliens for yourself, don't you? What's wrong with you? Normal people want to kill those things, not sneak around to get a better look. Don't leave me alone, Dax. I'm stuck in here without a suit."

What should I say? Yes, I do want to see them and try to communicate with them if I can. I want to apologize for what my species is doing to them. Why is that wrong? "I *need* to check on our squad. You'll be fine."

She glances through the window. "I don't see any Piltrak ships. What if they killed everyone and left? Is that what you want to see? Dead human bodies?"

Does she have to be so dramatic? "Viga, the red light is still there. I think it's coming from their ship, which means they're out there. If I don't go outside, I can't find out if our squad is...dead or not. Look, I won't be long." I crouch near the hatch, open it and hear a soft, barely detectable hiss. The ladder deploys and I see the black rock below, covered in places with a thin layer of dust.

Before climbing down, I peek through the hatch first and see what I presume is the Piltrak ship behind Jarmella's, about twenty meters or so from me. It's hovering, like mine, but is absolutely round, not streamlined like our fighters. It has a small bar-like window wrapped all the way around and it's glowing red, but not as bright as it was before. There are symbols around it above the window, similar to the symbols on the Jurale Electromagnetic Resonator's container back on the transport. I pull the weapon from my pocket and it vibrates in my gloved hand, giving off a very mild electric shock through the fabric. Did I activate it somehow? Better not tell Viga or she'll panic for sure.

There aren't any weird aliens wandering around, but my squad is still in place behind Jarmella's ship and mine, each of them standing on the asteroid's surface. They must be terrified. I have to get to them. When I climb down the ladder, my feet touch the asteroid and I feel a pull of gravity, just like Viga said. Here I am, Dax Orwan, a worthless smudge, standing on a chunk of rock in outer space. None of my friends or teachers at school would believe it. I hardly believe it.

Parna's at the end of my ship's tether line. I wave, but I don't think anyone sees me because they're all looking in the same direction, at the Piltrak ship. It's strange, but I don't see any aliens at all. They must be inside the ship, with Jarmer. What are they doing to him? I have to help him. There must be a way inside their ship. I walk slowly to avoid kicking up dust plumes that would draw attention to myself, and go behind my fighter to my squad.

"Parna, can you hear me?" I tap her on the shoulder and she startles.

Her eyes are huge and she's talking, but I can't hear her. I thought I'd have a communication channel with everyone. I mouth Jarmer's name and she points to the Piltrak ship. I nod and start toward the enemy. I have no idea what I'm up against, but I have to get to Jarmer and do whatever I can to save him. He did that for me.

The Piltrak ship doesn't seem to have a doorway or hatch, but when I get only a meter from the pulsing glow, it changes from red to purple. There's definitely no hatch, but the light is mesmerizing and I want to feel it all over me. I *need* to feel it. Even the vibrating weapon in my hand has a purple glow to it now.

I take one step into the light and immediately it flashes red again. I'm hit with a stinging jolt of some sort and I'm plunged into complete darkness. Am I floating or on the ground, inside the ship or on the asteroid? Or maybe I'm flying out into space. My head's spinning and I'm tingling all over. Am I dying?

"Prrrshhhh," someone or something says. "Prrreeeb."

I'm queasy. "Hello? Who's there? Where am I?"

"Prrrkkkk."

"Are you a Piltrak?" They're going to kill me, I realize that. I'm nothing to them, an insignificant human. "I don't mean you any harm. I've come for my friend."

All I can do is wriggle my body without going anywhere. I think I'm suspended in mid-air. If they want to hurt me, I can't stop them. I still have the weapon in my hand, although it's stopped vibrating and is glowing again, this time blue. My eyes adjust to the blue light it's giving off and I see that I *am* floating on my back in a room with rounded walls. The Piltrak ship. But where are they?

The voice speaks again, "Prrrkkth."

"I'm sorry, but I don't know what you're saying. I'm here to bring my friend back. Can you understand me?"

My whole body stiffens when a bolt of electricity shoots down and strikes me in the chest. The pain is intense and my hand involuntarily squeezes the weapon. It's difficult, but I manage to run my thumb up and down the groove until sparks splutter out of the front. Since I have no idea how to use it, my only hope is to make the Piltrak believe I do.

Another bolt, stronger this time, shoots through me. I can't control my muscles and I drop the weapon; it crashes to the ground with a loud metallic clang. The electricity finally stops and as much as I try not to, tears drip down my face.

"Please stop!" I scream.

The interior of the ship lights up and I see the walls are covered in the strange symbols. What does that mean? The Jurale and Piltrak have the same language? If only I knew how to talk to them, I could explain that I don't want to hurt them, so long as they let me take Jarmer back.

"Prrr...hum...an. Huuumannn."

"Yes, I'm human." I move and reach down, but can't get to the weapon, it's too far away. "Let me go. Just let me go!"

"Human," comes the voice again. "Cease your hostile actions or die."

Where is the alien? I don't see anyone? And why does it speak my language now? "What hostile actions? I told you I mean you no harm."

A strange purple vapor appears on the wall nearest my head and begins to collect into a form that is short, really short. I remember what Jarmer said about the Piltrak; they're small, hunched, with four arms and six eyes. As the form takes shape, I don't see four arms, but two, and it's not hunched at all, but standing upright. After a moment, I see a Piltrak, my first alien. It's a little less than a meter tall and looks surprisingly like a human, except for its face. It has three eyes in a column in the center of its face, a sort of snout-like nose, and a rounded mouth.

It walks slowly to me, bends, and picks up the weapon. "Human, you have a Jurale resonating translator. Why?"

Translator? It's not a weapon? "I found it. Is that how you can speak my language?"

The Piltrak comes closer and looks up at me. "I am not speaking your language. You are speaking mine." It holds the translator up high. "Humans are dangerous. Our Jurale brothers have told us of your attacks on the innocents."

Innocents? "I haven't attacked anyone." That's not true, I attacked the Katarga, but the Piltrak doesn't have to know that. "I already told you I won't hurt you. Where's my friend, my companion? What have you done with him?"

There's a bright flash and the inside walls transform into regular, square-shaped walls and I fall to the floor, but instead of slamming down hard, I land gently. The Piltrak points at me and I feel another electric shock. I scream and curl up when it stops.

"Why are you doing this to me?" My whole body hurts and all I can think of is getting back to my ship and taking off. I sit up. *Please don't shock me again.*

"Human, you will die and all Piltrak-Jurale fleets will destroy your planet."

Piltrak-Jurale? So they've joined forces for the sole purpose of killing everyone on Earth? There must be something I can do to stop them. "Where's Jarmer, my companion?"

"Gone."

What! That can't be right. Not Jarmer! It's my fault. He saved me and all I did was get him captured and killed. And my squad will be next. What have I done? I'd give my life for his in a second. But the Piltrak doesn't care about that. It wants to exterminate us all.

Chapter Twenty-One

My head's spinning and my mind's going in a thousand different directions. I'm stuck inside the Piltrak ship and my squad is out there on the asteroid, close to suffocation. And Jarmer's dead. I'll never see him again. My tears fall and I scream as loud as I can. Who cares anymore?

The Piltrak comes beside me. "Human, why do you cry? The ship is oxygenated if you wish to remove your protective gear."

It's probably lying, but what do I care. I unfasten the helmet and tug it off. I *can* breathe and it's fresh air, not stale like in my helmet. After sucking in a few breaths and wiping my eyes, I stand and look down at the Piltrak.

"I have a name. I'm Dax. And I'm crying because you killed my friend and you're going to kill the rest of my friends and everyone on Earth. That's why I cry. You can't just kill us!"

The Piltrak emits a faint purple mist all around it. "We know enough about you humans. You killed our Jurale brothers while they were on an exploratory mission and you stole their translator. That is not a reasonable species. I know all I need to know about the humans."

When the mist drifts over to me, I feel strange, relaxed. It's the same sort of feeling I had when I was in the light outside of the ship. "What are you doing to me?"

"I am called Prentak. I am commander of the First Defense Legion and what you are experiencing is called Bliss. We project peace, not hostility. But do not mistake our peaceful intentions with cowardice."

I'm in a weird daze, yet my mind is still clear and for some reason, I trust Prentak. "I would never. So, you weren't going to attack Earth?"

Prentak takes my hand. "Not at first. When our Jurale brothers reported to us how they were mercilessly assaulted without provocation, we joined with them to protect our worlds. Now Earth will be destroyed before we lose any more of our kind."

The purple mist fades away and I feel normal again. "What about the Katarga? Are you friends with them, too?"

"No." Prentak lets go of my hand, walks to the wall, and presses his hand against it. "Katarga do not communicate much with us. They are what we Piltrak call pralthsm."

"I'm sorry, what?" That didn't even sound like a real word.

"Pralthsm means they prefer to be with their own kind. They are settlers. Your war with them started as self-defense, but now humans will not allow them to retreat. They are stuck fighting in your war."

That sounds *exactly* like what the commanders are doing. "Prentak, can't you help them?" I watch him carefully to see what he's doing, but he's only standing there with his hand on the wall.

"If we assist them, which they do not want, we risk endangering ourselves even more. I have determined that it is better to conquer Earth and then allow the Katarga to withdraw in peace."

That makes a lot of sense, except for the conquering Earth part. "So why do you want to kill me? And why did you kill my friend Jarmer? He did nothing to you. He was a good person, a very good person."

Finally, Prentak takes his hand off the wall. "Jarmer is his name?"

"Yes. He was my friend." I feel the tears starting up again.

The wall where Prentak had his hand slowly dissolves into a wavering curtain of purple light. "Go and be with your friend, Dax."

Oh, no! So this is how I'm going to die, suffocated in a toxic purple cloud. I want to live, I honestly do. I can learn to be a soldier or if they won't take me back, I can find a safe planet somewhere and live the rest of my life in exile with my squad. They deserve to live.

"Please don't kill me or my friends. Please."

Prentak just stares at me. "Go."

If only I could hug Ma one last time and see Da's smile, but I'll never see them again and I'll never see my squad. "Will you let my friends outside return to the transport? They're innocent and I brought them here. If not for me, they'd be safe, at least for a while." My heart's beating so fast. I'm seconds away from dying. Nobody on the transport or back on earth will ever know what happened. "If you haven't killed them already, please let them go. They're innocent."

With a strange look, Prentak motions to the purple curtain. "Go into the veil, Dax."

"You won't even consider letting my friends go? But why? None of us here want to harm anyone." My stomach hurts and my heart aches. "We ran away so we wouldn't have to kill, or get killed ourselves."

"Do you not understand the veil, Dax?" Prentak comes to me, reaches up, and puts his hand on my arm. "We are not so different, you and I. I wish to save my people as well. We do not kill without good cause. Unlike your kind. Your friends are already safe inside the veil. I have killed no one. Go through yourself and you will see."

What's he talking about? How can my squad be in a veil of light? "I don't understand. Prentak, what is the veil? Does it hurt?"

"Hurt? It is life. It is all. It is nothing. It is whatever you need. The Jurale translator you have acts in a similar way to the veil. They can both give or take away."

Give? Take away? "I don't understand." So it is a weapon? What exactly does Prentak mean? "Can you explain it to me?"

Prentak motions again to the veil. "A veil is created out of necessity. The Particles of Preedithantha collect together when they are needed for a specific purpose. In this case, your friends require oxygen and Bliss to reduce their anxiety. The Preedithantha detected this through the translator and flowed over your fighter vessels to supply oxygen to your people. The Piltrak and Preedithantha work in harmony; we protect them and they serve our needs."

"Are the Preedithantha alive? Living beings?"

"They most certainly are. They reside within a host, especially Piltrak bodies, and we provide them with the living host as they require. It is a beautiful conjoining. Now, Dax, enter through the veil before your oxygen is depleted. I do not require much oxygen, therefore my ship does not have a large supply, but the Preedithantha increased it for you."

"Wait. The probe. I came here for the probe. It can generate oxygen for us."

Prentak points again to the veil. "You do not need the probe. I seized it so it cannot be used against us. It tracked our movement and that is how your people found us. But once my First Defense Legion was discovered, I used the veil to hide the rest of our ships."

The rest of his ships? How many does he have? "Oh. Then keep it. I don't want anything that can be used for war." I take a breath and realize the air is a bit thin because I'm getting slightly lightheaded. I'm going to have to trust that Prentak has saved my squad. I either walk through the veil or die from lack of oxygen. "What happens when I go into the veil?"

He makes a sound that I think is laughter, but it sounds more like a snort. "You are full of questions."

"I know. I've been told I ask too many."

"That is not a bad thing, Dax. Now, go." He stands to the side of the veil.

Right before I step into the light, he hands me the translator. "Keep this with you. The Preedithantha will come to you through it whenever you need them. They have infinite knowledge. But remember, what the translator gives, it can also take away."

I nod, even though I'm not sure what he means, and take the translator. The veil is truly beautiful; shimmery and giving off that feeling, the Bliss Prentak talked about. I feel good just being near it. With the translator clutched to my chest, I take two steps and I'm bathed in the purple light.

"Dax!" shouts a voice. I recognize it, it's Viga.

The light's dim now and I see Tablon, Viga, Kova, Briett, everyone. They seem relieved to see me, although Jarmella is frowning and glaring at me. "Are you all okay?" I ask.

Nobody is wearing helmets either. I can't make sense of where I am. It's another room, larger than the ship, with square walls, a ceiling of red, and a floor the color of the asteroid. How did I walk through the veil and end up in a room that's bigger than the Piltrak ship?

Viga smiles. "We're fine." Her smile drops. "Dax, Jarmer's not here."

My joy fades away instantly. "I know. Prentak told me."

Viga rushes over and embraces me, squeezing way too hard. "Who's Prentak?"

"The Piltrak who helped us. He's friendly and doesn't want to hurt anyone. None of the aliens want to hurt us."

Jarmella stomps to me with her hands balled up into fists. "Really? Then where's my brother?"

Tablon comes forward. "You're trusting aliens, Orwan? These things have to be killed. I can't believe you don't know that by now."

Briett groans. "Dax, I don't like aliens. They scare me because they want to eat our brains. Don't let them fool you. We have to go and warn the commanders."

I manage to wriggle free from Viga's grasp and go to Briett. "Absolutely not. Look, Prentak said these things called Preedithantha can keep us alive." I suddenly realize that I'm not sure if that means we can leave or if we have to stay within the veil for the rest of our lives. Why didn't I ask Prentak more about the veil? It was the damn Bliss! I couldn't think straight.

As if reading my mind, Prentak appears right in front of me. "Dax, I shall provide safe passage for all of you to your destination of choice, however, I implore you not to rejoin your leaders in their attacks or you too will be destroyed."

"Destroyed!" shouts Kova. "What's going on? Dax?"

With a sharp shake of his head, Tablon gets in my face. "I should have stayed on the transport and taken my chances with Viteri."

Why won't they listen? "Calm down, Tablon. Nobody has anything to worry about." I motion to Prentak. "This is Prentak, a Piltrak commander of the..." I can't remember what he said.

"First Defense Legion," he answers. "You humans are unpredictable and self-serving, but I am willing to cease our attack, providing your leaders cease theirs. I have healed that human there, Tablon, as a show of good faith."

Tablon looks at his leg. "Maybe it healed on its own," he mumbles.

Jarmella still has her mouth set in a scowl. "You killed my brother. We're not listening to any vile garbage that comes out of your mouth. If I get the chance, I'll blast you into space dust."

I get in between Prentak and Jarmella. "Wait, Jarmella, I'm sure it wasn't intentional that Jarmer..."

"Don't defend these creatures, smudge!" Tablon growls.

Prentak interrupts, "Your friend and brother Jarmer is not deceased. The Preedithantha detected a disease in him and are healing him. He will be returned once the procedure is complete. We repair what is broken."

I look around. "What? What disease? Where is he?" I glance at Jarmella. "He's all right, did you hear that? Does he have a disease?"

She shakes her head. "No. He's fine. They're lying."

Tablon stands with Jarmella. "Of course they're lying. That's what they do."

Prentak comes toward me. "Your friend had a defect in his heart that would have ended his life before the span of one of your Earth months passed. Flying in space strained his heart. The more he flew, the worse it became. He was likely unaware of it. He will be returned soon. When you are ready, I will permit you to leave. Where is the destination you wish to go?"

I'm shocked to hear about Jarmer, but thankful Prentak is treating him, even though he has no reason to be nice to us. "Thank you for taking care of us all, especially Jarmer. And Tablon." As for the question of where to go, I have no idea. I just want to get back in my fighter and leave the solar system, but that's impossible. "Prentak, we have nowhere to go. I betrayed the leaders of our world by escaping and we can't return to Earth because they're waiting for us. Because of me, we're all exiles."

Tablon groans. "We have to go back to the transport, smudge. There's no other choice."

Prentak places his hand on my arm. "Ask the Preedithantha for what you need. Use the translator to achieve peace. I must leave you now to prepare for our attack."

Achieve peace? How? He's going to attack Earth no matter what. "Wait! Nobody can achieve peace while Earth is at war. Our leaders are creating this war. They're planning to attack your ships so you will attack Earth and there'll be another war going. They know you're here, they're prepared."

"Dax," Prentak takes a step backward. "I am aware of the tactics and have therefore declared a preemptive attack. I have five fleets concealed within the veil, undetectable. Your planet will never see the attack until it is too late."

Tablon points at Prentak. "I told you we can't trust aliens!"

I glare at him. "Be quiet, Tablon." Prentak's words roll around in my head. The people on Earth have no idea what's going on, or that they're so close to complete annihilation. "You don't have to declare war on Earth, Prentak. Why not talk to our people and explain how they've been betrayed by the commanders? You can't kill the whole population. You just can't. Most of the people are like us." I motion to my squad. "We don't want to fight or kill your people. We're being forced to fight and that's why we've escaped, to tell everyone the truth."

"I know what is on your mind because the Preedithantha have conveyed your feelings to me. While I understand, there is nothing I can do. I will protect my people at all costs and I cannot allow the Piltrak species to become embroiled in an ongoing war with Earth, like the Katarga. The Piltrak and Jurale together will destroy your planet and take no prisoners. I regret you will become orphaned from your home planet, but that is how it must be. This is why you must not return there."

"I can't accept that, Prentak." I have to do something before we're the only humans left alive in the universe.

"Dax," whispers Briett. "I don't want my family to die. It's okay if I do, but not my ma and da."

Jarmella stomps to me. "Do something, Orwan. You can't let this *thing* kill everyone."

I get eye-to-eye with Jarmella. "Prentak's not a thing. His people have every right to defend themselves. You know what the commanders are doing. Who can blame any alien for wanting to stop this lethal bullying."

"Lethal bullying," Briett repeats. "Is that a real thing, Dax?"

Jarmella pokes me in the chest. "Siding with the enemy, *smudge*? I should have known. We're not bullies, we're protecting our planet."

A bright red flash lights up the interior. Briett yelps. What now? As soon as the light dies down, I see Jarmer standing beside Prentak. He's all right! "Jarmer? I was so worried...but you're okay, right?"

Jarmer wobbles slightly. "I'm, ah, fine. Good in fact." He draws in a deep breath. "I feel really...strong."

"Jarmer, what did those *things* do to you," Jarmella says as she goes to him. "You don't look any different."

I glance at Prentak to gauge what he's thinking, but it's hard when he doesn't seem to have any expressions. If he can see that we're caring people who love each other, maybe he'll call off the attack.

I have to try to get through to him. "Prentak, as the commander of the First Defense Legion, can't you contact Earth and give them an ultimatum? Explain what'll happen if they don't stand down. Isn't a peaceful solution better than a war?"

Prentak shakes his head slowly. "There will be no war. We will not give Earth the chance to attack, or defend themselves. Our attack will be swift and final. I am sorry this upsets you."

"Wait." Jarmer waves his arms. "You speak our language. When I was...wherever I was...I couldn't understand what the other Piltraks were saying. But you can talk to our people."

I hold up the translator. "Jarmer, this translates. Prentak hears us speaking his language and we hear him speaking ours. He doesn't actually speak ours." The translator vibrates slightly in my hand; I still have no idea how to use it. A translator is a fantastic device, but incredibly worthless in a battle. Or is it? According to Prentak, it's also some sort of weapon. If only I can figure out how to use it, I can stop him from destroying Earth. The commanders think it's an electromagnetic resonator and that it dissociates things. Maybe it does. But I can't kill Prentak because that'd mean I'm no better than the commanders.

What was it Prentak said? The translator acts like the veil and the Preedithantha are there when they're needed. Therefore, if I have the translator and need help, the Preedithantha should be there for me. Great, but how do I let them know what I want? All I need is for Prentak to stop his attack on Earth. But how can I do that?

A second later, the translator vibrates and fires a burst of purple light right at Prentak. He's just standing there, blinking and breathing, but not moving. He's immobilized! We have to escape and warn Earth, although that would require dealing with the commanders. My squad is looking at me, expecting me to do something, and all I can do is look back. I don't even know how to get out of the veil. I don't know what the veil is or where it is. We could be floating around space for all I know.

Viga's mouth gapes. "Dax, what did you do? What do we do now? Did you kill him?"

The translator isn't vibrating anymore, yet it's glowing a faint purple. "Um, why don't you...ah...let me...give me a minute." Not that a minute is going to solve anything. Prentak is looking right at me. Any feeling of Bliss I had is gone and replaced with panic. Did I just declare war on the Piltrak?

Chapter Twenty-Two

I have absolutely no idea what to do or what to tell my squad. I wish they would stop looking to me for all the answers. All I want is for us to be back in the fighters on our way to Earth.

"Dax!" Viga shouts.

What does she want now? I turn, but all I see is purple and right away, that feeling of Bliss washes over me. "Viga!"

"Right here, Dax. Where are you? I can't see anything. Why don't I care?"

"I think I'm scared. I think," says Briett. "Are they eating my brains? If they are, I don't seem to mind."

With my arms outstretched, I feel around. "Nobody's eating anybody's brains, Briett." Apparently everyone is feeling the Bliss. There's something hard in front of me, hard but rounded. My fingers trace along the surface and I think I recognize it. The shape reminds me of my fighter cockpit. That can't be right though, we couldn't all fit in there.

The purple fades into a light mist and then vanishes altogether so I can see again. I *am* in my fighter and Viga, Kova, Briett, and Tablon are crowded next to me. Well, this is great. How am I supposed to pilot the ship with all of these people? There aren't enough seats or helmets, and I don't have the probe.

Briett is softly whimpering. "Dax, I don't want to go back to the transport."

The Bliss must have worn off because everyone is visibly upset, at me. I have to get help from the Preedithantha, but I don't know how I did it last time, other than thinking about what I wanted. Is that all there is to it?

"Don't worry, Briett." I hold the translator in both hands. "I'll keep you safe."

If you can hear me Preedithantha, can you help us? We need to fly to Earth, but our ships won't hold everyone and we don't have enough oxygen.

The translator vibrates and glows, but there's no veil this time, only the soft purple coming off the device. What does that mean? In the next second, my helmet is on the pilot's seat. After putting it on and activating the synap-trodes, I call for Jarmer.

"Is that you, Dax?" he asks.

"Yes. Are you in your ship? What about Jarmella? Where's the rest of my squad?" It's so good to hear his voice again.

"I'm all alone in my fighter. What's going on, Dax? Where's that Piltrak?"

Jarmella responds, "I have the same three that I had before, but they're inside my ship this time."

At least everyone is safe. "I don't know where Prentak is." And I hope with all my heart he's not dead. What if I got him killed when I asked the Preedithantha for help? I stare at the translator. I've become what I detest, a soldier. I wasn't thinking about Prentak or the Piltrak, all I wanted was to save myself and my planet. That's thinking like the sort of soldier I was trained to be. But that's not me. Not by a long shot. The aliens don't want to hurt us, or at least they didn't. These stupid wars have to end before more innocent people, and aliens, die. *Preedithantha, can you transport Prentak here with me?*

In a brilliant flash of purple, Prentak appears right in front of me.

He nods. "Dax, you are wise. I had hoped I was not wrong about you. You are the one to lead the attack on Earth."

"What? I'm not going to attack Earth. I brought you here to make sure you weren't dying. I don't want *any* wars."

He's looking at me and lets out one of his laughs. "I said lead the attack. I did not say attack. The Preedithantha agree that you can effectively inform the people of Earth how imperative it is that they cease all hostile actions and allow the Katarga to withdraw. You have what we Piltrak call praltah."

Briett grabs my arm. "What's going on? Are we going to attack Earth?"

I shake my head and pry Briett's fingers off my arm. "No." I turn back to Prentak. "What does praltah mean?"

Prentak places his hand over the translator. "Praltah means a force within that drives one to do what is correct. War is not correct and you know this and will do what is necessary to end war. That, Dax, is praltah. Your leaders do not possess praltah."

Praltah or not, I can't do what he wants. "Prentak, all we have are two fighters and a poorly trained squadron of soldiers. Not to mention, we don't have an oxygen supply for all of us. I won't jeopardize my friends. I've already put them in danger more times than I can count." I glance at Viga, who's holding Briett's hand. They all deserve to be back home with their families. "I can't do this, Prentak. Look what I did to you. I didn't think about what would happen to you, I just acted. That's not praltah. That's selfishness."

"Dax." Viga comes to me. "You're not selfish. If this Piltrak says you should lead us, then lead us. We've trusted you in the past and we still trust you. I don't want to die fighting against a species that wants nothing more than to be left alone. I want the Katarga to go home and I want to go home. If all of the aliens go away, then we won't have any more wars."

Prentak takes his hand off the translator. "Dax, I was never in any danger, but you did not know that. You were worried for my life and beseeched the Preedithantha to save me. That is not selfishness. That is bravery. Without knowing what would happen if you brought me to your ship, you did it anyway."

"But that move put my squad at risk. I'm not a soldier, Prentak. I have no special skills or talents other than the desire to end all of this and go home." I take off my helmet and slump into the pilot's seat. "And I'm riddled with guilt. Soldiers don't feel guilt. I killed innocent Katarga when I was caught in the vortex. All I thought of was crashing and taking them with me, so I opened fire. Taking a life is easy, Prentak. Saving a life is hard and that's what makes someone brave."

Prentak continues, "That is quite true. You have a deep understanding, Dax. And that is why you must lead my fleet, at my side. As a human co-leader of the fleet, you can explain to your people what will happen if they do not agree to peace. If you do not lead with me, I will lead alone. And you know the outcome if I lead. I offer you this opportunity only once."

Tablon's been quiet, but now he speaks up, "I think the Piltrak's right. You've managed to avoid death so far and you escaped from a fortified transport, with your entire squad. I can send an open communication broadcast to Earth using my Lead Communicator and let everyone know who you are before we arrive."

"You'd do that?" I'm shocked. "I suppose if the people see how badly we're treated and how the Piltrak and Katarga don't want to fight us, maybe they'll listen."

"Young lady!" screams Trab through the cockpit speaker. "Dax!"

I jump. "Trab? I can't believe it's you! I thought you shut down communications."

"I did, but this is an emergency. Commander Viteri has sent a battalion of fighters to your location with a lethal directive. That means you have to get your butts in launch mode right now!"

Lethal directive? I can't stand any of this. Viteri's solution for everything is to kill. This is crazy, expecting me to somehow save my squad, the aliens, and the human race at the same time. It's impossible, yet I have to figure a way to do it.

Through the front window, I see distant lights, lots of them. I know exactly what they are; Jarmer's fighter squadron, sent to destroy us. "Trab, can you program Earth's coordinates into our fighters?" I slip on my restraints and secure them.

"Of course."

"Then do it!" I shout, feeling my panic rising. "Take us right to Global Command's headquarters!"

Trab gasps. "You got it, young lady. They won't expect you to knock on their front door! Good luck, Dax."

I slip on my helmet and a moment later, my heads-up display flashes on and shows a set of coordinates. The approaching lights are closer now and too many to count. "Jarmer! Jarmella! Launch!"

Jarmer shouts, "I hope you know what you're doing!"

My synap-trodes activate and I order my ship to launch, without bothering with the preflight checklist.

Viga puts her hand on my shoulder. "Dax, we'll die. The cockpit doesn't have near enough residual oxygen to support all of us on a trip to Earth."

"I know. I'll share my oxygen with all of you. We'll trade the helmet back and forth." I force a smile and hope she believes it.

"Wait, Dax," Jarmer says. "You can't. You need full oxygen or the synap-trodes won't work. You can't donate any of your oxygen supply. It's a failsafe to keep the pilot in top condition."

"Just launch, Jarmer, and let me worry about that." The lights are so close now I can make out the vague outline of the fighter ships. My ship's engine starts.

What can I do? There has to be something I'm not thinking of. How can I provide oxygen to everyone without sharing mine? *Think, Dax, think.* I can't let them die. *Preedithantha, save my friends and give them oxygen. I told you my ship can't support us all.*

"Dax, what's...happening?" Viga gasps and disappears in a cloud of purple.

Soon, everyone is gone, except for Prentak and me. Within a few seconds, the cloud of purple mist dissipates.

Prentak sits in the co-pilot seat. "Be careful, Dax. You are using the Preedithantha too much. You must rely on yourself. They are with you to help, not solve every problem."

"Okay. But where did everyone go? They're all right?"

Jarmer shouts, "What happened? Jarmella said everyone but her disappeared!"

I shout back, "Be quiet, Jarmer!"

Prentak cocks his head. "Of course they are all right. The Preedithantha would never do harm, but the translator can."

My ship points straight up and launches off the asteroid. This is when I feel safest, when I'm flying in my ship, into the wonderful freedom of space.

"There's too much to know, Prentak. I'll forget something and end up destroying the whole universe." I close my eyes for a moment to process everything. "Where are they, Prentak?"

"Within the invisible veil. You are smarter than you know. Do not doubt yourself. You are an exceptional human, perhaps even more so now. I detect that you have recently received an influx of additional knowledge."

I open my eyes. "I think that's from a device called a cerebral interpreter. I used it back on the transport. But I don't feel any smarter."

"Not all knowledge is beneficial, but I believe you will always know how to use what you have."

"I hope you're right." I check the heads-up display to make sure we're on course. "What's an invisible veil? I thought it was that purple mist. How can my friends be invisible?"

"Invisible to your eyes, Dax. There are many dimensions in time and space. The invisible veil is not understood by you humans. Your friends in both fighters are still here with you, but in another plane of existence where you cannot see them. They are in Bliss, in stasis, until the Preedithantha release them."

"That's amazing." I place the translator on my lap. "Prentak, what if I'm no good at leading? I'm trying hard to have confidence in myself, but I've never been in charge of anyone, or anything."

He's watching me, but not saying anything, although he's tracing his fingers in circles on his right palm.

Jarmer's and Jarmella's ships are on my right. On my left, the fighters from the transport are heading straight for us, closing in. We'll be in range soon. We need to go faster.

If we can gain enough distance between us and the fighters, they might be recalled to the transport. If only I'd had more training in battle strategy. Regardless, we need to gain some distance from the fighters. "Jarmer, we need to accelerate to 2% lightspeed."

He responds right away, "You want us to speed-jump? That's a dangerous maneuver for three fighters in close proximity. Our anti-collision systems could cause us to change course to avoid an object and impact one another."

I know he's worried, but something's telling me it'll be fine. "Don't worry about anything. Just fly your ship. You, too, Jarmella. I've got this." I end communications so neither of them can object, and I press the black star-shaped button twice.

Prentak snorts. "You have lightspeed? That is something I did not know. It must be a well-guarded secret for our intelligence gatherers to have missed it. You humans continue to surprise me."

Was that a compliment? "I'm constantly surprised, too, but usually not in a good way. Like the Jurale translator." It's on my lap, softly glowing a muted purple. "My commander had it and he thinks it's a weapon that will dissociate people around it. Will it? If it does, how does it work?" My ship accelerates and I'm pushed back into my seat.

Pentrak keeps drawing on his palm. "The Jurale are powerful, Dax, more powerful than any lifeforms in the galaxy, except for perhaps the Preedithantha." He motions to the translator. "That, my friend, contains the Jurales' power. But enough of that. I have ordered my fleet to maintain secrecy and follow us to your planet, but not to act until I give the command."

When did he communicate to his fleet? "I don't understand. Prentak, are you telepathic?"

"Not as you would understand, but I shall try to explain. Piltrak are all linked together through a neural-molecular signaling system. Our bodies contain transmitters that produce a signal that transcends time and space."

"Is that what you were doing on your hand? Signaling your fleet?" It's incredible how little we know about other beings.

He holds his hand up, palm facing me. There are fine red lines crisscrossing his hand. "By activating the neural transmitters, I can communicate. It is similar to how you speak through your devices, except our devices are ourselves, not an artificial creation."

"That's incredible, Prentak. I wish I could do that." I like him. He's not anything like what I imagined aliens to be like. "How is your fleet maintaining secrecy? They'll be seen by Global Command as soon as we're close."

"The veil protects them and conceals them."

"Oh. They're invisible? Is that why our intelligence officials saw thousands of your vessels and then only fifty-one? You hid the others?"

He nods and draws again on his palm. "They believe it was an anomaly and still believe we only have fifty-one."

"Dax," Jarmer says. "Get ready, because once we enter Earth's atmosphere, we'll be airborne targets. Whatever happens, I believe in you and I've got your back. Jarmella's with us, too."

That's exactly what I needed to hear. "Thanks, Jarmer. I just hope I don't let you down."

According to the heads-up display, we'll pass by Mars soon and then we'll be back at Earth before long. There's no sign of Jarmer's flyboys. They must have given up. We're close now and I'm scared, more scared than I was leaving Ma and Da or getting on the shuttle or when I was beaten by Lenora. This fear is completely different. I'm leading an invisible enemy alien fleet right to my planet and risking not only my entire squad but everyone on Earth. I'm either a hero or a traitor. There's no gray area in between. Yeah, this is definitely a different type of fear.

Chapter Twenty-Three

My focus is on the heads-up display because I don't want to make any mistakes. I'd be more comfortable if Trab was still with me, but at least I have Prentak, although he's quiet and is still doodling on his palm. There's no indication on my heads-up that his fleet is anywhere around. Is this the only way?

"Dax, I feel your reticence," he finally says.

"Reticence?"

"You are unsure. The Preedithantha have judged you as compassionate, and I agree, although you harbor insecurity deep inside you that you must eliminate."

Of course I'm insecure. What does he expect? I've never had an alien sit beside me as a sort-of friend as I zoom to Earth with his attack battalion behind us. This is all very strange and more than a little intimidating. I'm no commander, yet here I am, joining with the Piltrak to threaten Earth into submission. That doesn't seem right. I'm human, so shouldn't I be siding with my own kind?

Jarmer suddenly shouts, "Dax! You have to slow down! Cancel lightspeed or you'll crash through Earth's atmosphere too fast! Dax!"

"Okay, okay!" I slow my ship down using the synap-trodes and glance at my passenger. "Prentak, why didn't you say something? I could have killed us. And what did you mean when you said the Preedithantha judged me and I have to eliminate my insecurity? How can I do that? You've put your trust in the wrong person. Look what happened just now. I wasn't paying attention and we almost died."

He stares at me without blinking. "Almost is not actuality. When you took the translator, the Preedithantha were activated by your compassion. They will never assist those who are not deserving."

"But compassion isn't a good quality to have, at least not in my world. My friend Jarmer said girls can't be fighter pilots because we're too compassionate. Compassion equals weakness in the Global Forces. If my people think I'm compassionate, they won't listen to me. I can't convince anyone on Earth that these alien wars have to end."

His mouth contorts into what has to be a smile. "You managed to convince all of your friends to follow you by breaking regulations and risking their lives. Your friend Jarmer believes in you and that other human, Tablon. I sensed immense animosity against you from him, but that is waning now. That is an accomplishment. You have a special gift, Dax, one that you have not recognized because of your insecurity."

Again with the insecurity. Well, I'm insecure for a reason. I've lived my whole life being told I'm nothing and I'll never be anything. My parents are poor and I was forced into the Global Forces so I wouldn't *poison* anyone with my questions about the wars, and I've been marked for death because I'm a lowly AFGF smudge. Who wouldn't be insecure?

A flashing light on my heads-up catches my attention. The reading says we're only a hundred thousand kilometers from Earth's atmosphere. Everything happened so fast, I haven't thought of what to say when we land at Global Command. That is if we don't get shot down first.

"Prentak, can my squad get hurt if I'm shot down?"

"The Preedithantha will keep them safe within the veil. The Preedithantha will protect you, too, if you want them to."

What does that mean? Of course I want them to protect me. "How do I do that?"

He points to the translator in my lap. "You are already connected to them through the translator, but for protection, you must accept them *into* yourself."

It's like my blood just froze in my veins. The thought of an alien inside me is terrifying. Even if it means being safe, I just can't do that. "I don't want that, Prentak." I'll take my chances on my own. The reading says I'm ten thousand kilometers from the atmosphere, almost there.

"That is your decision." Prentak looks out the side window.

Am I making a mistake? I check the reading, one thousand kilometers to go. Global Command must know I'm here. *Okay, Dax, think of a speech.* It has to be something that'll make Global Command listen and pay attention. That's easy; tell the truth. Da always said nobody can go wrong if they tell the truth. So that's it then, I'll explain what I heard and how the commanders are causing wars to make money. My only hope is that Global Command isn't as corrupt as the commanders.

The protective screen slides over the front window and there's a slight shudder as my fighter slips into the atmosphere, but then everything is smooth again, although now I can't see anything. I'm flying blind.

My eyes are glued to the display. "Jarmer, are you there? Are you all right?"

"I'm fine, Dax," his voice is a bit shaky. "But..."

But? But what!

He continues, "I detected three fleets of fighters that were launched from the Arctic Training Camp. And five more from the East Training Camp. Dax, they're heading right for us. And the holo-energy mask is inoperable once we're through the atmosphere."

Why isn't Prentak saying anything? All he's doing is drawing on his palm again. I engage the synap-trodes and open the covering over the window. I have to see! When the cover slides open, all I see are clouds. Pure white fluffy clouds everywhere. I used to watch clouds drift by at home and wished I could grab onto one and go with it to Jewel or any place other than my outlier. For a minute, I forget where I am until a brilliant flash of red outside lights up the clouds.

"What's that!" I shout.

Now Prentak speaks, "My fleet has engaged the enemy."

The enemy? "Prentak, who's the enemy? Us? I mean, Earth?"

He nods. "Of course. They fired your friends and barely missed one of my veiled vessels. I cannot allow destruction of any Piltrak vessels, including this one."

"This isn't a Piltrak vessel, Prentak. You can't shoot..." I've made a terrible mistake bringing Piltrak ships right to Earth. "Those are my people out there. Did you kill them?"

"We always engage an enemy with lethal force, nothing less. You must convince your people to cease the attack or my fleet will annihilate them."

My stomach tightens and I feel sick. Someone just died because of me. I might as well have shot them down myself. The result would be the same. "Don't shoot at anyone else, Prentak. Please."

He looks over at me. "I will protect my people just as you wish to protect yours. Remember, we did not start this war, but we will end it. You brought me to this vessel and my people will protect me at all costs."

My ship banks sharply, levels off for a while, and banks again to the left. "Are you controlling my ship?"

"Yes. I am commanding your ship to take evasive action."

We're clear of the clouds now and I see several fighters swooping up and around us, then an exchange of fire from invisible Piltrak ships. Our fighters don't stand a chance against ships they can't see. It's so unfair, yet I'm torn between who's right and who's wrong. Prentak is absolutely right about the fact that the Piltrak didn't start the war. But does that entitle them to kill fighter pilots? People are dying and I can't do a thing about it.

Jarmer screams out, "No!"

"Jarmer! Jarmer, are you hit?" I glare at Prentak. "Did your people fire on him?"

"They did not, but *your* people have destroyed one of *your* fighters."

"What?" I can't breathe. "Jarmer?"

There's a pause. "Our fighters shot down my sister." Jarmer's voice is faint. "She's...gone."

What can I say to him? Nothing will bring her back. "Prentak, what about my squad that was with Jarmella?"

He looks straight ahead. "Your squad is still within the veil."

At least they're safe. For now. I never liked Jarmella, but I certainly didn't want her to die.

The ground, brown with scrubby bushes and trees, is below. Mid-World. All I can do is sit and watch the battle as the ground gets closer and closer. There are a few burning scraps of fighter ship tumbling through the air, and in my heart, I know it's Jarmella.

My ship drops to ten meters above the landscape and I see a fortified area that has to be Global Command; dark stone walls surrounding a large round building. As I get closer, we're fired upon from hidden weapons. The shots somehow explode before they hit me.

Prentak turns to me. "Dax, the Preedithantha have installed a temporary shield around both of your fighters to keep us, and your friend, safe. It is with regret that the other ship was not protected soon enough. The shield will be disabled once you disembark. You will be vulnerable unless you request protection from the Preedithantha."

Cold sweat drenches me and I remove my helmet to wipe my face. "I don't want an alien species in my head." I feel numb. "I want to see my parents. The Piltrak are killing humans. And humans are killing humans. This is insane. I can't make a difference at this point."

"Dax, is it better for a few to be sacrificed with the *hope* of ending the war and therefore saving the majority, or have the entire human population eliminated, thereby ending the war with *certainty*? You can bring that hope to reality and end the slaughter."

I'd rather see nobody dead, ever, but deep down, I know he's right, if it's not too late. "Promise me you won't kill anyone else. Those fighter pilots had families."

"The Piltrak have families also."

I nod. "This has to stop. I'll speak to my people and I'll do everything I can to make them understand." I peer out the side window and see Jarmer's ship on my left. "Jarmer, are you all right?"

He's quiet for a moment. "They killed her like she was nothing. They didn't care. They knew we weren't aliens, but they shot her down anyway."

"I'm so sorry, Jarmer."

"If it takes my last breath, I'll make them pay." His voice is stronger now, more determined. "I counted at least eighty fighters that were shot down by the Piltrak. One of them better be the one who killed my sister."

"I hope so. What if I fail, Jarmer? What if nobody listens to me."

Jarmer comes back right away. "Fail? You won't fail. This battle just reinforces why we need to denounce the Global Forces. Our lives mean nothing to them. They wanted to kill you just to keep you from telling others about the stupidity of these wars. I believe in you, Dax. Don't make my sister's death be for nothing."

Before I can take a breath, I hear an explosion close by and my ship flips end-over-end. "Jarmer! A shockwave got me! I'm out of control!" I turn to Prentak. "I don't know what to do."

"I cannot help guide your ship any longer. I only have so much control. Accept the Preedithantha."

What choice do I have? "Fine! Preedithantha, I accept you!"

A thin purple mist drifts around my ship outside; the Bliss. Without me doing anything, my ship straightens out and flies directly to Global Command where it hovers over the main building. I have a strange buzzing in my ears, not uncomfortable, but annoying. Nobody fires on me and the soldiers that are rushing about scan the air like they can't find me. Am I invisible?

Inside my head, I hear a high-pitched voice, *You are within the veil and cannot be seen. Take the translator.*

Where is it? It flew off my lap, but I don't know where it went. I look around and see it on the floor near Prentak. Miraculously, it rises and floats to me. Did I do that? I grasp it and sparks scatter from it in every direction. Prentak makes his little laughing sound. "You are now one with the Preedithantha, Dax. Fully integrated with them. Talk to your people."

"How am I supposed to do that?" The buzzing is gone, but I don't feel any different. It's not like the Preedithantha are controlling me or making me do anything. "I have to know..."

The Preedithantha reply silently, *All is well. We are with you. Keep the translator close.*

Okay, but why? I don't need it to translate my language. So what else am I supposed to do with it? It's still sparking. I slip my helmet on and use the synap-trodes to open the hatch and command my ship to drop to two meters above the ground. I unfasten my restraints, remove the helmet, and motion to Prentak to follow me.

I peek outside. The purple mist is all over my ship and although it's right there in front of everyone, nobody bothers me.

With my foot on the rung of the ladder, I glance at Prentak, who's still in his seat with no hint that he's planning to come with me. Fine, I can do it on my own. I can't see Jarmer's ship, but I'm willing to trust the Preedithantha when they said *all is well*. I climb down and when my feet hit the ground, I realize the purple mist hasn't extended to ground level. In an instant, I hear shouting and a second later, something strikes me in the back. My body goes limp and I fall onto the dirt, unable to move. From my vantage point, all I see are boots, lots and lots of boots stomping in my direction. I've been captured. I thought the Preedithantha were supposed to protect me.

Chapter Twenty-Four

My ears are ringing with voices screaming and heavy footsteps everywhere around me. They're telling me not to move, like I have a choice. My entire body is completely numb from my neck down. I'm on my side, but can still look around. Above me, I can see into my ship through the hatch, but otherwise, it's invisible. I can't see Jarmer's ship, so he has to be invisible as well.

A small man wearing a clear helmet crouches a short distance from me and glares. He's got broad shoulders and a huge mustache that goes around his mouth and down to his chin. "Where did you come from? What's that purple cloud? Tell me right now if it's toxic because we *will* test it and it'll go easier for you if you confess. Who are you?" He's shouting the words rather than speaking them.

I cough and swallow to clear away some dust that blew into my mouth. "The cloud isn't toxic. My name is Daxella Rose Orwan, AFGF recruit from the Mid-World Equatorial Training Camp. What have you done to me?" My heart's thumping and sweat's dripping down my face.

The man is still crouching. "AFGF? What are you doing here? How did you get here? You dropped out of that cloud." He points up. "Explain yourself, recruit!"

His shouting is giving me a headache. "I can't move." I wish Prentak would come and explain everything so I don't have to.

The little man gets up and presses a button on a metallic box on his belt. A slight shock hits me and I can move again. I scramble to my feet, staying out of the Bliss cloud since I need all my senses at this point, and salute.

"I'm Commander General Samson Rikter. Now, tell me everything or you'll end up a smudge at my feet."

Smudge? Seems like I can't get away from that word. I hold the salute and take a breath before answering. "Are you the commander in charge of Global Command, sir?"

He eyes me and circles around me. "Of course I am." In one quick movement, he takes off his helmet and hands it to a young man who scurries up next to him, and whispers in his ear. He continues, "I just received confirmation that the cloud is indeed non-toxic. You've told the truth, recruit. So how did you come to be inside the cloud? Is it a new weapon or transportation device I don't know about? Answer carefully, because I am to know of every single weapon we have in our arsenal, human or alien."

I don't like the way he's looking at me; his nose is wrinkled like I'm a piece of garbage. "Sir, I must talk to you about what's really going on with the wars. I found out information I think you need to know. The whole system is corrupt and the commanders..."

He lets out a belly laugh. "The commanders?" He stops laughing and pokes me in the chest. "You are an AFGF, a worthless pile of manure destined to die on the moon. You don't tell me anything!" He turns to the young man. "Take this recruit to a cell and question her. Then open fire on the purple cloud until you obliterate it from my sight."

"Wait!" I'm not going to jail. I can't. I have Prentak literally floating above my head to worry about. "You have to listen to me." I drop the salute and don't even bother about standing at attention. "The commanders are staging these wars to make money. The aliens don't want to fight us."

Rikter slaps me across my cheek so hard that I stumble backward. He's red-faced angry. "You do not speak to me unless spoken to." His finger moves to the metal box on his belt.

I know he's going to numb me again. "Preedithantha! Save me!"

Inside my head, I hear them: *You are protected. Enter the ship.*

"I don't understand," I mumble.

With a step forward, Rikter presses the button, but I don't fall down this time. He presses it over and over again, then shouts at the young man, "The simu-sleep isn't working! Fix it and take this recruit into custody!"

The young man points a laser gun at me. "Come with me or I'll blast you."

I stand my ground. "No. I'm not going anywhere with you. Commander Rikter, I'm telling you the truth. These wars are invented, forced, so the commanders can make a lot of money off their investments in the manufacturing plants. I'm not lying. I heard this straight from Commander Viteri himself. You have to believe me."

Rikter is still pressing the button, but stops and stares at me. "I don't know what game you're playing, recruit, or how you left your transport and appeared here, but if you do not obey me, you will be executed as a traitor to Earth. You choose. Surrender immediately and live, or refuse and die." He withdraws a blue-glowing object about the size of a laser pistol, with the same Jurale markings I've seen before, and a barrel that looks more like an old-fashioned bullet-firing gun I've seen in my history books. "This will vaporize you."

I think to myself, *Preedithantha, what is that?*

An answer comes: *That is a Jurale child's toy that fires bursts of air in the shape of ancient Earth projectiles called bullets. It is harmless. Enter the ship.*

Wow, the commanders think they know everything and assume every Jurale object is a weapon. Idiots. And these are the people running our planet and making all the decisions. Well, no more. I'm taking charge right now.

Even though Rikter doesn't have a weapon, the man with him does. *Preedithantha, can you prevent those laser weapons from hurting me?*

As said before, you are protected. You must enter the ship.

I turn and hurry under the cloud to the ladder, but before I can grasp the rung, I hear Rikter give the order to open fire on me and the cloud. I wrap my fingers around the rung and hear ear-splitting explosions all around me.

Rikter orders a cease-fire and approaches after a moment but doesn't get too close. I keep my grip on the rung but face him.

He lowers his voice, "Recruit, I don't know how you managed to stay alive, but I cannot have you spreading these vicious rumors about our war strategy. Come with me now and we can discuss the terms of your surrender."

"War strategy? It seems more like treason to sacrifice children for the sake of making money. And you want me to surrender?" Does that mean Rikter is in on everything? I abandon the ladder and run to him, grab the Jurale toy from his hand and point it at him. "Preedithantha, make the toy fire!"

A series of air-bullets fly from the barrel and hit Rikter in the chest with a soft puffing sound. He staggers backward, staring at his uniform. I smile and toss the toy on the ground.

"I'm not surrendering. Ever. You've tricked the people of Earth long enough and you need to stop the attack on the Katarga and the Piltrak. If you don't, the Piltrak will attack and destroy the entire planet."

"What?" Rikter motions to his men. "Take this recruit into custody. She disabled my weapon and is threatening the world."

Really? Is that all he can think of? Arrest me and ignore everything I just said? "Listen! You have to declare that every war is over. The Piltrak are ready to attack. Do you think I'm lying?"

He nods slowly. "Of course you're lying, you pathetic child."

I don't have a choice now. Reasoning didn't work, so maybe a show of force is all that's left. "Preedithantha! Remove the veil!"

A bright red flash lights up everything as far as I can see and within a second, my ship, Jarmer's ship, and lots of Piltrak ships are visible, hovering over and around Global Command. Not all of the Piltrak ships are like Prentak's. Some are big, maybe three times as big, and others have extensions coming out of the back and front. I feel someone next to me and glance to my right. It's Prentak.

"Bold move, Dax," he says. "They will not listen because they already know to be truth what you are saying. By exposing them, you are a danger to them. They will try to kill you to silence you."

"I know. I'm used to that." I put my attention back on Rikter.

Prentak touches me on the arm. "Preedithantha are here to help you, but use them carefully."

I nod. "I will. Hey, why do you understand me? I don't have the translator, it's still in the ship."

He makes the little laugh sound. "The Preedithantha and you are one and they connect you to all those likewise linked to them."

"Alien!" shouts Rikter. "Open fire! Open fire!" He runs toward the building with his hands covering his head.

I jump in front of Prentak. "They're going to shoot!"

"Dax, I cannot be harmed by them. But my people will see the threat and act accordingly."

"No, wait. Please tell your people not to attack. I think I can still convince *my* people to end the wars. Just not these people."

"You cannot, Dax." Prentak begins doodling on his palm. "This was your last chance."

Jarmer climbs out of his fighter and runs to me. "Dax, are these the people responsible for Jarmella? I can destroy this entire compound with my priz-spec." He's breathing hard. "Just give the word."

Laser fire explodes all around us, but nothing touches us.

"Jarmer, I don't know who's responsible. But we can't murder all of these people. I'm sure most of them are just doing their duty."

"Maybe, but they're on the wrong side and deserve to die."

I understand his grief, but..."Jarmer, if you level Global Command, the commanders will come at you with everything they've got. Do you want to die at the hands of these people or do you want to stand up to them and fight against injustice? Fight against what they did to Jarmella?"

The assault continues and at least twenty soldiers advance on us with large laser weapons, firing directly at me and Jarmer.

Jarmer shakes his head slowly. "I know you're right, but I have to make them pay."

Prentak steps in between us. "Get back to your ship, Jarmer. The Preedithantha cannot protect us all for much longer."

Jarmer glares at Prentak. "And leave Dax here with you? I don't think so."

I put my hands on his shoulders. "Jarmer, you're safer in your ship. You have to stay alive for Jarmella, so you can tell what happened. That's what Jarmella would have wanted."

"Yeah, but she's not here, is she?" A tear trickles down his cheek. "I can't leave you here alone." He wipes the tear away and glances around.

"I'm fine. Besides, I've got help from the Piltrak and the Preedithatha. But I do need you. Can you contact Trab and see if he can send out a communication to all of the fighters telling them not to attack the Piltrak. If they don't attack, the Piltrak won't fire on them. Right, Prentak?"

He doodles for a moment and looks up. "I have given the order to only destroy those vessels attacking them. For now."

"Can you help us, Jarmer?"

Jarmer thinks for a second and nods. "Yeah, I can. This is for my sister. Stay safe!" He dashes to his ship.

The laser and pulse fire continues and other than the incredible noise, it does nothing.

I watch Jarmer climb back into his ship. He's so strong and brave, exactly the type of soldier we need for this strange rebellion.

"Thank you for all your help, Prentak."

He stops doodling. "Do not thank me yet. As I have said before, I will not allow my people to become victims of Earth. I have issued a time limitation."

"What does that mean?"

"You have ten Earth minutes. If you cannot convince your people to cease the attacks, my battalions will commence total annihilation."

Only ten minutes? How can I get my message out in only ten minutes?

Jarmer climbs down the ladder of his ship. "Dax!"

I rush to him.

"Dax." Jarmer removes his helmet. "Trab said he'll need twenty minutes. The training camp has been shut down and he's under house arrest, well, camp arrest. But he said he can still manipulate the communications system even though they shut it all down. He knows how to get into it by doing a back-end security breach." He shrugs. "I don't know what that means, but he needs twenty minutes."

"We don't have twenty minutes." I wave to Prentak. "Twenty minutes! I need twenty minutes!"

Prentak moves his finger around his palm. "No. In less than nine minutes, your people will have thirty-two war battalions in place directly over us. Their fleet is assembled and mobilized. Even the Preedithantha cannot protect against that. We must destroy all humans before that happens. I will not jeopardize my fleet. You now have eight minutes and forty-nine seconds."

Preedithantha, can I see my squad? Can you bring them out of the veil?

I have to explain to my friends what's happening and how everyone on Earth is about to die because of me. They'll hate me, but they need to know.

You were told to return to your ship. You did not listen.

212

I was a little busy trying to prevent Earth from being destroyed. *Preedithantha, release my squad from the veil.* In a brief flash of purple, all of my friends, as well as Tablon, appear around me. They're obviously confused, Briett most of all judging by the way he's shaking his head and blinking. It's so good to see them.

"Dax?" Viga asks. "Where are we? What happened? Why is the Piltrak still here?"

Time to try my skills at explaining everything I've done. "You were kept in the purple veil of the Preedithantha, but it's time to let you out. I tried to make Global Command see what's happening, but it didn't do any good. They already know. It's not just a conspiracy among the training camp commanders, but Global Command, too. We've only got..." I glance at Prentak.

He looks at me. "Seven minutes and 23 seconds."

I continue, "Seven minutes and 23 seconds before the Piltrak attack."

Briett cocks his head to the side. "Before they attack what? Us? They're going to eat our brains, aren't they? I told you they would!"

Oh, Briett. I shake my head. "No, they're not going to attack us or eat our brains. The attack is on..." I stop. I don't want to say anymore. Here I am, back on Earth, the place I never thought I'd ever see again, and it's about to be turned to rubble, a dead planet devoid of all people. And it's because I can't do anything to stop it. Where will we go when everyone is dead? "Prentak! My parents! I have to save them."

The explosions stop for a moment and the soldiers group together as if they're strategizing.

Prentak holds up his right hand and I see the crisscrossed lines on his palm are bright red. "My orders have been confirmed. There is no time to mount a rescue mission."

His voice is flat, unemotional. Doesn't he understand how important my parents are?

Return to your ship.

What? *What good will that do, Preedithantha?* Everything and everyone I know is about to...

Fly your ship. Your family is our family. Your friends are our friends. Bring us your family. You were told to return to your ship.

I'm getting tired of this voice in my head being so cryptic. *Yes, you did tell me, but you didn't tell me why! I don't have the coordinates to my outlier, so what am I supposed to do? What do you expect from me?*

We are one with you. Pilot your ship and your thoughts will guide us.

I'm not exactly sure what that means, but if there's a chance of saving my parents, I have to go along with the Preedithantha. "Prentak, I'm going to fly to my outlier. Will you keep my friends safe until I get back?"

He stares. "You think you can get back here in under six minutes?"

"The Preedithantha are helping me. Keep my friends safe!" I scamper up the ladder and into my ship, strap myself into the pilot's seat, jam my helmet on and activate the heads-up display. I start the engine and launch, hoping Prentak will protect everyone on the ground.

Our Piltrak brother will not harm your friends as the Piltrak are sworn allied friends of the Preedithantha. Your friends are our friends.

I don't know why I was reluctant to have the Preedithantha with me. They make me feel like nobody can ever hurt me again. My ship levels off and accelerates so fast I'm pushed into my seat. The heads-up says I'm going at 2% lightspeed! That's impossible, I didn't do anything. Before I know it, my ship slows and plummets to the ground, stopping suddenly in a hover a few meters above the ground. It's strange, but I wasn't even jerked around by the abrupt movement. And right in front of me is my house. I'm home!

Chapter Twenty-Five

I can't wait to see Ma and Da and tell them how much I love them, but not just yet, I need to secure the area first. The street is eerily quiet, nobody rushing out even though my fighter ship is hovering on our dirt patch of a lawn. Where is everyone? By the position of the sun, it's early morning. There should be people leaving for their jobs and kids heading to school, but there's not a single person anywhere.

I open the hatch and climb down the ladder. "Ma! Da!"

Where are they?

In a sprint, I get to my house and bang on the door, but it swings open. That's not right, it's never unlocked. We don't own much, but these days even poor people can be victims of theft. I remember a neighbor who got robbed of the small amount of food they had so Ma gave them a basket of carrots and a frozen chicken. We still had a few potatoes, onions, and some leftover soup for the rest of the week, which was fine for us. Our family was much smaller than theirs and we managed. Desperation makes people do terrible things.

"Ma!" I call after pushing the front door open. "Where are you?"

I can't believe it, I have a matter of minutes to save them and they're not here. What if they were chased off by prowlers? Where would they go? There's no time to go to the factories to look for them. *Preedithantha, where are my parents?*

There's a pause. *They cannot be reached in time. Return to your ship and leave the planet.*

What? What! *Wait. I'm not leaving until I have my parents.*

The entire outlier population is gone and your parents are imprisoned in the city of Jewel. Once you arrived on Earth, your parents were seized. You cannot help. Return to your ship. Piltrak brothers are about to attack.

The population is gone? Does that mean dead? All because of me? "Why didn't you tell me this before I came here?" I shout as I run through the house.

You guided your ship here. The position of your parents was unknown until you asked. All from your outlier have been captured.

So the Preedithantha don't think for themselves? Great, I wasted what little time I had coming home. But I still have to try to get to them, even if I run out of time. At least I'd have tried. "I'm going to Jewel." I rush to my ship and scamper up the ladder.

You will not make it in time. When our Piltrak brothers attack, your parents will die.

"I can't let that happen." I strap myself in and shove my helmet on. "Can't you put my parents inside the veil like you did with my squad?"

The Preedithantha veil can only project in the immediate vicinity of the Preedithantha or a host of the Preedithantha such as a Piltrak or in this case, yourself. Launch your ship and leave this planet.

I'm not leaving Earth until I know Ma and Da are safe. And then there's my squad to think about. Prentak will abandon them as soon as his people start their attack. I have to get back to them. All within...what, seconds? How long do I have?

Time has expired. War is imminent.

No! This can't be happening. I command my ship to launch and ask the Preedithantha to take me to Jewel. My stomach's tight and I'm sweating like crazy, but if Prentak begins his attack at Global Command in Mid-World, I might have some time to find my parents before his fleet makes it here. I hope.

It doesn't take long for my ship to zoom through the air above my outlier and fly on a heading due north. How does it know where to go? I've never been to Jewel.

Your thoughts inform Preedithantha.

I don't know what that means because I have no idea where Jewel is.

Preedithantha can access everything on Earth.

Oh. So you can find any place that I think of?

Indeed, so long as the location is known within accessible Earth records.

216

That's amazing. And frightening. The ground below is mostly brown and dry with an occasional blue or greenish waterway with colorful vegetation lining the banks, interrupting the dull landscape. But before long, there's green everywhere ahead. It has to be the grassy lawns inside Jewel's protective walls. We learned that Jewel has walls, but it never made sense to me why, and of course our teachers never explained the reasoning behind it. I always assumed it was to enforce a separation between the city and the outliers. I think I was right.

My ship flies to the center of the city, right over an open square with the brightest green grass I've ever seen and flowers of every imaginable color spilling from an array of planters. There are towering buildings and huge, lavish houses made of colorful stones that look more like gems, and as the sun catches them, it hurts my eyes. No wonder it's called Jewel. The ship settles into a hover and without any warning, is the target of laser fire. A couple of laser bursts hit my ship, but then the rest of them explode before striking the fuselage. There's no purple cloud, so I'm not in the veil. *Preedithantha, are you doing this?*

Preedithantha will always protect Preedithantha.

I guess that means I'm safe, for the time being anyway. The attack is coming from a gigantic, multi-story pink, yellow and blue building overlooking the garden square. There are banners of gold fabric fluttering from the rooftop. That has to be the City Chief's headquarters. In our Politics and Society class, my teacher taught us how the City Chief lives and works at the heart of Jewel. That building certainly looks like the heart of the city to me.

So, where are my parents and the rest of my outlier? The headquarters building can't be large enough to hold everyone and I have no idea if there's a prison within the city limits. One thing I do know for sure is that I won't let everyone on Earth die. They have to know about the attack and get to safety. If there is anywhere safe.

"Dax!" It's Jarmer's voice through the communication system.

"Jarmer, you're okay? And my squad? What's going on? Are the Piltrak attacking?"

"Dax, Global Command...is gone," his voice is flat.

Gone? My heart's racing and I feel sick. I got them killed. Me. Nobody else. "My squad?"

"Safe." There's a pause. "We're all here, but everything around us has been leveled. *You* brought the Piltrak right to Global Command. Those Piltrak ships flew off in all directions and shot down every one of our attack fleet as soon as they were in range. I have no idea if Earth has any defenses left. I'm going to fly to my outlier and find my family, if the Piltrak don't shoot me down first. Please tell me you can stop this."

What does he expect? He pushed me into this and now he's blaming me. I can't stop it, because nobody will listen to me now with Global Command gone. There's no one around to negotiate with the Piltrak anyway. "What am I supposed to do? If I could stop the Piltrak, I would. I'm at my outlier's city right now. Jarmer, they rounded up my village's entire population and have them locked up somewhere. It's because I escaped. They're punishing me by taking my parents and everyone else."

"This is a galactic mess. It won't do them any good to punish anyone, don't they know that? Do you think your outlier was evacuated for safety?"

"No. Jarmer, I was told everyone was *captured* and my parents are imprisoned at Jewel. But that's just my outlier, I'm sure your family is okay. Go and find them before it's too late. Tell my squad I'll come back for them after I find my parents." I open the hatch and rip the helmet off.

Since the Preedithantha protect themselves, they won't let me get hurt. I hurry down the ladder as laser bursts explode all around me. I move away from my ship and wave my arms around.

"Stop!" I shout as loud as I can. "Stop your shooting! Let me speak!" I raise my hands in the air to show I have no weapons and take a few more steps toward the building. After a couple more lasers bursts, the attack ends and all that's left is the ringing in my ears from the explosions. "My name is Daxella Rose Orwan from Village 77. I'm an AFGF recruit and I have to see the City Chief!"

Piltrak attack fleet to arrive in four Earth minutes.

Four minutes? Not long, but better than nothing. I keep my hands raised and wait. After a few seconds, the smoke clears, and a bird chirps from its hidden perch among the branches of a leafy tree. It seems like forever since I've heard birds singing. A gentle breeze brings with it the perfume of flowers mixed with the acrid stench of the explosions. This is my home, was my home, before it was taken from me by Viteri and Global Command. I can never go back to my normal life. That's a distant memory now.

I put my arms down when ten guards dressed in helmets, body armor, and heavy boots march out of the building in two rows. Behind them is a lanky gray-haired woman wearing a black suit. The guards stop and the woman strides between them and comes to me.

"I am Shallane Magro, City Chief of Jewel. Before you are taken away, I will allow you to speak." She stares at me with such hatred, I can actually feel it.

I know the Preedithantha will protect me, but I'm still scared. "Bring my parents to me."

She laughs and shakes her head. "Making demands? Commander Viteri said you would come here looking for your parents. You have the mind of a fifteen-year-old, but the gall of someone much older." She gets close to me. "You are a traitor and a non-conformist, and you brought the enemy to our planet. You think I don't know who you are, Orwan? Your outlier was decommissioned last night for their part in producing a traitor, and once you arrived at Global Command, your parents were locked away where they'll rot away slowly, each deplorable day a reminder that you are their daughter."

"You can't do that. Take me and let them go. Don't you have a conscience?"

"Under any other circumstances, you'd be imprisoned for speaking to me like that. But prison is too good for the likes of you."

My heart is thumping and I'm trembling, but manage to hold my shoulders back and lock eyes with the City Chief. "Release my parents and the rest of my outlier."

With narrowed eyes, the City Chief scowls. "Village 77 no longer exists. It will be flattened. The residents have been sent to live in the destitute housing areas of the neighboring outliers. Your parents, however, will never again see the light of the sun."

My knees shake and threaten to collapse and my throat is so dry I can't swallow. "I'll only say this one last time. Bring me my parents."

"You make no demands, Orwan. You side with the alien menace and assist them in their attack. You are a traitor. This beautiful city has been evacuated and her residents are in a secured secret location that neither you nor your alien friends can find. I protect my own kind, unlike you."

I'm not sure I can get through to the City Chief or not, but I have to try. "Don't you see what's happening here? These wars are constructed by the commanders and Global Command. They don't want me speaking out against them, that's what this is all about. My parents have nothing to do with any of it. And the aliens don't want..."

The City Chief smirks. "The aliens have attacked Global Command because you helped them. Commander Viteri himself sent an alert to the cities and marked you as a shoot-on-sight enemy target. Once the war is won, great rewards will be handed out to the hero responsible for killing you. I am that hero."

So now I have a bounty on my head. "This is ridiculous! I'm just a girl. The real enemies are the commanders. Because of them, nobody will survive!"

She shakes her head and waves to the guards. "You're too naïve to understand, Orwan. The most valuable people will survive. That's what matters. The puny, worthless, weak children are sent to the moon so they won't have the chance to reproduce. It's a global culling, if you will. Troublemakers like you are eliminated along with the pathetic children. But you somehow survived. Not for long. You, and your poverty-stricken parents, will not survive this war. And you, my dear, will die at my hands."

Two guards run to me and grab me by the arms. They're too strong and I can't pull away. "Listen to me! In a couple of minutes, the Piltrak fleet will be here and they'll open fire on you and destroy the city. I came here for my parents and to warn you to evacuate!"

The City Chief shrugs. "Well, Jewell has already been evacuated and your parents will not be released. Seems like you made a poor decision, Orwan. On your knees." She motions for the guards to force me to the ground. "The Piltrak might destroy Jewel, but her people are safe, and I shall make my escape as soon as I've dispatched you. Earth will rise up and defeat those barbarians once the transports return. Shame you won't live long enough to witness our glory."

I'm pushed to my knees and my arms are twisted behind my back. "Transports? There was only one transport sent to Saturn. One transport could never defeat the entire Piltrak fleet. Commander Viteri was going to attack the Piltraks to cause a war with them. He was sacrificing everyone on that transport. That's why I escaped. Why won't you listen to me!"

"You are a lying child." The City Chief brings out a laser pistol from under her jacket. "We are at war with the Piltrak and the Katarga because *they* attack *us*."

Preedithantha, help me! "That's not true. None of it's true. You've been lied to. We all have. It's all about making the commanders rich. Children die so the commanders can buy bigger houses."

"Your words truly are dangerous. I didn't believe it when Viteri said you spewed venom and had to be advanced to keep you under control. But now I hear it for myself." The City Chief raises her pistol and brings it close to my forehead. "Hmmm, change of plans." She nods to a guard. "Bring me Minka and Drabon Orwan."

Did I hear right? That's Ma and Da! They're here! I can't believe I'm going to see them again. I'm going to give Ma the biggest hug ever, if I can get away from the guards. *Preedithantha, keep me and my parents safe.* We'll take off in my ship and fly to Global Command, rescue my squad and go...somewhere. Anywhere.

Preedithantha will assure your freedom by assisting our Piltrak brothers once they arrive. The enemy will be eliminated.

I tug and twist my arms, but I'm held firmly. "No! Don't do that!"

The City Chief squints. "Don't do what?"

I ignore her. *Preedithantha, listen. Innocent people will get killed if the Piltrak come. I just want to take my parents away from here.*

Preedithantha cannot otherwise assure your safety. Preedithantha must protect Preedithantha. You are one with Preedithantha.

"I know that!" I shout.

The City Chief stares at me. "What are you talking about? You're delusional."

"I wasn't talking to..."

Piltrak brothers will destroy all cities and outliers.

No, no, no. Is my only choice to let the Piltrak kill everyone in sight? Enough people have died already, I can't let anyone else become a victim of this war. *Preedithantha, leave me, I'll do this on my own.*

Jewel will be vaporized like Global Command was. At least my squad and Jarmer are safe. They'll have a chance to rebuild their lives and I'll be nothing but a bad memory. If only I could still expose the deceit to the world. But how can I do that? I need help. *Wait, I changed my mind, Preedithantha! Don't leave!*

"Dax!" It's Ma!

I turn my head and see Ma and Da in shackles, being led toward me. Ma's crying, but also smiling. I find myself smiling, too.

"Ma! I'm so sorry. I didn't mean to escape." I don't care that I'm crying. It doesn't matter anymore. We're together again. Whatever comes next won't be so bad now that I have my family back.

Ma and Da are shoved to the ground next to me. If only I had a weapon, I'd make sure nobody ever hurt my parents again. Ma's face is drenched in tears, but she's still beautiful.

"Oh, sweetie, don't apologize for anything. When they said you escaped, I knew you must have had a good reason. Are those bruises on your face? Did they hurt you?" Ma wipes her cheek on her shoulder.

I glare at the City Chief. "Yes, Ma, they did hurt me, but bruises heal. There's another pain that won't heal though. They've hurt my heart and taken away all of my trust and faith in the leaders of the world."

"Enough!" The City Chief presses her pistol to my forehead. "Your entire traitorous family will die together. There's no point in prolonging the inevitable and wasting resources keeping your family alive. A romantic end to a tragic tale, no?"

A burst of ground-rumbling pulses strike the building so violently that the guards and the City Chief lose their footing and stumble. This is my chance! I spring to my feet, wrestle the laser pistol from the City Chief and point it at her. She falls to her knees and glares at me as a shadow drifts over us. I look up; it's a fighter passing overhead, but it's one of ours! It settles into a hover and the ladder extends. What now?

I keep the pistol trained on the City Chief, my finger on the trigger button, ready to do whatever I have to. One person descends from the fighter and my breath freezes in my throat.

"Hi, Orwan," Tablon says as he sprints to me. "Need a ride?"

Chapter Twenty-Six

I've never been so excited to see someone who hates me. But at this point, anyone who's not threatening me with death is my friend.

Tablon takes the pistol from my hand, aims it at the City Chief, and smirks. "I don't know how I know this, but I sort of knew you needed rescuing and had the coordinates in my head. Jarmer's not happy with me because I told him he had to bring me here at 2% lightspeed."

Daxella Rose, we listened to your true desire and brought your friends instead of the Piltrak, but be warned, the Piltrak are near.

Thank you, Preedithantha. A crackling sound makes me look over at the smoldering building. "Tablon, I think you took out Jewel's weapons."

"That was the plan." Tablon is still smirking. "I kind of like being a rebel. It really wasn't me though, a mechanic from the training camp told us what to do."

Mechanic? Trab! "Well, it was you who fired at the weapons, Tablon. Ma, Da, this is Tablon Neemiss, Senior Lead Recruit."

They stand and give him a nod. The City Chief, however, is not at all pleased and scowls at him.

She snorts and gets up, brushing grass from her suit. "You will never get away with this. The Piltrak are coming, you said that yourself. They'll kill us all."

"Dax?" Ma's looking up. "What's that?"

Something is blocking out the sun. "Unlock their shackles!" I yell at the guards. It's not one single thing blocking the sun, but lots and lots of things. "Tablon, those are Piltrak ships. We have to get out of here."

Jarmer climbs out of the ship and runs over to me. "Get in your fighter, Dax! Your Piltrak friend said he can't protect us if we're still on Earth. Tab and I got away before Commander Viteri's battalions arrived. We have to launch now!"

"Jarmer's right," Tablon agrees. "If we can get out of the atmosphere, we're safe. Once Commander Viteri knows we're here, he'll send a battalion our way for sure."

"I can't go." I hug Ma. "We can't all fit in two fighters. There's not enough oxygen and I'm sure not leaving anyone behind." *Preedithantha, can you continue to protect all of us?*

Preedithantha can, at great risk to you.

What does that mean? What risk?

The City Chief lunges at me, but I'm too quick and jump aside. She shakes her head. "Release me and I'll allow you to come to the bunker. It's impenetrable. Not even the Piltrak bastards can get through. Our battalions will finish this war once and for all."

I glance at Jarmer and Tablon. What were they thinking? They came to save me, yet they don't have a plan to stop the war. And the City Chief has every intention of still fighting the Piltrak. So what was this all about if we just run away and the wars continue? I'm not going to let anyone shoot down the Piltrak. Prentak is my friend and I trust him when he says his people don't want to fight. This war has to end, and not by both sides obliterating one another.

"You're the City Chief, not a leader in the Global Forces. What makes you think you can order me around? And what makes you think you have the right to kill an alien species? You have no idea what the Piltrak are like. But I do."

"I knew you were a traitor!" she yells.

Tablon grabs a key from the guard and unshackles Ma and Da, then steps in between the City Chief and me. "Dax, we have to go." He points to the sky. "Right now."

The Piltrak ships have to be less than twenty or thirty kilometers away and the ones in the front of the triangular formation are glowing red. I'm sure that means they're ready to fire. "Tablon, take my parents to my ship." I glare at the City Chief. "If a traitor tries to stop senseless killing, then yes, I'm a traitor."

Tablon hesitates. "You just said there's not enough oxygen."

"I know, but I don't have a choice, do I?" Even if I manage to keep Ma and Da alive, what about everyone else from my outlier? And the other outliers. The Piltrak are prepared to kill everyone. My head's throbbing. I don't know what to do. I hate the idea of running away like a coward, especially since I'm sure that's exactly what Viteri expects from me. That's what everyone expects.

I'm done running.

I grab the pistol from Tablon and aim it at the City Chief while I wait for Ma and Da to get inside my ship. "Tablon, go with Jarmer."

He stares at me for a moment. "You're getting bossy, smudge."

With a slight smirk, he rushes to Jarmer and they get into their ship. I walk backward to my ladder. I only need a few seconds to get up the ladder, so I fire a couple of laser bursts at the ground in front of the City Chief. She yelps and runs toward the smoldering building with her guards close behind. That gives me time and I rush into my ship.

Ma is standing near the pilot's seat, wringing her hands. "Dax, Da and I agreed that we'll stay behind so you can escape."

"No." I grab my helmet and as soon as the synap-trodes activate, I close the hatch and activate the heads-up display. "As long as we don't go above about 3,800 meters, we won't need oxygen. That's the altitude I'll hold. We'll make it."

Now Da speaks up, "But that boy said we have to leave Earth. Dax, I won't risk your life." He takes my hand. "Let your mother and me out. I'm your da and I'm telling you to leave us and get off this planet before it's too late."

I squeeze his hand. "That's not going to happen. Da, I'm not only your daughter, I'm a soldier, and I've lived more in these past few days than I would have in a year at home. I'll think of something, but for now, we have to launch."

If I need to, I'll have the Preedithantha put Ma and Da in the veil.

He continues, "Do you even know how to fly?"

"I sure do. Ma, sit in the co-pilot's seat, and Da, sit on the floor, but hold onto something because the ship goes very fast, straight up."

After I'm in my seat and have my restraints on, I wait until Ma is secured and Da is seated next to her with his arms looped around the armrests. In a flash, Jarmer launches and heads in the opposite direction to the Piltrak fleet.

I follow him but keep my eyes on Ma and Da. They're terrified, but they're safe. I saved my parents and it feels good. Now I have to get to my squad.

From an altitude of 3,500 meters, I can see the destruction below. Fires, explosions, and air-to-air combat between the Piltrak fighters and Earth's larger battleships. Wait, that's not right. Prentak said he was going to destroy Earth before our battalions had the chance to attack. That didn't happen. So where is Prentak and what went wrong?

"Young lady, is that you?" Trab says in a raspy voice.

"Trab! Yes, it's me. I found my parents and have them with me. What's going on? Why is there a battle? The Piltrak fleet was…I mean, I thought they had the advantage."

He coughs. "Not quite. They did, but…" He coughs again. "The Piltrak leader refused to attack any other target after he destroyed Global Command. He said he wanted to speak to the head of Global Forces. I intercepted his global communication." There's a pause. "It took a while to translate his language with some old diplomatic programs I had, but when I did, he said he would negotiate a mutual surrender, in the name of Dax, the only human he's ever trusted."

Me? "Trab, where is he? What happened?" My heart's thumping. "Where's Prentak?"

Trab has a fit of coughing. "Young lady, I made an awful mistake. I sent a message to Commander Viteri conveying the Piltrak's translation and when Viteri arrived, he said he was open to negotiation. But as soon as your Piltrak landed, Viteri ordered…" More coughing. "Dax, your friend was captured and the Piltrak opened fire on the training camp. There's not much left."

"Trab, are you all right? I'm coming there to get you. Is Prentak okay?"

"No, don't come! I'll be fine, don't you worry about me. You *can't* come here, Dax. Viteri survived the attack. He's alive and still has his lethal directive on you, a shoot-on-sight directive, and he's holding the Piltrak hostage."

"So what do I do? Prentak won't let his people surrender." The thought of Prentak as a hostage makes me sick. Especially because he was trying to do what *I* wanted. I'm sure Viteri is torturing him. The only logical thing for me to do is find a solution to make up for all the trouble I've created. "Trab, can you punch in the coordinates to the training camp?"

"Why? What good...you can't come here, young lady. Viteri's here, using that Piltrak as bait to flush you out. You'll fly right into an ambush."

I glance at Ma and Da. They're staring at me, probably wondering who I'm talking to. I can't risk getting them hurt or captured again. If only I could put them somewhere safe, but where? The whole planet's under attack.

"Dax, honey," Ma says, reaching out and taking my hand. "Do whatever you have to do. Don't worry about us. The City Chief was going to execute us anyway. I'd rather die here with you than down there."

"That's brave of you, Ma, but you're not going to die. Neither am I. I'll think of some...wait. Our outlier was evacuated. There's no reason for the Piltrak to attack it now." I smile and squeeze her hand. "You can go home."

Da speaks up, "And what about you? You're coming, too, right?"

As much as I'd love to go home and pretend none of this was happening, I can't. I have my squad to think of and a war to win. "I'll be home as soon as I can. But I have some business to take care of first."

After asking Trab to put in the coordinates for Village 77 and giving him our address, I lean back as my fighter heads off, away from the Piltrak fleet. Behind me is Jewel, but it's no longer a beautiful gem in the center of our outliers, but a charred mass of broken buildings. It's strange to think that all my life I'd been so anxious to go to the city, and now that's the last place I want to be. Below my ship, the landscape turns brown and dry, and I couldn't be happier. My little outlier is just ahead and that desolate, dead place is right where I want to be. It's where I belong.

Chapter Twenty-Seven

Back on my front lawn again, and after a check of the airspace around me, I open the hatch. Thankfully there aren't any ships, ours or Piltrak, anywhere in sight. Once Ma and Da are safely inside the house, I can race off to the training camp. I still have no idea what to do when I get there, but something will come to me, it has to. It's tempting to ask the Preedithantha for help, but Prentak's warning keeps echoing in my head.

With my restraints off, I go to the hatch. "Okay, hurry up and get inside and stay there. I'll come back as soon as I can. I love you both so much."

"Sweetie," Ma says with tears clouding her eyes. "Stay with us. We'll manage somehow. Once this war is over, things will return to normal and we'll all be together forever."

What does she mean by *normal*? There is no normal anymore and I doubt there ever will be. Everything's changed. I've changed. "Ma, I can't do what I have to do unless I know you and Da will be all right. Lock all of the doors. I'll be back before you know it."

Ma nods and takes off her restraints while Da gets up and comes to me. "Dax, are you sure you know what you're doing? You threatened the City Chief. She's probably put a catch-and-kill on you."

"Da, I'm responsible for leading the Piltraks to Earth and I already have a lethal directive on me from Commander Viteri. It was stupid of me to think Earth would ever negotiate. Now I have to find my squad and get them to safety, rescue the Piltrak fleet commander and end this war before it's too late. I don't care what the City Chief thinks she can do to me. She was going to kill you and Ma just because I'm a non-conforming AFGF recruit. She scattered our outlier's population and doesn't care about anyone but herself. I bet you anything she makes money from the wars, too." I motion to the ladder. "Go into the house and don't worry about me. I have friends now.

Good friends. I'm not alone anymore. And I promise you, I'll make sure every single person on this planet knows the truth."

With a shake of his head, Da objects, "I'm your da. I'm supposed to keep *you* safe, not the other way around. I feel so helpless."

I hug him. "You kept me safe my whole life. Now it's my turn to take it from here."

He flashes a brief smile and winks. "All right, but you'd better not get in any trouble or I'll never hear the end of it from your ma."

Ma grabs me and hugs me tightly. "I love you, sweetie. Be careful. Promise me you won't get yourself killed."

I force a smile. "I promise."

She lets go and gives me a nod, then climbs down the ladder, followed by Da. I poke my head through the hatch and wait until they're both inside before I rush back to my seat, squeeze on my helmet and fasten the restraints. Within a few seconds, I'm airborne. It takes a few tries before Trab answers and even though he sounds weaker than ever, he plugs in the coordinates for our training camp. After I go there and rescue Prentak and Trab, I'll swoop into what remains of Global Command and get my squad. Deep down, the impossibility of the situation is churning, but that line of thinking has to stay buried.

"Dax? Where the hell are you?" Tablon shouts. "I don't see you anywhere."

Amazing! Tablon and Jarmer haven't been shot down. "I'm okay, where are you? Did you make it through the atmosphere?"

Now Jarmer responds, "Of course not. We went to my outlier and then Tablon's and told our families to stay inside. Dax, I'm not leaving until I have revenge for my sister. Viteri's alive and fighting off the Piltrak at the camp. We're heading to Global Command, but I'm staying in the stratosphere so the Piltrak won't get me. Did you escape the planet?"

At least our families are relatively safe, unless the Piltrak open fire on people's houses. "Jarmer, I'm not running away. I have to make a slight detour and then I'll meet up with you at Global Command." My ship punches through a layer of clouds and bursts into the bluest sky. I'll level off in the stratosphere, too.

"What detour," Tablon asks, sounding suspicious.

"Viteri is holding Prentak hostage." My ship levels off and cruises across the ocean toward the Mid-World continent.

Jarmer yells, "You are *not* going to the camp! Dax, I'll give you my coordinates. Come to me and we'll go together to Global Com..."

"No! Prentak put his trust in me. I can't leave him there. He's got a good heart, Jarmer, and wouldn't hurt anyone if he wasn't forced into it. This is something I have to do for him." I'm about to disconnect transmission but hesitate for a moment. "Get my squad and take them away from Earth."

"Hold on, Dax," Tablon says. "You're being stupid."

I hear Jarmer mumbling and grumbling. "Tablon's right, you're not thinking. You're just a girl, Dax, and you don't know anything about flying into a battle zone.

Pain shoots through my jaw from grinding my teeth so hard. "Are you serious? You don't think I'm qualified? Listen to me, *flyboy*, I have alien creatures in my brain, I'm friends with the Piltrak fleet commander and I learned to fly a fighter with only a couple of lessons. Not to mention the fact that I have a lethal directive on me and I've managed to stay alive! You know what, *boys*, I am qualified and I'd appreciate it if you'd stop saying I'm not!"

I press the black star-shaped button once and accelerate to 1% lightspeed. To hell with them and to hell with Viteri. I'm not a stupid girl or a worthless smudge. Sure I'm marked for death and flying a stolen fighter ship on a mission to save the entire world, and the Piltrak species, but I can do it. And then there's the Katarga. I'll set them free while I'm at it. I'll accomplish all of that, or die trying.

"Dax!" Jarmer shouts. "Dax, what are you going to do? Give me your coordinates."

"I don't need you, Jarmer. I'll get Trab and Prentak on my own." The heads-up display says I'm almost over the training camp, but still high in the stratosphere. I'll have to descend soon, probably right into the fighting. That's a terrifying thought, yet it's not terror I'm feeling, but excitement. The very idea of being in a real fight makes my heart race, in a good way, and a rush of adrenaline is spiking through my veins. Maybe I am a soldier after all.

Jarmer continues, "I'm sorry for treating you...like a...I don't know. It's just that I'm...worried about you. Look, I want to come with you. Two fighters are better than one. Tab agrees with me. Trab's my friend, too, and

I don't want him to die. He was hit during the battle and he's in bad shape, Dax. I'll change my heading and meet you at camp. Okay?"

Should I trust him? "Just go and get my squad. I can handle Viteri."

"Smudge!" Tablon blurts. "We're coming whether you say we can or not. You'll get killed by yourself. What will that prove?"

As much as I don't want to admit it, Tablon's got a point. Taking on Viteri and whatever's left of his battalion by myself is reckless. I can't be reckless at this point. "Fine. I'm in the stratosphere over the camp now and I'll begin my descent in five minutes. And don't call me smudge."

I hear Tablon snicker a bit. "No problem, *Dax*."

Jarmer lets out a whoop. "The fight's on! I'll drop to the troposphere and come in low and fast. Dax, don't open fire unless fired upon."

"I know, I know." I use the synap-trodes to set a descent pattern. "Jarmer, how do I use the priz-spec weapon?"

"Easy. When you're engaged in battle, you use the control stick to fire the priz-spec weapons and the synap-trodes to guide the ship. When you order the ship into battle mode, a green button on the control stick will pop up where your thumb will be. Press it once to fire, hold it down to fire multiple pulses. If it goes red, wait until it recharges and turns green again. Got it?"

"Ah, sure." It's actually not too difficult. "Jarmer, don't you dare shoot at the Piltrak ships. If we don't shoot at them, they won't shoot at us."

"Is that true?" Tablon asks.

I have no idea if it's true. "Of course it is. Don't fire on them."

Tablon clears his throat. "Um, smu...Dax, what's your final plan here?"

Final plan? Is he kidding? I don't even have a starting plan. Although, if I turn the tables and capture Viteri, perhaps whoever remains in charge of Global Command will finally listen to me. With Prentak freed and Viteri my prisoner, I might have the best leverage ever.

"I'll let you know when I work it out."

Chapter Twenty-Eight

When I finally tell Jarmer and Tablon about how I'm going to capture Viteri and free Prentak, they both make it known that they think my plan isn't a plan at all, but they agree to stand with me. I stay in the stratosphere while Jarmer gets into position.

"Dax!" It's Jarmer and he sounds excited. "I dropped down into the troposphere over the equatorial area of Mid-World. It's crazy down here. I evaded several of our fighters and *five* Piltrak ships and didn't even take a single hit. Tab almost vomited when I had to spiral in a dive!"

"Shut up, flyboy!" Tablon shouts.

Poor Tablon. I really shouldn't feel sorry for him after the way he treated me at training camp, but I can't help it. He's changed, at least I think he has. Could it be that he understands me a bit better because of how Lenora treated him?

"Dax, are you there?" Jarmer asks.

Damn, I let myself get distracted. "Yeah, I'm here. Jarmer, do you know if there's a way to coordinate our trajectories so we arrive at the same time?"

There's a pause and then Jarmer shouts, "I'm under attack and lost my synap-trodes! I'm switching to manual."

He's been hit? If only he hadn't insisted on coming with me.

"Get back into the stratosphere, Jarmer. You won't stand a chance against the Piltrak or the battalion."

"I can hold my own, Dax." He sounds angry. "If I can shake these Piltrak black holes, I'll program in a dual-approach pattern for both of us." He grunts. "Tab, we've got a Piltrak on our tail and I can't let go of the control stick. I need you to press the black star-shaped button once. Now!"

He wants to jump to 1% lightspeed during a battle, which means he's desperate. He needs help. Thankfully, my synap-trodes are working, so I can descend to the troposphere. "I'm coming, Jarmer. Program in your coordinates."

After a moment, he says, "Done. But be careful, it's bad here, Dax."

My ship turns sharply to starboard and dives so fast that I'm pushed into my seat and can't move, not my head or my arms, and it feels like my heart is being crushed inside my chest. *I don't want to crash!* Within a few seconds, I see brilliant flashes all around me and flinch as two Piltrak ships zoom by, followed by one of our fighters. I'm in the middle of the battle, but still heading straight for the ground.

"Dax, pull out of the dive!" Jarmer shouts. "Disengage the synap-trodes and go hands-on. You can disable the synap-trodes in an active firefight. Only use them when you shoot the priz-spec."

I've never used the control stick to maneuver, he never showed me how. Why didn't he tell me this before? If I don't do something soon, I really will be a smudge. "I'll try." After concentrating on turning off the synap-trodes, my ship suddenly flips and rolls out of control. "Jarmer!"

Jarmer responds right away, "Grab the control stick and ease it forward, then press the two green buttons above your horizon on the heads-up. That'll level you off."

I manage to do what he says, although without the synap-trodes, it's hard to manually press the green buttons. Sure enough, my ship's under my control. "Thanks. I wish you'd explained how to do that before." My fingers hurt from gripping the control stick too tightly. I have to loosen my grip so I can make small corrections instead of stiff, jerky movements. Before long, I've got the hang of it and I'm flying my ship without the synap-trodes. It's amazing to bank and roll, avoiding the other ships that either haven't noticed me or don't care because they're focused on the fight. I don't see Jarmer anywhere.

"Jarmer, where are you?"

"I'm behind you. I'll put my ship in mimic-mode. Everything I do, you'll do. It's a tactical maneuver that casts a shadow over your ship on tracking devices so you'll be practically invisible and all they'll see is my ship, but I'm controlling your ship as well."

"I don't understand." Now I wish I'd learned tactics and how these ships really work.

He groans. "If a ship is damaged during a battle, a rescue ship goes into mimic-mode and escorts it back to base. The enemy trackers see only one ship and can't see the damaged one. It doesn't work for long because they realize pretty quick that the damaged ship is in a projected shadow. Damaged ships are easy targets, so we try to hide them from the enemy. Get it?"

"Yeah." In only a few seconds, the control stick freezes in place and I can't budge it no matter how hard I try. "Jarmer?"

"I've got your ship, Dax, don't worry. This only works for a few minutes, but I'll guide us both through the battle zone and straight to the training camp. I'm going to have to disengage mimic when we're about ten kilometers from the target landing area. Can you handle it on your own?"

Is he being condescending or concerned? Of course I can handle my ship. I flew to the moon, to the transport, to Jewel, and to my outlier, and other than taking a shot from the Katarga, I managed to stay alive, all by myself without help from any flyboys. "Yes, Jarmer, I can handle it. In fact, if you want to disengage mimic right now, I'll be fine. I'm a big girl."

I hear snickering and know it's Tablon. Through his laughter, he manages to talk. "Yeah, Jarmer, she's a better flyboy than you are! You're nobody's smudge, are you, Dax? Remind me never to cross you again."

I don't understand boys at all. One minute they're vicious and hateful and the next supportive and kind. I remember when Manti and I would talk during breaks at school and she'd tell me how boys thought girls were crazy. Well, I've come to the conclusion that it's the boys who are crazy.

"Shut up, Tab." Jarmer's mad. "I didn't mean to underestimate you, Dax. I get it, you're as strong as any boy and can fly a fighter, but you can still get shot down. Being a good pilot doesn't make you invincible. Okay? Be careful or I'll never forgive myself."

What does he think, I *won't* be careful? "Don't worry about me." All I can do now is hand my ship over to Jarmer and hope he doesn't get us both shot down. I'd rather be in control of my own ship, but he *is* more experienced.

Exploding ships, laser bursts, and Jarmer's priz-spec pulses are everywhere around me. The priz-spec emits a colorful rainbow of energy that quickly turns bright white. Anything hit by a blast disintegrates. Miraculously, nothing hits my fighter. Jarmer's an amazing pilot and has managed to keep us both out of harm's way. As I'm descending, I close my eyes to block out the horror of what's happening. Humans and aliens are dying right before my eyes. If only the people on the ground could see for themselves how awful, and real, war is, maybe they'd listen to reason and end it.

I open my eyes. There might be something I can do, something that's stuck in my head that I must have seen when I used the cerebral interpreter. I somehow learned a lot from using it, like how the propulsion packs regenerate oxygen. I guess it's a learning tool of sorts. If I'm remembering correctly, the fighters have a type of image capture device to use for future training. Problem is, I don't know how to use it.

"Jarmer, I'm going to try something." I re-engage the synap-trodes, wrap my fingers around the control stick again and bring up my ship's operations manual on the heads-up.

"Dax, what are you doing! You separated from me," Jarmer yells frantically. "Dax!"

I don't have time to deal with his hysterics. "Keep on your heading, Jarmer. I'll only be a minute."

After scrolling through a few pages, I find what I'm looking for, instructions on how to use the image capture. It's easy. Just press a hexagonal blue button in the center of the display and aim my ship where I want to record. No problem. I tighten my grip on the control stick and press the button. A small image showing the scene in front of me pops up on my display.

"Trab, are you there? Trab, can you hear me?" *Please be there.*

"Is...that you, young lady?" His voice is faint and weak.

"Yes, it's me. Trab, Jarmer and I are coming for you, but right now I'm using the image capture and need to broadcast it to every household and personal broadcast viewing system on the planet, as well as the recruitment broadcast projections in the outliers. How do I do that?"

He groans and gasps, but answers, "Give me...a second."

I shouldn't ask him to do anything, he's injured. "Trab, never mind, take care of yourself. I'll figure something out."

"Too late, it's done. Every broadcast receiver on Earth will get your image feed. No idea who might be watching or even if the receivers are still operational, but it's done. If you, ugh, want sound, press the blue button on your control stick and speak. Good...luck, young lady."

A bright flash catches my eye; a large Earth fighter is heading straight for me with the sun at its back. I shove the stick forward and to starboard, diving and rolling to avoid a collision, but I'm not fast enough and my ship shudders as a pulse slams into my fuselage. If the damage is bad enough, I'll crash and nobody will know why I'm sending the images of the battle. It's hard to control the ship and it keeps descending even though I'm accelerating and trying to gain altitude.

I have to add my voice to the feed before it's too late. I move my thumb into position on the blue button and take a breath. "People of Earth, this is Daxella Rose Orwan. I'm a recruit in the Global Forces and what you're seeing is the result of a supermassive deception by Global Command, the World Military Leadership, and the Council of Commanders."

Another shot hits my ship and I'm sent into a spin. I thought the Preedithantha were going to keep me safe. *Preedithantha!* As I'm spiraling down, I see at least three or four more of our fighters coming right for me. Can't they tell I'm not the enemy? My ship looks nothing like a Piltrak fighter. I manage to pull out of the spin, but my ship's shaking and it feels like it's about to break into a million pieces.

This might be my last chance. I press the blue button again and continue, "These wars are created by the commanders to generate money. The more wars, the more kids they need, which means more uniforms, weapons, and ships." Another hit to my ship's nose causes sparks and small fires around the cockpit. At least I'll die doing the right thing. "I hope you can see how our own people are trying to bring me down to shut me up. Human life is as unimportant as alien life to these people. They make it impossible for families to survive unless they produce more and more recruits to keep these wars going to generate money. The death toll is so high because they don't want us to survive. We die and they destroy our uniforms and weapons so the factories have to make more. Your children are dying to make the commanders rich!"

"Recruit Orwan, I've been waiting for this moment." It's Viteri. "I've got you in my sights."

I instantly feel cold and can't breathe. My hands are shaking and sweat is dripping into my eyes. He's here, in one of the fighters. I feel sick.

He continues, "I disconnected your transmissions. I'm going to personally put a priz-spec pulse through the center of your ship and scatter your miserable body into the atmosphere. I should have ended you when I had the chance at training camp. I knew you were toxic."

What am I going to do? Everything's unraveling and my mind's completely blank. I want to be home in my bed with Ma singing me a song and tucking me in. I want to eat my birthday cake and have a stupid job and go back to how things were before I was advanced. But I can't, that's all in the past. I'm here, now, about to die at the hands of Viteri. If he kills me, the wars will continue and more kids and aliens will die. It could even get worse because Prentak is a prisoner. His people will come to Earth with everything they have.

I take a deep breath and focus. Out of the corner of my eye, I see the Jurale translator on the floor near the co-pilot's seat. It's within reach and I stretch to grab it. *Preedithantha, I need help.* "Commander Viteri, you're nothing but a greedy black hole without a conscience. You intimidate everyone into believing you're stronger than them. But I see you for what you are."

"Really? And what do you think I am? Cancel that, Orwan. I don't care. I'm locked onto your ship. You have five seconds, you worthless *smudge*."

Preedithantha, where are you? I don't want to die! Prentak's voice echoes in my memory: *what the translator gives, it can also take away.*

"Three, two..."

A blinding, searing red light fills the cockpit and a huge explosion pushes me hard against the seat. Everything is muffled and even with my eyes shut, the light stings. Am I dead? Is this what it's like to die? Did Viteri win yet again?

There are sparks everywhere, but with limited oxygen in the cockpit, there aren't any fires. I have to find out where the ship was hit and assess any damage. The good thing is that I'm heading away from the moon and hopefully out of range of the Katarga. The damage doesn't seem too bad, a few charred places on the walls, and a couple of broken instruments. Thankfully the heads-up display is still working.

The ship's mine again, so where do I go? If Trab lied to me and programmed in the lunar coordinates, then he'll gain control again and turn my ship around. But I have no idea how to stop him or how to reprogram new coordinates

Chapter Twenty-Nine

The light dies down and I open my eyes, expecting to be greeted by Manti and my other dead friends, but instead, I'm still in my ship...alive. The view outside my front window is horrifying. Pieces of burning aircraft are scattered in the air, falling in broken chunks all around me. My ship's tumbling slowly, like it's a controlled descent. What's happening?

Preedithantha are here to assist you. Our Piltrak brothers believe you have praltah, therefore, we will now assist when needed regardless of whether you ask or not.

Praltah? A drive to do what's right? But I don't know what's right or wrong anymore. "Are you controlling my ship? And...was that Viteri's ship that was destroyed?" As much as I hate him, I don't want him dead. I want him to account for everything he's done.

Affirmative on both counts.

I rip the helmet off my head. Viteri's dead. How can that be the right thing? "But I thought you wanted peace. I didn't want you to kill anyone."

You required help. You did not wish to die. We helped. The attacking ship was ready to fire a powerful weapon. With no possible escape, destruction of the aggressor was necessary. We activated and enhanced your prismatic-spectrum weapon.

So basically, I shot down a commander of the Global Forces. That's not what I wanted. Or was it? I knew the consequences. What the translator gives, it can also take away. It can protect *or* destroy. I used it to connect to the Preedithantha and didn't think about what that meant as long as I survived. Why did I do that? And what about Jarmer and Tablon?

Preedithantha will continue to protect your friends. Your enemies, however, are our enemies.

"Wait. What do you mean by that? You're going to kill my people? You can't do that! Stop!" I'm shouting, even though I know they can read my thoughts. It just feels good to scream.

You accepted us.

"Yes, I did, and I'll have to live with that for the rest of my life." My ship drifts down to the center of my training camp and settles softly a few meters above the ground. Immediately, recruits and what I assume to be more seasoned soldiers judging by the way they seem to be bossing the recruits around, rush out and surround my ship.

"Preedithantha, do *not* hurt these people!" I shout again.

They hold our Piltrak brother.

"I know. I'm here to set him free. Give me a chance. Please." And I need to find Trab. "Where are my friends, the boys in the other ship? Where are they?"

Within the veil. You have five Earth minutes and then we will destroy all.

Five minutes? Thank goodness Jarmer and Tablon are safe. Okay, fine, I can do it by myself. I hold onto the translator and rub my thumb along the groove until a few sparks shoot out. "Can I control Bliss with the translator?"

Preedithantha control Bliss. We can allow Bliss to flow through the translator at your request.

That's all I need to know. I open the hatch, translator in hand, and peer outside. My ship is covered with the purple cloud of the veil. It's obviously not invisible though because there must be a hundred laser guns pointed at my ship. One rung at a time, I descend the ladder and step away from the ship, but stay within the cloud.

"You there! Throw down that weapon and drop to your knees!" shouts a tall man who I recognize as the commander I saw with Viteri on the transport. "We will open fire if you do not comply."

As if I'd comply. "Bring me Prentak, the Piltrak prisoner, and Trab, the mechanic and I'll leave." Five soldiers take up positions beside the commander, each with a really big laser gun aimed right at me.

I shake my head a little to keep the sweat out of my eyes and continue to make sparks shoot out of the translator. The commander and his soldiers don't move, although I see one soldier twitch his finger. He's going to shoot me.

The commander speaks again, "Last chance, recruit. I have orders to comply with Commander Viteri's lethal directive if you do not surrender."

Whether I surrender or not, he'll still kill me. That's what a lethal directive is; shoot on sight. There's no negotiating or surrender. I'm amazed he hasn't already shot me. "Bring me Prentak and Trab." I extend my arm and make the translator spark more. "This is a Jurale weapon and I will use it if *you* don't surrender to *me*."

The commander squints in the sunlight. "Where did you get that?"

"Off your level on the transport. And Commander Viteri is in no position to give orders any more." I shouldn't have said that. Damn my mouth.

"What have you done to him?" The commander motions for his soldiers to lower their guns. "Where is he? Did you hand him over to the Piltrak?"

I have to choose my words carefully. "I won't repeat myself again." I might as well use the Bliss and make them do what I want.

The Preedithantha speak to me: *Exercise caution when using Bliss. You do not control Bliss or its effects.*

Great, a warning without explanation. I should be used to that by now. So what do I do? The commander isn't going to give me Prentak or Trab and I'm not leaving without them. And, I'm running out of time.

Tap your thumb four times in the center of the groove.

Why? What'll that do?

Tap your thumb...

Fine! I do it and in an instant, the ground shakes and rolls, and a tremendous boom echoes everywhere. I almost lose my footing, but manage to stay upright.

Preedithantha, what was that?

The concentrated energy of the Preedithantha. The Earth's crust beneath your feet will disintegrate in one Earth minute unless our Piltrak brother is brought to us. We will repair the damage at that time. However, if he is not delivered, the crust will continue to degrade. This message has been conveyed to all humans within a fifty-meter radius.

My whole body trembles and I look at the ground. There are spidery cracks in the soil going in every direction. This isn't a bluff, the Preedithantha are serious.

I shout to the commander, "Bring me Prentak and Trab!"

He's pale. "You've sided with the enemy and have betrayed your people." He turns to his soldiers. "Bring the Piltrak and find that mechanic." He glares at me. "Traitor."

I can't breathe, I'm so scared, but it worked. I'm getting Trab and Prentak. The only way to get anyone to listen to me now is if I clear my name. But how can I do that? Viteri is dead and I've been labeled a traitor.

Before long, Prentak is brought out, shackled and bruised. The shackles are taken off and he's given a shove toward me. He stops, bends, and looks at the ground. A moment later, Trab is transported out on a hover-stretcher. He looks bad, with cuts and scratches all over him, and his head and left arm are bandaged.

"Prentak," I call. "Get into the ship."

He straightens, gives me a nod, but instead of coming to the ship, he walks over to Trab. "I will help this man first." He places his hands over Trab's chest and casts a red veil that covers the stretcher completely.

The medic who brought out the stretcher runs away and doesn't look back. After only a few seconds, the veil withdraws and Trab sits up with a confused expression.

He sees me and smiles. "Dax?" He climbs off the stretcher with help from Prentak. "Young lady, what's going on?"

I keep my eyes on the commander. "I'll explain later, Trab, but for now, get into the ship. Quickly. We don't have much time."

Prentak points to the ground. "Indeed we do not have much time."

With a shrug, Trab jogs to the ladder and climbs into the ship, followed by Prentak. I walk backward until I'm at the ladder. "Commander, please don't try to follow me or the Preedithantha might do something terrible."

"Preedi-what? You won't make it far," he spits the words. "You're as good as dead."

"What else is new," I mumble as I rush inside my fighter.

Prentak is in the co-pilot's seat and Trab is behind him, holding onto the back of the seat. Once I'm in my restraints, I initiate the launch procedure. The engine fires up and I activate the heads-up.

Trab runs his hands over his body and peels off the bandages. "How did all of my wounds get healed? Viteri had his men fire on me. He wanted to kill me and left me for dead. But now there's not a single wound." He leans over the seat and says to Prentak, "Was it you?"

Prentak nods. "Contrary to what your people think of us, we do not enjoy killing. We possess the ability to heal and would gladly help your people, even now, if only they would cease their hostilities toward us and the Katarga."

"Thank you, Prentak." I glance at Trab.

With a laugh, Trab shakes his head. "We never gave you Piltrak a chance, did we? I think it's too late now, though. But thank you for fixing me up." He turns to me. "What's the plan here, Dax? Any words of wisdom?"

"Yes. Hold on tight." I launch and the ship points straight up and accelerates toward the sky.

Trab groans and is pushed against the back wall of the cockpit. "A little more notice would be good next time, young lady. Don't go too high, I don't have oxygen."

"I know, I know. Don't worry, we're only going to Global Command. I don't need much altitude." *Preedithantha, did you repair the Earth's crust?*

"They did," Prentak answers. "Dax, you must stop requesting help from them. They also possess praltah and will not stop until they believe they have taken the necessary steps to make Earth no longer a hostile planet. Do you understand?"

I stop the ascent and level off the ship at 3,000 meters altitude. "I think so."

Trab clears his throat. "Hold on there, young lady. Global Command? Praltah? What are you two talking about?"

I make sure we're on course before answering. "Trab, a lot is going on right now and it'd take way too long to explain it all. Can you give me the benefit of the doubt here and just trust that I know what I'm doing?"

"Sure. But *do* you know what you're doing?" He raises an eyebrow.

"Of course I do." I turn away and concentrate on my heading.

Only forty kilometers away, time to start a quick descent. It's been an easy flight with the veil protecting me, but what if I do what Prentak says and stop using the Preedithantha? I won't have their protection anymore. That's not a very comforting thought, especially since everyone wants me dead. I don't think they'll give up looking for me. I need the Preedithantha.

The cockpit's quiet as we drop down over the jungle and speed a few meters above the tree canopies until we halt over the smoldering ruins of Global Command. Jarmer's ship is on the lawn and I see several recruits wandering around. We're still too high for me to see who they are, but I can definitely pick out Briett. He looks up and points.

I bring my ship down next to Jarmer's, shut down the engine, and take off my restraints. "So, Trab, what do you think? Do I know what I'm doing or not?"

He grins. "Well, as far as flying, you bet. But I meant long-range plans, young lady." He looks at me expectantly.

Prentak stands and glances at Trab, then me. "I am curious also to see how you expect to bring peace between your people and mine. So far, the situation has proved to be as expected. Humans are a violent, self-serving species without regard for others. As I said before, I cannot allow my people to suffer any more than they already have."

I watch Prentak for a moment and realize he's right, but not about all humans, only the ones who've been fooled by Global Command's propaganda. Well, I have to set the record straight, even if I die trying. I'm marked for death anyway, so what have I got to lose at this point? "Prentak, you can't lump everyone into the 'violent and self-serving' category. That's not fair. You said you'd give me a chance and that's all I need. A chance."

He shakes his head and traces his finger on his palm. "I gave you a chance. One hundred and five of my fleet have been destroyed. It is over, Dax. I have ordered the remainder of my advance fleet to enter the atmosphere and destroy all Earth vessels immediately, without hesitation or consideration. Once the vessels are eliminated, a complete cleansing of the planet will begin. All human lifeforms will likewise be eliminated. If you could have stopped your people from warring with us, there would be no need to do this. You and your friends will remain safe, concealed within the veil until you exit Earth's atmosphere. I give you that promise. But you must go now."

My head's spinning. "You can't...we can't...we only have two fighters. I can't drag my squad behind our ships again."

Trab speaks up, "Young lady, this is war. You're fighting a losing battle here. You've been given the opportunity to escape with your life. I'd take it."

How can I? Ma and Da are at home, not to mention all of the innocent people in every city and outlier on the planet. There's no way I can abandon them all and run away like a coward. "Trab, go with Jarmer and take my squad somewhere safe. I'm staying to fight. I have to try...something. Prentak, you said I have praltah, which means you know I can't leave."

Prentak goes to the hatch. "I know. But heed my warning, Dax. My fleet is on the way and will arrive within thirteen of your Earth minutes. I had truly hoped you could have convinced your people that we desire peace, not war. This saddens me, but I have to protect my people. If you choose to stay, I cannot guarantee your survival. The veil will only protect your ships for as long as it takes to leave the planet. If you do not launch, the veil will withdraw. I do thank you for rescuing me, but I cannot turn my back on my people. There is more at stake than you or I." He looks at me one last time and climbs down the ladder.

Thirteen minutes to come up with a solution. Through the front window, I see Jarmer and Tablon coming toward my ship. They were supposed to leave.

"Young lady? What's on your mind?" Trab nudges me. "I owe you my life, you know. Where I come from, that's a debt that has to be repaid. I've got your back, no matter what crazy idea you come up with." He flashes a smile. "I'm with you to the end."

I nudge him back. "Thanks, Trab. How's this for a crazy idea? I'm going to save the world."

Chapter Thirty

I have a million thoughts rushing around in my brain, crashing into one another and skittering away when I dismiss them as impossible. Not a single one is feasible and I'm quickly running out of ideas. While Trab sits in the pilot seat and fusses with the instruments and control stick, Tablon comes up the ladder into my ship.

He stares at Trab. "Hello, I'm Tablon Neemiss. I don't think we've met."

Standing, Trab gives Tablon a nod. "No, we haven't. But I know all about you, Senior Lead Neemiss." There's a sour expression on Trab's face.

I move in between them. "Trab, Tablon's helping me, remember? Anyone willing to help is a friend of mine."

With a shrug, Trab goes back to fiddling with the control stick. "Sure."

Tablon lowers his voice, "He doesn't like me much, does he?"

"Don't worry about him. He'll come around. I did." I point out the window. "How's everyone doing?"

"Well, your squad is fine, except for Big Pig who keeps whining that he's hungry and thinks he'll starve to death long before the Piltrak or the commanders kill us. Dax, Jarmer wants to launch and go back to his outlier to be with his family. He wants to tell them what happened to Jarmella. Truth is, it's not just him who wants to leave. We all want to go home until this blows over."

Does he really think this war will "blow over"? I thought he understood the severity of it, but maybe he doesn't. "Tablon, this is an all-or-nothing war. The Piltrak are coming to Earth in force now with one purpose; to destroy every living human. They won't spare the innocent people, including our families. If you go home, you'll die. My parents are lying low, just like everyone else. But that won't save them. I've come too far to let them die."

Tablon's jaw twitches. "Then what are you planning to do? You'll get us all killed. I don't see any wonderful solution you've come up with, so what are you going to do? Tell me. I came with you because I woke up once I learned what Lenora was up to. I didn't want her to kill you and I figured you'd know what to do. But you don't have any ideas, do you? All your great ideas about telling the world the truth were just fantasies. Nobody will listen to you. You know that and so do I. If this is the end of the world, then I want to be with my family when I die."

"Here now, Senior Lead Neemiss," Trab edges past me.

"Don't call me that! I'm not a Lead anymore. Rank is meaningless now. We're all traitors!" Tablon's face is red and he's sweaty.

I hold up my hands. "Okay, okay, enough. Calm down, Tablon. I do have an idea if you'll only listen to me. And trust me, I have no intention of getting splattered into a billion molecules." I face Trab. "Can we still access that broadcast footage I made of the battle?"

He thinks of a moment. "I think we can, it should be stored in your ship's files. Why?"

I put my hand on Tablon's shoulder to keep him under control. "Viteri shut down the transmission, right? Which means nobody can receive a signal."

Tablon nods. "Yeah, so?"

My mind's spinning. "Trab, can we create a huge projection, so big that anyone on the ground can see it? Maybe one projection over each of the cities?"

His brow's pinched. "I don't...you want to...it would require linking up with the computer tech in each city." He smiles and nods. "It might work. But I'm not so good with computer applications, much better with mechanics. I can fix almost any fighter, even if..."

"Trab! *I'm* good with computers." I watch Tablon. "Are you still with me, Senior Lead Neemiss? The people need leadership and that's what you're trained in."

He's shaking his head. "Even if you can project the broadcast, what good will it do? You're not thinking straight. By now, the commanders would have told everyone that you're the enemy and should be shot on sight. The people are so brainwashed by the commanders, and frightened of us, that they'll listen to whatever they say. Is this all you've got? If it is, it's a galactic waste."

A voice comes from the hatch, "It's a good plan." Jarmer climbs into the ship. "You don't give Dax enough credit, Tab. We *can* clone the projections and set them up over every city, globally. People will see them, but we have to do more. We need to record a declaration of what the wars are really about, and play it at the same time. Like you were trying to do, Dax, but on a larger scale. This time, we can put in a security protocol to prevent Viteri or anyone else tampering with it."

Tablon groans. "Okay, but a declaration from who? We can't get close enough to anyone at this point."

"It's *whom*, Tab." Jarmer smirks. "I guess Leads don't have to be very educated. Did you even graduate from school? I did, top of my class."

With his fists balled up, Tablon takes a step toward Jarmer. "I scored perfect on my exits, for your information. And I can snap your spine without breaking a sweat. Want to try me, flyboy?"

Jarmer raises an eyebrow. "I can outfly and outfight you. I'm ready when you are." He glances at me. "Stand back, Dax, so you don't get hurt." He turns back to Tablon. "I know how you and Lenora teamed up against Dax for no good reason. You won't ever get the chance to hurt her again."

Tablon puffs out his chest and runs his finger along the big scar on his face. "My Da gave me this with a laser-blade when he was teaching me to fight and I never flinched once. Not once."

So that's how Tablon got his scar. I would never have guessed that. What sort of family does he come from?

Jarmer turns his left wrist over where there's a jagged raised scar about four centimeters long. "See this scar? I got this on my first day of training when I hit a tree with my fighter. And I didn't flinch either."

"Hit a tree with your fighter? You've never even done hand-to-hand combat!" Tablon laughs. "When I go after you, you'll never see me coming."

Enough is enough. I shout, "Hey! Stop."

"You'll never have the chance to try, recruit." Jarmer lunges toward Tablon, who ducks out of the way.

What's wrong with them? Why do boys always want to fight? "Stop it! We've got less than ten minutes now before the Piltrak arrive in force. What are you thinking? This isn't the time to argue about who's better at what or whose scar is bigger. We've got work to do. Tablon, relax, and Jarmer, what do you mean about getting a declaration? I recorded a statement with the projections. Is that good enough?"

Jarmer's breathing hard. "Yes, I heard it. It's perfect. And for your information, Tab started it."

"Lies! You did, you pile of galactic dust." Tablon points at Jarmer. "Dax, if you listen to him, you'll get yourself killed. Look, we can all fly away from here and find a safe planet or moon to live on. It's the only way."

Trab shakes his head but goes back to the controls.

I look at both Tablon and Jarmer. "What's gotten into the two of you? You can go ahead and leave, but I'm staying. Trab and I will figure something out."

With a scowl, Jarmer glares at Tablon. "He can leave, but I'm staying with you, Dax. We have work to do."

Tablon narrows his eyes at Jarmer. "I'm staying, too. Dax, I'm only thinking of your...everyone's safety. But stop for a minute and think. How can we accomplish anything? It's just us and those AFGFs out there. That's not exactly a seasoned squad. And we only have two fighter ships against aliens and the Global Forces, who all want to see us dead."

Tablon has a good point, but I'm used to being outnumbered and marked for death. Through the cockpit window, I see trails of smoke and explosions everywhere in the distance. I can't tell who's who up there or if Prentak's fleet is almost here. One thing I know for certain, I'm not going to stand around chatting, I have to act.

"Boys, I don't need anyone to worry about me or my squad. We might be AFGFs, but we're the only hope the world has. Earth is my home and I'm not going to let my home get destroyed."

"You tell 'em, young lady!" Trab laughs.

Jarmer smiles. "I'm with you there, Trab. And I'm with you, Dax, but..."

I return Jarmer's smile. "You'll have to trust me. Tablon, if you want to leave, I won't hold it against you."

With a firm shake of his head, Tablon frowns. "I'm not leaving you alone with this flyboy."

"Okay then, that means we have a Lead, two pilots, a mechanic, and my squad." When I say it out loud, I realize how ridiculous it is. Us against all of the Global Forces and the Piltraks. Even without Viteri leading a personal vendetta against me, it's an impossible task. Am I being unfair to Jarmer? He wanted to go home and be with his family. But as much as I miss Ma and Da, I have to finish this war and make sure it never happens again.

"Young lady," Trab says. "I've found those recordings you made, stored in the deep-stash files of the fighter. Hard to locate, but I got 'em."

Jarmer has a confused expression. "Deep-stash files? Never heard of them. I know everything there is to know about a fighter, but nobody ever told me about any *deep-stash* files." Now he looks angry. "What else didn't they tell me?"

"Don't get all upset, Jarmer." Trab gives him a wink. "I'm not even supposed to know about deep-stash. It's a system used to store information about the fighter, the pilot, the mission, and whatever else the commanders might want to look into. They developed it to collect information, if they needed it. That's how they figured that most girls would hesitate before killing an enemy. I found out about deep-stash accidentally when I tapped into a cerebral interpreter once. Almost got caught!" He chuckles.

What if all commanders have the interpreters? "There's one in camp? A cerebral interpreter? I used one, too. That's how I learned the truth about what the commanders are doing. Those things are filled with information." If I had one, I'd have proof of everything. "Trab, I need to get my hands on one of the interpreters. Do all the high-up people have them? Could there be one here?"

Jarmer and Tablon look completely lost and for once, have nothing to say.

Trab taps the side of his head like he's thinking. "So this is Global Command, where we are right now?"

I nod. "Yes. What's left of it. I only came back here to get my squad."

He continues, "I've never been here before, but I can guarantee that the upper echelon has cerebral interpreters. Is there anyone left?"

Tablon answers, "No. There were a few survivors, but they got away in escape shuttles. It's just us here."

"That's good. Nobody to get in the way." Trab motions to the hatch. "Let's go."

With a groan, Jarmer shakes his head. "And do what? I still don't know what a cerebral interpreter is or what it can do."

I give him a pat on the arm. "I'll explain it later. Trab, do you know the layout of Global Command?"

He moves to the ladder. "Not at all. And to make it even more difficult, we'll have to sift through a bunch of rubble. That'll take time, young lady."

He's right, it won't be easy to find a cerebral interpreter, if there's one here and if it isn't damaged. Before I take a step, Prentak pokes his head up through the hatch.

I nod to him. "I thought you left us."

"Not yet. My ship will arrive momentarily, but I thought I could help you one last time before I go." He has something under his arm as he climbs onto the cockpit. "You wanted this." He hands me a cerebral interpreter with its screen attached.

I take it. "How did you know? We were just talking about trying to find one."

"I know. The Preedithantha communicated your wishes. I would suggest you leave now that you have this device. Remember, the veil will only protect you for a short time and then you will also become a casualty of this human-caused war. I do not like the thought of that. My people will not fire upon you as long as you stay in the upper atmosphere. Remain there until the battle has ended. It is the only way for you to stay safe. Take care of yourself, Dax." He turns to go, hesitates, and turns back. "You are one of the few recognized by the Preedithantha, Dax. Find others like you. You will need them." With a slight grunt, he climbs down the ladder.

"What did he mean by that?" I look around, but everyone shrugs. "What others?"

Trab's brow is pinched. "Cryptic little thing, isn't he?"

"Yes, he is." I sigh and hold up the cerebral interpreter. "At least we don't have to scramble through the rubble."

A sudden roaring sound makes us all look through the window. It's a Piltrak ship settling onto the ground. My poor squad is running for cover! I've forgotten all about them. "Tablon, go and tell my squad that it's just Prentak's ship and we're okay. For now."

"Sure." He puffs out his chest and shoves his way past Jarmer. "Out of my way, flyboy."

An explosion lights up everything outside and a moment later, a shock wave hits my ship with a violent shake and we all lose our footing. A series of smaller explosions pop all around us. I stumble to the window and look out. Right above us are four Global Forces fighters exchanging laser bursts with Prentak's ship. I have no idea if he's inside it or not or if my squad made it to safety. What am I supposed to do now? I don't want Prentak to kill everyone in the fighters, but I also don't want them to kill him and his people. I have to end this once and for all, but I need help. I can't do it on my own.

Chapter Thirty-One

I run to the hatch and peek out, but with all of the explosions, I can't really see what's happening. Trab's yelling at me to stay back and Jarmer's shouting that he has to get to his fighter. As soon as I start down the ladder, Tablon grabs my arm.

"Get back in here, Dax, you can't go out there now!"

"Let go." I pull free and hurry down. A quick scan of the area and I find my squad taking cover behind a pile of rubble. The purple veil is covering both ships and although it can't protect me in the open, I rush across the lawn and throw myself to the ground near Viga. I can't believe I didn't get hit by the laser blasts.

"Dax!" Viga reaches out for my arm, her hand trembling. "What should we do?"

"Well, we can't stay here. Prentak said we'll be safe inside the fighters if we leave the atmosphere, so that's what we'll do."

Kova crawls to me. "And then what? I don't want my family to die. How are you going to save *them*?"

"Kova's right." Viga cowers when a laser blast strikes behind us. "Are you going to tow the squad behind again? I get to ride inside, right?"

I hadn't thought much about it, but they *will* have to be towed, although now Trab's with us and I need him as my co-pilot. "Change of plans. We now have a mechanic, Trab, from the training camp. He knows everything about the fighters and Global Forces."

Viga groans. "So he'll be in your fighter, not me. Damn it, Dax, I'm scared. I don't want to float through the air on a tether line. We're at war now, with fighters and lasers."

If things go wrong, I'm not only dooming my squad but the entire population of Earth. My chest's tight and my stomach feels weird. "Don't worry, Viga. Everything's going to be fine. I have a plan, and once everything settles down, we'll rebuild our outliers and have nice, safe lives to live. It'll all work out."

"Really?" Briett's on his stomach with his hands covering his head. "I hope it's a good plan and you end the war because I'm really hungry and I have to go to the toilet. Can I have a job teaching kids in a school? I'd like that." He turns his head and smiles at me. "Little kids. Not teenagers. Little kids aren't as mean as they are when they get older."

"Sure, Briett. You'll be a good teacher." I smile at him. He deserves to have a great life, far away from danger and fighting. "AFGFs! We can't stay here, it's too dangerous. We have to launch and get out of Earth's atmosphere. Once we're in the ships, we have protection from the veil, but only for a short time. Get suited up and in position behind the fighters!"

From my peripheral vision, I see Jarmer rushing in my direction, followed by Tablon. Jarmer dives to the ground and blocks me from a nearby explosion. Tablon shoves Jarmer and they scuffle in the dirt.

Briett's sobbing and is curled up in a ball. "I don't want to die," he cries.

"Enough!" I shout above the sound of explosions overhead. "You're scaring everyone."

Tablon rolls off Jarmer, breathing hard. "This flyboy's too weak to protect…"

"I can take care of myself, Tablon." I motion to Prentak's ship still on the ground. "Did anyone see if Prentak got inside?"

Kova raises her hand. "He walked to it and just disappeared. That was right before our battalion started firing."

Good, that means he made it safely into his ship. I look up and the first thought that pops into my head is how the sky looks like the old photographs I've seen of parades where fireworks, little incendiary rockets, exploded in gorgeous colorful displays for nothing more than the entertainment of people watching. How different things are now. I've never seen real fireworks and the only parades in my outlier were of empty coffins for the children who'd died in battle. It must have been such a happy time a hundred years ago.

I'm thrust back to reality when Prentak's ship fires a strange blue-colored pulse at one of the fighters above him and a shower of small pieces of metal from the ship fall all around us. The fighter crashes down maybe half a kilometer away, close enough to make the ground shake. We're all quiet, and I know why. We're all thinking the same thing, the human crew didn't stand a chance.

This is what my life's about now. Wonder who'll survive and who won't. But there's no time to mourn. "Get into your spacesuits and onto your tethers! We're out of time."

Nobody moves for a few seconds, but then Tablon bellows, "Recruits! We launch in thirty seconds, with or without you!"

That gets everyone moving, except for Briett who's still curled up in a tight ball. I crawl to him and give him a shake. "Briett, get up. Come on, I'll help you in to your suit. It'll be all right."

"Big pig!" Tablon shouts.

"Briett?" I shake him again and again. That's when I notice the dirt around him is soaked with blood. "He's hit! Briett, can you hear me? Somebody help! Hurry!"

I shake him again. Nothing. His face is pale and his eyes are closed, almost like he's sleeping. Kova and Viga rush to him, look under his uniform for a wound and find a small piece of metal lodged in the side of his neck. Without looking closer, I know from my anatomy classes that it sliced his carotid artery. He bled out before any of us knew he was even hit.

"Oh, Briett," I whisper. My tears drip and mix with his blood. Why Briett? He never did anything to anyone. "No!"

Without a word, Tablon rushes over, lifts Briett onto his shoulder, and hurries to Jarmer's ship. He struggles up the ladder and vanishes inside. I'm numb and can't think straight. Sweet Briett's gone. An explosion brings me back and I watch as the fighting between Prentak and Global Forces continues, but after a few seconds, Prentak launches and accelerates so fast, he's gone from sight before I can blink. The Global Forces battalion follows and we're left alone in abrupt silence. My ears are ringing.

"Dax." Jarmer puts his arm over my shoulders. "We have to go. We can take care of Big Pi...Briett, when we have a chance. Okay?" He turns to my squad. "I'm really sorry, but I need you all to suit up and get in line behind my ship and Dax's. Don't argue with me, this isn't the time. You'll be safe." He strides to the tether lines and straightens them out.

Viga draws in a deep breath and wipes her eyes with her shirt. "Did that Piltrak launch so the battalion would follow him and leave us alone?"

I stare at her for a moment, not sure anymore what's going on. It's a struggle to comprehend everything. I shrug. "I don't know." The sky's empty, no ships, no fighting, just a smoky haze hanging motionless against a vivid blue backdrop. We're at war and Briett's dead. Is any of this worth it?

Scraping her boot in the dirt, Kova covers most of the bloodstain and runs off to the pile of spacesuits near the tether lines. Everyone goes and does the same, although Viga hangs back a bit until Jarmer yells at her.

"Young lady," Trab calls to me. He's standing near my ship. "One of the tether lines is secured to your ship and I've programmed in coordinates that'll take us into a low orbit for the time being. Jarmer's ship, too. And the propulsion packs are fully recharged with oxygen."

With a last look at the spot where Briett died, I wipe my eyes and shuffle to my fighter. "Thanks, Trab."

"Ah, please accept my condolences. Big Pig was a good boy." He sniffles and hurries up the ladder.

"Yes, he was," I say to the empty space around me.

Once I'm in my ship, I ready for launch and use the synap-trodes to look behind my ship to see if my squad's tethered. It all seems so hopeless now. Where am I supposed to go with all of these people?

"Looks like we're good, young lady." Trab nods and slips his helmet on. "Take it slow on the launch, Dax, so the squad isn't shaken around too much."

"Okay." With the ship in regular launch mode, I watch Jarmer's ship and see him initiate his launch. "Here we go, Trab." We take off at the same time.

At about five kilometers altitude, we encounter a thin layer of clouds but burst through as we pass out of the troposphere and into the stratosphere, where there's a battle raging between the Global Forces battalion and a bunch of Piltrak ships. I know we're in the veil, but it's still frightening to think we're flying so close to the fighting. We zip through the mesosphere and into the thermosphere, and I say a silent goodbye to Earth, and Ma and Da. If my plan doesn't work, I can't go back, ever. Not that there'll be anything left to go back to.

"You're doing great, young lady, keep your acceleration steady and hold your course. When you exit the exosphere, I'll take over and you can use the cerebral interpreter."

"It'll take me a few minutes." I can't see Jarmer anymore, but my heads-up display shows both of our trajectories and coordinates, and he's keeping a steady pace with me. "Trab, I was thinking about something. Prentak healed you, right?"

"Yes, that's true. And I'm grateful."

"Maybe he can bring Briett back. Do you think he can?"

Trab shrugs. "I don't know anything about the Piltrak. Sorry."

My ship's in the transitional space between the thermosphere and exosphere, and as I look outside, what I see makes me gasp out loud.

Trab points out the window. "Oh, that's not good."

Off to starboard are so many Piltrak ships that it's impossible to count them. Hundreds, maybe thousands, pushing through the exosphere, no longer invisible and all different sizes. Some are small and others are huge, maybe ten times as big. This is the rest of Prentak's fleet and that means it's too late, there's no time to do anything to save Earth. How can I sit here and do nothing? I can't.

"Preedithantha!"

"What's that you said, young lady? I know about those."

"You do?" I shouldn't be calling on them. Prentak warned me not to. *Forget it Preedithantha, I don't need you.* Okay, I'll try something myself first. "Hand me the cerebral interpreter, Trab."

He lifts it off his lap. "Be quick. Like I said before, I'm no pilot. Why did you say Preedi-whatever?"

"It's not important. But I need the cerebral interpreter. Just hold steady."

"Dax, I know a little about those Preedi-whatevers." He hands me the cerebral interpreter.

I place it on my lap. "How?" I check my coordinates and see both Jarmer and I are leaving the exosphere. About half of Prentak's ships have already dropped into the lower atmosphere. Nobody pays us any attention. So where is Prentak? "Trab, how do you know about the Preedithantha? It was the *Piltrak* that told me about them."

Trab leans over the taps the cerebral interpreter. "From inside here. Well, not this one, but the one I got into. There was a file, similar to the deep-stash in the ships, hidden way down deep. If I remember right, the file was dated March 2087 and said those Preedi-whatevers were virus vectors. Real deadly, carried viruses from outer space to Earth. That sound right?"

As much as I try, I can't swallow a lump that's formed in my throat. Vectors? That can't be right. Prentak said the Preedithantha would help me, and they did. They kept me, and my squad, safe. They're in my brain and I'm not sick with a virus. It has to be a lie.

"No, Trab, that doesn't sound right. They don't infect people." Although Prentak did say they could be dangerous. What if they've given me a disease and it hasn't surfaced yet?

"All right then. I suppose the information was wrong. But it's still buried inside the interpreter." He points to my heads-up. "Orbit's initiating."

"Okay. So how did the commanders know about the Preedithantha? Even if they had it wrong, I still don't understand. Prentak told me how it's like a symbiotic relationship. And he said nobody on Earth ever tried to communicate with the Piltrak. So how did anyone find out about the Preedithantha?"

What if they did infect me with something? I think back to what Viteri said, about me infecting everyone around me with my non-conformist behavior. Maybe I'm like the Preedithantha and I'm a vector, too. But I'm a vector of truth.

Chapter Thirty-Two

I watch Jarmer's ship on the heads-up and check on my squad. I honestly don't know what to do. They have limited oxygen, so I have to get them somewhere safe soon. But where? So long as we're in the veil, we can't be hurt. As much as I need to protect them, I can't leave Ma and Da.

Trab clears his throat. "Dax. Take a few minutes to breathe. You've been through hell. So what were you saying about the Preed-things?"

"I feel so helpless orbiting around Earth while so many are dying."

"I know you do. But we were told to come up here, right? We're where we're supposed to be."

I know he's right. I really do need a few minutes to wrap my mind around everything. "Trab, it was the Katarga who first attacked Earth, right?"

"Indeed it was. Back in 2087, a hundred years ago. It was February and by March, almost 2/3 of Earth's population was gone and our colonies on the moon were destroyed. Earth was so overpopulated at that time and spreading out into the galaxy. About 12 billion of us on this old planet and almost a million on the moon, not enough resources to support us all. Anyway, the Katarga even blasted our long-range transports that were going to colonize the rings around Saturn. That was another million people we lost. That's what depleted the population."

"So when did the Piltrak attack? I learned in school that fifty years after the Katarga attacked us, the Piltrak came. Is that right? I'm never sure anymore that what I've been told is the truth."

He nods. "It was, ah, 2137, November. I was just a young boy when it happened, two or three, so I don't remember much. My folks told me how families were evacuated and put in the subs sometime before the Piltrak got here."

"Subs? What are those?" I glance outside again and see even more explosions lighting up the sky below. How long can I wait up here without doing anything?

Trab taps me on the shoulder. "Hey, don't look at that. Let's keep talking. Ah, the subs, or sub-residences, were underground facilities designed as living spaces."

I turn away from the window.

He continues, "We all stayed underground for about ten years, and then the population was divided and put in different outliers or the cities. You know what? Those ten years were the happiest of my life."

"Really?"

Trab smiles at me. "For those ten years, families were together, working and surviving, spending time with each other." He glances away and says softly, "Best ten years of my life."

"Ten years? That's a long time. So what happened after that?" I glance out the window again. People are dying and I'm doing nothing.

"Dax, look at me. Everything's going to work out, you'll see. Someone like you is destined for success. I feel it in my bones. Okay, so let me finish my story."

I don't feel much like listening, but it's a distraction at least.

He continues, "The subs were already complete by the time we were moved into them. They were great, sort of like being above ground with trees and gardens, houses, schools. I can still remember when my family got to go back up top. I was amazed to see the sun and clouds. It was odd, although I'm not sure what I expected, there wasn't any rubble or downed spaceships. Nothing. We were told the Piltrak came and infected the people who remained above ground, but were ultimately defeated. That's all I know about that. I remember my parents explaining that we were put underground so we wouldn't get infected, but I still can't figure out how they knew the Piltrak had those Preedi-whatevers that could infect us. And if they knew that, why did anyone stay above ground? It's a mystery to me, Dax."

"Okay, so what happened when you were above ground? Did life just go on?"

An explosion close to us jostles my ship and I instinctively grab the control stick. Trab puts his hand on my shoulder.

"That was too close, young lady."

"I'm scared, Trab. What's going to happen to us? Humans, I mean. We almost died out fifty years ago and now it's happening again. We don't learn, do we?" I close my eyes and try hard to think of happier times when I was with Ma and Da. I'd give anything to be there again. I don't care if we're poor and we struggle, I want that time back.

"Young lady, listen to me. I'll protect you. You saved me, so it's the least I can do. I'll make sure nobody ever hurts you."

I don't think that's a promise he can keep. "Thanks, Trab."

"Shall I go on with my story?"

With a nod, I lean back and watch him.

"Life was okay for a while above ground. Not much changed from being in the subs, except about two years later, when I turned fifteen. I was taken from my family and conscripted into the military. Now it's called the Age of Classification and Conformity."

"Our Date of Fate."

He stares at me for a moment. "That's right. That's what you kids call it now. It was different then though. There was actually a lottery for boys when they turned fifteen. The winners were taken from their homes and placed in training camps to prepare to fight the aliens if they came back. The girls stayed behind and worked or raised families, at first. Nobody wanted to risk girls getting killed since we had to keep building up our population, you see. But eventually, girls were advanced too. The day I got picked in the lottery was a life changer for me. I never saw my parents again."

"I'm so sorry, Trab. But there's something I don't understand. I never heard about the subs. My grandparents should have been in them, right? Why didn't they ever say anything?"

He nods thoughtfully. "Well, everyone had to swear an oath never to mention the subs. Oh, dear, that means I just violated my oath!" He lets out a belly laugh. "Guess it doesn't matter at this point. Your grandparents wouldn't have told your parents, or they would have violated their oath as well."

"I guess. But it's only an oath."

"Oh, Dax, you've seen the reach of Global Forces. Even back then, the new military that formed was full of threats and intimidation. I was told that

265

if I ever told anyone about the subs, my parents would be imprisoned and I'd be executed. We all believed those threats."

"It's not much different today."

Trab shrugs and checks outside. "I suppose."

I wait until he turns away from the window. "Trab, I think I would have told *my* family. I've never kept secrets from my Ma and Da. How did Global Command, or whoever it was at the time, find out about the Preedithantha? Who told them? And who built the outliers if the people above ground were infected? They were trying to rebuild the world, weren't they?" So much history that I don't know.

"Of course they had to rebuild. I learned a little when I was sent to training camp. I was born in the northern part of the Mid-World continent, but it was still called Africa then. All of us from Africa went to the first camp, the Equatorial camp. Africa became the property of Global Command, which was already set up by the time we came out of the subs. The Council of Commanders was started soon after. Anyway, I stayed in camp ever since, as you know. Never saw my parents again. Security wasn't as tight in the beginning and it took only a bit of snooping to find out information. That's how I learned that the outliers were developed as a way to keep people in line. Something about how the city in the center was supposed to be the ruling class and the outliers were the workers. Weird, but then I don't know what the thinking was like back then."

"Trab, things haven't changed much. The wealthy live in the cities and the outliers are the working classes. Our outlier is poor and anyone who isn't advanced works in the factories or schools. We're purposely kept poor so we're forced to keep producing children for advancement. We all rely on the child-rearing subsidies and then the advancement subsidies. Without advancement subsidies, most families can't make it. When did they come up with the Status levels?" I look down because I can't bring myself to make eye contact. "I'm only a Status 2."

He puts his hand on my shoulder. "Status is a human invention, Dax. It means nothing. Don't ever be ashamed of who you are. I've seen more kids come through the camps than I can keep track of, and they're all damn near the same. Scared and homesick. But you're one of the special ones. That's why they want to keep you quiet. Non-conformists are silenced in one way or another. Viteri made sure you were advanced to control you. It's all about control, young lady."

I nod. "I've come to see that."

He continues, "As soon as I was indoctrinated into training camp, I was taught never to ask questions and to accept all orders without hesitation. I learned the hard way and had my share of punishments." He chuckles. "I fell for this girl pilot, Antalia, but she was shipped out to fly fighter missions on the moon. I missed her so much, I stole some of the commanders' alcohol, got drunk, and smashed up two fighters trying to launch to find her. I spent two weeks scrubbing toilets." He laughs again at the memory. "But I'd sneak off every night to fix the fighters so they'd take me off the toilet duty. It worked because when the commanders saw how good I was, they made me a mechanic."

My head's spinning. I can't make sense of most of what Trab's saying, but it seems like the tragedy of the alien attacks changed Earth forever. Instead of doing good though, Global Command and the Council of Commanders have made things worse.

"So, what happened to Antalia?" I ask.

He sighs. "She lasted almost six months before a Katarga blast got her, or so I hear. That was before we realized fighters were too vulnerable."

"I'm sorry, Trab." I watch him for a moment until his smile gradually comes back. "Wait, Antalia was a fighter pilot? And she flew missions for six months? She didn't wash out."

"Of course not. She was one of the best pilots we had. A lot of the girls outflew the boys back then. It was sort of experimental to see if girls could handle a fighter. Like I said, girls were advanced later on, in smaller numbers though."

"Well, if girls were good pilots *then*, why aren't they pilots *now*?"

He narrows his eyes slightly. "That's a good point, young lady. It never sat well with me that the commanders started washing out the girls, claiming they were too compassionate to be effective fighter pilots. It's a galactic waste of talent, that's what it is."

I see a series of explosions below us. "Trab! Look! The Piltrak are engaging the battalion." I've wasted too much time talking. "I have to plug into the cerebral interpreter and see what I can find." *Please, please, please don't let anything happen to Ma or Da.*

"Go ahead, young lady. Maybe you can figure out where we can go from here. A suitable planet or something. Remember, you have to take off your helmet to use the interpreter and you'll only have the small amount of oxygen that's in the cabin." He raises an eyebrow, obviously waiting for me to acknowledge that I understand.

"I remember." With my helmet off, I attach the button-like electrode to my forehead and trigger the cerebral interpreter. This is my only hope to reveal the truth and if I can't find anything, there's nothing else I can do. And we'll have to find somewhere to go like Trab said.

I want to know about the initial Katarga attack. Right away, text comes up on the small screen.

> *Katarga sought out habitation for their expanding population but found Earth not suitable. Earth feared an attack from the Katarga vessels in orbit and mounted a preemptive nuclear rocket strike. Katarga had powerful weapons and mounted a full-scale retaliatory attack, destroying most of Earth's population.*

Nuclear weapons? I suppose that was the only sort of weaponry Earth had at the time. I'm amazed Earth didn't destroy itself in the process.

> *Earth's technology was primitive, but effective, and brought down twelve Katarga ships before the Katarga attacked.*

That's horrible. The Katarga hadn't done anything hostile before they were fired on?

> *No. Atmosphere sampling was the only testing done. Earth later found out the Katarga had prepared to leave, but when Earth attacked and their ships were lost, the Katarga created a base on the moon since the nuclear rockets did not have a sufficient range to reach the lunar surface. They destroyed the Earth's moon colonies. War started and lasted for ten years.*

Then how did we survive at all? It sounds like the Katarga had an advantage.

Once Katarga had destroyed most of Earth's population, they withdrew their ships from Earth's orbit and prepared for retreat, maintaining a base on the moon for monitoring. But Earth's remaining leaders had secretly developed battle fighter ships with new advanced weapons using Katarga technology they captured. Manufacturing plants were set up in underground bunkers.

The sub-residences they used later. Is that when we trapped the Katarga on the moon?

Affirmative. Once Katarga began to withdraw, Earth leaders mounted an attack and killed thousands of Katarga. The remaining Katarga retreated to their moon base where they were trapped. They became an instrument for profit.

No wonder we were never taught this part of Earth's history. Why did the Piltrak come to Earth fifty years later?

Katarga managed to send out a small super-sonic signal with a distress and warning message. It had to travel for 25 Earth years before reaching the Piltrak planet.

Wait a minute. How do you know this?

The Katarga leader in charge of the moon base was captured and tortured. She explained how they wanted to withdraw completely and return to their home. Earth leaders chose to suppress this information from the public.

Her? The leader was female?

Affirmative. Her three daughters remained on the moon after her capture. Her daughters sent the call for help. Katarga communicate with one another through thought.

Like telepathy?

More advanced than telepathy. They understand one another's thoughts and feel emotion and pain from one another.

But how did Earth learn about the message if it was the daughters who sent it?

Under torture, Katarga leader confessed to what she discovered her daughters had done. She said her daughters felt her pain and with no means to stop it, they reached out for help. Prior to her death, Katarga leader said the Preedithantha informed her daughters that the Piltrak were on their way. Earth learned of Preedithantha from the torture. The Katarga leader was imprisoned for 25 years.

I realize I'm crying and wipe my tears away and glance at Trab. He's been reading the text as well and has tears in his eyes, too. "Trab, all the Katarga wanted to do was go home." Just like me.

He nods. "But they weren't allowed to. And we tortured and killed one of their leaders for no reason." His head droops. "All this time I thought the Katarga attacked us first."

"So did I. That's what we were taught. The Katarga leader's daughters could feel their mother in pain. No wonder they begged for help. Prentak said the Katarga don't want help from anyone, but this time they did. I feel sick to my stomach, Trab."

"Me too. And now they're nothing but a source of income for the commanders. I'm disgusted to say I'm from Earth." He shakes his head sadly.

I have to find out more, like when the Piltrak arrived.

Piltrak intercepted distress signal and sent a fleet to the moon to free the Katarga. It took them 25 years to arrive. They brought Preedithantha that inhabited half of the remaining population of Earth.

Half of the population? What sort of disease did the Preedithantha have? Do I have a disease now?

WAR AND MONEY

Piltrak sent Preedithantha to Earth after negotiations broke down. Preedithantha flooded the cerebral cortex of humans with Bliss.

Bliss? That's not a disease. But that can't be right. Prentak said Earth never attempted to communicate with the Piltrak. When were the negotiations and what happened?

October 2137, Piltrak advance fleet detected near Saturn. November 2137, Piltrak commanders invited Earth leaders to a dialogue using Jurale interpreter, but Earth still would not negotiate with what Earth leaders called the alien menace, and war was declared on Piltrak. At this time, Earth had prepared sufficiently for the arrival of the Piltrak since they had advance warning from the Katarga leader, and had a large battalion and arsenal ready for battle. In effect, negotiations were never initiated.

Prentak was right then. We never opened up any channels of communication, even when we could. And Earth couldn't stand that the people who were "infected" were content and happy. How could our leaders do this?

Earth saw more opportunity for income generation with another war, this time with the Piltrak, using the Preedithantha as a cause. Earth's population was informed that the Piltrak were infecting humans with a lethal disease.

I understand it all now, except why the Piltrak have come back fifty years after the start of the war.

When a Jurale scouting fleet was attacked by Global Command, Piltrak decided to return and destroy Earth to prevent further wars. Piltrak have developed advanced technology to allow them to travel faster than the last time. From their planet to Saturn took two months.

Such technology and we want to kill them. Who exactly are the Jurale?

According to intelligence from Global Command, Jurale are historians. They gather information throughout the universe.

But Prentak said they were very powerful. And their interpreter can also be a weapon. Are they only historians?

According to intelligence gathered from torture of additional captive Katarga, the Jurale have advanced technology and control of sub-atomic particles such as the Preedithantha.

More Katarga were tortured? Do the Jurale also have a symbiotic relationship with the Preedithantha?

They gather information through the Preedithantha network. They were coming to Earth to negotiate for the release of the Katarga and were then ambushed by Global Command two years ago. A new war was initiated against the Jurale with large human losses and zero Jurale losses. Jurale withdrew to avoid further conflict but did not leave the solar system.

And there are our three wars; the Katarga, the Piltrak, and the Jurale. Wait. The Jurale are still in our solar system?

Indeed, but location is unknown. It is presumed they are monitoring Earth's hostilities.

I pull off the electrode and place the cerebral interpreter on the ground at my feet. I don't have to know anything more, I've got all the information I need. It's an endless cycle of violence and the only people who benefit are the commanders, the wealthy factory owners, and anyone else who's invested in the wars.

The cities are off-limits to the outlier populations as a way to control us. Trab's one hundred percent right. It's all about control. Our leaders couldn't have the people "infected" with Bliss, because they'd lose control of them, so they declared war on the Piltrak. There's no money to be made if the people don't want to fight. No fighting, no money.

"Trab, why are only fifteen-year-olds recruited?"

He wipes his eyes again. "Like I said, it's about control. Children are easier to manipulate. Adults have fully-formed brains and tend to think and reason more. Kids can be molded and made to believe whatever authority figures, like the commanders, say. Propaganda works on teenagers and at fifteen, kids are old enough to hold weapons. Control, young lady. That Bliss that I read about in the text, what is it?" He stares at me for a moment. "Put that helmet back on, Dax, you're turning blue."

I nod and slip my helmet over my head, inhale deeply and look through the window at flashes of explosions everywhere. This is my planet dying. I can't just orbit up here while people are dying, but if I descend, my ship won't be protected.

"Dax, what is Bliss?"

I turn from the window. "Bliss makes you feel good. More than good. You feel like there's nothing wrong in the world, that you can get along with everyone and be happy. That's why Global Command doesn't like it. They don't want us to be happy and peaceful."

He shakes his head. "No, they don't. What are these damn wars doing to the human race?"

I know exactly what they're doing. I read once in a biological history class how animals have a pecking order. A type of stratified society where some were at the top, some in the middle, and some at the bottom. That's what we have. Our status system is a pecking order.

"I know what's it's doing, Trab. The wars are designed to stratify our society. The wealthy are at the top and the only way for them to stay there is to keep most of the population poor and dependent on them and to keep the people frightened of the aliens. The wars have to continue so the people will stay scared and trust that our government will save them, even though countless kids die each day. Parents are forced into sending their kids into battle to keep earning subsistence subsidies, and kids believe they're doing their part to save the planet. Tell me, how does Global Command have enough money to spend on the subsidies and supplies for the Global Forces?"

"Taxes. Wages are heavily taxed and every six months or so, there's an inflation increase in taxes. The taxes go straight to the Global Forces. Why?"

That's why paychecks get smaller and smaller. "The more kids advanced, the more kids that need equipment. And as each dies, a replacement comes along with new equipment. No wonder there's so much propaganda to advance. Global Command wants to keep the flow of recruits coming. I can't stand this, Trab. How many cities are there globally?"

He stares for a moment. "What? Oh, I never really thought of it. There weren't many of course when I came out of the subs, but the population's grown and there have to be plenty now. Do you think they stuck us underground so those Preedi-things wouldn't infect us with Bliss?"

I give him a nod. "I think so. Maybe they can't get underground." Wait, why not? If they're sub-atomic, they can get through anything, and it doesn't seem like the Preedithantha could be tricked into thinking only a few people were above ground. That's something I need to look into, but later. Right now, war's raging and my people are getting slaughtered.

"Young lady, I can include that information you just found out with the broadcast. That'll raise questions and get people thinking." He pointed out the window. "That Piltrak you know, Prentak, will he ever stop his attack? You know, I think it's time we got back to your plan."

"You're right. And I don't know Prentak *that* well. I have no idea what he'll do." Although Prentak was willing to give me a chance before, I have no way of reaching him and letting him know what I'm planning to do. "We can't waste any more time orbiting. Can you get the broadcast ready, and add in a speech I'll make?"

"Of course. Give me a few minutes to edit the feeds so we'll have your voice along with the broadcast of the battle from the deep-stash files and some of the cerebral interpreter text."

"Okay. But hurry. This is our only chance to stop the fighting and maybe, just maybe, get us all back to Earth." I check the coordinates and see that Jarmer is still in position. "Jarmer, are you there?"

There's a brief pause. "Yes. Dax, what are we doing? Are you seeing what's going on down there? I didn't want to say anything before, but does the squad have enough oxygen? We're still in the Piltrak veil, but I don't know if that gives them oxygen or not."

"They're fine." I hope. Prentak told me my friends would stay safe as we left the atmosphere. I bring up a view out back and see my squad. They're not panicking, but I do see some occasionally moving an arm or leg. "They're perfectly safe, Jarmer. But that's not why I'm contacting you. Do you know how many cities there are and is there some way to find the coordinates for the cities and outliers?"

Another pause. "Whatever you've got in mind, it better work because I'm about ready to reprogram coordinates for my outlier."

"Just tell me how to find the coordinates."

Tablon comes on. "Dax, if you can access the commanders' computer system at training camp, you can find whatever you need. I learned about it from the Early Training Simulation. They have data on all of the cities and their outliers for recruitment purposes. Are you sure you're okay?"

"Of course she is," Jarmer grumbles. "She's a lot tougher than you think."

"Shut up, flyboy. Don't go thinking you can..."

I cut them both off. "Thanks, I have all the information I need. I'm disconnecting communication."

Trab looks over at me and smiles. "*Two* boys, eh?"

"It's not what you think, Trab. They're just...being boys." I need to concentrate on a way to get into the commanders' computer system and not think about Tablon and Jarmer.

"You need the cerebral interpreter again?"

I shake my head. "No. I've had enough of that thing for now. If I can't find what I need, I'll use it."

After working with the synap-trodes for several minutes, I finally tap into the computers at training camp and locate a file that not only lists the cities and their outliers but each City Chief's name as well. I bring up the file on my heads-up.

Trab studies the display and fiddles with the instruments. "I'll plug in those coordinates now. You want the broadcast over the cities *and* outliers?"

I nod. "Yes, I do. We need to reach every single person who's still alive."

"All righty. This shouldn't be much harder than fixing a fighter's navigation communication system. I can get the projections up once I hack into each city's tech. I'll make sure the projections go up at 80 meters above ground level. That should allow people anywhere to see them. I'll need to record your speech now. You can speak like you are right now and I'll capture it and add it in. This time I'll set it up so the commanders can't disable it so easily."

I draw in a breath and think for a moment before saying anything. "People of Earth, I am Dax Orwan, an AFGF recruit. You've been fooled by Global Command and the Council of Commanders. We are fighting wars that were manufactured for the sole purpose of making money. Not for people like me, a Status 2, but for the wealthy classes. I have first-hand knowledge that the Katarga and the Piltrak don't want to fight us, they want to live in peace and return home to their planets. Global Command has not let them do this. They refuse to end the wars and go out of their way to create more. We are taught to blindly obey whatever Global Command tells us. The aliens are not hostile until they are provoked, and will leave us alone if we let them. Please watch the broadcast and you'll see. If you decide to do the right thing, go outside, kneel, and raise your hands in surrender. You will not be harmed by the aliens. I give you my word. The Piltrak are attacking because they refuse to be targeted like the Katarga. They will stop if you show them you don't want to fight."

Preedithantha, tell Prentak not to attack any human with their arms raised in surrender.

Trab grins and winks. "Well done, young lady."

My whole body is trembling. "When you're ready, transmit."

"Yes, ma'am. I've added in the text from the cerebral interpreter as well." He winks again. "Transmitting."

There's a moment of silence. I hope my message is getting through to Earth, and to Prentak.

"Is that really the smudge?" comes a voice I'd hoped I'd never hear again. Lenora snorts. "I'm going to personally shoot you out of orbit and then shoot down that traitor Tablon. But first, I'll kill your squad, one by one, and every single decayed black hole you told to surrender. You're dead, smudge. Dead."

Chapter Thirty-Three

I never expected Lenora to be here, but I suppose I should have. Now I've endangered everyone again.

"Lenora, you want me, not my squad."

She laughs. "Oh, no, I want you and your pathetic squad of traitorous alien lovers. I'll take you all down."

"Lenora," Tablon blurts. "Glad you found us. I'll transmit our coordinates to you, but only if you agree not to shoot us down. You can take the smudge as your prisoner and do whatever you want with her. Think about it, you'll get a commendation for sure."

I'm stunned. Tablon is betraying me after all we've been through. It feels like he's reached in and ripped out my heart with his bare hands. "Tablon..."

"Shut up, smudge!" he shouts.

There's silence. Does that mean Lenora is considering his proposition? Why isn't Jarmer objecting? He can't be with Tablon on this, he can't. Unless he blames me for Jarmella's death. I use my internal communicator. "Trab, I'll have to take the fighter out of automatic flight mode if I'm going to fight."

He's frowning. "I can't believe that girl's still alive. I figured her crew would have put her down like a rabid animal by now."

"She's the toxic one. She knows exactly how to manipulate Tablon and the Commander." I wrap my fingers around the control stick and disconnect the synap-trodes.

Lenora comes back on. "Okay, Senior Lead Neemiss, I'll agree to that. Give me your coordinates."

I glance at Trab just as a ship-to-ship communication comes in from Jarmer.

Jarmer's talking quietly, almost in a whisper, "Dax, don't do anything drastic. Tab's bringing Lenora to us. When she's in range, I'll blast her with priz-spec. Hold your position and don't let her find out you're off the synap-trodes."

Breathless, I look over at Trab. "Can she detect it if I'm flying without them?"

Trab nudges me with a finger on his lips. "Speak softly so the ship-to-ship isn't picked up. If Lenora's looking for it, she'll find that you disconnected the synap-trodes. But don't reconnect, because that'll give off an energy signature that she can easily pick up."

"Okay." At least Tablon hasn't betrayed me, that's something I guess. If Lenora knows my squad is vulnerable, that must mean we're not in the veil anymore. All she has to do is shoot at the tether and they'll go drifting away. I thought we'd still have protection from the veil, at least while we're in the upper atmosphere. "I'll keep on a steady course, Jarmer. But when she's in range, I want to be the one to fire."

"Wait," Tablon says. "We should capture her instead of killing her."

Jarmer grunts. "It's her or us, Tab. Lenora's out for Dax's blood, is that what you want?"

A pause. "Of course not. Fine." Tablon sighs. He sounds regretful or disappointed. "Do what you have to do, Dax."

Not that I need his permission, but it's good that he's still on my side. To stay on course, I track Jarmer's coordinates so I can mimic his movement and hopefully fool Lenora. I never thought I'd turn into a killer. I killed some of the Katarga and killed Viteri, and now Lenora will be my third kill. Maybe I am a soldier after all.

Trab taps my shoulder. "The Broadcast's now projected over every city and outlier in a recurring play loop. Whoever looks up will see it and hear you. I hope the Piltrak realize what you're doing and don't shoot the people instead of accepting their surrender. That is, if they surrender."

Preedithantha, did you reach Prentak?

We are with you and cannot transmit to Piltrak.

What does that mean? You're all linked, aren't you?

We are with you, focused on you as our host. The Piltrak veil has been removed to conserve energy, but now you are in danger. Use the Jurale translator.

I knew my ship wasn't protected anymore, but where is the translator? I must have dropped it. "Trab, do you see a silver..." Before I can finish, I see it on the floor near his feet. "Can you hand me that?"

He stretches his arm and grabs it. "Here you go. What are you going to do with that?"

"Whatever I can." Preedithantha, how do I get a message to Prentak?

Jurale interpreter can signal the Piltrak, the Jurale, the Katarga, and the Naroosha.

Who are the Naroosha? I've never heard of them.

Naroosha are within the X4 section of the Milky Way Galaxy, but none have ventured as far as Earth. Naroosha should not be contacted under any circumstances.

No problem, I don't intend to contact them. So how can I signal Prentak?

As a human, you do not possess a direct link to other species utilizing Preedithantha, so you will have to place interpreter to your forehead and allow your neural synapses to merge with the interpreter and communicate with any species capable of picking up signal.

I stare at the interpreter. What an incredible piece of technology. We could learn so much from these aliens if we'd only give them a chance. And if they'd give us a chance. "Trab, can you take over flying the ship for a while longer?"

"Of course. But don't forget, I'm no fighter pilot."

After taking a few breaths and removing my helmet, I shake out my hands to stop them from trembling and press the interpreter to my forehead. Right away I feel sharp pricks of pain all over my head, far more than the synap-trodes when they connect. It hurts so much, I almost stop, but after a moment, the pain lessens to the point where I can tolerate it, although there's this weird tingling all through my body, almost like an electrical charge going from the top of my head down to my feet.

There's a sudden, excruciating jolt of pain in my head and then a thousand voices talking all at once. I can understand the words I catch here and there, but can't focus on most. Maybe if I concentrate only on Prentak. With his image in my mind, I repeat his name over and over.

The voices fade until there's only one, and it's Prentak! But he's ordering his fleet to "cleanse the colorful city and its surroundings". That has to be Jewel, my city. No! Prentak, don't do this! Stop!

"Dax? Is that you? How can I hear you?" Prentak asks, sounding astonished.

"Yes, it's me. I'm using the Jurale translator. Please call off the attack. Look at the sky above all of the cities and outliers. I'm broadcasting the truth about the wars all over the planet. If the people believe me, they'll go outside and surrender to you. You don't need to kill them. You can concentrate only on the ships attacking you. If you defeat the Global Forces, you and the Katarga can return home."

"I cannot cease the attack. I am not the battle fleet commander, only the advance fleet commander."

"Then let me talk to the battle fleet commander. You said you'd give me a chance to make this right. That's what I'm trying to do."

I glance at Trab. He's staring at me with his mouth open. "Who are you talking to, young lady? I only hear you."

"I'm talking to Prentak." It must sound like a very strange conversation.

Prentak speaks again, "Dax, you must leave your planet and find another world. The Piltrak will help you. You can trust in me."

"I do, but you know I can't do that. My parents are down there, and the families of all of my friends. Not to mention every other innocent person. Families that just want to live their lives. Can't you contact the battle fleet commander for me, please? I'm doing what I can. I don't have long though because a girl who wants to kill me is heading to me and she'll be here very soon."

He doesn't respond right away. "I have located you. Stay in your orbit and do not fluctuate your path."

"Okay. And then what?" My heart's thumping.

"Battle Commander Prendrahl will arrive at your coordinates momentarily. I cannot guarantee the outcome. This is all I can do for you, Dax. Good luck." He's gone.

Once again, the flurry of voices ring through my head and the pain comes back. I remove the interpreter and slip my helmet on again. "Trab, Prentak's helping us."

"What are you talking about? Help us how? And where's Lenora?"

Before I can answer, my ship shudders violently. I check my heads-up and the artificial horizon is spinning out of control. "Trab! My squad!"

"We've been hit!" he shouts as he moves the control stick from side to side.

Lenora laughs. "As if I'd trust Tablon. You're vapor, smudge."

Chapter Thirty-Four

As Trab and I try to get the ship under control, Lenora keeps firing and hits my ship another couple of times. I hear Tablon yelling at her to cease fire, but she's not listening. My ship and my squad won't survive another hit.

Trab shouts, "Dax, engage the synap-trodes! Take us down into the troposphere! More control down there. Lenora's squad is in a fighter almost twice as big as yours."

After engaging the synap-trodes, it's a struggle to get the ship under control, but after a few more seconds, I have the ship again and manage to dodge an onslaught of laser bursts. Trab's keeping an eye on Lenora's position and added her ship onto my heads-up so I know exactly where she is. She's closing in fast.

I slip through the thermosphere, but the moment I enter the mesosphere, I see multiple ships appear on the heads-up. "Trab, are those more battalion fighters? Is Lenora surrounding me? Where's Jarmer?"

Trab shakes his head. "He's around. Those ships aren't ours, they have a different energy signature. They have to be Piltrak ships. Young lady, accelerate and get us down to the troposphere! Your squad doesn't have much oxygen left now that we're out of that veil thing."

Without hesitating, I open the acceleration-throttle to maximum and push my ship, not lightspeed, but still very fast. My fighter instantly dives and unless Lenora and the Piltrak match my speed, I'll lose them. I'm going so fast that I blast right through one of the broadcasts and although my eyes are blurry, I see the ground coming at me too fast.

"Dax! Slow down!" Jarmer shouts.

"Young lady!" Trab's voice is shaky.

Even though I slow my ship, we're going to impact. I squeeze my eyes closed and think of Ma and Da and hope more than anything that the broadcasts work and they'll be all right.

"Proud to have worked with you, young lady," Trab's voice is faint.

"Same here," I exhale the words more than speak them. I'm about to kill my friends tethered behind my ship. I hate myself.

With a whoosh in my ears and a tremendous burst of hot air, my ship rumbles and jolts, and the breath is knocked out of me. I can't breathe at all and I'm burning, so hot. Please let us die quickly. I don't want Trab and my squad to suffer.

You will not die. Preedithantha protect themselves.

What! My eyes fly open and I draw in a deep breath. Where am I? I can't see a single thing, it's too dark. I reach out and feel Trab in his seat, but he's not moving. "Trab! Can you hear me?"

"What...happened?" he mumbles.

"I don't know, but we're alive!"

There's no sound and my ship's not moving. The heads-up isn't working so there's no ambient light given off by the instruments. I slip off my helmet and restraints and feel around. We must have crashed and dug into the ground somehow. But why aren't we dead? An impact like that should have killed us and destroyed the ship.

After a moment, a single light near Trab illuminates enough for me to see him. He's out of his restraints, too, and messing around with the instrument panel.

"What are you doing, Trab? Can we get out of the ship? Are we buried? What about my squad? Did they make it? Are they out of oxygen?" I'm already getting claustrophobic and sweating like mad.

"Stay calm, young lady. I got one emergency light to work and I'm trying to bring up the backup display."

"Okay. But there's not enough oxygen..."

"I said stay calm."

I'm trying, really trying, but it's hard. My heart's thumping and I'm light-headed. How am I supposed to stay calm? "Why didn't we break apart on impact? Come on, Trab, what about my squad?" *Preedithantha? Where are we?*

Trab lets out a groan. "You sure don't know how to be quiet, do you? Just hold on." He flips a switch and a series of small recessed lights in the ceiling flick on, followed by a tiny display to the right of where the heads-up usually is. "There now, that's better."

"Why? We're still buried in the dirt, just waiting for Lenora or the Piltrak to come and get us."

He's studying the display. "I had a feeling...yep, I was right. Never thought I'd be here again." He laughs. "Dax, welcome to my home."

Great, Trab's gone mad. "Maybe you should sit down for a bit, Trab. Let me..."

"We're in the subs, Dax. I don't know how, but here we are. Since we're alive, I'm betting your squad is too. And look here." He points to a set of coordinates. "We're a kilometer underground, with a solid layer of rock and soil above us. No breaks or cracks, solid. Like we didn't crash through at all. Can't explain it." He shakes his head.

"I think I can. The Preedithantha. I heard them. I thought I was imagining it. So how do we get out? How did you get out when you went above ground?" I squint and stare out the window, but can't see anything. "So, this is under Mid-World?"

He nods. "From the coordinates, yes. This is the sub where I grew up. Hey, can you ask those Preedi-things what's going on?"

"I did, but they don't always answer questions." I concentrate again. *How do we get out of the subs? Preedithantha?*

Nothing.

Preedithantha, how can we get out of here? Are you there? Hello?

Still nothing.

"Trab, no luck. I think we're alone down here." *I'm so scared. I have to find out what's happened to my squad and get to Ma and Da.*

"Well, thanks for trying. Those Preedi-things aren't the most reliable, are they?" He takes a deep breath. "Let me check the sensors to see if there's sufficient oxygen in the sub before we go out."

"Hurry. My squad's out there. At least I hope they are." While Trab's working, I try to activate the heads-up display. It takes a few tries with the synap-trodes, but then it lights up and I locate Jarmer, who's flying in the troposphere with Lenora on his tail. "I have to help Jarmer. The display works, so do you think our communications will work as well?"

Trab doesn't look up from the instrument panel. "Not sure yet. The communications and display work on different systems. I'm still trying to figure out how we got down here without any apparent damage."

Preedithantha, where are you? Why won't you answer me? I need your help now.

Not a single word from them. I guess I've been relying on them too much as Prentak said. But if they'll help me now, I swear on the sun, I'll never call on them again. What was it they said? *You will not die. Preedithantha protect themselves.* That's right, they're always with me so if I die, they'll die. But why won't they communicate with me now? I grab the Jurale interpreter and rub my thumb in the groove. The usual sparks aren't there and there's no vibration at all. It's dead.

"Young lady, oxygen level in the sub is 98.4 percent of normal. Whatever oxygen manufacturing process they used, it's still operational. That's a very good thing. I've put on our external landing lights." He opens the hatch. "Shall we?"

Without waiting, I run to the hatch and practically slide down the ladder. "Kova! Viga!" My ship has multiple scratches over the fuselage from Lenora's attack, but when I get around back, I find the tether line missing. Where are they? My scream is swallowed up in the emptiness.

Trab rushes to me. "What's wrong?"

"Look."

He rushes to the rear of the ship where the tether line should be. "It's not here."

"I know that! What does it mean?" On my hands and knees, I crawl around for any sign that my squad was there, but there aren't any footprints or scuffles in the layer of dust that covers the ground. They didn't make it down here with me. That means they're either dead or soon will be when Lenora finds them.

Why did the Preedithantha bring me here and then ignore me? They said they protect themselves, so where are they? What good is it to save me and then abandon me? I can't live down in this hole, I have to find a way to get back into the battle.

"Young lady, tell me if this makes sense. You said those Preedi-things took us down here, well, what if there's something down here that killed them? Remember when I said we were all put down here to protect us from infection?"

"Yes, I remember. If they're dead, we have no help at all down here. They've always helped me." Was I relying on them too much? "I'm finding a way out because I'm not done with Lenora or this war. Find me an exit, Trab."

He winks. "That's my girl!"

While Trab walks around, peering into the darkness, I rush back to the ship and plug into the cerebral interpreter. At least it seems to work down here.

Where are the exits in the subterranean residences?

Text appears on the screen right away: *Sub-residences were sealed after they were decommissioned. No entry, no exit. Seal is permanent.*

No, I don't believe that. Wouldn't someone want to go down at some point? Is there something in the sub-residences that kills Preedithantha?

A sentence scrolls across the screen.

Viral vectors, Preedithantha, are blocked by energy shield twenty meters above sub-residences.

Blocked? So they're not killed. Then I just have to get above the energy shield. But how? Come on, there must be a way out. Are all of the subs the same?

Sub-residence designs are identical. Four sub-residences were originally designed on four continents. One sub-residence per continent.

Find me a schematic.

A detailed schematic flashes onto the screen. I keep the electrode on my forehead, carry the interpreter down the ladder and call out to Trab. "I have a schematic!" Silence. Darkness and silence. "Trab?" It feels like I'm swallowed up in the dark.

Trab went to the left of the ship, so that's where I'll go. As I go, I shout until there's a sound, like creaking metal.

"Dax! Dax, hurry!"

I peel off the electrode, put the interpreter down, and run full speed toward Trab, stumbling and tripping in the dark. "Where are you? I can't see anything!" The ground is soft under my feet.

"Stay to the right of the ship until you find a wall, follow it and turn a corner. You'll see light."

I stop and touch the ground. How can this be? It feels like grass. With my arms stretched out in front, I hurry along until I hit a wall, then follow it until I find a corner. Sure enough, there's light in the distance, enough for me to see the ground and start running again. The ground is solid, concrete, or stone now. The light's coming from a room with a huge glass door that's open. Trab's inside, moving something, a table or large box.

He turns. "Young lady, this makes me sick to my stomach."

What does? I'm afraid to look. When I'm close, I see a very large metallic rectangular box on top of a table. "What's that?"

"A coffin."

Now I know I don't want to look. "Is there somebody...inside?"

"You bet there is." He stands back and motions me forward. "I removed the lid, but it's still sealed with a clear covering. I think this was used as a display. I saw something like this once when I was in training. They put a coffin very similar to this in the Senior Commander's office and had all of the recruits march past it."

"Who was it?" I come closer.

"The first leader of Global Command. He was above ground during the first attacks of the Piltrak and got killed. But this is different."

I take another step. "Why? Who's in there?"

"It's not human." He stands back.

I look down through the clear cover and gasp. Inside is a pale yellow creature about twice the size of a human adult, with spiky black hair, three eyes straight across, and cuts, bruises, and wounds all over. I think it's a woman, judging by what looks like breasts underneath a torn sheer dress. "Trab, is this the Katarga leader?"

He nods and slides the metal cover back on. "I think it is. They tortured her and then put her on display for everyone to see. I guess when I was here, I was too young to see her. My parents never mentioned this, maybe they didn't know. Sometimes I'm ashamed to say I'm human."

"Me too." That image is implanted in my brain now. And to think her daughters could feel everything she felt. Even worse is the fact that she would have known they could feel her torture. "I've had enough, Trab. All of this suffering has to stop now. I've got a schematic of the subs and found out there's an energy shield twenty meters above us that blocks the Preedithantha. If we can get above that, I can reach them again."

"And do what? What can they do? Why would they help us? What's in it for them?" He shakes his head. "Maybe we should just stay down here and live out our lives in peace."

I take his hand. "No. My parents are up there, and my friends. If there's even a slight chance of saving them, I'll take it. Besides, I doubt there are any supplies left down here. Listen to me. The Preedithantha control Bliss. I know this is going to sound terrible, but what if I get them to infect everyone on Earth with Bliss? That'll end the fighting immediately and then the Katarga and Piltrak can leave without doing any more damage. It's extreme, but extreme is what we need."

"Hold on there, young lady. An infection is what they were trying to prevent way back when. That's the whole reason for these subs. I can't go along with that. Sorry, but I can't." He pulls his hand free. "You're a smart girl, Dax, and I've been willing to follow you, but count me out at this point. There's no way I'm going to infect humans with some alien virus."

"I don't think it's really a virus."

"Do you hear yourself? You don't *think* it's a virus." He shakes his head and clamps the metallic cover in place. "Besides, as soon as you get to the surface, Lenora and the commanders will blast you full of priz-spec pulses. I can't let you risk your life."

"How are you going to stop me? I don't need you or Tablon or Jarmer." I'm willing to bet the Preedithantha aren't dangerous, although I don't know for certain what Bliss is or exactly how the Preedithantha get into a host. All I know is that Bliss stopped me being afraid, and that's a good thing. How could it possibly be a bad thing? The old leaders were scared of Bliss because they would have lost control of everyone if nobody was susceptible to their propaganda of fear.

Trab is just staring at the ground. "You need to stop for a minute and think."

"Everyone I love is up there. I can't stay here, not knowing if they're all right or not. And if I get killed, I'll die knowing I tried. You can stay here and do nothing for all I care." I glance at the coffin, rush out of the room and backtrack to the ship where I find the interpreter. Once in my ship, I seal the hatch closed.

The schematic is still on the screen. The sub is a single level, with a series of compartments for living quarters all built around a park, very similar to the set-up of our outliers, except we surround a city, not a park. In the center of the park is a launchpad with a type of tube that carries people to the surface. It reminds me of the lift on the transport. If that was grass I walked on, my ship must be in the park, maybe even on the launch pad. But if the tube is sealed, I'll need to unseal it. I could sure use Trab's expertise right now, but after the things I said, I doubt he'll want to help.

The cerebral interpreter only has a small reference about how the launch tube was sealed. All it says is the energy field was drawn across it. That's not much to go on.

A sound near the hatch makes me turn.

"Young lady!" Trab shouts as he bangs on the hatch.

He's going to try to convince me to stay with him underground, but I can't. "Go away, Trab."

"Recruit Orwan, open the hatch right now!"

"I've got things to do, Trab. Please leave me alone."

He thumps on the hatch. "Open up!"

I put the helmet on and engage the synap-trodes so I can use the heads-up to view behind my ship. Trab is to the side, but I see him, and I see the coffin on a hover stretcher near him. What's he doing? I keep the helmet on so I can control the ship if I need to, and open the hatch. "What do you want, Trab?"

He pokes his head in. "This poor woman should be returned to her people." He shrugs. "I'm not going to live forever, might as well go out fighting alongside you."

"You mean it?"

With a nod, he motions outside. "Let me secure our guest into the payload bay and then we'll be good to go."

"Payload bay? What's that?" I've been flying this fighter and never knew there was a payload bay.

He answers simply, "Rear of the ship where the weapons are stored. There's enough room for more weaponry than you're carrying, so the coffin should fit. It'll be snug, but there'll be enough room."

"I could have put my squad back there instead of towing them around space."

He shakes his head. "No, there's some radiation back there from the weapons. Your squad was safer out in space."

"Oh. But we still can't leave. The exit's sealed with the energy shield. I have no idea how to break through it."

He doesn't respond and vanishes down the ladder for a few minutes. He pokes his head back in. "All done. Dax, I'm the best damn mechanic at the Mid-World Equatorial Training Camp. And the best damn tech hacker. Trust me. If there's a way out, I'll find it." He climbs inside.

It's good to have him with me. After studying the schematic, he uses the synap-trodes to bring up a row of coordinates and other things I don't understand and nods slowly to himself. Whatever he's seeing, I'm not.

If I can hug Ma and Da again before I die, I'll be happy. I honestly don't expect to survive this, but I want to say goodbye and try to make sure they'll be safe.

"All right, young lady, I've figured it out." He doesn't look too certain. "But..."

Do I want to hear this? "But what?"

"Well, we'll make it out just fine, but we'll have to blast our way out."

"With the ship's lasers?"

"Priz-spec." He wipes his brow. "Dangerous as all get-out using priz-spec in a confined area. We're directly beneath the launch tube, but once we enter the tube, you'll have to accelerate to 3% lightspeed and fire away with everything you've got. That should open a hole in the shield long enough for us to get through before it seals again. That's why you'll have to go at 3%. It'll seal really quick."

"I've never gone that fast, especially in a launch. Will my ship hold together? It's damaged remember. Lenora tried her best to shoot me down."

"I'm aware of that. The ship'll hold. These are the best ships in the Global Forces thanks to me. They're rubbish when they get to camp, but they're stellar after I've fixed them. It'll hold." He draws in a deep breath and gets into his restraints. "Launch, young lady."

I fasten my restraints, close the hatch and prepare my ship for launch. I should be terrified, but I feel alive, energized. Three percent lightspeed. What will that be like? I bet Jarmer's never gone that fast. With my concentration on the black star button, I glance over at Trab. He smiles and points up.

My finger is on the priz-spec firing button. I'll have to accelerate using the synap-trodes and press the priz-spec button at the same time or we'll never make it and we'll slam into the energy shield and disintegrate into a billion pieces. My breath is frozen in my throat. I press the black star button three times and hold down the priz-spec firing button simultaneously. Before I can exhale, my ship tilts vertical and roars upward as a pulse fires up into the tube. Everything's a blur and my eyes feel like they've been sucked into the sockets. When we break through into the open air, I know we've made it.

I'm going so fast, I'm already in the exosphere, still climbing, and still firing my priz-spec. I command the ship to reduce speed and take my finger off the firing button. I don't feel so much pressure on my body anymore and can inhale with no trouble. But, the moon is looming right in front of me. "Trab, did you program in the moon's coordinates? We're heading right for..."

"I told you we had to get this old girl back to her people."

"But they'll shoot us down! I shot at them last time I was there and it's not like they're going to be too receptive to see me back again."

"Young lady, can't you contact those Preedi-things?" He winks. "We're out of the subs now."

That's right! Preedithantha, we have the corpse of the Katarga leader onboard and want to take her back to the Katarga. Can you help?

Preedithantha are thankful you found a way past the energy shield to free us. We will attempt communications with the Katarga. If they are not receptive, however, communication will not be possible.

Please try, and tell them to allow us to land.

Katarga cannot harm you if you are again placed within the veil.

Put me in the veil.

"Trab, we're okay. The Katarga can't hurt us and the Preedithantha said they'll try to contact them."

"Excellent." He lets out a breath. "Excellent. While you're concentrating on not crashing onto the moon's surface, I'm going to see if I can use a tech link-up to access the Council of Commanders and see what's what."

"I hope didn't see me shoot out of the subs. When we're done with the Katarga, we have to find my squad. I have no idea what happened to them."

"If I know those AFGFs, they'll be just fine. Better kids than the most seasoned Leads."

"You're right about that." I smile at the thought of seeing my friends again, but the fight's not over.

If the broadcasts don't work, I'll have to ask the Preedithantha to get into the brains of everyone on Earth and activate Bliss. That's all I have left.

As I approach the surface of the moon, I see the AFGFs advance and retreat over and over again as the Katarga respond to their attacks. It really is a never-ending battle. But if I'm successful, it'll stop permanently and everyone, humans and aliens, can go home and have a future. I position my ship over the AFGFs. They all look up, but I'm in the veil so they can't see me.

Preedithantha, take me out of the veil.

The second I put the ship in a hover two meters off the surface, the AFGFs surround me and aim their weapons.

"Looks like they can see us. Um, young lady, I have good news and..."

"Give me the good news." I need something good to hang onto.

"The broadcasts worked and got the attention of approximately 35% of the global population."

I stare out the side window at the AFGFs. That was me not so long ago; afraid and trying to stay alive. "The bad news?"

"Global Forces is rounding up the people. The Piltrak were holding back because of the people surrendering, but are regrouping their attack formations now that Global Forces is in control again. It's over, Dax. You tried, don't ever think you didn't do everything you could. At least we'll return the Katarga leader."

"That's not good enough. What do we do after she's been returned? Surrender?" There's a wave of boiling anger that's building down deep and I'm trying hard to stop it from exploding, but I don't think I can. Everything I try fails. "I'll never stop trying!"

"Young lady, I didn't mean anything."

"I know. I'm sorry, I didn't mean to yell. Have you picked up anything about my parents? Jarmer, Tablon, my squad? Anyone?" I make sure my spacesuit and helmet are secure.

He shakes his head. "No news. Sorry." He motions to the hatch. "The neg pressure allows you to keep the hatch open. Not sure if Jarmer told you that."

"Yeah, I know." I open the hatch.

"That's so you can get back in quickly if you need to. Be careful, Dax."

With a nod, I slide down the ladder and plant my feet on the soft dust of the moon. My boots sink a few centimeters. This is exactly where Viteri wanted me to be. Nobody is shooting, but the AFGFs are closing in with their weapons trained on me.

Trab calls to me from the hatch. "I opened up a communication frequency. You can talk to the soldiers."

A boy with a hint of a mustache walks up to me. "Who are you? Why'd you land in the middle of our battle? We were gaining ground."

"No, you weren't." I point toward the Katarga stronghold. "You'll never gain ground. It's designed that way. They shoot, you shoot and kids die. Did your Leads ever tell you what to do if you managed to break through the stronghold?"

The boy looks confused. "Who *are* you?"

"Daxella Rose Orwan, AFGF recruit under Commander Viteri."

He's even more confused now. "Your ship was invisible. Who's your pilot? Why were you brought here in an invisible fighter? We don't have that tech."

"I'm the pilot and I'm here to explain to you why you have to stop fighting. Don't worry about the Katarga. Do you even know what's happening on Earth?" I turn and see Trab climbing down in a spacesuit that looks a size too small.

The boy lowers his weapon. "No. We haven't had any communications in days, but I saw those ships coming. Are they Piltrak?"

I nod. "Yes. But listen to me, the Piltrak aren't our enemy. Neither are the Katarga. Not anymore. If you stop shooting at the Katarga, they'll go home. That's all they want."

Trab stands beside me, tugging on the crotch of the spacesuit. "She's telling the truth. Do me a favor, young man, and tell your squad to put down their weapons and under no circumstances pick them up again."

The boy shakes his head. "Are you insane? You want us to unarm ourselves? We're the last squad here. The other four squads are all dead and we haven't received any replacements. We should have had a transport by now with more recruits."

I take a step closer. "That's because there's a war on Earth, ah...what's your name?"

"Harner. I'm the RIC."

"How long have you been here, Harner?" The rest of his squad gathers around. They're all girls.

"About four days." He points to Trab. "And who are you? Are you the pilot?"

I shake my head. "I told you I'm the pilot. This is Trab, he's a mechanic from my training camp. If he tells you to put your weapons down, you do it. Understand?"

Harner nods and places his gun on the ground at his feet. His squad does the same. He shakes his head. "There, now the Katarga can come and eat us and we can't fight back. Is that what you want?"

There's a flash of bright blue and Prentak appears next to me and hands me the Jurale interpreter. "Hello again, Dax." He circles Harner. "Katarga do not eat humans. They subsist on molecular elements they glean from their surroundings. Their planet was low on resources so they went on an exploratory mission and became your captives." Prentak's ship turns visible.

Harner backs away. "What are you?"

I kick Harner's weapon out of reach. "This is Prentak, a Piltrak fleet commander. Harner, I don't have all day to stand here and explain every little thing, so here's what I need. Take your squad back to your base and wait there. Don't communicate with anyone and don't arm yourselves. Can you do that?"

He's staring at Prentak. "What?"

"Can you do that? Don't you want to go home to your family?" I face his squad. "Don't you all want to go home? Imagine if these wars ended today, right now. You could go to your outliers or cities and spend the rest of your lives in peace."

A girl with black hair framing her face tilts her head. "Peace? How? We won't have any subsidies. We'll have to scratch around in the dumps for scraps of food and die slowly from starvation. I don't want my parents or baby sister to die."

I continue, "When the wars end, we'll have to put our societies back in order. The cities won't only be for the rich and the poor won't be stuck in the outliers."

Harner comes to me. "You're dreaming. It's been this way for so long, it's not going to change." He looks at his squad. "Come on! Back to battle!"

"No!" I grab his gun and point it at him. Preedithantha, can you give this squad Bliss?

A purple cloud descends and drifts over everyone except for me, Trab and Prentak. Harner and his squad stand still with contented smiles on their faces. I'm still amazed how fast Bliss works and feel a little guilty that I Blissed the AFGFs without their knowledge. But I had to, it was for their own good. And for the good of everyone.

The AFGFs slowly wander away toward their base.

Prentak touches me on my arm. "Dax, is this not what started the wars?"

What's he talking about? Of course it wasn't. The wars started because...because Global Command wanted...damn it. He's right. They were afraid of being controlled by Bliss and built the subs to stay safe. And that led to Global Command being created and the Council of Commanders and the whole manufacturing of the wars for money. Did it all stem from the Preedithantha's Bliss?

I'm doing a good thing by using Bliss. Right? "The Bliss is temporary. I'll have it withdrawn later. They were going to attack the Katarga. I have to let the Katarga come and get their leader and go home. Once the Katarga are gone, then you can take your people and leave as well. Isn't that what we agreed on?"

He turns and looks at the back of my ship. That's when I see that Trab has unloaded the coffin and has it on the ground. Since the Katarga aren't shooting, the Preedithantha must have contacted them and let them know what's going on.

Prentak takes his hand off my arm. "Dax, I came here to help the Katarga and make sure you would find a safe place to live. I thought you understood that it is too late to stop the destruction of Earth's human population. Your leaders will not surrender now. I must lead my fleet..."

"You can't do this, Prentak. My parents are on Earth, and then there are all of those innocent people in the outliers who surrendered like *I* told them to! You can't kill them. They listened to me and left their homes where they're exposed."

Trab comes over. "Hello there, Prentak. I have an idea if you'll give me a chance to explain." He tugs on the spacesuit again. "These suits weren't designed for a full-grown man."

Prentak gives Trab a slight nod. "I will listen to you."

"Thank you, sir." Trab glances at me. "Dax, it just occurred to me that maybe we can use the Preedi-things to get inside the commanders and make them stop the wars. Just the commanders."

Infect the commanders with Bliss? That's better than exposing everyone on the planet. "Prentak, can we ask the Preedithantha to inhabit a particular person or persons?"

With a quizzical expression, Prentak looks from me to Trab and Earth in the distance. "Of course they can, but I would not recommend doing what you are thinking of doing. This was tried before."

I stare at Earth with its beautiful blue oceans and white clouds covering portions of the land. "Right, fifty years ago. That's when the subs were used. So what exactly happened? Why didn't t work?"

He hesitates. "My people brought the Preedithantha to Earth. We did not mean for the Preedithantha to inhabit humans. We only wanted them to project Bliss to show the humans how they could feel at peace and allow the Katarga to leave. It did not work, the Preedithantha forced themselves into their human hosts because they could not survive otherwise. As the

Preedithantha settled into their human hosts, a group of uninfected went underground and created the energy shield to stop the Preedithantha. They'd discovered that once an infected person was sheltered by an energy field, the Preedithantha went dormant. The humans later removed the infected population and placed them underground as well. My people returned home after the Katarga refused our help. After approximately three of your Earth years, the Preedithantha died from starvation caused by the energy shield. All underground humans were cleansed from their Preedithantha."

"Oh." Now it makes sense. "But I have the Preedithantha in me and nothing's happened to me. In fact, they leave me alone until I ask them for something. Didn't my people know that? Couldn't your people have told them?"

"Dax," Prentak starts. "Humans do not want another species to inhabit them. Preedithantha live within Piltrak in a symbiotic relationship."

"I know, you told me that already."

He continues, "But they do not have the same symbiotic relationship with humans."

What does that mean? "But I'm okay."

Trab goes up to Prentak. "Those Preedi-things better not do anything to her."

"They will not harm her, but they will protect themselves. That means if Dax is attacked, they will do whatever is necessary to save themselves, and their host."

My body feels heavy. "That's why they blew up Commander Viteri. But they didn't destroy Lenora. How come?"

Prentak steps to the side to get away from Trab. "It was probably easier for them to transport you underground. They will do whatever is fastest and more productive. If they did not destroy a ship, then that ship is very fortunate."

As much as I hate Lenora, I'm glad they didn't kill her and her crew. "Prentak, is there any way for them to leave me?"

"By accepting their help when you were on Saturn's ring, you allowed them access."

"But you didn't explain anything!" I'm basically a weapon. Someone attacks me, the Preedithantha will kill them. This isn't what I wanted. I can't ever go home now. It's too dangerous.

"Young lady." Trab points behind us toward the Katarga stronghold.

Prentak announces, "The Katarga are arriving."

I spin around and see a bright yellow land vehicle like nothing I've seen on Earth. This one has black spikes poking out from every part of it and instead of wheels, it has a single, centrally located rotating tread similar to what I saw in a history book on something called a tank. But they had two instead of only one. When it gets closer, I realize how big it is, at least three times the size of my fighter.

Prentak walks away from my ship and stands with his hands raised. Are we supposed to do the same thing? Trab seems as confused as me, so we decide to wait near the coffin to see what happens and stay close to my ship's hatch. We can scramble inside if things go wrong.

The Katarga vehicle stops a short distance from Prentak and a door at the front slides open. A yellow Katarga jumps out and glides to Prentak, towering above him. It looks almost identical to the Katarga in the coffin, except its' spiky hair is white. Like Prentak, it doesn't have a spacesuit but does wear a sheer tunic in bright yellow fabric. The Katarga must like yellow. The way it moves is elegant and graceful, its feet barely touching the ground. Did I kill some of these beautiful things when I was in the vortex?

The Preedithantha speak to me, *No Katarga were harmed during your attack.*

That's the best news I could ever hear. I'm so happy I want to scream. Preedithantha, is my squad alive?

Alive.

Thank the sun and stars!

Prentak and the Katarga communicate for a few minutes, occasionally looking at Trab and me. Another Katarga, also with white hair spikes, comes out of the vehicle, glides to the coffin, and stops. I'm still holding the Jurale translator and decide I might as well try to communicate.

"Greetings. My name is Daxella Rose Orwan. I'm here to help you go home. My friend, Trab, found your leader."

The Katarga blinks all three eyes at the same time. "We give thanks that you return our beloved mother."

Mother? Unbelievable, this is one of her daughters. How old is she? "It's the least we can do for you. I apologize for all humans. Nobody should be treated the way she was. Please take her home."

"You have done a great service, human person Daxella Rose Orwan. We have been trapped on this rock for too long, although we did not wish to leave without our mother's remains."

"I understand. I've had to leave my mother and father and I miss them every second."

The Katarga bends down and places her hand on my shoulder. "I sympathize with you. I must go now and return my mother to our people. You are the first human I have encountered who has not tried to kill me. Perhaps there is hope for your species after all." She straightens, waves her hand over the coffin, and makes it hover.

Walking beside it, she takes it to the vehicle and loads it inside. A moment later, Prentak returns to us and the other Katarga gets into the vehicle as well. After only a few seconds, they drive off toward the stronghold. I'd love to stay with them and learn all about them, but I know they have to leave while they have the chance.

Trab has tears in his eyes. "Young lady, that was the most incredible thing I've ever seen." He wriggles in his spacesuit.

"Where did you get that suit, Trab? I didn't see an extra one."

"A spare is stored in a compartment on the back of the fighter seats."

"Well, that one doesn't seem to fit so well." I smile.

"It's for someone your size, not mine." He stares off into the distance. "Maybe you've set things in motion and no more kids will ever have to wear one."

"Maybe."

I'm both sad and happy that the Katarga are leaving, a bittersweet feeling that's settled in the pit of my stomach. "I have to go. My squad's down there somewhere and I have to make sure my parents are safe."

Trab is watching the vehicle. "I know. But the war's still going on. As soon as you head to Earth..."

I shake my head. "I have the Preedithantha. They can keep my ship in the veil. I'll be fine."

"Dax." Prentak looks up at my ship. "The Preedithantha cannot project the veil indefinitely. Each time they project the veil or Bliss, it uses their energy, which uses your energy because they are now linked with you. Remember, they will protect themselves at all costs. If you insist on them using the veil, they will require your energy to maintain it. All of your energy. They are not used to a human host and may not recognize the damage they can do. They likely chose to take the ship underground to use less energy, rather than destroy the attacking vessel."

"So I'll die if I try to use the veil for too long?" This just gets worse and worse, but I have to take my chances. So far, all I've accomplished is helping the Katarga leave the moon. That's not good enough. "I'm going to Earth anyway."

There's a groan from Trab. "I knew you'd say that. You'll need a co-pilot."

"I can fly the fighter alone, Trab. You should stay here with the AFGFs at their base camp."

Now he chuckles. "You can't get rid of me that easily, young lady. Besides, now that I'm standing on the moon, I can honestly say I'd rather be on Earth."

I smile at him. "I kind of like it here. But I'm ready to go back and I'm glad it'll be with you, Trab. Prentak, can you ask your people not to shoot me down?" I'll still have to worry about the battalion, especially Lenora, but at least I won't have the Piltrak after me. And if I need the veil, I can use it for a short time.

Prentak nods. "I will request your ship as off-limits, but if you do not remain on the moon or in Earth's upper atmosphere, there is little protection I can offer. My time here has expired and I must return to my fleet now, Dax. The Piltrak will not withdraw and will continue to eliminate the human threat. I wish you luck with whatever you do. I would suggest you quickly find your family and friends and come with us to our planet where you will be safe. We have the technology to build you a home with sufficient oxygen."

"Thank you, Prentak, but I'll be all right. *This* is my home. I belong here."

He continues, "I understand. My offer stands, but if you wish to remain on Earth, perhaps you can rebuild your lives once we have cleansed the planet."

That's an awful thought. "I'll figure something out. But I won't leave."

Trab puts his arm over my shoulders. "I agree with you, Dax. I was born on Earth and that's where I'll die sooner or later. Hopefully later. It was nice to meet you, Prentak. Tell your people not all humans are hostile."

With a nod, Prentak glances at me, goes to his ship, and vanishes. I'll never get used to how he gets inside, it's so weird. I hear rumbling and notice a yellow glow coming from the Katarga stronghold. The rumbling fades slightly as a cluster of yellow and blue ships rise. There are so many I can't count them. They're almost like Prentak's, round with no windows, but much, much bigger.

Safe travels, Katarga. My tears create a mosaic of color in my vision. At least the Katarga have their mother back now. "Let's go, Trab. I need to make sure *my* mother is okay."

We don't speak as we climb into my fighter and prepare for launch. No words are necessary, we both know there's a good chance we won't make it and we're both willing to take the risk. The priority is to get to Ma and Da. I only wish my broadcast hadn't backfired. Am I supposed to just watch my planet burn?

Chapter Thirty-Five

As we slip through Earth's atmosphere, Trab attempts to locate Jarmer but isn't having any luck, although he did find Lenora over my outlier. I know exactly what she's doing there. She's waiting for me at my house, trying to flush me out by threatening my parents. I'm not about to engage her over my outlier in case there are other residents who'd managed to return. I can't let anyone get hurt in the crossfire, so I'll sneak in low from Jewel with the advantage of surprise. If I'm in imminent danger, I'll put the veil around my ship.

In flight, I manage to evade detection from a battalion fighter that doesn't seem like it saw me as I dive under it, and I speed past three Piltrak ships that ignore me and zip right by like I'm not there.

"Trab, have you found Jarmer yet? I'm only twenty-four kilometers from Jewel."

"No. Either he's removed his tracking mechanism, which no pilot knows how to do, or his ship's..." he doesn't finish the sentence.

"He's out there, I know he is. I'll find him." I drop down to a cruising altitude of ten meters above the ground and slow my speed.

Trab points through the front window. "I didn't detect any battalion ships in or around Jewel. We should be good until we get to your outlier. Lenora has three fighters in a tight holding pattern and she's set her ship down right in front of your house. She's drawing you in, young lady."

"I know she's waiting for me. But she isn't expecting me to come from Jewel." I wink.

The view out the front window is strange. Colorful Jewel is deserted, not a single person on the streets or in the green parks. Nobody. Where is everyone?

"Dax, I hope you're right and she isn't looking in this direction." He sighs deeply. "Descend another four meters. You'll still be above the tree canopy between Jewel and your outlier, but not by much. Lenora shouldn't be able to track you that low. Hey, how did she suddenly become in charge? She's just a Lead."

"She got real friendly with Tablon, and since he was the Commander's favorite, she got noticed. That was her plan all along. And now that Tablon's joined up with me and my squad, she probably volunteered to be my executioner."

"Yeah, could be. But she's not going to stop you." He chuckled nervously.

Not if I have anything to do about it. I drop down another four meters, skimming the treetops as I go, and arm my laser guns and priz-spec. What I need is a distraction so I can swoop in and get Ma and Da before Lenora even realizes what I'm doing. It might work if I fire off a few laser bursts at the ground before I get too close to my house. And if I use the veil, she can't see my ship. That's a huge advantage.

I leave the forests and fly over the scrub desert land that makes up my outlier. Without trees, I drop down to only two meters off the ground and slow to what Trab calls walking speed. Before long I see houses ahead. This is it, no turning back.

"Young lady, get ready. Two of the ships just left the holding pattern and are heading this way. She knows you're here."

It feels like my whole body is caught in a gravitational sink and my heart is being squeezed so tight I can hardly breathe. I have to evade the ships.

"Trab, I'm going to accelerate to 1% lightspeed and stop right in front of Lenora before anyone can do anything." If I'm careful, I can fire a couple of laser bursts a few streets away to draw her fighters in a different direction.

"Wait. Wait! Stopping so suddenly after that kind of acceleration will..."

"No, it won't." Preedithantha, protect my ship with the veil.

Preedithantha will offer protection.

Right away, the purple mist drifts in front of the window. I'm in the veil. I ignore Trab as he keeps complaining that we'll break apart, and press the black star button. The force of the acceleration shoves me into the seat for the blink of an eye, then the deceleration jolts me forward hard against the restraints. But the ship's intact. I'm directly in front of Lenora's ship, our noses are no more than a couple of meters apart.

"You okay, Trab?"

His mouth's gaping. "This shouldn't have happened. It can't happen. I know these ships better than anyone and…"

"Don't over-think it, Trab." Using the heads-up, I position my laser guns so one is aimed right at Lenora's ship and one is ready to fire a burst a kilometer away. I'll save the priz-spec for an emergency. I open the hatch.

Trab's out of his restraints. "You're not going out there."

"I have to." I push past him. "When I give you the signal, fire laser gun 2. Laser gun 1 is aimed at Lenora's ship. Don't touch the priz-spec unless we need it."

"What? Who am I firing at?" He shakes his head. "You're not thinking straight. It's that purple cloud, it's doing something to you. It's toxic, it has to be."

"It's not. It's the veil, not Bliss. And I'm fine." That's not totally true. I'm still feeling the compression all over my body and my head hurts. But this isn't the time to worry about space sickness or whatever it is. If it's the Preedithantha using my energy, I should retract the veil. *Preedithantha, remove the veil.*

The mist vanishes immediately. I take off my helmet, and with the Jurale interpreter in my hand, I descend the ladder and come face-to-face with Lenora holding a laser gun in her hand.

"You're an easy one to trap, smudge," she says with a sneer. "And using alien invisibility tech is illegal."

"Bring me my parents or I'll open fire on your ship."

She smirks. "No, you won't." She points to her ship and I see movement in the cockpit. Two men approach the front window. They have Tablon by the arms. He's struggling and shouting something. "You fire on my ship, Tablon dies."

What do I do now? This isn't what I was expecting. "Where are my parents, Lenora?" I rub my thumb along the Jurale interpreter. "You can't do this to Tablon."

"Put down that stupid alien weapon. And as for Tablon, he's a stinking traitor. I should have killed him in the transport when you told him I beat you and he had the nerve to tell me he'd report me. I convinced him not to, but I never trusted him after that. Even sex didn't work on him. What sort of boy isn't swayed by sex?"

"You're decayed, Lenora. Tell me where my parents are and I won't hurt you."

She motions behind her. "Your parents are inside the house, safe and sound, with a soldier guarding them of course. There were also a few idiot residents in this disgusting outlier hiding out. But I have them and if you attack, they'll all get their throats sliced open, starting with your Ma and papa. It's up to you how you want this to end. Give up, or attack and lose Tablon, your parents, and every single resident. Your move, smudge."

I can't breathe. My lungs aren't expanding properly. I look from Tablon to my house. Surrendering is the only option unless I use the Preedithantha to Bliss everyone. "Trab!" Now I feel sick and weak.

"Right here, Dax!" he shouts back.

My knees shake and I collapse before I have the chance to tell him not to fire. Lenora's laughing, actually laughing! I hear 'stupid smudge' ring in my ears and then an explosion. No! He fired the laser gun! I struggle to stand, but Lenora shoves me over and kicks me in the ribs.

"You've got your traitor friends firing on us? Say goodbye to your parents, smudge. I'll snap their spines myself."

Chapter Thirty-Six

Another explosion shakes the ground and Lenora tumbles down next to me. Her laser gun is within reach, so I grab it, but I can't stand because my legs won't move, and my head's spinning. Two more explosions thunder around me and I instinctively close my eyes and cover my head with my hands. What's Trab doing, blowing up my whole outlier? I open my eyes to the sight of Lenora's ship on the ground, out of its hover, smoking.

"Smudge! You're dead!" Lenora screams, crawling to me.

I manage to draw in a breath and yell, "Trab! Cease fire!"

He calls back, "I didn't do anything!"

Then who did? I glance at my ship, again bathed in the purple mist. Preedithantha, I said to remove the veil.

Preedithantha will protect our own.

Yes, I know, you've said that before. But I'm fine.

The mist dissipates and vanishes from my ship, and I feel a burst of energy. It was the veil taking my energy. I'll have to be very careful from here on. I get to my feet as a fighter speeds overhead, swoops down and around, and comes to a hover over Lenora's damaged ship. Maybe I acted too soon in removing my veil. My ship's vulnerable.

Lenora grabs my arm, wrestles her laser gun away from me, and points it at my head. "Told you I'd kill you." Her finger moves to the trigger button.

The hovering ship fires a small pulse at the ground about half a meter from Lenora, which launches her into the air. She flails, drops her laser gun, and crashes down into a crumpled heap. Were they aiming at me and missed? I run for the ladder.

"Dax!" Jarmer's voice echoes around me. "In the ship, Dax. It's me."

I have one foot on the lower rung of my fighter, but stop and turn. The other ship edges closer and I see Jarmer in the pilot's seat, waving. He's alive!

Unfortunately, Lenora's squad also sees him and have their weapons trained on his ship, and they're not ordinary laser guns, but something that looks more powerful. Powerful enough to perhaps bring down a fighter ship.

Jarmer ignores me as I motion him to leave and doesn't move. Instead, he fires a few more pulses at the ground near the soldiers, knocking them all down. I can imagine him smiling and laughing and thoroughly enjoying himself. If he's safe, he might know where my squad is.

I don't get more than one step toward him when a huge blast hits his ship, making it shake and lurch violently, but Jarmer regains control only to get hit again. This time I can tell he's struggling to stop from slamming into my house and forces his ship to crash land in my neighbor's front yard. I see a battalion ship hovering a short distance away. There's too much going on, I can't think straight, my mind's all muddled. Another strike tips his ship upside down.

"Jarmer!" I scream.

I take off toward Jarmer's ship, but before I get far, one of Lenora's soldiers grabs me and tosses me to the ground. He presses a small laser pistol to my head.

Lenora comes over, limping and dragging her left foot behind her. "I'm going to make an example out of you, smudge. Just like Commander Viteri wanted."

"This is wrong, Lenora." I catch my breath and get up. "Wasn't it enough to attack and kill aliens, now you want to start killing our people? The Commander's dead. You can stop this if you put down the weapons and surrender to the Piltrak. That's all they want. Stop fighting against them and they'll leave here and go home. We can have peace. Isn't that what you want?"

She shakes her head and scowls. "Why would I want peace? War will bring me fame and get my parents money. Without wars, I'd be a nobody back in the outlier scraping out a living working in some galactically ridiculous job. I don't want that." She nods to the soldier and he places his finger on the trigger button.

"Wait! Let me see my parents before I die. Please." In my peripheral vision, I see Tablon and Jarmer, injured and supporting one another, heading in my direction. They're hurt, but alive.

Lenora continues, "Shut up, smudge. You don't get any favors. Your parents are going to die, and I'll make sure it's a slow death." She smiles. "Go ahead, turn the smudge's brains to liquid."

Preedithantha...

"Stop this now!" Trab shouts from the ladder of my ship. "This has gone far enough. Lenora, you're a Lead in the Global Forces, so act like it. A Lead doesn't kill other soldiers."

She glares at Trab. "Really? You think you know so much about the Global Forces, old man? Look at you, you're not even a soldier. Shoot him after you end the smudge."

I yell, "No!" Trab's right, this has gone on long enough. Preedithantha, protect my friends.

Preedithantha will protect ourselves and our host's friends.

In a bright flash of purple, the veil covers my ship and Jarmer's, making them both invisible.

"Where's my ship, Dax?" Jarmer glares at me.

Preedithantha, can you give Bliss to everyone here except me and my friends?

Preedithantha will cast Bliss in a half-kilometer radius, excluding you and your friends.

"Trab..." My head suddenly throbs and my legs shake to the point where I can't stand and drop to my knees.

"Dax!" Jarmer limps to me. "What's wrong? What happened to my ship? And yours? And why is everyone covered in a purple mist? What's going on? They're all...happy."

It's so hard to breathe. "The ships are still here. Invisible. And the cloud gives them Bliss. It's only on them though, not us. Find my parents." I roll over and try to suck in a deep breath.

Trab's beside me. "Young lady, what can I do?"

"Take my parents somewhere safe." My vision's getting blurry.

"Dax," Tablon says. "That mist is killing you."

I can't release it or Lenora and her soldiers will shoot us all. I'll keep the veil and Bliss up long enough for Trab to get my parents and take them away, and for Tablon and Jarmer to escape. I can hold out that long. My head hurts so much and now my insides feel like they're on fire. The voices around me are muffled and all I see are shapes and outlines of people.

In my ear, I hear a whisper, "Dax, sweetie. Talk to me. Dax." It's Ma.

My throat's so dry, it's hard to speak. "Ma. Is Da with you? Are you all right?"

"Yes, yes, we're fine. We have to get you away from here. This young man says that cloud is killing you." She's crying, I can hear her voice crack and sobs escape now and then.

"I'm staying...until you and Da are away from here. I tried, Ma, I tried so hard to get Global Command to listen." I blink to focus on her face. "The aliens don't want to fight us. Nobody will listen."

Now Da whispers in my other ear, "They did listen. And not just our outlier. We received messages over the computer system right before we were captured that people are banding together to stop Global Command. They heard you, Dax."

"They did?" I can't believe it. The broadcast worked. I'm so tired, I need to sleep, just for a little while. The pain's gone now and I'm warm like I'm wrapped in my blanket. It's a wonderful feeling. I'll close my eyes, just for a few minutes.

"Dax!"

"Dax, wake up!"

"Young lady!"

I don't know who's yelling or why. All I want to do is sleep and dream wonderful dreams. Now I'm floating. Maybe this is a dream. No idea where I am or how long I've been floating. I'll just take one more breath and then sleep. I think I might be dying, but it's not bad.

A loud clanging shocks me awake and I open my eyes to blackness. Am I dead? I never learned what happens when someone dies. I always thought the body decays and that's that, but I'm here. Wherever here is. I touch my arms, my face, my legs. My body hasn't decomposed, and I'm breathing. Does that mean I didn't die?

"Hello?" My voice echoes.

"Dax? She's awake!" Ma shouts.

Chapter Thirty-Seven

There's a strange smell all around me. Stale, musty air, but it's familiar. I hear footsteps running toward me, getting closer. More than one person. I'm sure I heard Ma or was that a dream? I feel around me. I'm on a bed, although the mattress is worn, like my mattress in my dorm at training camp. Where's my Jurale translator?

"Dax!" Da shouts.

Just where am I? "Ma, Da?"

A bright light flashes on and I sit up, shielding my eyes. This is a bedroom; small, dirty, and bare except for the bed and a threadbare carpet around the bed. Draped over me is my old, multi-colored blanket that Ma made so long ago. All around the room are strange glowing rocks pressed into the walls; the source of the light. I take a breath. A glorious breath. I can breathe again and I'm wide awake.

"Dax!" Ma rushes in from the doorway. "You're all right? Do you feel all right? Can you talk?" She sits on the bed, pulls the blanket up, and hugs me way too tight.

I swallow. "Yes, I'm fine. What's going on? Where's Da?"

"Right here, Dax." Da comes in and sighs heavily. "We thought...well, never mind that."

I wriggle out of Ma's arms. "Where is this? Am I sick? Is this a hospital?"

Ma shakes her head. "No. I'd better let your friends explain it to you." She gets up and motions to the doorway.

Jarmer stands there with a smile on his face, then comes to my bed. "Can't believe you're sitting here, Dax. You scared us all." His face is bruised with several half-healed cuts on his arms and a small nick out of his skin above his right eye. "You look good."

"I feel good. How are you?"

He continues, "Not bad. But we have to talk."

That doesn't sound good. "Wait, where is this? This isn't the training camp and it isn't my house. What happened? Where's my squad?"

He crouches at my bedside and takes my hand. "Dax, we're in a place that Trab calls the sub-residences. I've never heard of them, but here we are."

I retract my hand. "What? We're underground again? What about my squad?" My voice raises in pitch.

He takes my hand again and squeezes it this time. "Listen, they're fine, they're all fine. Except for Big Pig, but you already know about...and...Tab. But..." He pauses and looks away.

"But what, Jarmer? Where's Tablon?"

"Tab stayed above to fight. He said he couldn't come down here while Lenora's still in charge. The fight's in full swing above, Dax. We're down here for good. According to Trab, we can't get out. But we're safe."

"And Briett?"

Jarmer glances at the ground. "Prentak helped us bury him."

I look at the faces around me and while I'm thrilled they're all okay, I'm not happy about being in the subs again. But I got out once, I can do it again. "I'm not staying here. There's work to do and I'm not about to lie around down here while our people, and the Piltrak, are getting slaughtered. Plus, we can't leave Tablon alone up there."

"Dax, sweetie," says Ma as she smoothes my hair. "We don't know what state the world's in. Right before we came down, Trab said he intercepted a communication from the new Global Command to the battalion fighters that they'd detected Jurale ships approaching. Global Command has relocated somewhere and Trab doesn't know where. I hate to say this, but we might be the last humans alive, sweetie."

I jump to my feet. "What? What are you saying? How long have I been down here?"

Jarmer sighs and runs his hand over his hair. "A week. We got you down here right after the incident with Lenora."

I can't make sense of any of this. "I don't understand. Where is Lenora?"

From the doorway, Trab shakes his head. "She got away. That's why Tablon stayed. He said you'll never be safe until she's dead. He also wants to find out where everyone in the cities and outliers were evacuated to. No sign of them. His family is missing, too."

I can understand Tablon wanting to find his family, but now he's up there all alone. "I should have stayed with him."

"Young lady, this was the only way to save you. The Preedi-things had almost drained all of your energy using the veil and Bliss. I sent a distress call to Prentak using that Jurale interpreter of yours and he arrived just in time. It was his idea to have the Preedi-things transport you to the subs where they'd be blocked. Prentak said they will protect themselves at all costs, so with you dying, their only option was to go below so you wouldn't die. Without a host, *they* die. Prentak told me that humans aren't their normal hosts and we don't have enough energy to support them, and once they're in a host, they can't leave because they're integrated into the host. See the problem?"

With a half-hearted nod, I sit down on the edge of the bed. "But if I don't use the veil, I can still go above and find Tablon. And fight."

He shakes his head again. "Nope. Unless we find a miracle cure for Preedi-thing sickness. Your energy has to be replenished and we don't know how to do that."

"Then how am I still alive?"

He continues, "Prentak told me, right before he had them send us down, that once they're blocked, you'll recover enough to live, but it'll take some years for them to die. But if you go past the energy shield before three years, they'll activate again. Whether you use the veil or not doesn't matter at this point because what energy you have left will be used up before the Preedi-things even realize what's happened. You're stuck here, young lady."

This can't be right. It isn't right. "No, I don't accept that. What have you been doing for a week then?"

Da puts his arm around Ma. "Surviving, Dax. We're all together again. And the families of your friends, too. That Piltrak somehow got all of the families down here, except for that Tablon boy's family. We have a total of 49 people here. We've already set up gardens and got the water supply providing clean water. Trab helped us with that."

Trab smiles. "My job when I was down here all those years ago was to irrigate the gardens, so I know a thing or two about the water system. Dax, when you went unconscious, the veil protecting both yours and Jarmer's ships vanished and they were so badly damaged, the engines won't work. We have the ships, but I don't have any components to fix them. We can't fire at the energy shield and fly out even if we wanted to."

I lean forward with my head in my hands. What if Ma's right and we are the only ones left? What then? We spend the rest of our lives in the subs, never knowing what happened above? How are they all okay with that? I'm not.

"I'm going to find a way out if it's the last thing I do."

Jarmer sits next to me. "It will be."

I frown at him. "I have to know."

He touches my arm. "Know what?"

"Whether Global Command destroyed the Piltrak or if the Piltrak won. If Global Command won, nothing will change. They'll keep going and continue inventing new wars. It's not over, Jarmer, not until I know the universe is safe from humans. And I need to find Tablon."

As angry as I am, when I see Viga, Kova and the rest of my squad come in, I smile. They're a bright spot in all of this misery.

Viga runs to me and throws her arms around me. "You have no idea how good it is to see you up and around." She hands me the little playing cube she had when I first saw her. "In honor of Big Pig, we changed the game. It's no longer War and Money."

I turn the cube over. "So what is it?"

"Starting Over. The rules are now completely different. Want to play?"

I hold the cube and glance around the room. This is my family, my extended family. I'd do anything for them and they'd do the same for me. Except one is missing; Tablon. So here I am, in my new home, starting over. I give Viga a nod and toss the cube in the air. I'm ready to play.

End

Stay tuned for Book Two: War and Disorder

About the Author

Sofia Diana Gabel started life in Sydney, Australia, but her family moved to the United States when she was very young. Home wasn't settled for a long time and included living in Toronto, Canada; Henrietta and Buffalo, New York; Northridge; California; a short stint back in Sydney, Australia; Reno, Nevada; Dallas, Texas; Daytona Beach, Florida; Las Vegas, Nevada; San Jose, California; Ojai, California; Ventura, California; Salt Lake City, Utah; Pacific Grove, California, and finally to the Pacific Northwest.

Perhaps the unsettled, partial nomadic lifestyle is the reason she loves to travel and is never fully satisfied with where she's living. Moving around and travelling to different countries are adventures which serve as potential settings and backdrops for stories. As a multi-genre fiction writer, with degrees in wildlife biology and archaeology, and coursework in creative writing and criminal justice, she enjoys being out in nature, keeping up on archaeological discoveries and learning about the law, criminal behavior and police procedures (all leading to potential story plots!)

When she's not glued to her desk writing or researching, she loves to spend time with her family and hairless Sphynx cats. Writing is a true passion, born from a love of the written word and how those words can transport the reader to different places or worlds, and deliver them back to reality, safe and sound.

Please visit her website: www.sofiadianagabel.com[1] for updates or to contact her for interviews or presentations.

Other social media:

Goodreads https://www.goodreads.com/sofiadianagabel

Facebook facebook.com/sofiadianagabel

---

1. http://www.sofiadianagabel.com

Other books by Sofia Diana Gabel
Science Fiction
Two Brothers: Origin
Two Brothers: Heritage
Two Brothers: Species

All three books in one ebook: Two Brothers, A Ramtalan Trilogy

The Clean Slate Accord (Novella)
Environmental Satire
Pest Control
Historic Romantic Suspense
Charity's Heart
Paranormal Romance
Gracie, Dead or Alive
Historic Fiction
A Woman's Way

Don't miss out!

Visit the website below and you can sign up to receive emails whenever Sofia Diana Gabel publishes a new book. There's no charge and no obligation.

https://books2read.com/r/B-A-GPBBB-CXOPC

BOOKS 2 READ

Connecting independent readers to independent writers.

Did you love *War and Money*? Then you should read *Neanderball*[2] by Sofia Diana Gabel!

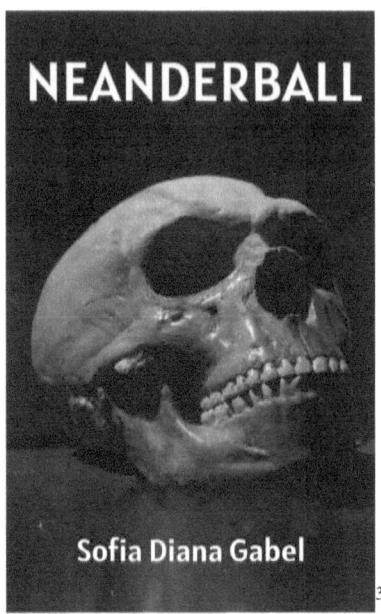

Geneticist Lucien Roux's cutting-edge experiment to clone Neanderthals blurs lines between ambition and ethics after the clones are stolen and forced to play a brutal and violent game dubbed Neanderball. Haunted by the realization that his hubris overpowered his morality, Lucien knows he must fix what he's done.

Racing against time as a military faction and a sinister adversary close in, he has one chance to expose the real reason his research was taken. With his ex-Marine girlfriend, he sets out on a dangerous journey to save the Neanderthals before it's too late. It's an all or nothing fight for redemption, leading to a showdown for his survival, and freedom for the Neanderthals. (92,000 words)

Read more at sofiadianagabel.com.

www.ingramcontent.com/pod-product-compliance
Lightning Source LLC
Chambersburg PA
CBHW020907200626
46814CB00001BA/211